PERIANDER
THE AVENGER

JOSEPH BRINGMAN

Periander the Avenger: The Final Son of Atlantis

Scripture quotation is from the *King James Version*.

Quotation of Plato's *Timaeus* is from Benjamin Jowett's translation.

Cover designed by 100Covers

Publisher's Cataloging-in-Publication Data

Names: Bringman, Joseph, author.
Title: Periander the avenger, the final son of Atlantis / Joseph Bringman.
Description: Seattle, WA: Bringman Publishing, 2025.
Identifiers: LCCN: 2025902607 | ISBN: 978-1-963006-05-6 (hardcover) | 978-1-963006-04-9 (paperback) 978-1-963006-03-2 (ebook)
Subjects: LCSH Atlantis (Legendary place)--Fiction. | Science fiction. | BISACFICTION / Science Fiction / Action & Adventure | FICTION / Historical /Ancient | FICTION / War & Military
Classification: LCC PS3602 .R56 P47 2025 | DDC 813.6--dc23

For all who never give up, who endure the trials and tribulations of an unrelenting world, and who strive to do what must be done because it is the right thing to do.

Now in this island of Atlantis there was a great and wonderful empire which had rule over the whole island and several others, and over parts of the continent... This vast power, gathered into one, endeavoured to subdue at a blow our country and yours and the whole of the region within the straits... But afterwards there occurred violent earthquakes and floods; and in a single day and night of misfortune all your warlike men in a body sank into the earth, and the island of Atlantis in like manner disappeared in the depths of the sea.

Plato, "Timaeus"

The righteous shall rejoice when he seeth the vengeance: he shall wash his feet in the blood of the wicked.

Psalm 58: 11

CHAPTER ONE

K ING PERIANDER TENDED THE flames of his fire. The stars of the
heavens shone upon the makeshift campsite, illuminating Periander's platinum hair while starry Leo up above observed the earthbound
band. All of his companions, after another day's trek across the Libyan
plains, had reached the nocturnal pastures of dreamland. Periander,
however, remained awake, the sweet embraces of sleep far-off from his
whirling mind.

His eyes—an emerald-green hue on the left and a right shining as
sapphire—watched the gently heaving body of his teenage son beside
him. With fatherly affection he pulled back up over the boy his tattered
blanket, which had shaken loose. Hot were the desert days yet the nights
were so cold! And as Periander kept watching him, it almost seemed as
if an outline of his wife appeared at their child's side, holding him close
so that nothing could dislodge her. He lifted his hand and grasped at the
air.

She was gone.

Periander clenched his fist and cursed it for its failure—not for this
time, for he knew that it had been only an apparition, a faint glow of his
memory deceiving his eyes. No, rather he cursed the hand that had let
Cornelia slip through its grasp, his beloved spouse, who ought still to be
with him.

Dreadful was that night, that horrible night when he was forced to flee
for his life—he, his family, and his closest companions too. The aban-

donment of hearth and home. Speeding in the hovercar. Flashes of lasers. Explosions. Running up the stairs. Panting. Just a few more steps! You can make it. Help! Cornelia hit. Falling. Grab my hand! NOOOOOOOO!

While these dark memories stewed in his mind's vengeful juices, Periander snatched up a purple flower from the desert earth. His fingers strangled it, pulverizing it into pulp; the liquefied plant bled out all over his hand, the sticky juice rolling down his wrist. He ground it so hard that his knuckles scraped against the palm. Finally, he stopped. With the slime sticking to his hand, he wiped the plant guts on the earth.

I will avenge you, Cornelia, thought Periander, his blazing eyes trained on his hand. *By the Deity Who created the world, I do swear that Critias and Eudoxia shall answer for your death. When I return to the land of my fathers, I will liberate it from their ravenous gullets. Every offense and insult they have committed against our family and our country shall be repaid double, treble, quadruple. By our son's head, Cornelia, which I will safeguard better than I did yours, your murderers shall pay life for life....*

***

THE HIGHWAY OF CERCYLON stretched far into the horizon, streaking across the Libyan plains. Beside the highway lay strips of grass and greenery; the palm trees lining the road, their lush leaves spreading outwards, provided a luxuriant sunshade. Journeying down this route were Periander and his men. The used hovercar that they had acquired from an itinerant merchant at an outrageous price, its gray sides shedding paint fragments like a drake molting its down in the summertime, was gasping its last puffs of air as it struggled to remain afloat. With a strident bang, the now smoke-engulfed engine died, and the ground raced to embrace the vehicle.

"Awww, this is just great!" exclaimed Agathocles, dismounting from the car. His bushy blond beard roaring in the breeze around his skinny neck, he pummeled the hood with his thick-fingered fist. "That swindler swore this would last till we got to Cyrene!"

"I agree it is unfortunate." Twirling the right full sideburn dangling several inches down beside his beardless chin, Demosthenes' hazel moustache rose as he remarked, "At least this canopy will shade us from the sun now that we must go on foot."

"But be vigilant," warned Periander, focusing his eyes on his son. "This land is a bastion of misgovernment and is notorious for its brigands and cutthroats; the shade may yet conceal an enemy. We opted to take a lightly trafficked path, so I doubt we'll be able to flag down a passerby. Only twenty miles separates us from Cyrene: if we pace ourselves well, we should reach the city before nightfall."

Hoisting his small bag of belongings over his shoulder, Jason scornfully wrinkled his long nose and rolled his green eyes. "What a *glorious* entrance we'll make—an Atlantean king and company arriving like a horde of beggars!"

"The important thing is that we arrive unharmed," said Periander, wrapping his right arm around him and running his left hand through Jason's spiky auburn hair. *What I wouldn't give to say the same about your mother...*

"Unharmed, indeed!" said Socrates, his stomach length silver beard flowing as he was helped out of the car by Philip. Straightening his small half-moon glasses, the forehead-bald old man ambled over to Jason and Periander. "Had that landing been any rougher, there would have been nothing left for our go-between to meet."

After gathering their meager belongings from the hovercar, Periander and his men marched down the highway, maintaining a steady pace while encountering no other souls along the way. When the sun was nearing the end of his daily circuit, filling the pink sky with his resplendent rays, the lofty walls of Cyrene began to rise high upon the horizon. Agathocles had proceeded farther up the road to a point that lay on the other side of a dune beyond his companions' line of sight. From his nearer vantage point, he started shouting back that their destination was within reach. While in the process of describing how many lights he could see emerging from the city skyline, his voice died mid-sentence.

"Agathocles!"

No response followed.

"Let's go!"

At Periander's urging, they raced towards the danger that had presumably engulfed their friend. Descending the dune on the other side, they walked into the middle of an armed standoff. Seventeen burly men, all armed with blaster rifles that were trained on Agathocles, blocked the road ahead. Agathocles, in turn, had his laser pistol drawn and was oscillating his gun-hand, unsure at whom of the many he should aim his weapon.

They're not uniformed, strictly speaking, but their apparel bares a certain similarity and their stances indicative of professional coördination. These aren't common robbers...

Demosthenes defensively stood in front of Periander as the others lined up across the path, brandishing their own weapons. Yet Periander, having surveyed the risks, brushed him aside and addressed the armed men. "Who are you and why do you obstruct us?"

There stood in the center of the opposing line a single man without a weapon drawn. His hand was casually working a toothpick. "I am Galba Antilles, Cyrene's chief highway patrolman."

"Galba Antilles? I've heard of that name. Weren't you the governor here?"

Galba narrowed his eyes. "Yes, I was once the governor of Cyrene before my scheming brother..."—he cast the toothpick down and ground it under his foot— "...before my city, in its wisdom, transferred the governorship to my brother Aeson and compensated me with the command of these fine patrolmen whom you see before you. Now, having obliged you by answering your question, answer mine! Who are *you?* What leads you to travel to Cyrene?"

"My name is Automedon Aretos from the city of Barca," improvised Periander. Quickly remembering that Cyrene was notable among the cities of Libya for being in possession of the continent's largest temple outside of Egypt, he folded his hands together as if in prayer. "We are pilgrims, intent only on visiting your city's famous temple to the Deity. We mean you no harm by our presence."

"You seem well-armed for pilgrims."

"We respect the principles of self-defense, and these roads are dangerous." Periander gestured his men to lower their weaponry.

The chief patrolman snorted. "Very well, you may go on your way. But," added Galba, "I'll send a couple of my men to accompany you, to ensure you reach your destination in safety."

And to see that you don't cause any trouble, thought Periander, finishing Galba's sentence for him. *This will complicate things...*

He nevertheless complied with what Galba had pronounced, not having any realistic alternative at the moment; and in the company of their minders, Periander led his men into the city.

Cyrene was a mid-sized city of thirty thousand souls, characterized by its bustling port from which its seafaring folk engaged in lucrative commerce with their Mediterranean neighbors. By now the sun had sunk into his western bed, and the fluorescent lights of the city blinded the heavenly lights. Periander and his men kept their cloaks' linen hoods drawn tightly over their faces, lest any merchant who did business in Atlantis should recognize them. For Critias, ensconced on the Atlantean throne of the High King, may not have held sway over the cities of Africa, but his money did; and from the time of Periander's flight, bountiful bounties had been posted for his capture and for his fellow outlaws too. The average passerby may be disinclined to lend a hand to strangers in need, but nothing stirs more interest in one's fellow man than the prospect of reward.

After spending several minutes at Cyrene's temple to conform to the story he had told, Periander led his men to the Phoenix Tavern. Here, he told their escorts, they had arranged lodging.

The tavern was squalid, its walls and stone floors befouled by spilled liquor and assorted fluids; shards of glass littered the floorboards, and many a nick and a scratch marred the furniture. Frequented by sailors, drunks, and pickpockets, the pungent smell of sweat and brine, complemented by overflowing spittoons, choked the air. As this was not the type of place that the authorities closely watched, it had previously been arranged for Periander to meet with his connection here.

"There," said Periander, pointing to the southwest corner of the room. There one man sat alone at a secluded table, wearing star-shaped sunglasses, and dressed in a burgundy cloak and a blue hat, the agreed upon sign. Periander told Jason and Socrates to wait at the bar along with their escorts. Making his way through the rowdy crowd, he approached the table.

The man was unfazed as Agathocles and Demosthenes sat down on either side of him. "Have you gentlemen tried the rum swizzle?" he asked nonchalantly, swishing his glass of rum. "It electrifies the souls of wanderers."

"Though I be a wanderer, I will never run to rum."

When he received the correct countersign, the man said, "I'm Thrallis." He handed Periander an envelope containing the transcriptions of messages forwarded to him from allies in Atlantis.

Periander avidly perused the letters, grimacing at the developments at home. After he finished reading it, Thrallis conversed with him about his journey, the state of his men, as well as asking among other things, "What is your plan from here on? Where should I forward your messages to?"

"I am enticed by our prospects in Egypt."

"Egypt... An excellent choice."

"Yes," continued Periander, stroking his well-trimmed beard. "As Egyptians are known for their hospitality to asylum-seekers, we should be able to dwell safely there for some time, without the incessant roving to which we have become accustomed. And based on my knowledge of Pharaoh Ozymandias, I am hopeful—the Deity willing—that by detailing the dangers the current régime poses not only to Atlantis but also to Egypt I may induce him to join us in... liberating Atlantis."

Periander lingered over the final two words. Then he sighed. His mind could, on the one hand, easily envision a triumphant outcome: the reclamation of his kingly rule and estates, his subjects restored to their allegiance to him, Atlantis freed from the cruel grasps of tyranny, vengeance wrought upon the House of Atlas.... Yet however simple it was to imagine the fruits of victory, something even the most slothful of dreamers could do, the daunting magnitude of the undertaking—the immense forces that would be necessary to invade Atlantis, the duration of the struggle, the concomitant difficulties—loomed over him as a hundred-year-old oak over a baby ant. The end is easily envisioned but the steps leading up to the end are always a struggle.

"I believe we have said all that is needed," said Thrallis, rising from the table.

"I thank you for your services," said Periander.

"Do not thank me for this," replied Thrallis as he walked a few steps away. "You owe me nothing."

"But you undertake great risks as our intermediary, do you not?"

"No, I don't."

Thrallis snapped his fingers. From the surrounding tables there rose seven men armed with blaster rifles, Thrallis' men, who went from blending in among the crowd to suddenly encircling Periander and his men.

"What's the meaning of this?" demanded Agathocles, swiveling his skinny neck around.

"I played you for fools," gloated Thrallis. A sardonic smile formed on his face. "I'm not your go-between: I am Governor Aeson Antilles's right-hand man, in charge of Cyrene's internal security. Your real contact fell into our hands, Periander, and before killing him we extracted what we needed from him for this little charade." He removed from his cloak an Atlantean wanted poster, depicting Periander and listing his accomplices and the corresponding prices for their respective captures. "Atlantis will pay well for you."

"You loathsome maggot," spat Periander. With his heart pounding, he calmly surveyed their foes. *Three on the right, two on the left, two in the center.*

"Away with them!" commanded Thrallis, turning aside.

As two of his thugs moved in to seize Periander, reaching for him with their alcohol-stained hands, the crimson bolt of a laser zipped across the room. Gore gushed from the first man's skull when the laser hit the left side of his head crosswise. Slashing straight into the brainy bark of his cerebral cortex, the laser killed the man instantly. Meanwhile the second thug, struck by his fallen comrade's corpse, bellowed a deafening screech as he fell backwards over a spiked-back metal chair that was poking out from another table, his bulky arms thrashing wildly and grasping the murky air in vain while the knifelike spikes ripped into his own back. The violent gyrations died down as soon as his head was impaled upon the jagged tops of several large, half-empty rum bottles that had been ditched beneath the other table. Wine-dark blood seeped from the man's head and intermingled with what remained of the undiluted liquor.

"Father!" shouted Jason, aiming his freshly fired gun as he and Socrates hurtled across the room.

Oh, no, thought Periander, gritting his teeth as their two escorts rushed up behind Jason.

The escorts drew their weapons, commanded everyone to halt, and barked at Thrallis' men to identify themselves. They received, as a reply, a round of laser fire that prompted them to duck behind the bar.

Periander, Agathocles, and Demosthenes flipped their corner table to use as a makeshift shelter while Jason and Socrates, now joined by their escorts who were compelled to fight alongside them to save their own lives, hunkered down behind the bar. From their respective positions, each group exchanged gunfire with Thrallis and his men who were divided into two groups: three (and then only two) men on the east side of the room and two others taking shelter in the southeast corner with Thrallis himself.

Socrates and one of their escorts stayed behind the counter to draw the enemy's gunfire while Jason and the other escort repeatedly darted out to shoot them from additional angles.

Outnumbered, Thrallis' men began to give way. Philip killed one of them with a shot fired from the west side of the room while Periander's group, inching their table forwards as their shield, forced Thrallis' party back towards the tavern's entrance.

"Lord Periander, watch out!" cried Socrates.

What?! Periander swung his head around. His jaw dropped.

A thug they had left for dead in their rear was alive! He held his panting, bleeding right chest in one hand and a grenade in the other. But before he could lob it at them, Socrates jumped out from the bar's counter and fired his gun as he raced across the room. Vomiting blood, the man dropped dead, and his grenade landed beside Socrates.

"Hurry! Dispose of the grenade!" shouted Periander.

Ducking the gunfire from Thrallis' remaining men, Agathocles charged over and, grabbing the explosive, hurled it out an open window leading to the alleyway.

BOOOOOOMMM!!!

Amidst the fighting, pandemonium had consumed the crowded room. Glasses shattered on the floor as bar patrons dropped them in terror. Screeching chairs ground the floor during the flight of their occupants. Whereas before the room had been more filled than empty, it was now more bare than populous even as the hemorrhaging of its clients continued. As when a starving cheetah catches two men unawares, and they turn to flee, each striving to outrun not the predator but his comrade, so too did the panicked mob exit the building, shoving and jostling and mercilessly trampling underfoot whomever impeded each one's path.

Resting with his back against the table, Periander clasped his pistol tightly. Its metal grip warmed his hand from repeated use. Clenching his teeth, he jumped up to fire the next round.

He was greeted by a room devoid of enemies.

"Cease fire! I think they've gone!"

The blasters of his men stopped. Over near the entrance came groans from several persons trampled in the frenzy. The alcoholic dispensaries behind the bar's counter, having had their guts shot through during the fight, were busy retching their contents onto the floor; the whooshing sound of all manner of liquor filled the air, which was likewise saturated with the intoxicating smells of sundry beverages. Yet no longer did gunfire resonate through the grim room.

"We must leave before Thrallis returns with reïnforcements," said Demosthenes.

"I know," murmured Periander, patting Agathocles on the back when he returned. "Is everyone alright?"

"Other than some scrapes from a shattered whisky bottle," said Philip, applying pressure to a minor cut on his arm. Although much blood covered his flesh, he added, "Don't worry: it's mostly theirs."

"My comrade is dead," called one of their escorts from the bar counter, crouching down over the cadaver.

Socrates said, "We sympathize with your loss."

Despite receiving positive responses from all his men and their surviving escort, one voice was prominent by its absence.

"Jason! Jason!" Periander frantically called his son's name when he did not appear.

His calls went unanswered.

"Has anyone seen my son?"

"I last saw him over there," answered Demosthenes, pointing towards a couple tables which were lying on their sides in front of one of the walls.

Oh, Deity, please, no...!

Periander staggered over to the tables. Inundated with dread, his throat barely able to swallow the saliva welling up in it, he peered over the bloodstained tabletops. His eyes widened out of fear that they were about to behold the body of his only child. "Jason..."

Blood and alcohol coated the floor behind the tables. Jason was nowhere to be seen. Periander braced himself against the wall with both hands as he felt his entire body quake from two contradictory emotions: joy because the absence of a body meant his son was not proven to be dead and terror because he did not know where Jason was. *Where are you, my boy? First your mother, and now...*

Periander's men exchanged glances with one another, unsure of what to say, when suddenly Agathocles shouted, "Look!"

Less than twenty feet away from Periander, in the spot where Thrallis' contingent had initially sought cover, one of his lackeys, wounded, crawling out from a table that had been overturned during the mayhem. They all sped to him.

"Where is my son?" yelled Periander, arriving first and yanking the man up from the floor. He thrust him against the hard wall. "What have you done with him?"

The man, his left arm dislocated, both his legs broken below the knees, and his crooked nose drenched with blood as a result of the fight, answered, "Fine, fine, I'll tell you." He coughed warm droplets of blood onto Periander's face. "While you were distracted with the grenade, my boss took the chance to escape. Abandoning me, of course—his life's the only one he's truly concerned about." Periander eased his grip on the man, who continued, "But as he left, I saw he managed to grab your kid by surprise, and had his other man drag him along."

Simultaneously relieved by this knowledge while also convulsing with rage, Periander demanded, "Where is he taking him?"

"I'd expect the governor's palace. That's where all the high-profile detainees are taken."

Periander let go of the man and started rushing to the exit. *I've got to get him back,* he thought, biting his lip. His feet stopped but his eyes continued rushing back and forth. *But they'll send reïnforcements after us; they could arrive any minute; we must take off and regroup. But what if they kill him before then, like the go-between? Overtake them before they reach their destination! But which way did they go? No, we should—*

His mind, spiraling with anxiety, began to stabilize when Agathocles' blunt but assuring voice hit his ears. "We'll get him back, my Lord. Count on it!"

"Just remember that they want him for the money," said Demosthenes, "and so will have to keep him alive and well to get the full reward."

Sighing and sagging his head, Periander muttered, "You're right, you're right," as he clenched his fists as if to force himself to accept that fact.

Then the surviving escort approached them. "I take it you're not pilgrims, Automedon—and that's probably not even your name." He spoke gruffly and with a high degree of scorn in his voice, his nostrils flaring as he gazed at the man who seemed responsible for all that had befallen him and his dead comrade.

Periander merely looked him in the eye. What words were equal to the occasion?

"I overheard them call you Periander. By any chance, you wouldn't be that Atlantean king who got driven out of his land and is now being hunted down like a mad dog by every lowlife this side of the Mediterranean, now would you?"

"I am the same."

"I don't care who you are, and frankly I don't think Galba will either. But if you want your son back, I think he'd be willing to make a deal with you...."

CHAPTER TWO

"**I** 'LL SEE TO IT that this is relayed to our king," said Lysander Besa as he received the envelope into his perspiring hands, his silver signet ring catching onto and nearly unsealing it.

"Careful, Son," warned Timaeus. Above his wrinkly cheeks, the old man's large brown eyes focused attentively on the letter and his voice resounded gently.

They were in the communal area of Lysander's apartment, located on the south side of the imperial palace. Though not too large in contrast to other palatial lodgings, they were spacious enough for the chief clerk of the High King's secretariat, sprawling out from the entrance into three additional rooms. As was true throughout this part of the palace complex, the floors were made of the most glittering vermilion marble and the walls of olive granite. Father and son gathered around an oaken desk lying beneath a window, from which one could perceive the palace's nut orchard ten stories below.

"I'm sorry." Lysander examined the still-intact golden seal and brushed the russet locks on his forehead aside to wipe his brow. This was the kind of message that induces sweat. It was neither a routine office memo, nor a letter to a long-absent friend, nor yet an epistle destined for maternal eyes and tears. This was a coded message for the exiled Periander.

Despite holding senior offices in the High King's government, Lysander and Timaeus defied the express prohibition against communicating with the High King's enemies not out of treachery but from sincere feelings of loyalty. They were by birth inhabitants of that sector of Atlantis which from time immemorial had been governed by Periander's family. Like all Atlanteans (apart from those in the continent's central subkingdom that was subject to the High King's exclusive jurisdiction), they owed a dual allegiance: both to the House of Eumelus that governed their tenth of Atlantis and to the House of Atlas which exercised a preëminent, but not absolute, authority over the whole continent. As Periander's subjects, Lysander and Timaeus regarded their allegiance to him as meriting a higher claim upon their actions rather than the duties they owed to them who had sought to murder him in defiance of the ancestral constitution. Nor did they remain faithful in thought only, which could by itself prove sufficiently dangerous in these times. Disregarding the omnipresent perils and heinous punishment that awaited them if they should be caught, they both utilized their positions in the imperial administration to further Periander's interests—collecting information and passing it along, via a network of go-betweens, to their exiled king.

As soon as the white envelope had submerged into the inner folds of Lysander' azure clothing, Timaeus said, "You will have to hold off delivering this to You-Know-Who until after the coronation."

Critias! cursed Lysander inwardly, the veins on both his hands bulging as he tightly clenched his fists. How he hated him!

Critias, the son of the queen mother Eudoxia, had borne the name of High King of Atlantis for many years but until now had not possessed the powers pertaining to his position. Having just attained his majority, oddly stipulated at nineteen years of age (despite being eighteen for all others), Critias finally was to be crowned this day and endowed with all the authority that came with it. Per the Regency Law, he could have been crowned last year if the regent, his mother, had deemed him ready to assume his kingly powers. Eudoxia, however, had chosen to continue as regent for one more year notwithstanding her son's many agitations to the contrary.

Critias' thoughts on the one-year delay were widely known.

On his eighteenth birthday, Critias had orchestrated a crepuscular coronation in the Throne Hall that perverted the symbolism of the rites. He and his young companions had crudely mimicked the ancient ceremonies which for centuries High Kings had undergone with dignity. Critias crowned himself with a wreath of coca leaves and accepted a splash of gin for his anointing. His harlots, donning priestly vestments, turned the cups for outpouring holy libations into receptacles for urine. And in lieu of royal hymnals, an impromptu chorus chanted bawdy drinking songs and other obscenities. Such had been the antics occurring when Lysander, drawn by their riotous ululations, entered the hall. As a party favor, he received a half-circle scar beneath his lower lip from one of the drunken revelers' wine bottles soaring midair. It was a small scar, scarcely showing a year later; nonetheless, it refreshed his revulsion for Critias whenever he met a mirror.

Lysander left his room with Timaeus, and they went to the Throne Hall. Fittingly adorned for the ceremony, the double row of grooved columns, which stretched through the center of the room up to the throne on the far wall, were decked with golden garlands. The throne itself, made of gilded orichalcum, stood ready to receive its monarch; eagerly-awaiting attendants surrounded it. All the Atlantean notables, dignitaries, and the dynasts from the other eight royal houses—no longer numbering nine as they had during previous coronations—were clad in their finest robes and jewels. Conversing with some other officials, Lysander ceased and stepped back to the wall as soon as the blasting of trumpeters heralded the royal entrance.

Critias entered to booming applause. His hair, whose ebony color he shared with his mother, shimmered as he held his wide forehead high. A huge smirk engulfed his ivory-colored face as he confidently sauntered towards the throne. At six foot six, Critias overshadowed his mother by a foot and a half.

Eudoxia, clothed in a scarlet dress sewed with black pearls, with egg-shaped diamonds fashioned into earrings drooping beside her narrow oblong face, scurried after her son while a dozen attendants suspended the dress's twenty-foot-long train. Throughout her procession, she was continually rotating her head, scrutinizing everyone with those little green eyes that bulged beneath her menacingly thick eyebrows.

Lysander gulped fearfully when her eyes happened to fall on his.

Coming to the area in front of the throne, Critias bade his mother step aside to a seat prepared for her while he remained at the focal point of the room. The ancient rites were duly carried out in their proper sequence until at last, from the hands of the high priest, Critias snatched the ruby-and-sapphire encrusted diadem and placed it upon his head. Rapturous ovations arose among the crowd and a long life wished for their High King. Then Critias recited a speech which had been written for him by his tutor before the latter had suspiciously fallen from a window to his death the prior day; his listless enunciation of grandiloquent vocabulary and the manner in which he strained the syntax jerky elicited yet more applause.

Lest he be conspicuous, Lysander played along by clapping in unison with the uncritical throng. Yet all the while his scar was prickling his lip. When Critias's voice suddenly became enlivened at the part of the speech describing the dissolution of Periander's royal house and the confiscation of all his properties to the imperial treasury, Lysander struggled to force a smile to suppress a snarl.

Critias had just finished speaking when two half-starved men with unkempt beards, clothed in nothing other than ragged loincloths, their bloody backs disfigured from chronic whippings, were dragged in front of him by a couple of guards.

Polycles and Donax! Lysander bit his lip when he recognized them.

The crowd murmured at this unexpected sight. What previous coronation had ever been desecrated by the presence of prisoners? Critias' nod to the guards, however, revealed that it was planned. Raising his arm for silence, he glared at his adoring audience and announced:

"These terrorists are guilty of treacherously conspiring against my crown!" He clutched the crown with one hand while pointing ominously at the convicts with the other. "They plotted my overthrow, conspiring to help that traitor Periander usurp my crown." He stomped over to them and pulled back the head of one of the prisoners by his hair. Putting a dagger to his throat, he shouted, "I am the High King of Atlantis!" as he slit the man's throat. "*Me*! I will not tolerate anyone who threatens my crown!" Then Critias breathlessly slashed the other throat, the blood splattering his fingers. Smiling at his handiwork, he held the gory blade beneath his nostrils and sniffed the life-giving fluid.

The crowd remained subdued as his mother Eudoxia walked over to his side.

"Let this be a warning to every miscreant," she hissed. She glowered at the crowd not only collectively but also, as it seemed, at all of them individually. "Whoever opposes us or plots against our rei—my son's reign." She corrected herself. "That person will be destroyed without mercy... according to law."

After a few more warnings against treasonous behavior, Eudoxia regaled the crowd with a summary of her outstanding regency—her strident voice roaring with pride as she catalogued her many, many, many achievements that had improved Atlantis so much. Everyone vigorously cheered whatever she was saying at any moment. Everyone, that is, except Critias. Indeed, standing in front of him, Eudoxia was completely oblivious that her son's black eyes were glaring at her.

When Eudoxia had at last finished speaking, the ceremony ended without more ado. She and Critias quit the room, flocked on all sides by their entourage and by the eight kings as hangers-on. Once all the royalty had left, the hall quickly became lifeless: all the others—lords and commoners, courtiers and servants alike—quickly made their own departures until only the slain prisoners remained.

Lysander reünited with Timaeus outside the Throne Hall and together they made their way back towards his apartments in silence. Lysander kept his head downcast, looking only at the floor while he thought about the executions; the tortured bodies and the coldness with which Critias had dispatched them kept flashing through his mind. Reaching his apartment, they unsealed and added a quick addendum to their letter. Timaeus at this point bade him goodnight and was about to leave when Lysander asked him to wait.

"Do you remember at breakfast, Father, when you prayed your daily prayer for Periander and the others' wellbeing?"

"Yes," said Timaeus, his voice a whisper.

"Well, I fear they ought to be praying more for *us*."

CHAPTER THREE

J ASON CRINGED AS GOVERNOR Aeson Antilles's chubby fingers, decked with ornate golden rings, seized his chin. The governor moved Jason's head from side to side in the same way as the prospective buyer of a mare might examine the horse's teeth. Beside him stood Thrallis like an equine huckster, smirking and visibly pleased with his human merchandise.

Near the end of the fight at the inn, Jason had had his back turned to Thrallis, his attention focused on Socrates' attack on the grenade-wielding enemy threatening his father's life. He therefore failed to see Thrallis when he slithered up on him from behind, gun in hand. With a single blow to the back of his skull, Jason abruptly lost a clump of hair, consciousness, and liberty too.

He revived to find himself being transported through the halls of the gubernatorial residence which, perched atop the highest hill of Cyrene, overlooked all that was below it. Inside was every conceivable luxury, its opulence most readily exemplified by the chamber into which he had been brought. This was Aeson's office, wide and receding deep into the building. The floor was polished marble, inset with mosaics made of precious stones and gems; the walls were plated with gold leaf; and the ceiling consisted of ivory that had been embossed with silvery animals skillfully carved therein. All the furniture exuded similar lavishness, and the platinum armchair behind Aeson's desk resembled a monarch's throne.

"You will fetch us a splendid price!" exclaimed Aeson as he clasped his hands together, his beardless, fatty jowls undulating with merriment. "Indeed, from your bounty alone I could outfit two more rooms like this. Servants! Contact the Atlanteans and—"

"Sir," said Thrallis, interrupting him. "I suggest you hold off on cashing in just yet."

"Whatever for?" said Aeson, his voice rising to a high pitch.

"In the interest of greater profit! True, the reward for the boy's capture is large—but the father's is larger, triple even."

"And? Why should that dissuade us from collecting this one's bounty now?"

"Because it will make it easier to capture Periander."

"But how will we get Periander? You lost him. We have no idea where he is now."

"Though he eluded capture the first time," mumbled Thrallis, gnashing his teeth, "so long as we have the son, we have the perfect bait for ensnaring the father."

"Oh, I get it! Brilliant! Use the son to lure the father. Trap him. Capital idea!"

All the while that Aeson and Thrallis were conversing, Jason was still present, observing them and listening as they spoke of him as though he were not there. *Your brother greatly exaggerated your intelligence,* thought Jason as he recalled Galba's mention of his "scheming brother."

When Aeson noticed the intense glare emanating from Jason, he casually beckoned the guards. "Take the boy away."

"Hey, hey, you can't do this!" shouted Jason, thumping his body around in an attempt to foil the two guards who were trying to subdue him. "I am a freeborn son of Atlantis, scion of the House of Eumelus! I demand you release me!"

"Oh, you may have been a prince once," scoffed Aeson softly, shaking his index finger at him dismissively, "but you're just an outlaw now, spurned by your own people. And as soon as I capture your father, I'll be rewarded handsomely."

"You couldn't capture a flea on your spittle-covered sixth chin, you born fool!" exclaimed Jason. Aeson gasped, his blubbery chin recoiling in shock. "It's obvious your underling has you wrapped around his finger!"

A blow to his face from Thrallis, who was bellowing, "Respect the Governor!" sent him flying towards the floor. Beset by several sets of arms, Jason was dragged out of the room. He was quickly ushered through the lowest bowels of the building and cast face-down into a prison cell. The thick metal door slammed behind him.

Heavily bruised, his right eye black and weepy, and with several scrapes on his arms, Jason rose from the mercilessly cold floor. It was a dank cell, compressed by its dark gray concrete walls. If no budgetary constraints had limited the expenditures made on Aeson's quarters, then the reverse was true for those of his prisoners. The cell's solitary furnishings were a pile of hay in lieu of a bed and an old, discolored chamber-pot.

Jason wearily plopped himself among the dry, prickly, brittle hay, still reeking of the bodies that had lain there before, and then looked up. From the slit at the top of the exterior wall, through which a modicum of light penetrated the dismal cell, came a buzzing mosquito. Attracted to the droplets of blood oozing from his wounds, it flew around Jason. He smiled at his little cellmate.

"O mosquito," whispered Jason, "if only you could fly me out of here, and restore me to my father; he would cover you with the kingliest of robes and give you a scepter to hold in your hand...."

✦✦✦

"I SEE," SAID GALBA. His man had led Periander and his men to their headquarters, a garrison adjoining the city wall, where he and Periander apprised Galba of all that had occurred. Boos and hissing had ensued from the ranks of the border patrol as they learned of their comrade's slaughter. "That sounds exactly like what my brother's thug would do. Thrallis values no one who gets in his way; he'd kill his own mother if she so much as delayed him thirty seconds. Many such incidents over the years are proof of this... and now one of my men has suffered at his hands."

"I must rescue my son," said Periander, stepping closer to Galba. "I will, no matter the cost. But despite your position in government and ties of blood, I have been led to believe that you would be willing to act against Aeson and save my son from Thrallis? Will you help me?"

Galba silently chewed a toothpick. He looked at Periander and his followers, then at his own patrolmen interspersed throughout the room. Hatred, indignation, and a longing for vengeance were discernible in their facial expressions, their obscenely violent gestures, and their intractable heckling of Aeson and Thrallis.

"Kidnapping is such a dingy way to get money," mused Galba. He sighed. "Then again, so is extortion, bribery, embezzlement, illegal taxation... There's nothing my brother won't stoop to if it means grasping another coin. And he'll permit his henchman to commit any abuse in the pursuit of it. I've tried to ignore it—to do my best in my own duties, to prove to the people that not all officials are corrupt. But with every passing day, the situation grows more intolerable."

"How did Cyrene's government fall into this state?" asked Periander. "As a boy, I recall hearing Cyrene to be a well-governed society despite its lack of a king to keep order."

"It's complicated." Galba looked down at the ground. "Yes, unlike Atlantis and the major powers, our city has no king. We call Cyrene a Republic: this means we have multiple magistrates, independently elected by our most prominent citizens, our commercial guilds, and other stakeholders, who rotate in office rather than ruling for life. I myself once served as governor; now I am in charge of patrolling our highways and hinterland. That is commonplace in a Republic. And regardless of which position I currently hold, I strive to serve my people the best I can."

"Evidently a foolish system if men of your integrity can be replaced with the likes of your brother."

"As a king, you scoff at this. But for many years this system worked for us."

"Until your system broke down."

Galba narrowed his eyes and held his gaze on Periander. "We come from different political worlds, Periander. (As a citizen rather than a subject, I will address you simply by your name without the titles of royalty and elaborate courtesies you are accustomed to receive from your countrymen.) I don't intend to start an in-depth debate over political philosophies with you and I don't think you want to argue the merits of monarchy and republics either, at least not now when your son's freedom is in jeopardy. But as a brief defense of my city, contrast your own land: Atlantis is under the rule of a hereditary monarch whom I venture you would characterize as a tyrant. I bet you wish you could vote Critias out of office right now, no?"

Periander flared his nostrils. "Although Atlantis is presently oppressed by a tyrannical High King and his regent mother, my homeland is a federal monarchy. We have multiple kings, of which I am one, who have been entrusted by our ancestors and the will of the Deity to jointly rule our land with justice and honor. All men fall short of perfect virtue, but from boyhood we are raised to regard no duty worthy of higher reverence than to honor the Deity by serving our people—the noble acts of our forefathers serving as our pedagogues and kept constantly before our eyes as ideals to be emulated. Wicked men inevitably come along among kings as among any class of persons. Critias, reared in his mother's wickedness, is proof of that. And while it is true we have no antiseptic procedure to depose a High King such as by 'voting him out of office,' we do have the precedents of our forefathers and the laws they bequeathed to us that authorize us, his fellow kings, to resist him by force if necessary. And that is the justification for the course on which I am now committed. Suffice it to say, our system also worked for many years; and, by the grace of the Deity, I will make it work again for me, my son, and his sons after him."

"An excellent rejoinder," said Galba, clapping his hands. "Periander, I fancy myself a good judge of men. Despite our different outlooks on politics, I'd wager we're pretty similar when it comes to our ethics and sense of duty to our peoples. And we're both faced with having to watch our societies chafe under the rule of evildoers. At least in your case you don't have to bear the added shame of watching your people suffer at the hands of your own kin..."

"What exactly happened between you and your brother?" interjected Agathocles from beside Periander.

Galba sighed. "My father was a prominent trader, whose fleet of cargo ships crisscrossed the Mediterranean and brought back great wealth to my city and family. His commercial ventures often kept him overseas for long stretches of time, supervising his business interests but without postponing pleasure. Shortly before he died, he confessed that he had another family in Syracuse. Despite my surprise to discover that I had a brother, I wished to meet him and invited him to visit Cyrene. That was my greatest mistake. Aeson eagerly came when he learned he had a relative with a far bigger house than my father had provided for his second family. While we're both sons of a merchant, our father left me his wealth but my brother the craving for gain. Once Aeson arrived, he stayed far beyond his welcome, refusing to be dislodged, pestering my associates and business partners in hopes of finding a get-rich-quick scheme. Then I was elected governor. I won't claim I was perfect at the job or good at finessing Councilmen; but suffice it to say, my tenure as governor proved ill-fated for those citizens keen to profit off sleaze. And no one coveted that more than my brother. When I rebuffed his attempts to turn my office into an engine of graft, he found a capable partner in that lowlife Thrallis who helped him quietly orchestrate my ouster. One way or another, Aeson and his henchman persuaded a majority of the

State-Council to vote to remove me from office. I and many of my supporters were relegated to border patrol, while that larcenous duo"—he spat upon the floor—"have been in charge ever since. Public office for them and their ilk is only a means for private enrichment. After a few membership changes on the Council, Aeson and his cronies muscled through self-serving reforms to the city's bylaws and totally corrupted our republican government, keeping themselves in office long after their terms should have expired; they have never been politically more secure."

"I take it, then," said Periander slowly, "that you can't simply vote your brother out of office?"

"You throw my words back at me." Galba lowered his head. "But I deserve that. Aeson has so thoroughly made a mockery of my city's customs that I can no more proceed against him by established channels than you can in your fight against Critias. Once again, I say, the two of us are alike." He raised his eyes to meet Periander's gaze and offered him his hand. "I think Cyrene has been corrupted and pillaged enough by Aeson and Thrallis: it's time for a change, one that must come from outside the political system. Periander, if you will help me overthrow my brother, then I'll help you get your son back. I expect he's being held in one prison or other, probably in Aeson's grandiose palace; after the coup, we'll liberate him."

Periander did not hesitate. He shook Galba's hand and immediately exchanged oaths with him. Each of their parties cheered for the new alliance, hoisting their weapons with thrill. All, that is, but Demosthenes, who took Periander aside.

"Sire," he whispered while twirling his right sideburn, "are you sure that this was the optimal path to take to save Prince Jason? It is one thing to seek collaboration from within hostile quarters; the history of bribing prison guards is a testament to its efficacy. But to go so far as to participate in a revolution, and to involve ourselves so deeply in the domestic affairs of a city which—"

"I am." The firm yet serenely calm tone of Periander's voice seemed to assuage any misgivings Demosthenes had. "My overriding concern right now is Jason's rescue. His captors control this city. With the assistance of inside collaborators who are heavily armed and able to maneuver freely throughout the city, we shall more readily succeed in freeing him. Besides," he added, his multicolored eyes blazing with intensity and radiating ardor, "if, without detracting from our main goal, we can simultaneously play a part in ousting Cyrene's oppressive, lawless régime, then I judge it not unworthy of our support. Tyranny anywhere is an affront to true kinghood everywhere." Although his mouth said Cyrene, Periander's heart boiled, and his hands sweated with thoughts of his native Atlantis.

"I understand," said Demosthenes, bowing his head. "May the king prosper in his undertaking and my hands prove useful to him."

"Yes!" interjected Agathocles, throwing one arm around Demosthenes' shoulder and the other into the air. "Now let's go defeat the bastards!"

***

B Y NOW HOURS HAD elapsed since the brawl in the tavern. All seemed peaceful in Cyrene, and quiet reigned in the city's streets; the stars alone appeared active. Quitting the waking world, governor Aeson had long since submerged into sleep, swaddled among cloth-of-gold bedding and pillows stuffed with the most exotic feathers. He was awakened by his servants amid a din of voices and, with the tip of his crimson nightcap collapsing onto his face, he was led out by Thrallis to the residence's main reception hall.

"Brother." Galba saluted him as he crossed the threshold.

"Brother," yawned Aeson aloofly. His drooping eyes shot open when they focused on the mass of men behind Galba.

"I have captured these desperados who entered the city," said Galba, extending his arm to exhibit his prisoners. Guarded by a throng of Galba's men, Periander along with Agathocles, Demosthenes, Socrates, and Philip stood in a row, their heads stooped low, and their hands weighed down by shackles.

"Ooh," murmured Aeson, rubbing his hands. "This is Periander and his crew?"

"The same ones with bounties on their heads."

Thrallis glared at Galba, his beady little eyes aglow. "How did you manage to catch them?"

"It was far too easy." Galba smirked as he flicked some gunk off his toothpick in Thrallis' direction, who responded with a crinkled nose and teeth-revealing snarl. "These fools actually came to me. To *me*! They thought I could be persuaded to help them. Sure. I helped them alright—right into chains! And all it took was a few deceptive words, some empty promises on my part and I had them totally outmatched. Such gullible fools Atlantis breeds."

"You double-crossing whoreson!" bellowed Agathocles, his sides heaving greatly.

Aeson passed by Thrallis and approached his brother. He gave him a split-second tap on his shoulder before continuing a few paces to survey the prisoners. "You've done me a great favor," he called back over his shoulder, although his attention was diverted entirely to Periander whom his eyes ogled greedily. "And here I was thinking you harbored a grudge against me for taking your job!"

"What I'm doing I do for the good of Cyrene," said Galba somberly, "and not for you."

"Whatever you say, Brother," murmured Aeson. He yanked Periander by his platinum hair so as to get a better view of his prisoner. "As for you, time to suffer the same fate as your valuable little brat. You'll garner a decent pri—uuuggghhhhh!"

Periander's shackles had unfastened by themselves. With his new-ly-freed hands, he grabbed a dagger concealed under a fold of his garment. Then, thrusting it with all his might like a wild boar who, frenzied from the sudden onslaught of a huntsman, spears his would-be killer on the ivory of his horn, Periander stabbed Aeson through his liver. Blood seeped from the wound as Periander withdrew his blade and penetrated the copious target again. Hurtling to the floor, Aeson grasped the air in vain; from his fist flew the hairs of Periander that it had clutched, each lifeless hair, now emancipated from its captor's hand, soaring upwards at Periander's face as though trying to reünite with its still-living brethren.

Aeson made the floor reverberate with his corpse's thud and his blood dripped down Periander's fingers.

As soon as Periander had cast aside his shackles, Agathocles, Demosthenes, Socrates, and Philip had likewise done the same. Behind each of them was one of Galba's men; the rest were dispersed throughout the room, a couple at each entrance, others flanking Aeson's guards who were stationed at several intervals here and there, and the last few standing alongside Galba himself.

Revealing the deception, Galba yelled, "Attack!"

The red flash of laser beams lit up the whole room as his men turned their weapons on Aeson's unsuspecting goons. Here a man was shot between the eyes, there through one ear and out the other. The heart, liver, intestines, groin, and hams were all prime targets, too. Despite the gravity of the scene, the slaughter itself lasted mere seconds. They died like sheep.

Thrallis was floundering on the floor, bleeding to death even as his hand urgently sought a pistol that lay in front of him. But the gray heel of Agathocles' boot dug into his wrist while the rest of him was restrained by Socrates.

Periander picked up the gun. "Where's my son? Where've you taken him, you filthy beast?"

Thrallis glared at him.

Periander knelt down and shoved the gun underneath Thrallis's protruding chin. "Where is he?"

"Cell. Twenty. Eight," spat Thrallis. He gave a crooked smile and chortled, "That's where you'll find your boy. Assuming my men haven't yet beaten him to death for trying to escape!"

Periander killed him with a single blast through the skull. He rose to his feet and glared down at the corpse. "That's for all the innocent people you've hurt."

"As soon as we've secured the rest of the building," said Galba as he approached, "I'll take you to your son."

Before he had finished speaking, one of his men rushed back into the room. "We've got complete control of the building!"

Wiping the sweat off his forehead, Periander turned to Galba. "Let's go."

Accompanied by several armed men, they raced through the corridors of the building until they reached the dungeon. All the while, Periander was gritting his teeth and silently praying to the Deity that his son was well.

Please, please let him be unharmed! I've already lost his mother. I can't lose my son, too.

When they arrived at Jason's cell, Periander solved his lack of a cardkey by placing his gun against the electronic lock's pad. With one press of the trigger, the metal door of the cell slid open. Jason was inside, lying motionless on the floor.

"Jason!" shouted Periander, sprinting over to him.

"What?" said Jason, his body jerking and his head rearing upwards. He blinked and covered his eyes as harsh fluorescent light from the hall flooded into the cell. "What's happening?"

"Jason, it's me, Son, it's me."

"Father? You're here!" exclaimed Jason while a great smile appearing on his bruised face.

Periander helped him to his feet, steadying him against his own body. "Are you alright?" Rage flooded through him and sweat rolled down his forehead as he examined Jason's black eyes and gashes on his cheeks. *Damn the vermin who did this!*

"Yes, I'm alright. It's just a few scrapes."

"Thank the Deity." Periander locked his arms around Jason in a deep embrace. *I thought I'd lost you...*

"I'm so glad to see you. But how did you get here? What happened to all the guards?"

"It doesn't matter. I'll tell you later. Are you sure you're okay?"

"I am now that you're here. That Thrallis and his minions roughed me up a bit, but I was man enough to endure their blows without breaking. I didn't disgrace our family name."

"I'm proud to hear that, Son. Many others would have cowered in fear upon being abducted, but you stood your ground to the best of your abilities. You are a credit to your ancestors."

"What I really feared, Father, was that they'd send me to—that I wouldn't see you again!"

"I know, I know," said Periander, holding tightly onto his son and stroking his head. "You are all that I have left in this world, Jason. I failed your mother and couldn't save her; but you, her best and lasting gift to this world—believe me, as the Deity lives, I would never have rested all my days until I got you back. There's nothing I wouldn't have done."

CHAPTER FOUR

"LONG LIVE THE HIGH King! Long live the High King!" chanted the crowd wildly.

Outside Critias' palace, thousands of Atlanteans thronged the western forecourts. Although nearly noontime, men and women, rich and poor, and all ages from the eldest graybeard to the youngest stripling had flocked here when rumor infected the whole body of the people with a wondrous report: Critias was scattering money from the palace.

Rumor did not disappoint the masses.

Perched atop the massive colonnaded balcony that dominated this side of the palace, each lucent pillar sparkling in the sunlight, the High King towered more than a hundred feet above his subjects. He merrily scooped up by fistfuls gold and silver coins out of the black ceramic barrels next to him—barrels overflowing with coins that nevertheless were so speedily depleted by Critias' munificence that his servants were obliged continuously to replenish their contents. With the flick of his wrists, down rained here, down rained there coins depicting the profile of their master (and of his mother Eudoxia, portrayed beside the profile of her son, on those that had been minted before his assumption of personal rule). The crowd, to a grinning Critias' delight, riotously accepted the royal gifts: everyone was shoving his neighbor and elbowing his friend's eyeballs as he madly fought to scoop up the coins in front of him and also those in front of everyone else.

Eventually Critias grew weary of this distraction. He tossed his last handful, blew kisses with histrionic gesticulation down to his audience, and withdrew into the palace. With a self-satisfied blush upon his ivory face, he boasted to the servants standing about, "My people love me! I am the king they have always yearned for!"

"They love your money," said a strident voice.

Critias snarled and turned around. There was his mother strutting down the hallway, her sickly green eyes as ominous as ever and her oblong face exhibiting its customary scowl. Bringing up the rear behind her, their heads lowered and eyes facing the floor, was Eudoxia's ever-present troupe of male courtiers dutifully following her in the same manner as dogs tail their masters' hindquarters.

"Are you envious, Mother?" asked Critias, putting his arms akimbo. His eyes narrowed into slits. "Do you resent that the people cheer for *me* but have never for *you* and your dour scowl?"

"I couldn't care less what the people think," sniffed Eudoxia as she tugged at the scarlet dress around her waist. "Squander some coins, and I too could buy applause."

"You object to how I spend my money?" said Critias, traversing the floor and looming over her.

"Hardly. Let the people have their token-cash today: we'll recoup it in taxation tomorrow."

Critias' flesh seethed and he grinded his teeth audibly. She always had a comeback to whatever he might say! The last word always just had to be hers! Before he could open his mouth to salvo another round of back-and-forth, Eudoxia stopped him by planting her little middle finger on his pale, thin lips.

"Hush! Enough of this prattle. We have more important things to do."

"Like what?"

"Just follow me and I'll show you."

She dismissed their servants and took him to her private helipad on the roof of the palace where a small airship awaited them. Its exterior was glossy white except for the blackness of its rear propulsion units. Inside was the sheen of gold and a rectangular row of red velvet seats. They went aboard, Eudoxia entered some coördinates on the computer panel, and with the starboard doors whisking shut the vehicle launched into the air.

"Where are you taking me?" asked Critias, crossing his arms, and glaring at her. "You just show up, start telling me I've got to—"

"To Dr. Anaxagoras' laboratory." Eudoxia did not even bother to look up from the computer screen on which she was typing. "He's in charge of our Experimental Weapons Development program. Now that you've begun to rule in your own right, there are certain things you must be made aware of, things which represent some of the most sensitive secrets our government possesses."

You mean my *government...* "What sort of things?"

"You'll see."

Critias reclined in his seat and stared out the oval-shaped port window. Having left the palace located in the center of Atlantis City, they flew southwards and passed over the many concentric rings, alternating between settled land and heavily trafficked waterways, that together made up the capital city. The outermost ring was itself inscribed within the city walls that enclosed more than a million souls. The royal airship traveled about twenty miles beyond the capital to an uninhabited glen beneath lofty Mt. Corax before gently descending beside the mountain.

After disembarking, Critias looked around perfunctorily. *Mountain rockery dotted with greenery; wild grass full of crows... that's all that's here.* He spat upon the earth and remarked, "I thought you were taking me to see a lab, not a nature tour."

Eudoxia, still inside the airship, wordlessly tapped the touchscreen once more. The earth shook as part of the mountainside facing Critias suddenly started to move, sending some birds crouched thereon into a squawking flight. When the movement ceased, the mountain revealed an entrance out of which emerged several lab-smocked scientists.

What on Earth...?

"Your Majesties," said one of them, bowing to both Critias and Eudoxia, who was exiting the airship. He was in his late fifties, sporting gray-hair that was disheveled and matted, and was extremely pale from lack of sunlight; his skin was nearly as pale as his spotless, wrinkle-free white lab-coat. His physique was so scrawny that he appeared a veritable dwarf next to Critias, and his right cheek twitched incessantly. Nevertheless, from behind his electronic glasses, his eyes seemed to exude vivacity itself, and he spoke with an animated tone.

"Anaxagoras," said Eudoxia, deigning to let him kiss her hand, "I have brought my son so that you may enlighten him about how our plans are progressing. Give us a tour of the facility."

"At once, my Lady."

Anaxagoras and the other scientists led them inside the hollowed-out mountain. Traversing the monotone, artificially-lit white hallways, Anaxagoras exhibited to Critias all manner of weaponry, whether completed or still in the embryonic stage. There were enhanced laser rifles, grenades, and other personal armaments; redesigned aerial warships and ground assault vehicles; massive force-field generators under construction; and many other experimental devices and prototypes were being tested with the intent of weaponizing nature's most miniscule secrets.

With each room they passed through, going ever deeper within the mountain complex, the visions became more and more extraordinary. Any lingering boredom yet plaguing Critias quickly perished. The sight of these fantastic weapons, and the scientists busily developing ever more lethal ones, mesmerized him: he stared and gaped as a woodpecker which, having been raised in captivity, is suddenly released into a virgin forest of the thickest trees and knows not where to begin.

Anaxagoras fawned over Eudoxia throughout the tour. Endlessly did he praise her to her son, saying, "Lord Critias, your mother's genius birthed this lab," and "her liberality and illimitable donations have financed the best weaponry," and "we owe everything to your mother and her passion for progress," and "this is science at its finest!"

When they reached the lab marked *Genetic Synthesis and Amalgamations*, Critias gawked at what he saw. Gigantic cylinders lined the room. Contained within them were organisms, encased in membranous sacs suspended in bubbling greenish fluid, whose bodies were linked in multiple locations by wires connected to the lab's computers. The creatures looked humanoid but had bestial elements: one had the head of a bull and the body of a man, another a woman's body on which were the limbs of a bear, a third with a leonine torso and boa constrictor tail, and another with a jackal's head.

"What are these things?" asked Critias, pressing his eyes up against one cylinder and focusing on the bull-man's extremely muscular mass.

"Here we are experimenting in genetic fusion in order to create human-animal hybrids," explained Anaxagoras. He stood beside Critias and pointed to the monster within. "Our intent is to grow a line of super-soldiers combining the best traits of the animal world—superior speed, strength, stamina—with human intellect."

"Wow. Are they ready for combat?"

"No, these are beta models. We've still got some kinks to work out before we can test them on the battlefield."

The tube fogged up from Critias' hot breath. "So, these super-soldiers will be even deadlier than regular ones?"

"Not these ones, but their successors will. Of course," added Anaxagoras, adjusting his glasses, "with ample safeguards ensuring that it is *we* who control them and use them as we will. We wouldn't want to unleash an army of mutants that might turn against us. (That would be as bad as suffering at the hands of one's own bacteriological warfare.)"

Despite her son's clear fascination, Eudoxia was unfazed by the monsters. "Enough of this. Anaxagoras, show us Project Heliocalypse."

Anaxagoras rubbed his hands together, a mad grin having swallowed his twitching face. He led them up to the highest level of the compound and into a gargantuan cylindrical room located below the peak of the mountain. Inside, suspended by cables from the ceiling, was a strange contraption. It was a gray cube measuring thirty feet in each direction; antennas, thrusters, blinking lights, and an assortment of other gadgets protruded from its sides in seemingly haphazard fashion. From two opposite sides there extended massive wings covered with solar panels, and a large tractor beam generator projected from beneath it.

Critias cocked his head and stared unblinkingly at the contraption. "What is it?"

"It's a satellite," said Anaxgoras, exchanging a satisfied glance with Eudoxia.

"A what?"

"A satellite," repeated Anaxgoras. "A spacecraft capable of orbiting the Earth. Ever since our ancestors developed airships, humans have been able to navigate the skies of our world but were prevented from going any farther because airships could operate no higher than the stratosphere owing to the designs of their engines. But a few years ago, we developed a superior engine that allows new vehicles to traverse the exosphere in safety. Satellites are unmanned spacecraft designed to operate independently in permanent orbit around the planet. Multiple prototypes have already been transported there and tested to satisfaction. In absolute secrecy, of course: we are the first nation to attain this technological capability."

"Yes, and from our spies' reports, the other great powers are years away from catching up to us," added Eudoxia with a grin.

"So what?" said Critias. He rolled his eyes. "What's the point of putting gizmos in space? All the good stuff's on Earth."

"But by controlling space, we will be able to seize control of the Earth!"

Critias licked his lips. "Really? How?"

"My Lord, if we were to make war against Athens, Memphis, Mohenjo-daro, or any other great city, what would be the greatest hindrance to our capturing them?"

"Well, wouldn't it be their force fields? Don't they have strong defenses just as we have here?"

"Yes, precisely that, my Lord. For over one hundred years, force fields have constituted at times formidable defenses for cities and other critical sites. It is no wonder, then, that when we fought our last major war over fifty years ago, it proved stubbornly difficult to breach the walls of Athens on account of their force fields: it took days of unrelenting saturation bombing to create an opening for an infiltration team to get in and bring down the city's generators. And this technology has only improved with age! The same means today would prove far less effective."

Snorting, Critias crossed his arms and said, "You make it sound impossible for us to defeat my enemies."

"No, not at all, my King. On the contrary, that is precisely what I have been working to resolve; and, funded and fully supported by your incredible mother, I have at last succeeded in overcoming the most recent round of one-upmanship in military technology. For you see, the history of war is the history of innovation and response. One man invents the sword, another man fashions a shield; one city learns to build a wall, another to construct siege towers and trebuchets; one nation discovers the secret to aerial transportation, another develops artillery and missiles to shoot them out of the sky; one side harnesses the power of lasers and constructs an armada of missiles, and the other side builds force fields to counteract those weapons. As far as the other great powers are concerned, we are currently at a technological standstill on account of force fields. But force fields have the same flaw as every previous iteration in military defensive technology: they are designed to counter the weapons of the previous conflict, not the next."

This is getting interesting... "So how do we counter the defenses?"

"This satellite"—Anaxagoras pointed excitedly to it—"is equipped with the strongest tractor beam ever built by the hand of man. It is so powerful that it will be able to capture any asteroid that passes near Earth's orbit and alter its trajectory."

"Sounds more like a shield than a sword," huffed Critias, folding his arms. *What has this to do with conquering nations...?*

"Not a shield but a shield piercer! This satellite will capture asteroids in orbit and then surgically redirect them to crash into our enemies' cities. Force fields operate by deflecting the directed energy of lasers or exploding bombs. An asteroid, on the other hand, is a large mass of matter: many asteroids weigh millions of pounds. When something of this magnitude impacts a force field, its matter will not be dispersed in seconds like a blast from a laser but will remain there, pressing down on the force field and requiring its generators to expend so much energy in a concentrated location that they will eventually fail. The mightiest force fields in existence would be hard-pressed to sustain an asteroid's weight for long, even if the asteroid hypothetically were to appear midair; but entering the outer atmosphere, a falling asteroid will be propelled by gravity and crash with an inexorable force that will make its impact on a force field even graver. In short, this satellite is a cannon capable of hitting any city on the planet with an asteroid that will smash through its force fields and annihilate it!"

"Just imagine the potential!" said Eudoxia, coiling her hands around Critias' neck as her bulbous eyes bored into his. Her breath was hot and smelled of garlic. "Project Heliocalypse will enable us to destroy any city at will. With the capitals of the world naked before us, our armies will be able to subdue all our former colonies... and Atlantis will again reign supreme as the only empire worthy of the name! Heliocalypse is the ultimate weapon. And *we and we alone* possess it! Once completed, the entire world will tremble before us and all will be ours."

She let go of his neck and he stepped back. Visions of skeletal bodies, cities depopulated, and all mankind weighed down with chains and groveling at his feet flashed through his mind. *Who would be able to make war against me,* wondered Critias, *the man who, like a god, rains fiery destruction down from the heavens?* Critias formed two fists and his body shook. "I will rule over the entire world! Posterity will remember me as the greatest High King in history. How soon can we attack?"

Eudoxia shook one finger while pushing his raised right arm downwards. Her voice tickling his ear, she said, "Patience, my son, patience. An enterprise of this magnitude must not be rushed. During all my years as regent, I steadily built up Atlantis's armed forces in anticipation of the greatest war ever to be fought. Our position is far stronger than it was when I began to rule, and we have already garnered victories over some minor nations. But more time is needed to finish preparations for conquering all the great powers—and the world!"

"Yes, and Project Heliocalypse still requires some fine-tuning before it will be fully operational," added Anaxagoras. He bowed his head. "But that day will come soon, Master."

Turning his head to look up at the satellite, Critias thought, *I can't wait to use this weapon to dominate the world.* His long tongue, marred by a minor cleft at its end, lubricated his lips. He threw his arms around Eudoxia, who welcomed his embrace with a kiss on his lips. "Mother," he gasped, his whole body vibrating with thrill, "you have finally given a gift not unworthy of me!"

CHAPTER FIVE

I N RECOMPENSE FOR THEIR assistance in toppling his brother's government and installing himself as the interim governor, Galba greatly honored Periander and his men. He housed them in the gubernatorial residence, where they stayed a week to convalesce, and he entertained them with all the luxuries that Aeson had acquired. Not since leaving his halls in Atlantis had Periander experienced such comfort or enjoyed greater security. The life of a fugitive, beset with unremitting dangers and deprivations—one's thoughts and energy devoted only to the current day, every face encountered a potential enemy—now yielded to feelings of quasi-security in Cyrene. Treated as the guest of honor at banquets and shown all the pageantry befitting his regal dignity, Periander reciprocated with his congeniality; and between him and Galba, king and citizen of a republic, there matured goodwill that birthed an oath-sealed pact of friendship.

Once they had recuperated, it came time to depart. Galba gave as gifts the most resplendent clothes formerly owned by Aeson and his cronies, armament, resources, and heaps of cash and valuable goods. He also gave them a protective escort to take them to the border of Egypt. Thus, the exiles, who had come impoverished and clothed in tattered garments, left richly equipped and in royal apparel.

When they arrived at the great concrete wall that enclosed Egypt's western boundary, Periander approached the border-guards at one of its checkpoints and he informed them of his identity and intention to seek asylum from the Pharaoh. With the capital duly notified of the situation and authorization granted by their higher-ups, the chief sentinel commanded the gate to be unbolted. The gigantic bifold gateway opened and through it passed Periander and his men, leaving the Libyan dunes for the Nile-nourished kingdom. On account of Periander's preëxisting relationship with the Egyptian government, they were even provided with transportation to the capital at Memphis.

"This is incredible," remarked Jason, looking out their airship's window as they made their way over the city.

Monumental buildings adorned with sculpted sphinxes lined the wide avenues that hummed with hover-cars. Open-air marketplaces sold silks, frankincense, and exotic fruits. Fed by the Nile, lush parks filled with aromatic flowers dotted the miles-long city, a wonder to behold.

"I know." Periander put one arm around his son's shoulders and began pointing out various landmarks. "I have been on diplomatic missions to Memphis several times," he said, "the most recent one not more than two years ago. Our Egyptian cousins have built an impressive civilization."

Periander referred to the Egyptians as their cousins because Egypt, like many other states, had been colonized by Atlanteans in the remote past. Despite their common ties of kindred, the relationship between Atlantis and her colony grew strained over the course of ages. After a war fought several centuries before Periander's time, Egypt won its independence from the motherland and had successfully maintained that independence to this day, notwithstanding occasional attempts by Atlantis to reässemble its primeval empire.

They soon arrived at the Pharaoh's palace. Unlike that of Critias, it was not a single vast structure but a complex of separate buildings which were nonetheless equally grand. The building to which they were brought was encircled with granite columns bearing an external awning. The entry had a golden threshold and palladium doors. Inside one passed through an atrium blooming with fragrant potted plants and trellises. Lining the pathway were life-sized marble effigies of the Pharaoh's predecessors, each monarch depicted in his prime, nude, with muscles bulging. And under the room's four skylights were four fountains of which the first flowed with red wine, the second gurgled with milk, the third poured out aromatic oil, and the fourth dispensed water.

Grabbing a cup from beside the milky fountain, Periander imbibed the cool drink. He looked up when a woman, attended by maids, entered the room. She was in her fifties, sporting an indigo robe and short coppery hair topped by a white-gold diadem. By her dignified gait and self-assured countenance, her eyes shining with warmness, it was clear to all his party that she was the queen. Approaching them, she said:

"Noble Periander, you grace our house once more. I regret only the circumstances of your visit."

"Lady Zenobia," replied Periander, dropping to one knee and kissing her gentle hand. "I come now as a suppliant to you and to your husband. Cast out of Atlantis like a lion's whelp by its mother, I seek the refuge of my Egyptian cousins."

"Arise, follow me." And leading him and his men into the next room, which was the Throne Hall, she showed them the royal court in all its splendor.

The pharaonic throne towered above the room, seventy gilded steps high. Thereon Pharaoh Ozymandias sat in state, robed in purple, and his hair covered by an uraeus-clad diadem. With a great baritone voice, he called down to Periander who, along with his men, had prostrated himself upon the floor. "Arise, O Periander. Prostration does not behoove a king."

Periander rose while his men remained prostrate.

"I have heard you seek my protection from the High King Critias and his agents; this I grant without reservation."

"I thank Egypt for its hospitality," said Periander with a bow of his head. "There is much which I must discuss with you concerning the fates of both our nations."

"Servants!" cried the Pharaoh. They scurried over to the throne's base. "Refresh our Atlantean guests and provide them with lodging. We shall not speak of business until they shall have been hospitably received."

Periander's men stood up and accompanied him as the shaven-headed menservants led them outside and through the palace complex to another building where they would lodge. There they were provided with baths, clean clothes, and refreshments. When the evening came, the servants again guided them through the maze of buildings, this time to a different one no less impressive than the Pharaoh's Throne Hall.

This was the banquet hall. Running down the hall's length below the chandeliers was a long wooden table engraved with scenes of Egyptian history, of battles and Pharaohs. All the courtiers and royal princes were sitting at this table, dressed in their most exquisite garb, and Periander's men were bidden to sit here. He, however, was led to the smaller table at the rear of the room, laterally bordering the main table and raised upon a daïs, where Ozymandias and his queen were seated. The Pharaoh himself offered Periander the head chair as his honored guest.

To the sound of harps, the feast began. The servants carried golden vases and basins from one guest to another so that they could wash their hands. Every delicacy imaginable—roasted flamingo, stuffed dormouse, peacock soup—ornamented the plates. Periander ate and he drank with Ozmandias and Zenobia, as did his men with the Egyptians.

After they had sated the desire for food, Ozymandias turned to Periander. "You first visited our realm, Periander, when you were hardly older than your son is now. In all the years I've known you, you have always been an honorable man and dutiful king, well-respected by your peers and subjects alike. How then have you come into your present state? To our dismay, we heard of your forced flight, of your denunciation as a traitor to your country, and of the bounty set on your head, but few details to explain the why and wherefore."

The room became silent. Periander leaned forward in his chair and exhaled heavily, collecting his thoughts. He raised his goblet, swished the residual champagne clinging to the bottom, and finished it off. Then he spoke.

"What happened to me was not the result of a single, recent action on my part. Rather, as when water gradually rises behind a dam, accumulating until eventually the dam is breached, so too was my undeserved exile years in the making and only recently came to fruition.

"It all started about two decades ago, when the then-High King Cuculus wed Eudoxia. I don't know why he chose her. Even then as a young woman she was vile and cold, full of guile and mistrustful of all. I doubt any thoughts of religion ever crossed her mind (her behavior certainly shows none). Yet such are the wiles of impassioned love, that mad emotion that no man can fathom, that Cuculus became wholly enchanted by her.

"Although his was not an exceptionally glorious reign, Cuculus was nonetheless a good enough ruler, a just man devoted to the Deity. But due to the vagaries of disease, deaths in battle, infertility, and unfortunate accidents in several preceding generations, he had the unlucky distinction of being the last living heir of Atlas' line, which had supplied the line of High Kings since time immemorial. His sudden death, not long after his marriage to Eudoxia, marked the extinction of the senior of the Ten Houses and, consequently, for the first time since the foundation of Atlantis, the devolving of the High Kingship onto a junior house. As it was, my father Themistocles, the scion of Eumelus, should have succeeded thereto—if Eudoxia had not claimed to be carrying Cuculus' child.

"She duly gave birth to a son several months later, whereupon my blameless father, who would never dream of retaining anything not his own, resigned his provisional imperial crown to the rightful High King, Critias. You know the rest. Eudoxia became regent. Invested with sovereign power that was legally hers to use until Critias' nineteenth birthday, she soon made clear what her intentions were. She redirected our national holidays from the collective celebration of Atlantis to the adoration of her and her house alone. She corrupted the priesthood with appointees as unethical as they are irreligious, showing more reverence for their mistress than the Deity Whom they purportedly serve. (She has nothing but disgust for the ancient customs.) Above all, she sought to concentrate all authority in her own hands by grabbing powers from the other nine kings and reducing the Council of Ten to a mere rubberstamp for her agenda. My father opposed her efforts to centralize power in the High Kingship contrary to our ancient federal system, and I took up his mantle on his death. But over the years, as fresh faces came and went on the Council, she steadily coaxed a majority to her side that effectively allowed her to do anything she wished.

"In foreign affairs, like the domestic, her goal was conquest. Not a year has passed since she took power that Atlantis's ever-larger armies have not been fighting in some portion of the globe, whether in the Amazonian jungles to expand our American colonies, in Britain to gain a foothold in Europe, or even waging war with the most far-off tribes of savages to exploit their lands' natural resources. Waging unjustified wars not in our interest, Eudoxia beggars our people with the taxes needed to pay for them—not to mention the vast amounts of money she devotes to the research and development of more lethal weaponry. She desires to have the world's largest military armed with the most advanced armaments, and I have zero doubts that she will limit its use to fighting minor conflicts with third-rate countries.

"Upon becoming head of the House of Eumelus, I added my disapproving voice to the Council Chamber. Yet despite Eudoxia's manifestly unacceptable conduct, the voices crying in dissent steadily shrunk until I alone was left to oppose her. All the other kings had bent their knees to her. Try though she might, she could not cajole me to her side: I guarded my integrity from all bribery and did not succumb to veiled threats that she is accustomed to deploy. Having long infuriated her by my resistance, which took a form no more violent than public opposition and refusal to go along with her demands, I guess I must have finally provoked her into calculating that she could get away with simply having me killed—and my family too."

"I was the one who discovered her plot," interjected Socrates, rising from his seat the better to be heard. Periander nodded to him to continue. "I, Socrates Hippothontis, was Themistocles' closest confidant and have watched over his son since he was a young boy. Along with my colleague, Philip Heraclid, I frequently visited the capital to conduct official business on behalf of our king. And I happened to have been staying in the imperial palace the night when Eudoxia convened nine of the Council of Ten's members.

"Passing by the Council Chamber, I beheld Eudoxia sitting in the center of the room on the High King's chair, her boy Critias standing beside her. Both their faces were contorted evilly: the mother was uttering vile falsehoods against Periander while the son, so animated that drool appeared to fall from his lips, kept urging for his death. As soon as I heard all the other kings meekly assent to condemning him and his whole family for treason—and to inflict the ancient penalty of burning them all alive—my whole body began quaking with dread. Recognizing the futility of confronting them and trying to dissuade them from their decision, I did not wait any longer but ran as fast away from there as these old legs of mine could run."

"That's when he bumped into me," said Philip as he stood up beside Socrates. "He told me what had happened, and at once I sent him to ready our lord's airship while I went to inform him."

"I was flabbergasted when I heard," said Periander. "In retrospect, I should not have been surprised: Eudoxia has proven herself to be an evil woman, and her son grew up marinated in her malign influence. But I was still clinging to the ancient norms governing relations between Atlantean kings, hoping against hope that I might still persuade her to abide by our ancestral customs (which certainly preclude assassinating one's fellow monarch). But Eudoxia respects neither the wisdom of her forefathers nor the rights of her contemporaries. As a result of my naïvety, I was utterly taken aback when I learned that my home would imminently be raided. I had so little time to try to save ourselves. It was a hectic flight." Periander's voice lowered as he recalled the events of that dreadful night. "My wife and son were with me in our home, as were my two chief officers, Agathocles Damonides and Demosthenes Pandionius. There was no time to pack any belongings; besides some weapons that we grabbed on the way out the door, of all my possessions the only thing I salvaged was the signet-ring of the founder of my House, and that only because I slept with it." He raised his right hand to show the ring on his fourth finger, which depicted a lion's head, his family's crest.

"Yet just as we were boarding our hovercar, imperial soldiers appeared on the horizon. We sped off at full speed, making a mad dash across my palace's grounds for my airship's landing pad as their vehicles chased ours. They fired their lasers; we retaliated with ours. The darkness partially screened us, and our vehicle got right up to the landing pad before their lasers hit the engine, causing the car to crash. But we were unharmed.

"With the wind blowing acrid smoke from the vehicle, we scrambled across the mossy plain towards the landing pad. It was located atop an elevated structure twenty feet high. Before we could ascend the steps circling its exterior, a gunfight ensued. Twenty soldiers pursued us. Critias, incredibly, was among them, the prospect of slaughtering innocents evidently too great to keep him home. Dodging the blasts of lasers, we climbed upwards. I sent Demosthenes and Philip ahead to get my son to safety, and Socrates was already waiting for us by the airship. But before the rest of us reached the top, Critias' troops had concentrated their firepower and obliterated the final steps, leaving about an eight-foot gap between us and our salvation. Those who had already made it up there exchanged fire with them to give cover to us trapped below, during which I made the jump across the void and was pulled up. Agathocles went next and we pulled him up to safety. But then Cornelia, my dearest wife, sweeter to me than my own life, she..."

Periander's voice faltered; the words he sought to say rose in his throat, drifted over his tongue, and thrice attempted to hurdle past his lips, each time missing their mark and falling backwards, in failure, down into his diaphragm. Yet if words could not escape him, teardrops did. Periander wept. He lowered his head and raised his red linen napkin to conceal his overflowing eyes and absorb their grief.

At last, drying his ducts, he resumed. "She was about to jump for it; but at the very moment that she did, I saw out of the corner of my eye a laser bolt flashing from Critias' gun and it... pierced her through her chest and... she toppled over the side. My hand immediately lunged as far as it could go, grasping at the air. I tried desperately to catch her... but I couldn't. I watched her fall to her death and couldn't do anything to stop it. I-I... I saw her motionless body, all that blood seeping out... I couldn't move. Agathocles had to grab me, carry me up to the airship. We left. Eluding the airships dispatched to shoot us down but not without sustaining damage, we had to make an emergency landing in Tunisia."

The whole room was filled with lamentation as all commiserated with Periander and his grievous loss of both his realm and his wife. Jason groaned for his dead mother, Periander's men for their queen whom they had failed. The Egyptians also tearfully bewailed Periander's plight; from the cupbearers and waiters to Pharaoh Ozymandias, clutching Zenobia close to his bosom, not an eye remained dry.

After Periander had narrated his journey across the north of Africa up to his arrival in Egypt, Ozymandias turned to him and said:

"O Periander, to hear such doleful testimony depresses all our hearts. My spies and informants have long reported similar tidings about Eudoxia's reign and character, and her aggressive wars are a concern to all. Your words themselves, and your wretched countenance, move my spirit. What then, Periander, Son of Themistocles, do you plan to do?"

"Lord Ozymandias," answered Periander, his recently-tearful eyes now burning with resolve, "during all my days, I never once committed perfidy against Atlantis, the High King, or regent. If I opposed Eudoxia's agenda, it was as part of the loyal opposition. Yet the present holders of imperial sovereignty have abused their powers, ravaged the customs of our ancestors, attacked a royal house with the intention of destroying it, and even now are devising yet more machinations that will imperil not only Atlantis but Egypt, too, and all the nations of the world."

Periander rose from his seat, planting both his hands on the tabletop; his eyes whirled with color and intensity. "It is my intention, by the grace of the Deity, to raise an armed force of sufficient size to invade Atlantis, overthrow Critias and his mother's régime, and establish in its place a government consistent with Atlantean tradition, one friendly towards all peaceful nations. This I seek, not merely to fulfill my sacred familial duty of avenging my wife's spilled blood, but also to ensure the peace of the world and a safe Atlantis for my son after me. I can assure you that Eudoxia means to make war on Egypt: her ambitions, endlessly reflected in the irredentist propaganda she feeds the people, are to reconquer all the lands that once belonged to Atlantis or even simply paid it homage. Her revanchism is no mere piece of official rhetoric but the guiding principle of a grand strategy bent on world domination. That is why I do solemnly entreat of you and request your assistance and participation in a grand coalition of kingdoms to liberate Atlantis and all mankind from the House of Atlas."

The Pharaoh sat for a moment, absorbing the words that had soared out of Periander's mouth. "Periander," he said at length, rubbing his chin, "I am not disinclined to agree with you about the danger posed by Critias and Eudoxia. As for a military alliance, well... impulsiveness has been the ruin of many a monarch. Permit me time to contemplate this with my advisors before we proceed further in negotiations."

"I fully comprehend the magnitude of what I am asking of you and respect your need to deliberate. Please consider it well."

CHAPTER SIX

THROUGHOUT THE DURATION OF Periander's speech before Ozymandias and the Egyptian court, from among the Pharaoh's children seated at the lower table, one pair of cerulean eyes gazed longingly at his commanding form while two ears devoted themselves to catching each passionate syllable that soared out of his mouth. These belonged to Psyche, the sole daughter of Ozymandias among his troop of fifteen sons. She was fair complexioned, long smooth red hair flowing down over her shoulders; a petite nose graced her face in between blushing cheeks which, like early-morning waves, bobbed gently as she breathed. Unlike her tablemates who were arrayed in the most colorful of costumes—purples, pinks, jades, indigoes—and sported much gold upon their persons, Psyche wore a simple black dress, bordered with white ermine, and not one piece of jewelry. She was in the traditional apparel of a mourning woman.

Ozymandias had betrothed his daughter to the firstborn of his grand vizier; but before they were bound together in wedlock, her intended husband was found drowned in the Nile, a victim of some cutthroat bandits. Although neither the timing of the engagement nor choice of groom had been arranged as she would have preferred, Psyche nevertheless was now conducting herself in virtual widowhood as Egyptian custom dictated she should.

When Periander had faltered over his words in describing his wife's death, Psyche clutched her chest and clenched her jaw. *The poor man,* she thought. *He must have treasured her so much! Even after suffering that blow, he still perseveres and seeks to avenge her. O Periander... How I wish I could comfort you and make things easier on you....*

After the banquet and its attendant festivities drew to a close, Psyche retired to her room to sleep. Beside the lower bedposts lay two handmaidens who, by their baggy red eyes, could well attest to Psyche's restless slumber that night. For Psyche dreamt that they were in Atlantis City, she and Periander together. He commanded soldiers from every nation whom he led in storming the imperial palace. There Periander slew Critias before the altar of the Deity whilst Psyche was stringing up Eudoxia with a noose from the palace's highest pinnacle.

The sun was still abed when Psyche sprang from hers. Not waking her handmaids, she donned her dark clothing in the darkness. Her feet, keen to rush to Periander's side and to intertwine with the tendons of his toes, whisked her to the threshold of her room. But stopping her hands from opening the door, she hesitated, conscious of propriety.

What if my mother were to catch me skulking about the palace at night? What would the women of the court say if they saw me sneaking into a man's bedchamber?

She turned back into the vestibule, but then made another start.

Yet I feel my whole body drawn to him like to no other man... I just want to be with him!

Again, she wavered at the threshold and retreated inwards.

But not this way, not like this. It's wrong.

Once more she lunged forwards like a fox from its den, only to recoil yet again. Trying three times and thrice failing, Psyche sat down on her bed and reflected for several moments.

"Awake, maidens, awake! I wish to offer prayers in the temple."

Ever quick to heed their mistress, Psyche's groggy handmaidens accompanied her through several courtyards to the palace temple. The temple was an open-air structure; forty granite columns on the sides and twenty both front and back held up its arched roof. Ascending its seven steps, they entered just as the rays of the rising sun burst forth to illuminate the temple. Inside were a couple of other rings of columns for the roof's support, each column fully covered with gold inscriptions written in the Old Atlantic dialect. The altar, a single rectangular slab of marble three feet high, lay within the innermost ring below a skylight in the temple's center.

As they entered, Psyche gasped. "Quick, quick!" she whispered to her handmaids, shooing them behind the nearest column. Pressing her back up against the same column, she cupped her mouth with her hands and steadied herself before she peered around it.

In front of the altar, flanked by Jason and Socrates on his right and on the left by Agathocles and Demosthenes, stood Periander. Jason held a cornucopia overflowing with juicy plums, apples, and strawberries as well as fragrant lilacs, daffodils, and roses. These Periander individually took and placed upon the altar, stacking them in a pyramid. Then he lit a match, set fire to his offering, and received from Agathocles' hand a golden chalice of blood-red wine with which he doused the conflagration. As he offered his libation, the fire crackled and grew until it had engulfed the whole sacrifice. Kneeling before the altar, Periander directed his eyes upwards, joining his hands while he uttered an invocation:

"O Deity, Invisible and Incorporeal, Omnipresent and Omnipotent, Thou Who knowest all things and art Creator of the Heaven and the Earth—to Thee I offer great thanks that Thou preservedst me, my son, and my men in our flight from Atlantis; that in Cyrene Thou didst snatch my son from out of the hand of Thrallis and Aeson; and that Thou hast brought us safely unto the Nilotic kingdom. If ever I pleased Thee and did justice and walked in Thy truth, then, I implore Thee, take up my cause and bless it—rouse Ozymandias to my side, and others of Thy cherished kings, to the end that I may oust that evil one now in possession of the Atlantean imperial throne."

He spoke in Old Atlantic, the language that was still used in all the ancient rites. But educated in that tongue, Psyche understood his words.

Such piety, she thought as the ritual unfolded. *So religious and devoted, like Father... holding his own private ceremonies because the public ones do not suffice the longings of his soul.*

Suddenly she crinkled her nose and puckered her lips as though tasting undiluted lemon when thoughts of Mycerinus, her betrothed, sashayed through her mind. Although a great devotee to the monarchy who was skilled in earthly affairs, Mycerinus had had no interest in spiritual matters: the name of the Deity was never on his lips, and always did he manage to proffer some excuse for his absences from religious rites and communal prayer.

Emerging from behind the column, Psyche acted as though she had just arrived. With a regal gait she strode down the temple, a handmaid on either side; halfway to the altar she encountered Periander's party as it was leaving. Bowing her head, she addressed him:

"Lord Periander, your speech last night stirred my soul, if not all Egypt's too. My sympathies are entirely yours. I wish you well in your negotiation with the Pharaoh."

Periander did not at once reply. He studied this black-clad figure, so conspicuous the night before in a room that had teemed with every possible color a prism can emanate. "Then my speech achieved its intended effect." He took her hand in his and applied his warm lips to it. "What is your name?"

Psyche blushed. "I see you have forgotten."

"What?" Periander's narrow eyebrows rose, and his eyes expanded.

Looking deeply into the green lake and blue lagoon that were his eyes, Psyche said, "We met before... when you came here two years ago on a diplomatic mission."

"I'm afraid I don't remember."

"In your travels, do you encounter too many princesses to remember all of us? Do we all blur together in your memory?" she asked softly, blinking her eyes.

"With all the royal houses out there, it's hard not to bump into a princess or two thousand," responded Periander with a chuckle, which caused her cheeks to blush. "So please forgive me if I forget. But if you're a princess, then you must be a relation of Pharoah Ozymandias."

"I am."

"Not one of his sisters, perhaps?"

She shook her head.

Grinning, he said, "I am a total fool. You are far too young to be one of his sisters. And I wager that rules out being an aunt, too."

Psyche giggled and shook her head.

"A cousin?"

"Not quite."

"Hmmm... Well, that leaves one option. By any chance, are you his daughter?"

"You guessed correctly."

"That explains it. Of course, Ozymandias would have introduced me to his children during my visits, especially one as fine as you."

"Yes. It was during one of the dances Father held in your honor. We were introduced—you were wearing an emerald-colored tunic interspersed with thin golden stripes, pleated navy trousers, and a short silver cape; I wore a white silk dress trimmed with yellow lace. You smelled of roasted chestnuts, for you had just come from visiting my uncle Rhampsinitus' study where that scent is ever present. We danced the *Nile's Overflow* for the full fourteen minutes, making our way down the breadth of the grand ballroom before the music stopped; you danced wonderfully despite favoring your right leg the whole time due to a discus injury you had sustained three days earlier."

Periander rubbed his bearded chin. "Your memory far outpaces mine, Lady..."

"Psyche."

"Psy-che." Periander leisurely articulated her name, each syllable falling from his tongue as honey from its comb. He took both her hands in his. "I am enchanted to be reäcquainted with you."

Her pallid cheeks flushed with rosiness and her eyes shone as the sea at noontide. Bidding him a farewell lest she say something silly, Psyche continued onwards to the altar, where she offered her prayers to the Deity.

***

M EANWHILE, PERIANDER AND HIS men quitted the temple and began to make their way through the palace's maze of buildings.

"So that was Ozymandias' daughter," mused Periander. "I recall most of his sons, but I'm surprised I don't remember our prior encounter..."

"Her beauty outstrips all the ladies at the court," said Jason, a giant grin spreading on his face. "Next to her, the rest of Egypt's women look like haggard frumps."

"Yes, she is quite beautiful. Her poise and grace were remarkable too," added Periander, nodding his head.

"She doubtlessly got that from her mother," said Socrates. "Zenobia was always a charming lass."

"How do you know so much about the Egyptian queen?" asked Jason.

"Because Zenobia is Atlantean. Her father was King Demophon of the House of Mestor, who was a good friend to your great-grandfather Aristides. Consequently, we had many occasions to interact with him and his family. In fact, your grandfather Themistocles and I once spent a whole summer with Zenobia and her brothers hunting lions in Africa. Well, she left the hunting part to us menfolk, but she made the rest of the safari pleasant by her presence. A most charming woman. And her daughter seems to have inherited that charm."

Jason nodded and murmured, "She'll make some man a happy husband."

Periander glanced at his son and smiled. *Has Psyche caught your eye, my son? She certainly has the potential to make a good wife, though I think she's a little old for you. But you are maturing into a man, only two years younger than I was when I wed your mother. We'll have to start thinking about finding you a bride after, Deity-willing, we liberate our homeland...*

Clearing his throat, Socrates said, "I fear her marital prospects may prove limited."

"What do you mean?" asked Agathocles, cocking his skinny neck. "What man in his right mind would be put off by that girl?"

"I heard from one courtier," explained Socrates, "that she had been betrothed last year but her intended died before the wedding. She is accordingly dressed in all black for the customary period of mourning, which should be almost over. But even once that period is passed, few Egyptian men will wish to marry her because their culture regards women in her situation as cursed. On the grounds that her bad luck has already killed one husband before the wedding, they believe any man whom she should marry will likewise meet an evil fate."

Agathocles' blue eyes brightened as he wordlessly mouthed *aha.* "Well, that explains why I kept hearing references to a 'Virgin Widow' last night. The Egyptians I was speaking with seemed quite spooked about the name."

"Oh, poppycock!" said Periander, gesturing his arms dismissively. "I encountered that same nonsense during my embassy. The Egyptians are far too superstitious about these things: they take a tragic, heartrending event like a young bride's loss of her fiancé and, reading an ill-omen into it, treat the poor girl as though she betokened some monstrous evil. It's not just irreligious: it's asinine and disgusting."

"It is, indeed," concurred Demosthenes. "But many diverse cultures have strange taboos which, in origin, presumably arose to safeguard against harm. Mutual association and ostensible correspondence are a common facet of such taboos. While there may be no scientific basis to refuse to marry a woman in the princess Psyche's condition, to a certain mentality there is a kind of pseudo-logic that makes avoiding a widow no less irrational than to avoid eating a type of berry after witnessing someone die from eating it."

"Whatever the rationalization, it's just wrong," said Periander. "Although I respect people who honor the customs handed down to them from their ancestors—and what I wouldn't give to have seen more of that in our own Atlantis!—those customs must not conflict with the teachings of the Deity or the principles of reason that He endowed us with. And this superstition flagrantly offends human reason."

"Couldn't Psyche marry a foreigner, if her own countrymen reject her?" ventured Jason.

Socrates pursed his lips. "Possibly... but in distinct contrast to how they seek out foreign princesses for their princes, the Egyptian monarchy generally refrains from giving their own princesses to foreign bridegrooms. (In fact, I can't recall hearing of any instance where a foreigner wed an Egyptian princess.) I doubt Ozymandias will upset precedent even in the case of his own daughter."

Chapter Seven

"WHY ARE WE HERE?" asked Critias, a sullen sneer around his lips.

It was midnight. His mother had rudely interrupted the card game he was playing, shooing away the other players, and insisted he follow her to the Progenitoreum, alone. This circular shrine, nestled between two craggy cliffs on the outskirts of the capital city's outermost ring, was dedicated to the founder of Atlantis. Off-limits to all but the chief priests and royalty, the building was eerily silent, and the roughness of its marble walls testified to its antiquity.

With his goose-pimpled arm holding a flashlight on account of the lack of electric lighting in the archaic structure, Critias brusquely looked around. Dominating the center of the room was a colossal solid-gold effigy of Poseidon, the legendary founder and first king of Atlantis. His image was adorned with a flowing beard, a muscular trident-wielding arm, and an orichalcum throne on which it was seated. Around the walls, facing their father, were golden statues of Atlas and Eumelus, Ampheres and Evaemon, Mneseus and Autochthon, Elasippus and Mestor, Azaës and Diaprepes—five pairs of twins from whom Atlantis's ten royal houses sprang. The flashlight cast shadows on the effigies in such a way that, every now and then, a golden man seemed faintly to shift in his seat. Between the statues of the father and sons were columns, gilded with gold, which alternated with the sons so as not to obstruct their view of their father; on these were written, in Old Atlantic, many ancient laws that tradition reported to have been ordained by Poseidon himself. Among the provisions were the prohibitions on the ten houses from waging unjust wars against each other or the dispossession of any one house of its inheritance by the others.

Critias put his free hand to one nostril and shot out of the other a mucous blob onto the bare earth floor. From its rocky crevices rose the strong sweet smell of ethylene gas. This oversweet aroma that permeated the room irritated Critias' nose, besides making him feel the beginnings of lightheadedness.

Eudoxia's scarlet dress glowed fiercely in the glow of his flashlight. "Son, the time has come for you to learn the truth about your father."

"What about Cuculus?" he said flippantly. "I never knew him, so why should I care?"

"Cuculus was not your father."

"What?" His eyes narrowed and his narrow chin lowered.

"Critias, your fa—"

Although she had been standing sideways to him, Critias grabbed her by her left arm and forcefully twisted her around to face him, his bone-crushing grip ripping her silken dress. Despite the chilly draft in the room, sweat started pouring down his face. His eyes were bloodshot. "Am I the bastard offspring of one of your lovers?!" he growled, the spittle flying onto her face even faster than his racing pulse. "Did you pass me off as *his* so you could seize the crown?!" *You've always wanted my power all for yourself... You'd tell any lie to get it.*

"Let go!" Eudoxia pulled free and slapped him hard, her scarlet-painted nails slashing his right cheek and drawing blood. Her bulbous eyes reflected fire. "Abort your anxiety. My conception and pregnancy were not as mundane as that."

"Then what is it? Why tell me now? Is this some sort of a threat to dangle over my head: that the crown isn't rightfully mine? So you can blackmail me?" He breathed heavily, becoming more lightheaded as he inhaled more ethylene gas. *If she tells this story to the people, even if it's a total lie, it could still raise enough doubts to... jeopardize my hold on power. There's only one sure way to prevent that...*

"Shut up and I'll explain!" Eudoxia glared at Critias, who was rubbing his blood-splattered cheek. "I conceived you, not from a mortal, but from a god."

"A god?" Critias threw his head back and guffawed, his laugh echoing menacingly off the walls. "What, you mean, like the Deity? Ha! You of all people don't seriously believe such myths. And you expect me to?"

"Not the Deity." Her lips moved to his ear. Her garlic breath overpowered the ethylene-filled air. "A true god: the Light-Bringer."

The flashlight went out and blackness consumed the room. Critias jumped back. The draft of air had suddenly become a whirlwind, surging throughout the room. His hair and clothing flittered violently. The air prickled his ivory face like icy claws that drew water from his eyes. "What is—?"

Critias ceased speaking when suddenly, in front of Poseidon's statue, materializing with increasing mass into what appeared to be a gyrating ball of light—or rather more like a wheel within a wheel, whose luminosity radiated almost so intensely as to blind even the sightless statues—there came forth into this world an entity cloaked in light.

"He's here!" shrieked Eudoxia, her face uncharacteristically ecstatic and relaxed as she staggered towards the ethereal light.

Critias blinked. The entity stood twelve feet tall and illumed the whole room with his presence. The body, shrouded in a snowy-white tunic that reached all the way down to the gargantuan nude feet, appeared like that of a young man in his prime, only larger. Beardless and with eternally youthful cheeks, the head was crowned with long flowing hair as white as chalk and as soft as the fluff of clouds. The eyes, sparkling as though all the stars of the heavens were contained therein, had platinum irises and gold sclera; the pupils were the size of pinpoints. A gracious smile formed on the entity's face, and the arms motioned for Critias to draw near.

Inching forward on wobbly legs, Critias placed his sweaty palm on his wide forehead and gaped. *This can't be real. Am I hallucinating? After all the times I've... This doesn't feel like...*

"Critias," breathed Eudoxia, touching him as he came beside her, "*this* is your father!"

Awestruck, Critias could only repeat, "Father?"

The entity, who emanated the scent of roses and infused the air with the taste of honey, looked down at him. "I am He-That-Brings-the-Light," he said in a soprano voice. "Azazel is my name. Your mother's words are true: you are my son."

"When—why—how did it happen?"

"One night I descended to this world, and out of all its women chose your mother to inseminate with my divine seed. You should be honored," said the Light-Bringer, "that an entity such as I should condescend to father a human."

His mind inundated with a cascade of thoughts, Critias first demanded, "What about Cuculus? Did he know any of this?"

"The cuckold had no idea," snickered Eudoxia. "He was so proud, thinking you were his. Three months before I gave birth, his life being of no more value at that point, I laced his favorite mushrooms with some aconite. The poison soon ended him without leaving any incriminating evidence."

He gazed at the Light-Bringer. "What is the meaning of my life? For what purpose did you father me?"

"For the enlightenment of the world."

Critias' heart thumped heavily as the Light-Bringer touched his forehead. In but a single moment of time there flashed before his mind's eye all the world and the nations thereof. He was above the globe, hovering in space and looking downwards. The planet kept revolving beneath his feet at an incredible pace: hundreds of times per second. Beside him stood the Light-Bringer, who said:

"Critias, since the dawn of existence mankind has dwelt in ignorance and darkness. Over the course of many ages, I have acted among the race of mortals, enlightening a select few with knowledge kept secret from the beginning of the world."

Critias gasped as there instantly materialized around him and the Light-Bringer dozens, no scores—hundreds! thousands!—of entities similar in appearance to the first. Focusing his eyes on his father, he asked, "Who are they?"

"My friends."

From among the host of entities that all stood about eight feet tall, seven separated themselves from the rest and took up positions behind the Light-Bringer. Being ten feet tall, their intermediate height sufficiently served to distinguish them.

A fleeting flash of light forced Critias to shut his eyes. When he reöpened them, the rocky floor of the Poseidoneum greeted him. Eudoxia was at his side, her green eyes frenetic and bulging from their sockets. The eight entities were now alone in front of them, all but the Light-Bringer levitating a couple feet above the floor.

"These seven," said the Light-Bringer, "are my lieutenants: Samyaza, Armaros, Baraqil, Kokabil, Chazaqil, Arakil, and Shamsil." He pointed to each in turn. "Critias, my son, at long last I have resolved to rescue humanity from the darkness of its own ignorance. I will illuminate all the peoples of the Earth with such powerful knowledge that they will never again suffer! This is why I begot you: you are my chosen vessel through whom I will remake your world."

Critias, kneeling on one leg before him, asked, "What am I to do?" His heart pulsated in his chest and in his throat his breath stifled. He had to know!

His father touched his shoulder and with one hand effortlessly raised him to his feet. "In order to create a future paradise, we must first clear away the present chaos. Therefore, you shall destroy the world as it now exists."

With his mouth watering so much that it overflowed onto his pale lips, revealing the jagged canine teeth that glistened in the light, Critias choked the air with his fists. If there were only one thing that could electrify Critias, it was the thought of limitless slaughter. To tell him to destroy was as unnecessary as to command a mole to burrow, a lark to sing, or a bee to pollinate.

The Light-Bringer continued. "Under my guidance, you will continue your mother's mission—and surpass her!—in remaking Atlantis and enlarging her armies. Soon you shall go forth conquering and shall subjugate all the nations. Out of the old world's ashes a new order shall spring! There shall be one world, one people, one language, one king, one god. At that time all humans, instructed in my hallowed knowledge, will share with you the enlightenment that my lieutenants shall impart to you. Yet before peace and harmony can reign, we must eliminate the systemic divisions plaguing mankind; and this can only come about by killing off the human flotsam responsible for perpetuating this iniquitous world order."

The Light-Bringer then spoke incomprehensible words to the seven, who subsequently materialized into white-hot beams of energy that departed the room through the crevices in the ceiling. The Light-Bringer himself lingered a few moments longer, glancing at Eudoxia and then at Critias, before following his lieutenants.

As soon as the Light-Bringer had left, the room became filled with darkness. Critias collapsed, his mouth foaming. Eudoxia took him by the hand and led him outside. He did not feel her, nor did he perceive his exit from the building; his mind, overwhelmed with all that had transpired, strained to process everything. Critias did, however, smirk because of one fact that simmered all-consumingly in him.

The urges for destruction that coursed through him on a daily basis, tingling his sinews and whetting his appetite for blood, were now no longer a mere eccentricity of his lacking any rationale beyond his private gratification: they were consecrated unto an otherworldly purpose.

Chapter Eight

T HREE WEEKS HAD PASSED since Periander made his proposal to Ozymandias. The day following their reception, negotiations began. Though Periander and Ozymandias conversed frequently with one another and saw each other at the palace's social festivities, most of the deliberations as well as precise details were argued by their respective aids and confidants.

Agathocles would stir souls by his emotional appeals, colorfully describing life under the Eudoxia-Critias régime and the horrors awaiting Egypt should they succeed in conquering it. Then the Grand Vizier Anysis would counter that no actual hostilities had been committed by Atlantis against Egypt; that Egypt was in a strong position to defend itself from foreign aggression; and that joining an offensive alliance, whose only other ally was tiny Cyrene, would not help Egypt but could provoke Atlantis into launching the very invasion that the alliance was intended to prevent. Demosthenes in turn would refute such objections by pointing out that a ruler bent on conquest, who already was swallowing up many minor lands, would soon be left with only greater countries to conquer; that Critias was following in the footsteps of many past aggressors; that an offensive war fought in foreign lands would spare Egypt the ravages of an invasion; that Egypt's affirmation would encourage additional allies to join; and that a pact forged in secret could in no way incite an enemy who did not even know of its existence.

While these and the like arguments were being debated in halls of state, Periander was reclining on a divan in his suite's large antechamber. Jason, Socrates, and Philip, lying on three other divans, were with him too, all resting after their eleven o'clock lunch. Turning his platinum head towards Socrates, he asked, "How do you think the negotiations are progressing?"

Socrates stroked the silver tip of his abdomen-length beard. "Fear not, Sire. Decades of experience have well taught me the tell-tale signs to watch for; irrespective of what some of his counselors may be angling for, I sense Ozymandias is moving our way."

"Do you really think he'll support us?" asked Jason.

"Yes. Your father framed our cause very forcefully, presenting a compelling argument to the Egyptians on why liberating Atlantis is in their best interests and not merely ours. And the Pharaoh's a reasonable man (not too surprising, as he is of my generation). I trust that an agreement acceptable to both sides can be worked out."

"I hope so," said Jason. He sighed and stared at the marble floor listlessly. "But why is it taking so long for the Pharaoh to make up his mind? Doesn't he understand how dangerous those two are? The people they've killed? And wish to kill?"

There was a knock at the door. Periander said to enter, and in came redheaded Psyche, no longer dressed in all black but an emerald-green attire, as well as a young man who apart from his face was completely covered by the long robes of a deep desert dweller.

"He says he has a message for you," said Psyche, motioning to the man to approach.

Sitting up, Periander accepted a letter from the man and generously rewarded him before he left. He opened the letter and smiled. *Lysander and Timaeus.* "It's from our friends in Atlantis."

"I suppose I should leave, then."

"No need," said Periander, sitting up and gesturing to her to sit alongside him. "Any developments in Atlantis we'll be relaying to your father anyway." Engrossed by the letter, Periander's eyes did not perceive the blush that surfaced on her fair cheeks as when twin dolphins breach from the depths of the churning sea into the sunrays above. He began aloud:

"Your Majesty, we are well if you and your entourage are well. The last few weeks have heralded several significant developments. King Critias' infamously strained relationship with his mother seems to be degenerating even more. He is becoming more vocal in his public criticism of Eudoxia's influence in his government and has been repeatedly overheard berating her in private. He has replaced many high-level ministers of his mother's with his own young companions and cronies, resulting in her scolding him for his impudence. He ignored her advice on the reörganizing of the new colony in Britain.

"Critias, in what is simultaneously a repudiation of one of his mother's major policies as well as grossly out of character for him, has suddenly transformed into a patron of religion! The altars and temples, which had fallen into decay or closed to the public under his mother, are being restored and reöpened. The priesthood is rapidly growing: new candidates are ordained daily (albeit for a price). Critias even secludes himself in the Poseidoneum, meditating, as he says, on his father's religion. For some inexplicable reason, however, he has taken to calling the Deity 'Light-Bringer' and it is by that novel appellation that he refers to Him in the sacrifices which he and his priests conduct. Rumors circulate that he and his new priests are devising further innovations in worship, so it is impossible to predict where his newfound love of religion will lead.

"Lastly, a nasty uprising is brewing in our American colonies. Word has come that some prominent, discontented colonists have combined with the native tribes and are attempting to sever their bonds with us. Troops and fleets are currently being mobilized to reïnforce the colonial garrisons and suppress the insurrection. Critias' reäction to the revolt, however, was a terror to behold! We and several other counselors were in Critias' bedchamber discussing other matters when an intelligence officer ran in and made the announcement.

"Critias oozed venom, bellowing both at us and past us as he hurled abuses upon the rebels, upbraiding anyone so 'audacious' as to rise up against him and his crown. His verbal outbursts were punctuated by the smashing of antique vases against the walls (necessitating our ducking to avoid being struck). Amidst his rage he swore several times that he personally would lead the army to quash the rebellion and exact, by fire, pale, and cross, the most gruesome vengeance on its perpetrators.

"Apprised of the situation, Eudoxia arrived and tried to placate Critias. Albeit equally furious at the affront, she remained composed and methodically went about defusing his unproductive temper. She also sought to dissuade him from his impulsive desire of taking personal command of the army, presumably fearing lest, by his death in America, her own influence (or what remains of it) over Atlantis would die with him. From appeals to reason and safety, logistics and strategy, to minimizing the rebels as being too worthless to merit his personal attention, Eudoxia gradually inveigled him to acquiesce (if only temporarily). She did not cease to utilize every charm at her disposal to retain his compliance but began coaxing him with emotional pleas. At that point, we were ejected from the room, leaving the two of them alone. But before the doors shut, we glimpsed the queen-mother sitting with her son on the bed, thrusting onto his lips an impassioned kiss such as bridegrooms are accustomed to give their wives on their wedding nights. (What further things she resorted to in order to influence him... the Deity only knows.)"

Finishing the letter, Periander, with revitalized vigor, dispatched Philip to inform Ozymandias of the latest incidents.

"This is good news?" said Psyche. Her warm breath caressed his neck.

"Absolutely," answered Periander, his colorful eyes flashing with excitement. "It's true the letter doesn't specify how extensive the rebellion is, or how they'll match up against the coming crackdown. But any resistance to Critias bodes well for us. We must pray that this may be the start of a protracted conflict, one that will drag Critias' war machinery into a quagmire, draining his forces and bogging them down on the other side of our ocean. An absence of armies in Atlantis would make the continent ripe for our invasion."

Jason, raising his right hand high, made a fist. "I hope they pay for Mother's death!"

"Is an invasion the only way?" asked Psyche, cocking her head. She fidgeted on the divan, betraying by her movements the awkwardness of what she was trying to suggest. "Couldn't you—like you did in Cyrene—infiltrate Atlantis with a special force, and take out the High King and his mother? Or some of your friends on the inside?"

"Alas, no." Periander took her soft, long-fingered hands into his much larger ones and gazed into her cerulean eyes. "Aeson and his associates first conned their way into power so they could loot the public treasury and then they illegally perpetuated their rule to hold on to their ill-gotten gains, making zero pretensions to the contrary. By eliminating him and his corrupt henchmen, Galba and his armed supporters were greeted with open arms by the much-enduring citizenry; the fact that Galba had previously served as governor bolstered our installing him at the head of an interim government. Yet Critias' kingship, on the other hand, enjoys legitimacy by right of succession. Although he has committed tyrannical acts, that does not detract from him being the people's hereditary monarch whom they are accustomed to obey. Eudoxia, moreover, spent her regency bewitching the people with her propaganda, and reports say Critias, far from being universally abhorred, is actually liked among the... more vulgar segments of the population. So, while I expect my own subjects to rally to my side, the remaining nine-tenths of the Atlantean population cannot be counted on to abandon Critias. It is possible someone inside could turn assassin. Eudoxia, however, thoroughly staffed the imperial administration with her acolytes as well as birthed an entire new class of magnates whose wealth and power depend entirely on the patronage of the High Kingship. In the event of her and Critias' assassination, I fear they would respond by naming one of their own

High King to perpetuate the régime and safeguard their own privileges rather than accept my claim to the throne. Killing those two monsters is absolutely necessary but it is not sufficient. We must also purge the whole imperial apparatus in order to establish functional control of government. And that can only happen by subduing the whole continent militarily." *Nor should either of those two escape the fury of my avenging hand....*

"And we'll need Egypt's help for that." Jason sat up and stared intently at Psyche. "Do you know what your father is thinking about the proposed alliance? Ask him when he'll decide?"

"Jason! Don't be so brusque!" said Periander angrily, hushing Jason who lowered his spiky head and apologized to Psyche.

"It's quite all right," she said. "I know my father very well. He'll most likely—"

"Sire!" Philip sprinted into the room, globs of sweat running down his face. "Ozymandias... contacted... by Critias... on holoprojector," he panted.

"What? Where are they?"

"Throne... Hall."

"Quick!" Periander dashed from his chair, Jason and Socrates behind him.

"Wait," said Psyche, raising her right arm to halt them, the green sleeve of her robe falling down to reveal the contours of her smooth arm. "My hovercart is just outside the building. It'll get us there much faster."

Following her, Periander and the others hurried outside where the gold-plated hovercart was parked against a shade-giving plane tree. They all boarded it except Socrates, whom they had to leave behind under the plane tree's well-trimmed branches due to a lack of space. Periander piloted the vehicle through the many winding courtyards of the palace. Arriving at the granite edifice of their destination, they dismounted, crossed the golden threshold, made their way through the atrium, and darted inside the Throne Hall.

Grand Vizier Anysis and other high-ranking Egyptians were present, lining up in two opposite rows from the wide steps of the throne's base to the entranceway. Agathocles and Demosthenes stood amid them. Ozymandias was perched on his throne. The Pharaoh's brown eyes were narrowed and pressed down by his bushy brown eyebrows, his nostrils flared, and his upper lip curled ever so slightly. In his left hand he held the royal scepter of Egypt, topped by a diamond-studded gold phoenix; he kept his right hand underneath a fold in his royal blue tunic, barely veiling a white-knuckled fist.

At the bottom of the throne's steps, a portable holoprojector had been wheeled in. Its steel outer covering was crisscrossed with horizontal black indentations across its fourteen sides; the two front sides displayed the control panels while the backmost one had the antenna. From this machine was projected a life-sized emerald-colored hologram of Critias, at whom Ozymandias was glowering.

"And I will repeat myself," insisted the Pharaoh through gritted teeth. "I have pledged to King Periander asylum in my realm. What I have granted I have granted. Threats shall not move me from that verdict which I, in good conscience, made."

When Periander's sudden entry prompted Ozymandias to move his head to see him, it likewise alerted Critias. His hologram body spun around, and his eyes grew big with devilish delight once they spotted Periander.

"Critias!" growled Periander. With the veins in his hands bulging in anger, he marched up in front of the holoprojector to confront his nemesis.

"Periander." Critias' thin lips expanded into a smirk. "It's been a while. How's the family doing?"

He glared at the tyrant. "You murderous fiend! What do you want now?"

"He wants you in chains," interjected Ozymandias, "and your son too."

"Yes, and in chains you shall be!" Critias leisurely doused his lips with his long, clefted tongue. The hologram's image quality was so explicit that one could see the drops of saliva trickling down his slender chin. "That outcome is predestined. I've already won this conflict of ours. No power on Earth can stop me, least of all your feeble self. So, give up! End this fugitive nonsense; it wearies me. Turn yourself over to my agents and come back home. If you do, there's a chance I might let you live, or maybe your son—you never know. (There's always room in my court for more jesters; my floors contribute all the crumbs one can eat!) Don't surrender, you'll die miserably. That's what happens to everybody who opposes me and the crown my father gave me."

Although his fingers kept rubbing against the cold metal of his gun, eager to remove it from its holster, Periander himself remained calm. "I knew your father. He demonstrated by his life that true kinghood is on the inside; a piece of metal about the head no more makes you worthy of the regal name than a crowned sow becomes a queen. What your mother's done, and what you're now doing, Cuculus would've never approved! If you truly wanted to honor your father, Critias, you wouldn't continue to persecute the innocent, nor violate that most basic law enacted by the Founder of our people: *Non bellabis adversus regem fraternalem.* 'Thou shalt not wage war against thy brother-king,'" he said, translating the Old Atlantic for Critias' benefit. "Cuculus would be ashamed to have fathered a murderous tyrant like you."

His retort was met by laughter. "Spare me the archaic rumblings of some bygone cavil-monger. I am 'living law!' I am the 'fount of justice!' Whatever I do is therefore by definition lawful and just."

The whole room erupted with gasps at his hubris.

He's becoming even more insane every time I see him. Shutting his eyes, Periander slowly shook his head. "You pervert the aphorisms," he declared, wagging his finger in disappointment. His eyes burst open with colorful intensity. "A king *is* living law because it is he who makes and unmakes all human laws. A king *is* the fount of justice because he appoints and authorizes all lower judges to right his subjects' wrongs and over him there is no earthly judge. But a king's laws are unjust—and therefore not true laws at all—if they do not conform to the Deity's Laws, which overrule us all. Without justice, a so-called king is nothing but the largest brigand in the kingdom, his pretended laws mere acts of violence. And I promise you this, Critias: no king, not even a high king, shall escape the Deity's righteous wrath if he butchers innocents with the very sword the Deity entrusted to him for their protection."

The court loudly applauded Periander, led by Agathocles whose thick hands easily clapped louder than all the others. Critias growled.

"I will *never* submit to a tyrant like you, Critias. You prize your beloved crown but are least deserving of it. Its regal sanctity is profaned by that stink seeping through the pores of your putrid skull, oozing out of your rotten soul! As the Deity lives, I will deprive you of your precious crown—not because I covet what is not mine, not because I suffer from god-sized delusions, not because I have an unslakable thirst for bloodshed—but because I refuse to tolerate all the wickedness you have committed, the wickedness you are even now committing, the wickedness you will commit. No, I will not stand by and watch while you and your mother tyrannize the people of Atlantis, while you drag the whole world down into the bilgewater of your insanity. In the name of the Deity and by the sweet soul of Cornelia, whom you *murdered*, I swear I will defeat you and eradicate your evil régime root and branch!"

In response to Periander's hearty oath, Critias murmured something unintelligible. His eyes were wildly zipping back and forth while his twitching face contorted with aggravation. Mere seconds later the hologram dissolved, its transmission terminated by Atlantis.

Periander flashed one last incensed glare at his enemy before the image had entirely faded. *He must be stopped... I will avenge Cornelia and free my people!*

Ozymandias, whose frown and wrinkled lip told well of his unease, appeared paler than before. Setting his eyes on Periander, he said, wearily, "Lord Periander, having heard the High King making multifarious threats against my realm, my person, and my family, permit me to consult with my counselors one final time. Then I will make my decision concerning your proposed alliance."

"Judge the matter well, O Pharaoh," answered Periander. He withdrew from the room, Jason and Philip beside him; and from the ranks of the Egyptians, Agathocles and Demosthenes rejoined their king. They began walking through the courtyards, retracing the journey to the guesthouse.

Grinning widely, Agathocles shadowboxed the air as they went along. "You certainly told him off, my liege!"

"You sure did, Father," said Jason, equally enthused.

"And did you see the way he looked at the end?" Agathocles laughed. "His face looked like he'd been constipated for a year! Oh, you skewered him good, Sire!"

"You reduced him to cutting off the holoprojector like a petulant child," added Jason. "You really knew how to tell him off."

Periander put his arm around Jason to draw him closer. "He infuriates me. Seeing him, hearing that monster's voice—my words just gushed forth of their own accord."

"Be that as it may, it was a potent indictment of Critias," said Demosthenes, twiddling his right hazel sideburn. "You brought out his worst characteristics: his egotism and shameless pretensions. He looked like the classic portrait of a tyrant. That, combined with how he sought to intimidate Ozymandias and issued threats, should prove decisive in concluding an alliance with Egypt."

Periander nodded. "I'm optimistic." Shielding his multicolored eyes from the sun, he scanned ahead. There, still under the plane tree, was Socrates. Periander waved, but the old man did not reciprocate.

With his back against the tree and his spectacles drooping down from his head, Socrates had clearly fallen asleep. He lay there, oblivious, as the playful breeze fingered the strands of his silver beard.

Chapter Nine

O ZYMANDIAS AND HIS COUNSELORS retired from the Throne Hall into the Council Chamber located behind it where they might discuss allying with Periander. In the meantime, Psyche returned to the women's apartments, which were situated two buildings south of the Throne Hall. This building was great both in size and grandeur, housing not only Psyche and her mother the queen but also the Pharaoh's three sisters, his nieces and daughters-in-law, and the aristocratic women of the court.

Psyche entered her mother's suite of rooms, a place where often she would linger when her mind was awhirl. Swaddled on four sides by thirty-seven-foot-high walls, the exterior ones parading five massive oval-shaped windows whose centers displayed stain-glassed doves, she felt secure here, here in her mother's presence.

At least that is how she would normally feel. With her father about to make his decision of whether to ally with Periander or not, however, Psyche fretted for the future, abhorring the too-soon images of having to part with Periander. For regardless of whichever choice her father made, Periander would be off to proposition his next likely ally once he had Egypt's answer. There he would go voyaging to some far-off land, contracting alliances, marshalling armies to reclaim his paternal estates, overthrowing Atlantis's oppressive régime... whereas she, languishing in Egypt, would be fulfilling nothing abroad or at home, a widow not yet twenty, a byword to be shunned by superstitious men.

Zenobia sat among her daughters-in-law, weaving a half-finished tapestry depicting the Mediterranean surf and clash of the waves in several purple hues. About twenty feet away, at a silver-studded desk, Psyche had opened her chest of chemicals. Fascinated by chemical reäctions and the compounding of elixirs, and with her father's encouragement, Psyche had been trained in the arts of the apothecary. Spending her time at this, she would often mix elements and vary dosages in her experiments, producing results varying in color, odor, and chemical stability. Yet now her hands only shifted the bottles back and forth, some blue or green, some red or yellow. Her mind's concentration was elsewhere.

Not too far away to see her daughter's idle conduct, Zenobia walked over to her and said, "Darling Psyche, what is troubling your mind? Is it our visitor Periander?"

"W-what? Whyever do you say that?" Sheepishly Psyche feigned surprise. She raised her right hand in front of her mouth to conceal that self-conscious grin which, waging a two-front war, rammed both her blushing cheeks upwards. From her left hand she let slip a bottle of hydrochloric acid, which duly shattered upon the floor. A pungent smell rose as the colorless liquid congealed into a puddle.

Her mother, glancing first at the spilled fluid before peering into her eyes, said, "Do you think I am oblivious? I've seen how you've been since King Periander arrived—the way you look at him and act when he's around. Have you fallen in love with Periander?"

"I... I... Yes. I've loved him since he visited Egypt two years ago. His charm and wit, his strength and gallantry, his piety and dutifulness, they all moved me." Psyche clasped her mother in an embrace, with locks of her red hair obscuring her face. "Now that he has returned, and I've been able to get to know him better these last few weeks—I crave him even more! It wasn't any youthful misperception: he's really all the man I thought he was, if not more so... I see how he has persevered despite all the pain he has endured; watching him work tirelessly to realize his goal, the deep respect his men have for him... I just want to be always at his side to help him as best I can."

Zenobia hugged her daughter. She pushed back the red hair, her warm hands locking onto the sides of Psyche's face. "You are quite right about his virtues, Daughter. Periander is a good man. And why not? He's of good stock." She paused a moment. "I was born an Atlantean, a princess of the House of Mestor, and so I knew his father Themistocles. There, too, was another good man. Not unlike you, I was smitten with Themistocles: savoring the moments I had with him, counting all his best qualities, picturing ourselves at our wedding..."

Psyche gaped in disbelief. "You were in love with Themistocles? Why have you never mentioned it before? What happened?"

"We royalty have duties that we owe. For diplomatic purposes, to strengthen relations between our countries, my father had pledged my hand in marriage to your father the king, who at that time was only crown prince. So, in spite of my personal feelings, I let that fancy pass and came to Egypt."

"And Themistocles just let you go like that, without a protest?"

"I'd never even gotten around to telling him that I loved him, at least not in words... Did he perhaps sense my feelings for him? I don't know. At this point, it doesn't matter. What's done is done."

"Oh, Mother! It does matter if you still feel regret for losing a lover."

"No, no, no, it's not like that." Her mother blinked slowly. She inhaled a deep breath. "I have had forty-one wonderful years with Ozymandias, given him sixteen children. Throughout this time, I came to love him with more love than I ever daydreamed I had for Themistocles. It's been a long while since I last thought of my love for him. After all, to fixate on counterfactuals—to obsess over what might have been—is unhealthy. We must look ahead on the path that we have chosen. But still... I know you were not thrilled when your father betrothed you to Mycerinus."

"Not at all. What I knew of him before the engagement did not please me, nor did spending time with him appease my heart. I am ashamed to say it, but... when I heard Mycerinus was killed, I silently rejoiced at my good fortune before my conscience could condemn such selfishness. And now this, this accursed widowhood..." Tears began to inundate her fair cheeks; her lips formed a melancholic smile. "Except for my father and brothers, what Egyptian man will talk to me, let alone wish to marry me?"

"The Egyptians and their foolish superstitions!" exclaimed Zenobia. She rolled her eyes. "That is the one thing I've never adjusted to in all my years here. O Psyche, I don't want *you* to regret missing out on your chance at finding happiness with the man of your dreams, least of all to forsake the opportunity merely to be forsaken and left manless. If you love this man, if you want to accompany him on his quest, then go entreat your father: he can make it happen."

Psyche embraced Zenobia and exclaimed, "I love you so much!"

"And I, you."

Thanking her mother for her heartening words, Psyche exited the bedchamber and scampered from the building. She made her way to the Throne Hall, passing through the fountain-filled atrium. In the rear of the room there were two large doors, each studded with amethysts and emeralds arranged in a variety of geometrical shapes. Two guards stood on either side of the doorway, grasping laser-lances in their hands. Seeing Psyche, they stood aside to let her pass, as they were accustomed; for she, with Ozymandias' assent, often attended the meetings of his council.

The room was L-shaped, with the shorter alcove forming its antechamber in which were file cabinets and portfolios, computer monitors and transmitters, lining the left and right walls. Psyche walked ahead and turned leftwards. An elongated ivory-carved table dominated this longer section of the room, around which sat twenty-three of her father's counselors. Ozymandias was seated at the end of the table on a golden throne which was beneath a crimson canopy; on the wall behind it hung a tapestry depicting sedges and bees. Facing the table, located in the room's L-joint, were four empty rows of benches. Psyche took a seat in the second row, sinking into the ruby velvet.

The Grand Vizier was speaking. "I defer to Your Majesty's judgment and the verdict of my peers." He bowed his head, rose from the table, and left the room, an emotionless expression on his face as he glanced at Psyche on his way out.

"Then," said the Pharaoh, clearing his throat, "having heard all opinions and considered the ramifications of joining the coalition King Periander is proposing, here is my decision. It seems best to me to enter into a military alliance with him, effective upon the expansion of the coalition, and to commit all of Egypt's resources to the aim of establishing a more benevolent government in Atlantis. I shall inform Periander of this myself."

With that Ozymandias dismissed his counselors. They began pouring out of the room, all streaming past Psyche, who remained like a turtle, clinging onto a bank amid a surging river, which stays put while the water carries off everything else. Once the last counselors had left, and Ozymandias was pushing his chair out from the table, Psyche galloped over to him to make her request.

Before her father could rise up, she had knelt down before him, her hands tightly clasping the linen fabric around his knees. With a solemn calm in her voice conveying certitude of purpose, her head erect with resolve, and her eyes wide, she began:

"Papa dear, may I ask something of you?"

"Psyche," said Ozymandias bewilderedly, "whatever is the matter? Why have you assailed my knees like some conquered soldier begging his captor to spare his life?"

"Oh, Father! Bashfulness restrains my words, ensnares my voice in its box."

Ozymandias' stumpy arms, leaner with age yet very much still thick with vigor, took hold of her beneath her upper arms and boosted Psyche up onto the warm paternal lap. "Has your father ever begrudged his little princess anything? Did I not give you, a mere toddler just learning to verbalize requests, a high-roofed wagon drawn by mules when you asked for it? Therefore speak, Child."

"Father, as soon as you conclude a treaty with Periander, he'll depart from our home."

"Yes, he will have to go recruit additional members for our alliance."

"After being around him these last few weeks, seeing and conversing with him—I do not want to part with him. Father, please don't make me have to say farewell."

"You must get used to his absence because he will be going."

"There's a way for you to spare me that."

Ozymandias raised one eyebrow. "I cannot detain him here, nor make him my prisoner: to do so would be a violation of my word and all laws of hospitality."

"No, but... you can send me with him."

"Wh-what?" Bounding from his seat, Ozymandias compelled Psyche to step off his vanishing lap and recoil from the throne. "You, Periander—marry?!"

"That is what I wish."

"A daughter of Egypt to be yoked with a son of Atlantis? It's absurd! Inconceivable! I forbid it!"

"Why? What is absurd about me marrying an Atlantean?"

"That is not a suitable union."

"Yet you married an Atlantean," Psyche pointed out. "Do you deem Mother 'unsuitable'?"

"That was different," huffed Ozymandias, turning his eyes away from her intense stare. "It is not Egypt's custom to give her princesses away. We take wives from others but do not ourselves give women in marriage."

Psyche pressed on. "But Father, I love him."

"Are there no males left in Egypt—no somber men, no strapping youths, not one lone boy still sucking his mother's breasts—that you desire to marry an outsider?"

"What Egyptian, with all his superstitions, would desire to marry a *virgin widow*?"

"I don't believe in the superstitions."

"But your subjects do."

Ozymandias, his body jerking and sweating, tersely replied, "I am Pharaoh: I can order anyone to marry you."

"Even Pharaoh cannot scrub men's souls of their beliefs, nor can you command my heart." Without weeping or crying, Psyche stared intently into her father's eyes and took him by his hands. "Please, Father, let me marry whom I wish."

"An exile from his homeland?" Freeing his hands, Ozymandias threw them up in the air. "How can I entrust my daughter to such a man, a man without a country, forced to travel from kingdom to kingdom in search of allies? What sort of a husband would a man like that make?"

"Did you not just esteem him worthy to entrust him with the fate of Egypt? To commit Egypt to wage war against Atlantis on his behalf?"

"A kingdom is not a daughter. Your comparison fails."

"But if a man is dependable in a thing as great as deciding the fate of kingdoms, is he not also dependable in so comparatively small a thing as receiving a wife? Even peasants take care of their wives. And Periander is head and shoulders above the hordes of common men: I would have no fear to trust him with my life."

Ozymandias whacked both palms upon the ivory table. "Look how he took care of his last wife!" He started panting while facial muscles madly distorted his expression.

"Father!" The appalled look in her eyes and the high-pitched tone of her gasp had their effect upon him.

Rendered speechless, he leaned against his throne to steady himself. His eyebrows unscrunched, his pupils contracted, and his drooping jaw closed. "I'm sorry. That was uncalled for, a cruel thing to say. It's just..."

Ozymandias placed his hands on her shoulders and delicately touched one of her cheeks. "Psyche, *I* love you. You say you don't want to be separated from Periander. Well, I don't want to be separated from you! That's why I betrothed you to Mycerinus: so you'd still be here at court, with your father and mother, where I'd always be able to find you. I love all your brothers, even Chephren after the incident with the shepherd Philitis. But you, my only girl, have always been dearer to me than my own eyes, my ears, my lungs. To lose you… the grief, excruciating—"

Psyche interrupted him with a hug. She delved into his bosom, and he hugged her tight. "I'll always love you, Father, here or a galaxy away! But I'll love you even more as the bride of Periander." She stepped back and rested her hands at her side. *Please, Father, let me marry him!* she silently pleaded, her eyes focused attentively on his.

"What about your mother?"

"She's the one who sent me to you."

"She did? Of course she did." Ozymandias sighed in a manner similar to a defeated boxer who, after thirty rounds fraught with valor, ultimately is entombed in the dust of the arena, the back of his bloody neck depressed by his victor's reeking, fungus-infected foot. "I am vanquished… I grant you my permission to wed him. And my blessing."

"Thank you, Father! Thank you so much!" Psyche hugged him again, this time releasing a Nile-rising cataract of tears.

Her father wept too, appearing hard-pressed to limit it to a mist and not a deluge. "Yes, yes, Periander is an exemplar of kinghood, descended from a noble line. This is a good match. He *shall* marry you, Psyche! I'll see to that."

Chapter Ten

"I AGREE TO ALLY with you and to commit the armies of Egypt to the overthrow of Critias on two conditions. The first is that Egypt will not initiate hostilities against Atlantis unless a minimum of one other great power joins our coalition. Do you assent?"

"I do. And the second?"

"That, in confirmation of this alliance, we be bound together not only by ties of comradeship but also by affinity—Lord Periander, I offer you my daughter Psyche in marriage."

Oh, my! I never expected this. Periander, not knowing what to say, stared blankly at Ozymandias, who was standing a foot away from him at the bottom of the throne's seventy steps. Next to the Pharaoh was Psyche, whose bright eyes were diffidently turned towards the floor. *Why do I have a feeling she had something to do with this?* he wondered goodheartedly.

Having stopped his jaw from sinking like a millstone, Periander regained his composure. His men, however, appeared visibly stunned while the equally-amazed Egyptian courtiers started whispering among themselves.

"I've never known a Pharaoh to act thus," mused Socrates, adjusting his glasses and stroking his beard.

"That is true," said Ozymandias, taking hold of one hand from both Psyche and Periander. He brought their hands together and solidified their clasp by overlaying his hands over theirs. "But in view of the unprecedented undertaking we are planning, I give my daughter to you, Periander of Atlantis, Son of Themistocles, in token of that faith which I and all Egypt have in you, my son."

As Ozymandias let go and stepped rearwards, Periander continued holding on to Psyche's warm petite hand, sensing her long fingers caressing the top of his hand while he hurriedly reflected on the significance of what was happening.

Remarrying so soon, especially before I've avenged Cornelia, wasn't part of my plan... But diplomatic marriages are a hallowed tradition among royalty, having sealed many a pact throughout history; given Egypt's atypical situation, this is an even greater honor being shown to me and to my house. If accomplishing my mission requires marriage, then I must marry.

When her other arm, tender and perfumed with sweet rosewater, curved around his upper back, he smiled.

Besides... Periander pulled Psyche close to him and kissed her right cheek, which tasted like plums caked in cherry syrup. *A man could do far worse in choice of brides than this one.* Turning next to Ozymandias, he bowed his head and said, "Then, Father, I accept your alliance and your daughter's hand in wedlock."

At the Pharaoh's command, an impromptu wedding was straightaway prepared. Servants scurried to decorate the palace temple, ritually cleansing it, hanging golden garlands from the columns, and erecting beneath its outer awning tables for the banquet feast. Psyche was rushed away by maidservants so that Zenobia and kinswomen might array the bride-to-be, while Periander returned with his men to his room to dress himself suitably for the occasion.

Three hours passed between the betrothal and the wedding. Escorted by his men, Periander, having donned a golden robe and diamond-encrusted gauntlets, his platinum hair slick back with oil, made his way through the palace complex to the temple.

"I can't believe Ozymandias is forcing you to marry her," said Jason briskly, walking to the right of his father.

"I am as surprised as you. I certainly didn't expect it, let alone promote it."

"I know royal marriages are often arranged, but why does Ozymandias break with his kingdom's marital custom now? Why is he so keen on making you marry Psyche? Or is he not the real force behind this move?"

"What do you mean?"

Jason halted and looked his father in his eyes. "I've seen the way she looks at you. I don't think she's the one being forced into this."

Periander paused, deep in thought, before responding. "Regardless of the circumstances behind this outcome, we must accept what the Deity has prepared for our lives. I don't want you to misjudge anything, Jason. This marital alliance will bolster our position and hasten the day when I'll be able to avenge Cornelia: that is why I am agreeing to it. If you fear I'll forget your mother, don't. No affection you may see shown to the princess will ever diminish my passion for your mother or blot her from my memory, any more than your birth and the fondness it engendered lessened our love for one another; and had we been blessed to give you siblings, our love for you would have been just as strong as before. Yes, I will be encumbered with responsibility for a new wife and will have to treat her with due regards, but that is the duty to which a good man is bound. Remember that."

"I know, I know." A budding smile appeared on his face. "Yet if you'd like it, Father," Jason added wistfully, "*I* could marry her instead, relieve you of this burden."

Periander laughed. Giving Jason a lighthearted rap on his back, he said, "Oh, my boy, I have a feeling you'd be a closer match to what that woman wants in a husband (or should want)."

When they arrived at the temple, Ozymandias and Zenobia were there, they and their other children and near relatives who were around the palace—less than forty Egyptians all together for these spontaneous nuptials. Periander's men intermingled with the Egyptians while he took his place before the altar to the left of Ozymandias. Only a moment later

Psyche, attended by a dozen maidservants, entered the temple. Wearing the gown which had been intended for her precluded marriage to Mycerinus, Psyche appeared resplendent in a dress that was all white apart from some life-sized images of bees, made of cloth-of-gold, sewed thereon.

Psyche joined Periander at the altar and the high priest of Memphis solemnized their marriage. He commended the fruitful union of Psyche's parents and implored the Deity to bless hers and Periander's. Finishing the ceremony, in accordance with Egyptian custom, the priest handed them the cornucopia from which they adorned the altar with peaches and daffodils. They were then given a chalice of wine to share a simultaneous sip before jointly pouring the remaining wine onto the fruits and flowers. Receiving a torch from Proteus, his bride's eldest brother, Periander ignited the sacrifice just as the last rays of the solar sphere were fading. With the flames consuming the offering, everyone began singing a hymn to the new couple.

After the ceremony there was feasting, there was dancing, there was merrymaking—all the sorts of things which one might find at any wedding. Finally, at ten o'clock, Periander and Psyche were ushered into the bridal chamber that had been prepared for them. There was a great bed inside, whose frame was of gold, and which was covered in silken sapphire sheets. Above it was a mural on the ceiling. In one scene there was a maiden extracting honey from a hive; in another she was pressing olives; a third scene included a youth, naked from the waist up, whose lips the maiden saturated with her honey; and the final scene showed the twain embracing in a dimly-lit cave.

Then the ushers ushered themselves away, and the door was locked. Edging towards him, Psyche nuzzled her cheek against his and whispered, "Periander, I am so happy to have married you."

"You love me although you scarcely know me."

She blinked. "I know enough to know I love you."

Periander took her in his arms and glued his eyes to hers. "I hope this love of yours will blossom and grow deeper with age. I promise to cherish you always and to give you the honor that befits a wife. Every husbandly duty I will perform...."

***

B Y THE TIME THE slugabed sun was finally hauled from his bed on the following morning, Periander had been awake for a couple hours. Enthusiastic after securing an alliance with Egypt and keen to be on his way to recruit even more allies, he had accordingly been arranging for their departure, coöperating with Ozymandias' servants in the preparations and preparing his own men for the journey ahead.

It was nine o'clock before his whereabouts were discovered by his new wife. He was at the main gate of the palace complex, overseeing servants loading his belongings and supplies onto a large gray hover-transport through its rear door. The vehicle was just taking off as Psyche arrived to greet him.

"Good morning, Psyche," said Periander, kissing her cheek.

Psyche wore a light pink dress reaching down to her ankles and was crowned with a thin white-gold diadem studded with rubies. "I woke to an empty bed and for a moment was afraid that last night had only been a dream..."

"Never fear," urged Periander, placing his palm over her left cheek which promptly blushed. "It was no dream nor was your husband fleeing you out of remorse. I had things to take care of, but you looked so peaceful I didn't want to wake you."

"What have you been up to?"

"Making arrangements for us to depart later today."

"Today? I knew you wanted a quick departure... but are we really to leave so soon?" she asked, cocking her head.

"Yes. I told you we'd be heading out promptly."

"Would it not be possible to linger for even one day, to enjoy our first full day married?" she asked, gently running one finger up his arm.

"As tempting as that is, I can't. I promise you I'll have plenty of time to show you the most romantic sights in Atlantis once I am restored to my land and have vanquished my enemies. In the meantime, I must act to accomplish that goal: I feel only restlessness until it's realized."

"I understand. What time will we be leaving?"

"Your father's already given us an airship and crew, and the preparations are nearly complete. We should be out of here in under three hours."

"Oh, my," exclaimed Psyche, obscuring her gaping mouth with her right hand. "Then I'd better go make my goodbyes to everyone."

Periander smiled as she rushed off, her dress billowing in the breeze so that it revealed her beautiful, supple ankles. *At least she's willing to fall in line, even seems eager to please. I don't know if she fully understood the magnitude of what she's signed up for. I never asked her to join me; now that she has, I can't ease off pursuing my mission just on her account. Hopefully, she won't prove a hindrance...*

***

PERIANDER'S ESTIMATION FOR THE timetable was not mistaken. Seventeen minutes before noon, he and his men, dressed in their finest apparel, were beside a lime-green sided, lemon-roofed hovercar, awaiting Ozymandias' farewell.

Psyche was the last of Periander's party to arrive. Looking at the others, she asked her husband, "Where is your other man, Philip?"

"He has already left," interjected Socrates, "for India."

"India? Is that our destination?"

"No, no," said Periander, coming over and putting his arm around her. "I've selected Philip to open negotiations with the king of Mohenjo-Daro since he has acquaintances in the royal court. We, on the other hand, shall go to Athens, where I can count on the help of a mighty friend."

"Oh, you are friends with King Athenagoras? I've heard he's quite crusty."

"With his son, the crown prince Leonidas." Periander smiled and felt a rush of warmth as he spoke his comrade's name. "We've been friends nearly two decades, and I'm sure he'll help prod his father—who is, as you put it, 'crusty'— to our cause."

Their conversation ended as Ozymandias and Zenobia appeared, grave in face, and trailed by courtiers and servants. Psyche and her mother went aside to share a few last words and intermittent embraces whilst Ozymandias addressed his son-in-law.

"Lord Periander," said the Pharaoh, "I pray to the Deity that you fare well and prosper in all your undertakings."

Periander bowed his head. "I thank you and Egypt for everything you have offered. May you likewise flourish."

"There is one more thing I wish to give you." His hands' signet rings momentarily tangling on each other's metal, Ozymandias summoned a couple servants with a clap.

They were carrying by four silver handles a large golden chest, the sides of which were entirely inscribed with words in the Old Atlantic dialect. The lid depicted foreign soldiers cowering before a colossal Pharaoh who, bow in hand, was effortlessly killing them. The servants, setting the chest down before Periander, opened it.

Periander gaped in amazement and his eyes became iridescent lakes. "This is—"

"The Astrap," said Ozymandias, completing his sentence.

Originally fashioned in the workshops of Atlantis, this ancient weapon had been in the Pharaohs' possession since Egypt's secession from the Atlantean Empire. The Astrapë was a bowstring made of orichalcum whose complex inner workings were powered by a rare elemental crystal, extracted from a primeval mine long since exhausted, that permitted a projector in the rear of the bow to generate laser-arrows. These luminous arrows were as blue as fresh sapphires. Yet unlike guns, which shoot their laser-bolts as soon as they are generated, the Astrapë's twined orichalcum bowstring contained stabilizers by which its arrows could be momentarily maintained in place once formed. This allowed greater amounts of energy to be concentrated into a single point than is typical with handheld arms, vastly increasing the arrows' power as well as giving the Astrapë's wielder ample time to aim it at his target. Despite the antiquity of this device, the Astrapë was still capable of holding its own with modern weaponry in close combat.

Ozymandias placed the prized weapon in Periander's hands. Sleek but firm, cold to the touch yet almost still warm from the hands of all the warriors who had wielded it, Periander was awed by the gift. "I wholeheartedly accept this. I've heard stories of the Astrapë since I was a boy—always wanted to test it out myself. Are you truly parting with it?"

"Yes, Periander," said Ozymandias. "I foresee its services will be needed in the war that is to come. But since I am too old to take the field of battle myself, I am lending you a weapon that many pharaohs have found most dependable in combat. I pray it may aid you in your fight."

"You can count on me to use it well. It is a great honor which you bestow upon me."

"Do not consider the Astrapë the token of my confidence in you: it is merely a gift, precious though it be." He cast a glance at his wife and daughter, still chatting in the distance. "No, I've already entrusted to you something far dearer to me than some weapon. *That* is what testifies to the faith I have placed in you."

Periander followed his gaze and understood. He thanked Ozymandias and exchanged farewells with him and his wife. The Astrapë was loaded into the vehicle, and Periander, his men, and Psyche all boarded it.

The hovercar lifted off and, surrounded by others to escort it, sped through the crowded streets of Memphis. The people shouted and excitedly waved their arms, bidding farewell to their princess. They proceeded to the outskirts of the city, where a royal dockyard had a landing pad awaiting them. Once they arrived, Periander and the others were directed to a saucer-shaped airship, three hundred feet in length, whose exterior was coated with reflective ice-colored metal. From the rear, a part of the hull opened, and a staircase descended.

Ascending it, they first entered the bridge where the ship's three crewmembers, dressed in blue jumpsuits emblazoned with golden phoenixes on the front and sphinxes on the back, greeted them. The deck was functional, not ornamental; the walls and floors glimmered with white metal and plastic interspersed by grayish colors and flashing green lights. Rising up in the middle of the craft, this was the ship's topmost section, whose single panoramic window provided an unbroken three-hundred-and-sixty-degree line of sight.

Periander and the others quickly progressed down to a lower level of the ship, all except Psyche. She remained on the bridge to gaze out the windows as the ship rose vertically into the sky. Traveling at five hundred miles per hour, it was not long before the ship had left the shores of Egypt behind and was zooming over the frothy Mediterranean. Then and only then did Psyche, taking one final glance at her native land that was already receding from view, leave to join the others in a lower-level cabin.

"What are you talking about?" she asked, interrupting a heated conversation. She sat down in the chair beside Periander's.

"We were debating what our next move should be after we make an alliance with Athens," said Periander, putting his arm around her shoulders.

"King Athenagoras is well-known for his neutrality and reluctance to become entangled in international deals. You're confident your friendship with his son will help persuade him?"

"I am." Periander leaned back against the wall and nodded his head several times. "Leonidas is no mere acquaintance or friend of convenience. More than a friend, he is like a brother to me. Our ties are as deep as the ocean floor, born of adversity, fostered by toil."

Theatrically folding his arms and thrusting his head back, Jason quipped, "Ah, now you've done it! He's about to tell *that* story again." The words, though disapproving, were contradicted by the good-natured tone in his voice and the smile on his face.

"What story?"

"About how he and Leonidas became friends saving Mother."

Periander flicked his hand. "I doubt she is interested in hearing about that."

"But I am." Her pupils growing in curiosity, Psyche exclaimed, "Go on, tell it!" as she gently prodded her husband's side.

"Alright, then. If you insist. It all started eighteen years ago..."

CHAPTER ELEVEN

"**M**Y FATHER THEMISTOCLES HAD arranged for me to marry a princess of the House of Mneseus. Her name was Cornelia, a most beautiful and sweet woman... Besides our families, princes from the other Houses as well as from Egypt, Athens, and other foreign lands—a huge gathering of royalty—had come to witness our marriage ceremony.

"On the day of the wedding, I, our companions, and families, arrived at my ancestral temple and waited for Cornelia to arrive. A slight delay was not unforeseen because she had made a last-minute trip to Athens to fetch her aunt Aspasia. But then the delay persisted. Four hours after the ceremony was scheduled to begin, we finally received a brief frantic message from the captain of her airship: mechanical difficulties had led them off course and forced them to make an emergency landing on that forty-thousand-square-mile slab of ice to the north known as the Isle of the Heliolaters. Furthermore, the island's inhabitants—those brutal savages who sacrifice human beings in order to propitiate the sun lest, according to their insane beliefs, he abandon their foul arctic land entirely due to lack of blood—had begun an attack upon Cornelia's airship!

"Wasting no time, I asked my father to ready a company of our soldiers so that I could lead them in rescuing my bride. But, his face drooping with agony, he told me that the last of our troops, along with the rest of all Atlantis's, had been diverted to suppress the rebellions then ravaging our Caribbean colonies. Consequently, we had no troops at the ready.

It would take much time to outfit a proper expedition; but by then it would be too late.

"Dumbstruck, I didn't know what to do. But then Leonidas approached me. Pointing to the princes gathered behind him, he said: 'Periander, your soldiers are absent, but we princes are present. Polycrates here has an exceptionally fast airship. Let us help you rescue your bride.'

"I hesitated. Leonidas' proposal sounded reasonable; but at the time I scarcely knew this Athenian, or that Egyptian, or most of those other princes aside from a few of the Atlanteans. I asked them what they wanted in return.

"'Only to fight as equals,' they replied.

"As crown prince of my House, I was used to either commanding subjects or obeying my father, not collaborating with peers. Yet, without much choice, I assented to their precondition.

"Gordian, Hiero, Polycrates, Marius, Cleisthenes, Peisistratos, Pindar, Pheros, Maneros, Domitian, Leonidas, and I—twelve valiant princes in all—hastened to where the distress signal originated. It was appalling! Cornelia's airship was still burning when we landed. The beach, its gravel red from blood, was strewn with bodies. The ship's crew had been hacked, stoned, clubbed, shot with darts. Aunt Aspasia's head lay over there, her body nowhere to be found. About twenty corpses belonged to the Heliolaters, cut down by gunfire. Whatever deficiencies in technology their war party had, they had clearly offset it by sheer numbers.

"While I despairingly searched the beach for Cornelia's body, Domitian discovered that one corpse was still half-alive. It was the copilot, his body riddled with darts. We managed to rouse him to a state of consciousness. I asked him if he knew what had happened to Cornelia.

"'She's alive,' he gasped. 'They're gonna sacrifice her to their god!'

"'Where is she?' I pressed. He demanded water; we gave it.

"'They took her,' he murmured, 'that way—' He died as he spoke. Before that, however, he did manage to point in one general direction.

Unfortunately, there were five paths into the island's interior in that direction and he hadn't specified the correct one.

"So, with the lone survivor dead and Cornelia about to be sacrificed in a pagan rite, I wanted a couple of princes to take the airship and search for her abductors from the air while the rest of us took the middle path inland. The princes disagreed. Yes, they accepted sending two men on aerial surveillance but, urged on by Cornelia's brother, insisted we split up.

"'United we stand a better chance against the savages,' I protested, fearing what would happen if another war party attacked us along the way.

"'My sister hasn't time for us to try one path that might be wrong,' Domitian declared. 'If two of us each take one path, we're sure to find her. Armed with guns, I'm sure we can handle some club-wielding barbarians.'

"I didn't share his outlook after seeing all the passengers and crewmembers massacred despite fighting back. But, outvoted, I relented, and we split up, two-to-a-path. I chose Leonidas as my partner because, after his earlier performance, I wanted to get to know this Athenian better.

"We proceeded along our path through the mountainous terrain. It was very narrow and rocky, enclosed by steep crags on either side. After two miles, the second crag receded, and the path began winding around a cliff overhanging a hot, bottomless drop. Harsh clouds of steam rose up from it, making us both sweat. We had not yet encountered any Heliolaters; but the broken weapons and charred bones of animals we encountered testified that it was a path well-trod by their people.

"Suddenly, as we approached a bend in the path, a dozen Heliolaters sprang out from behind the mountainside and began charging at us. Leonidas and I whipped out our guns, killing several in quick succession. The rest fled. But, unbeknownst to us, one of them had climbed up the mountainside above us. From there, the sniper fired a dart at Leonidas, which only grazed his shoulder but nonetheless caused him to fall backwards over the side of the steamy cliff. Seeing what happened, I quickly shot the villain dead and leapt to grab Leonidas before he was gone.

"I managed to catch him with one hand, wrapping my other arm around a rock jutting out of the ground. Lying face down, I tried to pull Leonidas up but couldn't with just one arm. I needed both my arms to haul him up; but if I were to let go of the rock supporting me, then we both would go over the side. We were in a predicament. And if you were thinking things couldn't have gotten worse, they did.

"While I was holding on to him, pebbles and rocks from the ledge I was on began to crumble due to our combined weight. Frantically, I looked around for anything that could help us. There was nothing.

"'Periander,' Leonidas called out at that point, 'just let me go. There's no use in both of us dying. Go, find your bride and save her; tell my people I died bravely.'

"I answered him through gritted teeth, 'No, I'm not leaving you. Don't think you can weasel out of the mission that easily. You're going to come and help me save Cornelia!' Although I spoke assertively, I plain didn't know how I was going to do it. I asked him what he could see. The thick steam blocked his view. I told him to kick his legs and feel around for anything.

"'There's a small ledge a few feet to my left,' he said.

"I asked if he would be able to jump for it if I swung him towards it. He said yes, and so, swinging him back a few times to build momentum, I hurled him over to it. He managed to catch onto it while I scrambled over to haul him up.

"We rested several moments, panting, after that ordeal. Leonidas thanked me profusely, vowing eternal friendship. I told him he was welcome. Our conversation, however, was cut short when we heard Cornelia's heartrending scream in the distance.

"Wasting no time, we rushed forwards around the corner of the mountainside.

"The path opened up to a plateau filled with over sixty Heliolaters. About two hundred feet away from us was a large opening that led to the hottest geothermal pool on the whole island—hot enough to cause instant death. Two men, priests by the look of their garb, were dragging Cornelia towards it. She shrieked when she saw us and flailed her arm desperately at us. Clenching my first, I asked Leonidas if he'd fight to the end with me no matter how bleak things looked. He placed his hand over mine and swore that he would.

"We charged forwards, guns a-blazing. We had taken two guns apiece with us, one for each hand, and our double firepower sped us through that evil horde. Yet there were so many of them that the necessity of killing all who stood in our way retarded our advance to Cornelia. Eventually I tried rushing past several of them to make a dash across the plateau, hoping thereby to sidestep the warriors and reach my bride before she was ritually murdered by the priests; but as I did, I caught my foot in a fissure in the ground and fell, spraining my leg. Unable to go on and seeing those savages getting ready to throw Cornelia into the hot pool, I yelled 'Leonidas!' at the top of my lungs.

"He looked where I was looking, and he bolted. He sprinted straight across the plateau, eluding the Heliolaters who came after him. Still fifty feet away, he raised his gun and in quick succession killed both priests just as they were about to cast sweet Cornelia down to her watery death. As soon as the priests were killed, the rest of the Heliolaters immediately turned tail and ran off, shrieking and hollowing barbarous gibberish.

"It was over.

"I merely remained where I was, thanking the Deity, as Leonidas led Cornelia over to me. She was deathly pale from fright, weeping and whimpering. My heart ached to see her like that. I hugged and kissed her and did what I could to comfort her after her harrowing trauma. It was also now my turn to thank Leonidas.

"As the rays of the dying sun set (destined to return in spite of no superstitious offering up of female blood), we swore oaths of eternal friendship with one another. No matter how our lives might turn out, Leonidas and I promised always to be loyal and to help one another. We radioed the other princes and regrouped with them. Then we all returned to Atlantis where a joyful reception awaited us.

"After a brief postponement, Cornelia and I were wed in the sight of all our princely friends. Although Leonidas afterwards had to make a prompt return to Athens and (which is something I only found out later) be harshly rebuked by his father for 'recklessly going off on some wild escapade,' that was by no means the last time we were to meet. Our friendship has matured over the years. We've stayed in contact, exchanged gifts, made frequent visits to each other's homes.

"Those murderous Heliolaters wreaked great harm that day, killing many good persons, and almost costing me my dear Cornelia... Yet, the Deity be praised, even some good can come from evil. For from the labors we performed that day, Leonidas and I became the greatest friends, friends closer than any brothers. If the ancient proverb that 'a true friend is another self' is correct, then Leonidas is my other self and I am his."

CHAPTER TWELVE

C RITIAS LOUNGED IN HIS room on a silky-smooth black divan, being himself clothed in equally black silken robes. His black-haired head reclined upon a pillow and from this position his mouth deigned to accept peeled grapes, juicy and sweet, from the hands hovering above him. These hands belonged to one of his maidservants, a petite brunette who was wearing only a few meager fragments of chartreuse cloth. On the other side of his divan there stood a harpist, rasping an extemporized tune on his instrument; the notes screeched, alternating between high-pierced twangs and bellowsome low thumps, but the music nevertheless enamored a smiling Critias. Such was his taste.

Critias turned his head towards his new aide-de-camp, Thrax. Characterized by a thick protruding jaw sheltered by a scraggly brown beard, a right ear larger than the left which constantly oozed pus, a deep scar that ran unevenly from the bridge of his nose across his left cheek, and a mouth seemingly locked in a perpetual snarl whose yellow canine teeth were bared, he inspired fear in all who beheld him. Only three years older than Critias, Thrax had been his companion since boyhood, always encouraging him at every turn. Now that Critias could exercise his regal powers unhampered, he had appointed Thrax to head the Atlantean military, sacking his mother's appointee whom he reässigned to lead a suicide mission against a rebel-held stronghold.

The rebellion in the Americas was precisely what Thrax had come to brief him on. Ninety Atlantean troops killed in this engagement, so-and-so many enemies killed at that battle; that town captured, this village liberated. Blood, bodies, battles. So it went. The rebels' momentum, once so infectious in its spread throughout the American colonies, had been quarantined. In the newfound stalemate, Critias' death-giving physicians now started amputating the gangrenous limbs.

While Thrax was still speaking, a soldier rushed in with a holoprojector. "Majesty, General Brasidas has an urgent message!"

"Put him on," replied Critias, lazily batting at his single skull-shaped earring.

"Majesty," said Brasidas, "Teotihuacan is ours!"

Critias bolted upright, a savage smile on his face. "Excellent!" He licked his lips. *That accursed city shall now feel my wrath!*

It was in this prosperous city of a half million souls, one of Atlantis's finest imperial jewels, that the patrician ringleaders of the revolt had first issued their call to arms. Unlike much of the inland countryside, principally inhabited by an indigenous population which had been subjugated to Atlantis since time immemorial, Teotihuacan was populated by Atlantean colonists. The fact that it was his own countrymen rebelling against him, spearheaded by their colonial well-to-do who ought most to treasure their ties to his crown, incensed Critias to no end and compounded his hatred for this particular city.

Critias rubbed his hands together so fast that his palms began to chafe from the scorching friction. "Send us photos of the carnage. Nothing exemplifies the futility of rebellion quite like a city's annihilation!"

"There was no bloodbath or killings. The city was retaken through peaceful means."

"WHAT?!" roared Critias, his eyes bloodshot as he leapt to his feet, causing both his maidservant and her loincloth to fall. "I ordered you to destroy it upon capture! ALL of it!"

"Yes, Sire, but—"

"To make an example of it! Punish them! Show the world what happens to those who defy me!" Critias' whole body shook, sweat seeping from his armpits and dripping from his forehead. His mouth convulsed, almost foaming; his teeth glinted. "HOW DARE YOU DEFY ME! Who said you could spare them?"

"Yo-yo-your m-m-mother," stammered Brasidas. "Sh-sh-she said to—"

"MOTHER!" *I should've known... She's* always *undermining me!*

Ignoring the rest of Brasidas' pathetic pleading, Critias bolted from the room, his heart seething with rage. Down the hallways of the palace thudded his feet, striking the floors like a blacksmith's horseshoe-fashioning hammer upon an anvil. He brushed past courtiers, servants, everyone. As he passed by them, they all cringed and with moist palms clasped their heaving chests. When he arrived at Eudoxia's apartments, he barked at the two crimson-clothed, gold-helmeted guards stationed outside the door to open it and then stormed inside.

His mother's suite of rooms, spacious and open, had a gold leaf floor; antique black lacquerware cups, ladles, and statuary were displayed on the white marble walls along with portraits of past Atlantean sovereigns; and crystal chandeliers hung from the thirty-foot ceilings. Eudoxia was sitting at a mahogany desk, reviewing official reports and documents of all sorts. Clad in scarlet and sporting a diamond-studded tiara larger than any she had worn before (similar to the imperial crown in its shape and proportion), she played the part of queen well.

As was her wont, Eudoxia was not alone: the room swarmed with a gaggle of thirteen male courtiers. Some fanned her with palm leaves, others handed her documents pilfered from high commanders, and the one who was stooping down on his knees held a glass of champagne up to her mouth. Critias howled "GET OUT!" at them and, dropping all that they held onto the floor, they scattered like mice fleeing before a Bengal tiger.

"What is the meaning of this?" demanded Eudoxia, scowling. She rubbed out of her eyes some champagne that had sprayed her when her cupbearer dropped the now-shattered glass in fright.

"What is the meaning of what Brasidas just told me, that *you* commanded him to spare Teotihuacan when *I* expressly ordered it destroyed?!"

Eudoxia cackled. "Is that what this is about? Teotihuacan?" Her scowl softened almost into a half-smile.

"Explain yourself!" Critias slammed his fist down upon the table, and a few glass shards from her cup pierced the bottom of his hand. Regardless of the droplets of blood trickling out, Critias was numbed to the pain.

"Don't throw another tantrum," said Eudoxia coolly, dabbing her strawberry-scented lips with a handkerchief. "A party of citizens overthrew the rebel-controlled government and offered surrender in return for the safety of their city. It was a reasonable offer; I told Brasidas to accept it."

"But I ordered it destroyed to make an example of it!"

Eudoxia's bulging green eyes narrowed and stared unblinkingly at him. "Large tracts of our colonies are infested with rebels. It's in our interest to retake a city—in which only a minority favored rebellion—speedily by peace so that our army can move on to combat rebel troops in the field, not bogging it down in a long siege just to gratify someone's bloodlust. Clemency can on occasion prove more pragmatic than rote reprisal."

"But it was *I* who ordered it done! Me! Who are *you* to countermand my orders, to go behind my back and tell *my* generals what to do?" Sweat droplets fell from Critias' forehead onto the desktop and mingled with the drops of his blood. *What else is she doing to me behind the scenes? And why are my generals listening to her when I am High King? How far does her grip on my servants go?*

"I am your mother. And lest you forget, I ruled Atlantis for nineteen years. All our generals know my expertise in statecraft and policy, and they properly value my judgments and heed my advice."

"How did you even know about that proposal? Even I wasn't told."

"Brasidas' transmission was intercepted, and I contacted him."

Critias gritted his teeth and skimmed over the papers spread out on the desk. "I see your hands are as skilled as ever at snatching information. Or should I say, your *paramours'* hands?"

Eudoxia slapped his face hard. "Don't talk to me that way! I must have accurate information if I am to make accurate decisions. You're not adequately supplying me with what I need, so I'm forced to seek it out myself."

"But you're not the one to make decisions! I AM!" Critias instinctively started to clasp his hands around his crown before he lowered them and lunged for his mother's tiara. Lifting it higher than his mother's flailing arms could reach, he dashed it to the ground. Tiny diamonds flew in every direction as though a hailstorm had engulfed the room. "I'm the High King! I should be learning everything concerning the military from Thrax—that's why I appointed him!—and then *I* should be making the decisions. Not you or anybody else. Me!"

Eudoxia merely rolled her eyes and muttered "Thrax!" derisively, with her lips curled.

"Do you object to who I choose?" asked Critias crossly, grating his teeth. He clenched his fists. The blood in his veins was pulsing heavily.

"Thrax is but a mere boy, hardly a man. He may serve you excellently as a booze-chooser or for making a trial run of some whore; but, when it comes to matters of state, he is absolutely unqualified. I would be remiss if I did not help you govern this empire."

Usurping my authority is your idea of help? Critias began to pant. "He's older than I am and has been at my side since childhood! We were brought up together, educated by the same instructors, undergone the same experiences. Are you perhaps really saying that *I* am 'unqualified' to rule?"

Her eyes swiveling gently, Eudoxia chortled. "Such an active imagination."

"Arrrrgghhh!" yelled Critias, his nostrils flaring and his whole body convulsing with hatred. He grabbed the metal lamp on his mother's desk and pummeled the lower side of her skull with it.

Eudoxia was thrown backwards onto the floor, her wooden chair snapping in two from the force of the blow. Out of her mouth a single canine tooth tumbled, and blood rained down upon her upturned dress, the hue of her life-giving fluid harmonizing perfectly with the scarlet fabric. Slivers could be seen devouring her legs like piranhas' teeth.

"What are you doing?" she screeched, her body slumped across the floor.

"Something I should've done from the get-go," said Critias. Reaching into the innards of his clothes, he extracted a dagger: the same dagger he had used to execute the prisoners at his coronation. "I've had enough of your incessant meddling. I'm going to rule Atlantis without interference from anyone, *especially you*." He spat out the last two words with acrimony.

"You ungrateful brat! I am the reason you're king. It was my regency that left you where you are now, my work that strengthened the High Kingship! You *need* me!"

"I don't need you anymore, Mother. I have Father now." Critias glared at her. "He'll provide me with all the advice I need and without you scheming for my crown."

Her eyes grew wide as they focused on the rising blade. "You can't do this! I'm a queen of Atlantis!" Her face was pale.

"You're a lady of the evening, not a queen. Cornelia was a true queen, and a far better woman than you, but I didn't spare her. So why should I spare you?"

"I'm not any old hussy," hissed Eudoxia. "I'm your mother!"

"I've killed many women who were mothers. What's one more to me?"

"Because it's a horrible sin to kill your *own* mother."

Critias tilted his neck and folded his arms. "A sin? You mean like husband-killing?" He laughed, resting the blade mockingly close beside his slender chin. "Yeah, it's a sin alright. So what! That never stopped you. Your whole life is an endless string of one sin after another. It's a good thing you never believed in the old morality: the guilt would've killed you long before I could."

"No, no, you misunderstand," she murmured, her harsh tone softening and her abrasive words gone. Pleadingly she raised an arm to his knee and looked him in his eye. "Yes, yes, I have committed many crimes to get to where we are, to obtain the level of power we now enjoy. But don't make the mistake of thinking it was all an act of selfishness on my part. Whatever I may have done, it was all for you! I *love* you, Critias. I did everything for you, *you*, my darling little angel. *You*."

"Love? Ha!" Critias kicked her arm onto the ground and trapped her hand beneath his heel. "Exactly what 'love' did you ever have for me? You were always too busy sitting on *my* throne, exercising *my* powers till the last possible nanosecond, to care about me. I scarcely saw you in childhood—a few minutes once a month, maybe twice if I did something bad enough to catch your attention. Even puppies spend more time with their bitch than I ever had with you."

"You must understand. Running an empire is time-consuming."

He ground his heel into her palm, causing her to howl in pain. "Don't try to fool me! It won't work on me now. My earliest memory is wondering why my mother hated me, why she never wanted to be with me. I thought I was unworthy of your love. But when I grew older, I learned it was *you* who was unworthy! I learned you had plenty of time to share pleasures with your lovers, just no time for me. You made me hate you. And after all that, you have the gall to speak to me of *love*?" He spat in her face.

"Ugghhh," moaned Eudoxia, her wrist being crushed beneath his foot. Raising her other hand, covered in blood, she gazed beyond the ceiling and stridently exclaimed, "I have nursed a viper in my bosom!"

"Nah, you pawned him off to a two-bit wet-nurse from the moment he was born. The only thing you've ever nursed was a lust for power. *My* power." Critias raised his dagger high.

"No, no!" Eudoxia gaped, her body wincing on the floor. But suddenly, blinking, green flames bulged forth from her hateful eyes and spit from her mouth as she shouted, "Fine! Go ahead and do it, you little bastard! Kill, kill." Her free hand's sharp nails ripped the lower part of her dress away, revealing bare flesh. "STAB ME IN THE WOMB THAT BORE YOU!"

Clutching her throat with one hand, Critias obliged his mother with the other. Into her womb he plunged his dagger. Her whole body writhed, and foul-tasting blood sprayed onto his face. Extracting his steel plunger from the filth, he thrust it into her again. And again. And again.

Withdrawing his dagger from the corpse, Critias wiped the bloodied blade on Eudoxia's pale cheeks. A sardonic smile spread across his face as he thought, *Funny. I often wondered if it would kill you to bring a smile to my face. Looks like it did.*

He rose from his deed just as Thrax entered the room.

"What's going on?" He stopped when he saw the lake of blood seeping from what moments ago had been the queen-mother.

"Just taking care of something," replied Critias nonchalantly, putting his arm around Thrax and grinning.

"I see you finally killed the old shrew. About time."

"Yes. Now let's decide how best to dispose of it...."

CHAPTER THIRTEEN

A COUPLE HOURS AFTER departing Egypt, the airship carrying Periander and the others reached Athens, the capital of Athenagoras' kingdom. Athens, as the largest city in the realm, dominated its hinterland, extending ten miles in every direction from its highest hill on which the Acropolitan Palace was situated. Overflowing with more than a million people, the cityscape was characterized by thin buildings, each ten to twenty stories tall, densely packed together; they were uniformly encased by gray metal, clustered in identically sized city blocks, with each crossway sporting a large circular fountain from which water, illuminated by neon-green lights, flowed. The wide bustling streets of Athens were overshadowed only by the occasional skyway connecting some of the taller buildings.

The airship docked at the exposed landing pads south of the palace. On account of the intensity of the rain that was irrigating the city, Periander and company dashed from their craft into the palace. His body drenched, Periander shivered as he tried to wring as much water as he could out of his sleeves. In spite of this atmosphere, however, he felt the disquiet in his soul dry up when Leonidas appeared to greet them.

Standing under the marble portico, Leonidas wore a gold-tasseled purple tunic and red moccasins rising halfway up his legs. Thick, inch-long russet hair crowned his head, and wide shoulder blades gave him the appearance of being larger than he was. His large blue eyes jumped when they spotted the guests. "Periander!" he called, raising his hand.

"Leonidas!" answered Periander. His hand embraced Leonidas's in salutation, and they exchanged a quick, jovial hug.

"I am so glad you've reached Athens safely. Ever since I heard you were cast into exile, I've feared for you and the others; but I knew you'd make your way here eventually." Glancing at Jason who had come up beside him, he lowered his head and added, "My heart grieves for Cornelia. She was one of the finest women ever to grace this world."

Periander thanked him for his consolation.

Leonidas subsequently greeted Socrates, Agathocles, and Demosthenes, all of whom he knew. After that he noticed Psyche, lingering in the rear. "Who is this?"

"This is Psyche, daughter of Pharaoh Ozymandias," replied Periander, strolling over and putting his arm around her lithe waist. "She is my new wife."

"Oh... well, uh..." His ascending eyebrows and descending jawbone communicated his surprise. "I didn't imagine you'd be so quick to remarry."

Neither did I.

"It's a pleasure to meet you." Leonidas took Psyche by her hand and kissed it. "I wish you and Periander many wonderful years together."

She reciprocated the salutation with a curtsy. "Where is King Athenagoras?"

"Father is presently out of the city, but he will be returning before supper."

Leonidas commanded the servants present to provide his guests with rooms and dry clothes. As the others were led away by the scurrying servants, Leonidas stayed with Periander to speak with him. They walked down one of the palace's many corridors; the walls were lined with portraits of preceding Athenian kings, all vibrant and gloriously portrayed except for one whose portrait was painted over in black. After exchanging a few pleasantries, Leonidas stopped walking and remarked, "From first impressions, you seem to have done well in finding yourself a new queen. An Egyptian princess, no less. I'm just disappointed I couldn't attend this wedding, too."

"It was not my intention, when I entered Egypt, to wed the Pharaoh's daughter," said Periander matter-of-factly as he halted beside his friend. "Or anyone, for that matter. My concentration is firmly fixed on freeing Atlantis from the tyranny of Critias and Eudoxia. But Ozymandias insisted I marry her as a token of our alliance. And you know the importance of diplomatic marriages."

"In the abstract, yes. Though in Egypt's case it's odd, given the Pharaohs' reluctance to give their daughters to foreigners." Leonidas put his head back and let loose a chuckle while thumping Periander on the back. "But then again, that's the Periander I know. Who but you could have won over Ozymandias so much that he'd want to rope you into the family? You must have electrified him!"

"We have had cordial interactions for many years. Yet I wouldn't have dreamt of him so flagrantly violating his land's ancestral customs (however foolish some of them may be): Ozymandias is no Eudoxia. Frankly, I suspect Psyche may have played a bigger role in arranging it."

"Really? What makes you say that?"

"During my stay in Egypt, she not only paid me respect that was obviously more than what formality dictates but she was also finding ways to frequent me. She has fourteen brothers, and I believe I spent less time with them as a whole than I did with their sister."

"Well, you couldn't blame her if she found you alluring. Remember that time we visited Indra's court—how those two young princesses from Harappa kept throwing themselves at you?"

"Do I ever! They were far more aggressive in proclaiming their desires than anything Psyche ventured. I'm still thankful Cornelia wasn't there to witness their antics."

"So, are you going to ask Psyche if she plotted to ensnare you in matrimony?"

Periander shook his head. "No, it would be unseemly. Regardless of the circumstances, we are lawfully married, and I intend to keep our marriage acceptable to the Deity's eyes. Voicing suspicions is out of the question."

After several moments of silence, Leonidas said, "Anyway... as to that alliance you mentioned. What is your exact plan to retake your rightful place in Atlantis?"

"I see no viable path except deposing Critias, which will sadly require making war on my own country to free her from her tyrants. Ozymandias has pledged the armies of Egypt for an invasion of Atlantis with the proviso that we have at least one more major power on our side." Periander heaved a sigh, staring at the floor. He blinked and formed a fist. "I must topple Critias and Eudoxia: no compromise is possible. Only a complete overthrow of their evil régime will be able to heal Atlantis. The undertaking will be immense, but that is the path I must walk."

"I concur with your assessment. Only sweeping changes will win back your House's estates, avenge Cornelia, and restore justice in your land."

"I pray there is a House left to restore," murmured Periander, thoughts of his son entering his mind. "Since his mother's death, I have constantly worried about any harm befalling Jason. Despite my best efforts to protect him, he was taken prisoner in Cyrene. Had we not rescued him in time, he could have... I feel partly responsible that he even had the chance to fall into that hazard because it was my opposition to Eudoxia that led to our exile... and to Cornelia's death. Had I capitulated like the other kings, my family would still be intact and safe from danger. Yet I did my duty to my country. I keep telling myself: there was no other course that I could have, in good conscience, taken." He sighed again.

Leonidas halted Periander. "Don't blame yourself for anything that has happened. It is those misbegotten cretins in Atlantis who are to blame!" He clenched both his fists; his nostrils flared, and his eyebrows soared. "I've been watching Eudoxia for years, and scrutinizing every-thing Critias has done since assuming power. They are despicable tyrants who create death and destruction wherever they go; no one is safe with them around. I don't have one scintilla of doubt that they're a danger not only to you but to my own people too. That is why I will help you in any way I can, not just as your friend but as an Athenian patriot as well. Athens needs you just as much as you need us. You're not alone in this fight, Periander."

"I knew, Leonidas, I could count on you." He smiled. "Now, I hope your father will be swayed to my cause. How is Athenagoras?" he asked as they resumed walking down the corridor.

Leonidas snorted. "Father is his usual self. Stubborn, bigoted. Yet, in light of all that has happened—especially the Egyptian alliance—I'm hopeful he'll come around and do what's right, join with you. No matter how inflexible he may be, I promise you, I will bend him to your side."

✳✳✳

HAVING CHANGED AND REFRESHED, Periander and his en-tourage made their way to the palace's banquet hall. On the east wall were paneled windows, small but endowed with a vertical view of the city below, while the colonnaded west wall led out to a red-bricked courtyard that led to another wing of the building. In the center of the room was a semicircular table, composed of adjacent slabs of solid black marble, stretching from one end to the other; the white chairs resting alongside it provided an excellent visual contrast.

Before Periander and his party were seated, King Athenagoras, flanked by several courtiers, appeared. In his late sixties, Athenagoras was slim-built apart from a mildly protruding abdomen. Ashen and thread-like hair fell from his head almost to his shoulders, even as his copious beard dropped halfway down his stomach. His eyes were gray, his face pasty, and his crusty nose aquiline. He wore a full-length silver robe embroidered with figures of roses in red and white velvet. Mounting the lone silver chair situated at the midpoint of the table, Athenagoras sat down, followed by all the rest.

The feast began. Periander was seated at the right hand of Athenagoras while Leonidas was at his left; Jason, Psyche, Socrates, Agathocles, and Demosthenes were in turn seated near to Periander. Servants brought forth washbasins for the guests, then the plates and glasses. In front of the table, entertainers delighted the guests: jugglers juggled flaming torches, a troupe of acrobats formed human pyramids six levels high, and belly dancers clothed in translucent silks gyrated wildly to the clashing of cymbals.

For over an hour, the merriment continued. His face beaming, Periander toasted Athenagoras and then Leonidas, with whom he reminisced about events from their youth. He was in high spirits. At last, with the final entertainers finishing, the servants cleared the table. It was time to commence business.

The whole room focused on Periander while he detailed his journey to Egypt, the incident in Cyrene, the trek across North Africa, the flight from Atlantis and the lamentable death of his queen. During the narration of these painful ordeals, Leonidas wordlessly expressed his anguish by the buckling of his face and the fisting of his hands beneath his chin; at the mention of Cornelia's death, he had to dab his eyes. His father, however, maintained a cool countenance throughout. Athenagoras' sullen look, even at the most pitiable parts of Periander's story, never subsided any more than they had risen during the jolliest portions of the feast.

When Periander had finished speaking, Athenagoras spoke. "Why have you come under my roof, Periander, Son of Themistocles?" he asked dispassionately, his lips smacking each other as he talked.

Periander explained the alliance he had made with Ozymandias and its intended goal, offering the reasons why Critias should be overthrown. "Lord Athenagoras, I entreat Athens to join this grand coalition, to become a partner in freeing the world from the cruelty of Critias and Eudoxia, its would-be masters."

There was silence. Everyone eyed Athenagoras, who remained in his seat, transfixed as ever by his own unmoved expression.

O Deity, Periander prayed silently, lightly biting his lip and grasping his knees, *please let Athenagoras look favorably upon us.*

"Periander," said Athenagoras, looking at him, "you are an exiled king, a wanderer in the Earth whose death is sought by his own people (who would reward me considerably for your capture). But you are a guest in my house, and a friend of my son. I am therefore not loathe to permit you to stay within my realm for as long as you may wish. However..." He paused, turning his pasty face away from Periander to Leonidas, and then back to Periander. "I will not join in this, this absurd, puerile scheme of yours—to imperil my kingdom by choosing to start a war with a state that has not attacked us. Athens will *never* make unprovoked war against Atlantis!"

"But Lord Athenagoras, while it may not yet have attacked you, there is every indication that—" Periander interjected before Athenagoras interrupted him.

"No, Periander. I do not care what Atlantis might be planning, or what they are doing in other parts of the world. That is their business. They have done nothing to harm my kingdom, so I will do nothing to harm them. I recognize that your assessment of the situation is clouded both by a burning lust to avenge your wife's death as well as the yearning to reclaim your patrimony as a king of Atlantis. Those are natural and understandable thoughts, even if imprudent; I recognize that, and I can respect your feelings. But I will not jeopardize the welfare of my country merely to further the insane vendetta of some dethroned monarch. As it is in your interest to agitate for war, so is it in my interest and the interests of Athens to uphold the present peace."

Athenagoras rose from his seat to leave the room, followed by the rest of the Athenians. With a perturbed shout of "Father!" Leonidas chased after him. From the waving of his arms and his irate voice that echoed over to the table, it was clear that he was making no progress at persuading his father to reconsider.

With a sigh, Periander slunk into his chair, his feet pushing against the black marble while his knuckles dug into his cheek. His body felt as heavy as a rhinoceros, his spirit as limp as a midnight morning glory. *I knew Athenagoras would not be easily persuaded. But to receive such an uncompromising rejection right off the bat...*

Psyche, standing behind his chair and wrapping her fragrant arms around his neck, said, "O Periander, what he said was wholly untrue! You're not irrational because of what you believe, what you hope to accomplish. Your plan is rational. Athenagoras is the one allowing prejudices to cloud *his* judgment." She kissed his forehead, leaving a burgundy lipstick imprint.

Periander stroked her long-fingered hands. "Thank you, Psyche, for your kind words."

"What are we to do now, my Lord?" asked Agathocles. "Try again, or move on to another realm?"

"I'll have to think about it." *It would be foolish to waste time here if it's a lost cause to persuade Athenagoras. Then again, Athens is the only kingdom in the world with a navy comparable to Atlantis's; we'll need sea power for an invasion and to help transport our armies...* He rose and the others followed him towards the exit.

Leonidas came running back into the room, raising his arm to halt them. "Periander, wait! You can't know the magnitude of my sorrow for what my father said. It's completely inexcusable."

"It's alright. At least—"

"No, it's not alright!" Leonidas' nostrils flared and his eyes broke wide. He formed a fist. "My father's an old fool, so blinkered, so... so... irresponsible. Whatever you do, don't leave Athens just yet," he implored. "I will continue to cajole him until I've made him realize what a fool he's being. I promise you." He held his hand out and Periander shook it.

"You are my most faithful friend in all the world, Leonidas. I thank you."

***

Periander and the others left, leaving Leonidas alone in the room. Alone, that is, except for one man, a certain parasite ever present at banquets to fill his unquenchable appetite. His name was Gnatho, a corpulent, clean-shaven fifty-eight-year-old whose skin oozed the richness of the food he habitually consumed from the bountiful royal table.

Approaching Leonidas, he bowed his greasy head. "Prince Leonidas," he began, his voice extremely guttural and grating.

Leonidas, curling his lip, snapped, "What do you want?" at the man whom he daily saw feasting on the spoils of Athens despite having no position in the government; nor did Leonidas ever witness any act on his part to justify his leisurely existence.

"I am moved by your audacious support for your friend—so forceful, so devoted as to lead you to confront your mighty sire. I believe you are right, my prince, and I would therefore be honored, if it pleases you, to assist you in any way I can."

Looking angrily at him, Leonidas put his arms akimbo and asked, "What can a cosseted little lickspittle, who knows nothing save how to gorge himself without toil, do that a king's son cannot?"

Whereas Leonidas' invective might have had its intended effect upon others, Gnatho was unfazed. Twisting his oblong mouth into an uneven, crooked smile, he boasted, "To retain a spot at a king's table—defending it against newcomers year after year—requires much dexterity in a man and leads him to learn all the mysteries of courtly life, even if necessity compels him to apply his skills only behind the scenes. Thus, his political acumen, though great, goes undetected and unrespected by the world at large."

Leonidas huffed. "Fine phraseology notwithstanding, I doubt there's anything your words could do to remedy my father's stubbornness." He lifted his foot to go.

Following him, Gnatho's glinting eyes slanted whilst he murmured, "Oh, there is always something that can be done...."

CHAPTER FOURTEEN

N INE DAYS HAD ELAPSED since his arrival in Athens. King Athenagoras still rebuffed Periander's proposed alliance and his arguments about the inevitability of war. After a few days of failure, Periander, lest by constant nagging he make himself so abhorrent to Athenagoras that he end up expelled from the realm, ceased trying to persuade him, trusting that Leonidas would stand the greatest chance in convincing his father. Leonidas did his best, championing his friend's cause by making repeated intercessions to his father, although without results.

Periander waited in the palace's communications hub. He and Jason had been out in the discus yard, playing in the heat of the noontime sun. A favorite pastime of the Athenians that was popular in Atlantis too, both father and son were equally matched. Or so they would normally be. Jason, sneezing more than would be expected, betrayed symptoms of a budding cold or else allergies to the poplar trees encircling the courtyard.

Just as Periander had scored his seventh hit, which left him needing only one more to win, Leonidas arrived to announce that there was an incoming transmission from Philip. Periander and Jason quit their game and hurriedly followed Leonidas to the communications hub. Socrates and the others were not then in the palace, but Psyche was, strolling through one of its ivory-draped porticoes. Seeing their vibrant expressions and learning of the transmission, she asked if she could come too, a request which Periander granted.

The communications hub was a massive room filled everywhere with the reflective glow of warm metal. Large egg-shaped computer monitors lined the walls, manned by dozens of technicians typing away at keyboards and busily speaking into their headsets. The many voices of communication officials receiving and relaying intelligence—ranging from Aegean shipping to events in foreign lands—produced a din of white noise.

Leonidas led them into a connecting room, passing through a wall of one-way glass. The room itself was soundproof and specially constructed to receive encrypted transmissions. With the shutting of the door, there was quiet. They took seats around the octagonal table on whose top was a built-in holoprojector. Leonidas hit the appropriate buttons, and a green hologram of Philip appeared.

Periander began. "How go the negotiations?" *May they be faring better than ours...*

Philip looked somber. His eyes were lowered heavily, his face was inert, and his voice carried itself weakly. "Majesty, King Indra wishes to speak with you himself about it."

Philip stepped aside and in his place King Indra appeared. "Your envoy has saddened us all by the woeful tale of your hardships and the loss of your queen," he addressed Periander. His baritone voice echoed sympathy that quickly turned to skepticism. "As to your proposed anti-Atlantis alliance, however, I am not yet convinced that the danger represented by the current government is grave enough to warrant action on our part. Perhaps the contrary may be proved later, but I am not satisfied that it is the case now. Neither am I persuaded that this alliance would be sufficient to defeat Atlantis in war. Mohenjo-Daro and Egypt, alone, against Atlantis? Even combining our forces, the struggle would be difficult. I therefore cannot join this coalition."

Periander gripped the table as he rose to his feet. He clenched his teeth, determined not to lose another potential ally. "Lord Indra, let me first say that I am not proposing anything 'anti-Atlantis.' Rather, it is out of love for my country that I have embarked upon this long, perilous trek—an inexorable drive to purge Atlantis of the elements that threaten not only its own destruction but untold destruction for the whole world."

"I merely meant the war would be against Atlantis: I did not mean to impugn your motives."

"I apologize if I misconstrued your words," said Periander. "But as you can see, this is something I treat with the utmost seriousness. While the peril posed by Critias is always before me, I do recognize that, from the perspective of Mohenjo-Daro, it is far-off both in space and time. Your realm is distant from Atlantis, even more so than Egypt; so far, no aggressive actions have been taken against it or in its vicinity. *Yet.* That is the point. The ambitions of the current régime are boundless: I should know, for I had to flee due to my opposition to them. Atlantean forces are already occupying territories in northern Europe, the western coasts of Africa, and have made further inroads into the American continents (which only recently was halted by rebellions in those colonies). The only reason no aggressive activities have been undertaken in Asia is precisely because they are still expanding outwards and have not yet reached the shores of Asia. Do not be deceived. Conquest on a global scale and the erection of a universal monarchy are the stated goals of Eudoxia and her son. If you do not join with us now and stop Atlantis's tyrants before it's too late to stop them, then there will come the day when Mohenjo-Daro is threatened with extinction and there will be none left to help you."

"Inactivity always leaves open the possibility of future developments contrary to one's interests," conceded Indra mildly, nodding his head. "Yet one cannot reäct aggressively to every potential threat: to do so would mean eternal war; or attending to one potential threat to the neglect of another one; or even, by confronting one potentiality, provoke the very result that the preventative measure was meant to prevent."

Oh... I've heard all this before. Periander, shaking his platinum head, began to amass his words for a verbal counterstrike; but before he could respond, Psyche unexpectedly addressed Indra.

"Lord Indra," she said, sitting calmly composed in her chair, her hands in her lap, as all turned their gaze to her, "you do raise legitimate objections: objections to a theory of seeking to extinguish every possible danger in existence or that might come into existence, a theory that brooks no distinction regarding a threat's magnitude or the likelihood of its materialization. But this is not theory we are speaking of. The malignant government of Atlantis is real; its High King desires my husband's death to such a degree that he threatened all Egypt with desolation for sheltering him; and if the present occupants of imperial power have no hesitation to destroy one of their own kings and to repress all resistance, both foreign and domestic, in pursuit of world domination, then they will never voluntarily stop unless they are made to stop."

Silence followed her words. Then Indra, rubbing his chin, said, "You've made a fair point." He chuckled. "I see that in addition to many sons, Ozymandias also sired a perceptive daughter, Princess Psyche of Egypt. Or rather, Queen Psyche, as you are now Atlantean royalty. It's manifestly true that first Eudoxia and now Critias are intent on enjoying an absolute despotism over their own people; and under them Atlantis has been exerting dominance on territories bordering the Atlantic (which, after all, is its ocean). While Atlantis's neighbors may have reasonable fears of succumbing to conquest, why should Mohenjo-Daro fear wars on the other side of the world?"

The lighting of the room reflected brilliantly on Psyche's ruddy face. Combining this with the unflinching serenity of her expression and the forceful yet calm pitch of her voice, she exuded judiciousness and appeared as a jurist explaining a verdict. "Atlantis dominates the Atlantic due to its central location in that ocean: geography directed the course its expansion would take. Yet there is no reason why Atlantis must be content with one ocean only. Some of its American colonies already border the Pacific; expansion westwards beyond that would be a logical course. In fact, if you search the chronicles of the world, you will find that at the peak of its strength the old Atlantean empire pursued that very goal. As my husband could attest, ever since Eudoxia assumed the regency the current régime has used every manner of propaganda to extol the restoration of Atlantis to the zenith of its power—they even held a three-day aquatic drama celebrating Atlantis's colonization and conquest of the ancient Earth. You know, as well as I do, that Mohenjo-Daro traces its origins to Atlantean settlers, as was Egypt and every other major offshoot of civilization. As far as Critias and Eudoxia are concerned, every nation that ever belonged to Atlantis is rightfully theirs and must be brought back into the empire."

So astute and forceful a description of our common menace, thought a nodding Periander while he eyed his wife. He smiled, particularly impressed that Psyche, at whose insistence he had recounted so many details and minutiae of his life in Atlantis and opposition against Eudoxia, should remember more than a week later the aquatic incident, a triviality that he had spent only thirty seconds describing. *Those weren't idle questions to kill time but the systematic inquiries of a statesman's mind. Psyche has fully committed herself to furthering my cause... and the results are impressive.*

"I'm aware of their pretensions..." answered Indra. "But talk is one thing, action another. They have yet to act concretely against any great power; the sincerity of their aggressive ideology is not yet proven. And even if all you say is true, could this alliance of yours stand a chance at defeating Atlantis?"

"Yes!" Psyche replied before he had scarcely finished uttering the last syllable. "Periander knows the inner workings of Atlantis better than anyone else; you could find no more perfect a guide for the invasion force than he. Furthermore, he can supply us not only with crucial military intelligence but also bodies: he will rally his own subjects to his side, and they will assist us in overthrowing the High King. The armies of Egypt are recognized worldwide for their strength and my father, whom none would dare label a fool, has pledged them to this cause. Your kingdom, Lord Indra, is renowned for specializing in aerial warships and the skill of its pilots; your sky fleets would prove invaluable in assaulting Atlantean defenses."

"And the Athenian navy is as large as the Atlantean, and its submarine forces are without equal!" interjected Leonidas as he rose from the table and slammed his fist onto its top. "United, we will defeat Atlantis!"

Indra's narrowing eyes focused on him. "Is Athens a partner in this endeavor? Was I told incorrectly that your father rejected this alliance?"

"He has yet to finish considering the matter fully," huffed Leonidas, forming a fist in defiance even as his eyes darted to the side.

"And hasn't *your* father conditioned his support on the recruitment of other allies?"

"He did," admitted Psyche, "but only to ensure we begin the war from a position of greatest strength. Do not judge his prudence as reluctance on his part. My father has such great confidence in Periander and his strategy that, contrary to Egyptian tradition, he entrusted me—his only daughter—to him in marriage."

Indra nodded approvingly.

"And," she added with a grin, "if Mohenjo-Daro joins, Egypt will immediately commit full-heartedly: by your decision, you have the power to activate this alliance."

Clearing his throat, Indra said, "Lady Psyche, you display Ozymandias' tact and thoughtfulness. He undoubtedly must be proud of you. And *you*, Periander, are fortunate to have acquired such a treasure. Now then, I am not yet moved to endorse this alliance; my reservations still exist. Nevertheless, you argued the matter well, Psyche. Perhaps... perhaps my reservations are not quite as compelling as they seemed. Further deliberation is in order. I therefore withdraw my rejection for now and return to being undecided."

With the final diplomatic particulars said, the holoprojector transmission ceased. His face beaming, Periander rose from the table and took hold of his wife's soft hands. "Psyche, wherever did you learn such skill in negotiation? How to interact with kings?"

Blushing, she rose from her seat and said, "Father always allowed me to attend sessions of his council and to witness how he conducts diplomacy. I learned, I suppose, from watching him."

"Whether taught or intuited, you certainly aided this negotiation," said Leonidas, coming up behind them.

"Although you didn't actually persuade him to join us... just not to reject us," murmured Jason, casting his green eyes upon the ground.

Responding to Jason's comment, Leonidas said, "Well, we're better off than we might have been. She kept Indra from outright rejecting us like..." He sighed. "My father's so stubborn! I know what I told Indra, but it will take a lot to make him change his mind."

"Well, I have faith you will do it," said Psyche.

"As do I," added Periander, putting his right arm around Leonidas as he held Psyche in his left. Clasping two persons dear to him, he said, "We still have a difficult journey ahead of us. But, together, we will reach victory's conclusion. We must, and *will*, prevail."

Chapter Fifteen

"**H**AS HE NO HUMANITY at all?" exclaimed Periander. His pupils intensified in shock and his dry mouth hung in disbelief. He glanced first at Socrates, who bore a stoical expression; then to Agathocles, whose facial twitching revealed his own revulsion; then to Demosthenes, who by the back-and-forth shifting of his eyes and the twining of his sideburn disclosed that he was already making mental calculations. Periander let fall onto the blue-green tiled floor of his chamber the message received from Lysander, in which his spy detailed the slaughter of Eudoxia.

The room resounded with tomblike silence. Not even a fly buzzed. The loudest clamor originated from the blinking of eyelids.

Finally, Agathocles spoke. "I for one am glad that tyrant is dead. Frankly, I don't care how she died; she richly deserved it."

"I am of two minds on this." Periander rested his finger above his lip. "On the one hand, I am jubilant that Eudoxia, a villain who disturbed the world, corrupted our homeland, forced us into exile, issued the wicked orders that directly led to… Cornelia's death"—he grimaced as poignant images swept through his mind—"has at long last paid for her wicked deeds. On the other hand, she did not forfeit her life on account of just retribution but was herself the victim of evil. For her to be struck down by her own child… I knew Critias inherited his mother's malevolent nature, her murderous inclinations. But still, what special variety of evil does it take to murder his own mother?"

Periander's mind turned to thoughts of his mother Aretë, of her smiling buttery face, her energizing laugh, the sweet-smelling apricot perfume she always wore, that time she missed attending a friend's wedding in Egypt when he was sick with measles as a boy.... "How can any man kill the woman who bore him? Even the beasts of the field show greater respect to their dams."

"Evil begets evil," said Socrates matter-of-factly, his long beard shifting from side to side. "When not inhibited, the offspring will imitate its parent's examples and grow unchecked in the ways of evil, at last overwhelming even its parental source as when a virus multiplies and kills its host."

Demosthenes nodded his head. "Having addressed the natural repugnance of matricide, we must not neglect the practical effects that Eudoxia's death will henceforth have on our plans."

"You're entirely correct," said Periander, "which is another reason I don't fully welcome her murder. No matter how fervidly I opposed Eudoxia's proposals, I always understood the reasoning behind them, even if they were wicked and fallacious. Though lacking in morals, she had her virtues in other spheres: calculating, conniving, she was quite versatile at scraping up every last bit of power and wealth she could grasp. I could almost predict what she would do in a given circumstance." *And if only I'd predicted she would attack me and my family...*

"And that was an asset for us." Demosthenes leaned forwards in his chair, placing his left arm on his knee and his hand on his naked chin. "To understand one's enemy is invaluable in war, and her predictability gave aid to our strategizing against her. Had she been able to maintain control over her son, Critias might have proven to be as predictable as she. He preferred murder to being controlled: there will be no bridling him from the inside now. Our experience of him, and not his mother, as the directing force in government is too limited to fully understand his reasoning and, therefore, how best to counter his plans."

"That boy's erratic," huffed Socrates, crinkling his nose. "The only consistency I have observed in him is a relishing for destruction. If you ask me, reasoned strategy and the exhausting mental load necessary for its implementation simply elude him."

Periander snorted. "Audacious, too." He referred to the part in Lysander's report of how Critias, for several days after slaying Eudoxia, had initially attempted to delude Atlantis into believing that his mother's death was natural. With pure hypocrisy he lauded her regency and political acumen; he adorned her statues with flowery wreathes of mourning; and he was preparing, during a closed casket funeral, to hail Eudoxia as the "Mother of Atlantis."

This charade notwithstanding, as happens with all monumental lies, the truth of Eudoxia's death was eventually exposed by one of her toadies (whose mangled body was afterwards discovered in a barrel of rum). Then, with equal gall, Critias reversed himself and spun a new tale as though he had never articulated the contrary: from a devoted mother who had served Atlantis with all her heart, Eudoxia transformed into an odious traitor. Her statues were destroyed throughout the world with iconoclastic zeal, and her decaying body was unceremoniously dumped into the Hydrocleptae River in the dead of night.

Rising from his seat, Agathocles asked, "Do you think this will affect the negotiations?" His chest was rising faster; a sweat droplet fell down his oval face into his bushy blond beard. "I mean, Eudoxia's actions, both past and present, were the starting point in all our talks."

"Now all her intentions are defunct," sighed Socrates, "as are our arguments against them."

"Psyche's father shouldn't back out because of her death; he heard enough threats from Critias to know the son is just as dangerous, if not more so. Critias certainly hasn't given any inclination of disavowing his mother's aggressive imperialism." Periander worriedly thought of Indra and Athenagoras. "Less than three days have passed since Indra agreed to reëvaluate our alliance… How will this affect him? I don't know. As to Athenagoras—"

Periander was interrupted when the door flew open.

"Periander!" shouted Leonidas, panting as he leaned up against the doorway. His eyes were wide and radiating alarm. "Come quickly! It's your son, Jason! He's deathly ill!"

Panic washed over Periander. His mind, which had been whirling with thoughts of war and foreign affairs, instantly snapped back to domestic anxieties, abandoning all wide-ranging contemplation for the constricted outlook of fatherhood just as swiftly as his body had abandoned its chair. On his feet, with the chair falling backwards and loudly cracking several tiles from the force of his standing—three, four, five shattered tiles splintering every which way—Periander scurried to the door. As they rushed down a portrait-lined hallway and then a green-carpeted stairway, he demanded, "What's happened?"

***

After breakfast, Psyche went to Jason's room, accompanied by a maidservant. Her breakfast had been served in one of the many posh dining rooms in the palace, this particular one located in the eastern wing wherein sunlight streamed through its floor-to-ceiling picture windows. Planning to eat with both her husband and stepson, Psyche had set two chairs around the table. Periander arrived first; but before he had taken so much as a bite of the eggs Benedict, Socrates, Agathocles, and Demosthenes interrupted them to announce that a messenger had arrived from Atlantis, and off he rushed with them.

Psyche had not minded. She understood how much Periander yearned for his homeland, how impatient he was to be informed of developments there, always darting off whenever something new occurred, eternally hopeful that things would come his way. His zeal and devotion to his country's welfare were two qualities of his that especially warmed her thumping heart. Besides, had Periander not been spending more time with her these past few days? Since her foray into the diplomatic arena and demonstration of her knowledge of politics, he had begun speaking at length with her concerning his alliance and plans to topple Critias and Eudoxia. Psyche therefore was not bothered that he eagerly ran off without a word to her. One meal was unimportant compared to her deepening ties with him that could only continue to intensify as their marriage matured.

Yet what about Jason? He never showed up at all. Out of concern for him, Psyche had her servant Chloë page Jason's room via the intercom system. When there was no response, Psyche decided to go see whether he was in his room, or if not, where he was.

Chloë knocked on Jason's door.

"Jason!" called Psyche. "It's me, Psyche! Answer if you're okay!"

"Madam, I hear breathing inside," said Chloë, her ear pressed against the door.

Psyche likewise pressed her ear to the cold metal door. There was faint groaning inside. *Something's not right.* She tried to open the door, but it was locked. Glancing down the hallway, she signaled a courtier emerging from behind the corner. "Quick!" she shouted to the tall, muscular man bounding towards them. "I think he's hurt in there!"

Three blows to the door later, they rushed inside. Psyche gasped.

Jason lay collapsed on the floor beside his bed, still in his nightclothes. His face was red with scaly skin, his eyes puffy and watering. He was visibly struggling for breath as his chest violently heaved up and down. In front of him was a puddle of putrid vomit reeking with an acidic stench.

Rushing to his side, Psyche felt his sweaty forehead. It burned hot with fever. "Fetch a physician!"

While the courtier darted out of the room, Psyche and Chloë carefully lifted Jason onto his bed. Psyche fetched some towels, and after soaking them in cold water she began applying them to Jason's forehead. "There,

there," she said soothingly as he moaned weakly at her touch. "It will be alright." *At least I hope it will be. His symptoms seem severe. Please help him, Deity! Please heal my husband's child.*

After what seemed like hours but were in fact mere minutes, the courtier returned with two physicians who soon were crowding around Jason. Leonidas, attracted by the hubbub that the courtier had raised, followed behind them.

Seeing him enter the room, Psyche called, "Find Periander! Quick!"

Mouthing "Oh, my!" when he saw Jason's appearance, Leonidas raced off just as Psyche had bidden him.

"What happened here?" demanded one of the physicians whilst removing a thermometer from his bag.

"I don't know," answered Psyche as she was brushed aside by the physicians. She wiped her sweating palms on her dress. "We found him this way just now. He seemed fine yesterday." Frantically recalling all she could of the past few days, she added, "Actually, I have heard him coughing for about three or four days."

"It looks like a viral infection," said the second physician, a man in his late fifties who was older than the other physician but whose grayish hair and large bushy moustache still retained its auburn color. He put his stethoscope to Jason's chest and listened. "His lungs sound congested."

Involuntarily placing her hands over her lungs, Psyche felt the throbbing of her own anxious breathing, inhaling less air than she normally would. The slight lightheadedness this engendered undermined her memory. She had seen a case like Jason's before, the same signs and symptoms, but where and what disease? Not influenza, for she had seen so many suffer from it in the Egyptian court, and this was clearly not it. Pneumonia, perhaps? Her aunt Nitocris had contracted that condition only seven months earlier, but there had been no flaking of the skin or inflammation.

Hmm, what can it be? wondered Psyche, chewing her lip. Redness, peeling skin, watering eyes, gasping for breath... *That's it!* "Could this be pseudonosis?"

"What?" said the younger physician, casting an annoyed glare at her.

"An infection transmitted by mosquitoes," said the elder physician matter-of-factly. "It occurs only in Libya and western Egypt. I saw one case of it many years ago, in a patient who had recently traveled in those parts."

Psyche nodded her head. "Yes, I've seen several of my countrymen come down with it."

"A good diagnosis, Ma'am."

"Well, we don't know that for sure. If it is pseudonosis, this will tell us." The younger physician took out a syringe and drew a sample of blood from Jason's arm. "I'll run it down to the lab."

Suddenly Periander rushed through the door. "Jason!" His blue and green eyes almost went white when he looked upon his son. "What's the matter with him?"

The younger physician, carrying the vial of blood, brusquely said, "We're going to find out," as he brushed past him and quit the room.

Periander knelt beside the bed and Psyche knelt beside him.

"What's wrong with him?" he murmured, staring down at his son who had only days before been in the prime of health and now was oppressed by disease. He briefly touched Jason's inflamed cheek and gulped. "I've never seen him look so sick..."

Psyche edged closer to him and rested her red-haired head on his shoulder. *He's trembling.*

"Psyche, I lost his mother. I couldn't bear to lose him, too."

"He'll recover." She kissed Periander's pale cheek; he took her hand in turn, holding it tight.

CHAPTER SIXTEEN

A S HIS SHAKY FEET dragged him towards the chamber to which he had been beckoned, Lysander's heart was beating as fast as a hummingbird flaps its wings. It was midnight, and the palace hall's lights shone dimmer than usual. Having returned victorious after suffocating the last embers of rebellion, Atlantis's High King was in high spirits. This in turn dispirited Lysander, who had wished disaster to befall him in America; although far too tactful to let such feelings slip in public, he could only let his imagination run wild and dread as to why Critias had summoned him at this unseemly hour.

Could he have discovered my loyalty to King Periander?

He entered the room. Gloom was all-pervading; some candles placed here and there provided the only faint flickering of light without dispelling the feeling that this was a black hole into which he had come. In the middle of the dark room, seated around a circular table, were about thirty other officials.

Whew, thought Lysander, exhaling deeply. *I'm not the only one summoned.* While his skin erupted in goose bumps, he seated himself in one of the cold metal chairs. Among the other officials present, he knew a few personally and thought he knew of a few more: court advisers, executive bureaucrats, and administrative cogs in the palace's hierarchy. The rest he did not recognize.

Minutes passed, and nothing happened. Murmurings were exchanged repeatedly between these merchants of ignorance, compounding the mystery of their summons with each trade; but no one knew the purpose for this meeting or when something would happen. The state of suspension gnawed at Lysander's nerves while his teeth gnawed at his lips with the passing of each additional minute. After a long wait, there suddenly exploded from the doorway heart attack-inducing blasts of trumpets as a smirking Critias sauntered into the room, flanked by oozy-eared Thrax.

Critias was clothed in his now typical all-black robes. In addition to two skull earrings, he also sported new imagery atop his hands that were similarly-ghoulish: a tattoo of a pile of skulls on the right hand and a tattoo of bones on the left. There was a tapestry hanging on the back wall that graphically depicted stake-bound men engulfed in fire, flames shooting out of their melting eye sockets. It was the chair angled in front of this that Critias chose for himself.

"Welcome, my guests," said Critias with a smile. "This is one evening you'll not soon forget!"

Lysander gulped, transfixed by Critias' roving black eyes that scrutinized them all.

"You wonder why I summoned you, am I right?" He licked his pale lips and laughed loudly. "Be of good cheer. I called you not for business, but for pleasure! To celebrate my triumph in America, my glory, and my power. Now let's have us some drinks!"

Upon Critias' thumping of the tabletop with both hands, a troupe of boys began streaming into the room. First five, then ten, soon fifteen... one boy for every guest. They were carrying goblets and bottles of wine, and comported themselves well as cupbearers. Yet the most striking thing about these children was their costumes. Wearing only black aprons which were decorated with white crossbones and black forehead bands that sported large, jagged horns, their bodies were likewise painted black. From their darkly-dyed scalps to the soles of their feet, the entire surface area of their bodies, all their skin, was covered by a thick layer of black paint that in conjunction with the horns lent them the appearance, in this shadowy room, of what underworldly spirits were said to have.

What is the meaning of this getup?

Lysander, rendered speechless by this strange spectacle, could only vaguely nod when his personal cupbearer asked if he wanted wine.

The boy set the goblet down in front of him. Formed in the shape of a skull, it was proportioned exactly to the human cranium. The sides were scorched brown, the eye sockets filled in, a nick on the bottom where a blade had cut through the neck of the—no, wait! Surely that could not be... Or was it? Yes, yes. This was no replica: it was a real human head! Not an imitation of a skull, but a genuine skull that had been fashioned into a goblet.

His mouth agape, Lysander gawked at his cup's innards. The cranial cavity, albeit thoroughly cleansed of its original contents, kept reminding Lysander about its initial usage. Then it was obscured when the boy filled the goblet with wine, pouring it all the way up to the brim until some of the blood-red fluid overflowed and gushed down the sides.

Critias carefully observed his guests' reäctions to the cups. "I see you marvel at these goblets, the fruits of my victory." He lifted up one skull-glass and slurped loudly. Wiping the scarlet liquor off his mouth with his skull-pile hand, he said, "The rebel leaders bequeathed their heads for our enjoyment. Drink up! Don't be shy!"

Picking up the goblet and staring at the undulating alcohol, Lysander, feeling a lump in his throat, hesitated to follow Critias' example. Yet with all his fellow guests one by one putting their skulls to their mouths, Lysander, sensing the watchful eyes of the High King upon him, stifled a gag and forced himself to drink. Chilled and unusually sweet-smelling, with a tinge of blood orange in it, the wine pushed past his uvula and hurtled down his throat.

Any discomfort on his guests' part did not trouble Critias; in fact, he cackled at it. After glugging down a second round of drinks, he began recounting his exploits in America and his feats of glory.

"I repaid the people of Teotihuacan for their folly in rising against me. Their leaders, I disemboweled; the common people, I divided into three groups. The men were rounded up and marched from one end of the city's grand boulevard to the other. In the middle of the city I constructed over the road a colossal yoke, made of shackles and fetters welded together. I sat atop it, perched in a throne, to watch them as they came, forced to pass beneath it. I spat upon the traitors and cursed them by the Light-Bringer. Once they had been led out of the city..." Critias, smiling, gulped more wine. "...my soldiers crucified them all. *Every. Last. One.* If only you could have seen the glorious sight! For over a hundred miles—east, west, south—the paths leading from the city were lined with thousands of bodies twitching, convulsing. Some held out as long as three days before expiring. But under the sun's hot glare, the reek of rotting corpses began on the second day; there was no wind, so by Day Three the air was saturated with the scent of death."

Thrax, sitting beside him, clapped for him, and by this act induced Critias' guests to applaud, too. Even Lysander, nauseous from this gory tale, likewise felt compelled to play the hypocrite, outwardly congratulating Critias while in his heart he cursed him. *Cruelest tyrant, inhuman beast, villain devoid of all feeling! How you revel in destruction and human misery! May the Deity repay your wicked joy with rightful misery!*

Critias continued. "The women I first had shaved—what piles of hair they produced! Then, hairless all over, I impaled them on pikes erected around the city, piercing the wombs which bore such traitors or which would surely have borne them. Bloodied torsos and mouths tarnished with blood seeping up, the women made an excellent wall for the city's perimeter."

Again, applause ensued, more raucous than before. Lysander played along, gingerly clapping; yet some of his fellow guests sounded earnest in their praise, which caused his nostrils to flare from anger. Sloshing his goblet, wine pouring down his protruding chin, Thrax drunkenly shouted, "Tell of the children!"

"The children," replied Critias, his cheeks rising devilishly, "I massed in the field north of the city, the one that used to be used for festivals of fertility and of harvests come in. There my men built mass pits, filled them with fuel, and ignited them. We cast the children into the fire, and they were burned alive, by far the quickest of all of Teotihuacan's citizens to die."

More applause erupted, and so the scene repeated itself throughout the night. Hours more would pass before an uneasy Lysander, his facial scar burning all the while, was released from this deadly symposium. All the while Critias spoke ceaselessly of death and things deathly, of gore and blood, continually goaded by Thrax and the baths of wine that he imbibed.

Appalled by it all, Lysander inwardly choked the most when Critias gave his justification for the bloodbath: "The terror of me spread throughout all the colonies; the rebels knew what awaited them. Sadly, we had only time to destroy four more measly towns before people everywhere threw down their arms and fearfully recognized my authority. Thus, did I snuff out the rebellion and all challenge to my rule and in so doing provided my poets with abundant material for songs to celebrate my deeds." As he said the last sentence, his blazing eyes locked on to Lysander, who laboriously concealed his sweaty palms and tried to act nondescript.

With the clocks striking five and the sun shortly due to rise, Critias retired from his guests who were finally free to leave. Lysander hurried back to his apartments, his heart pounding, and locked the door behind him. He tried to go to sleep, hoping to awaken to find that this whole incident was but a nightmare. Yet with his mind whirling from Critias' words and his body irritated from too much wine, Lysander could only toss and turn in his bed.

Knock, knock.

Lysander startled. *Who could that be?* he wondered. It was six o'clock, and he was not expecting anyone. He rose from his bed, his skin cold and riddled with goose bumps. *I did everything the tyrant wished; he couldn't have sent an agent to arrest me...* He gasped as he recalled Critias staring at him. *No, he can't know! I've been so careful! There's no way he could have read my mind, know my true feelings...*

More knocks followed.

"I'm coming!" he called, nervously turning on the light. *But what if one of the others, maybe a go-between, revealed my communications with King Periander? Was tonight's party meant to detect disloyalists and conspirators...?*

The marble floor was cold on his naked feet. Walking slowly across the room, Lysander stubbed his toe on a chair that had fallen over; the throbbing hurt, but fear dulled his pain. He reached the door just as another knock came.

O Deity, if this is the end...

With trembling hands that made the handle wet, Lysander opened the door. Bracing himself, he held his head high and thrust it forwards to confront the knocker.

What the—? He glanced right, then left.

No one was there.

Who was knocking?

Perplexed, Lysander looked down. *Oh!* There was a child standing before him. Several seconds passed before he realized that this boy, now freshly bathed and clothed in a white tunic, was recently his cupbearer.

The blond-haired boy wordlessly presented him with a little box before scampering off.

Refastening the door, Lysander went to his desk to examine the gift. There was a dagger inside of it, steel-bladed, whose well-crafted hilt was made of solid ivory. He picked it up and discovered the following words imprinted on the hilt: COMBIBONI MAGNI REGIS. Which meant, in Old Atlantic, "For one who has drunk with the High King."

Lysander stared blankly at the dagger. It was ostensibly a present from Critias, and an expensive one at that. Yet as to what profounder significance the dagger might portend, however, who could know?

CHAPTER SEVENTEEN

ABOUT AN HOUR PASSED before the results of Jason's blood test were known. The younger physician entered the room, holding an electronic pad containing the diagnosis. Periander and Psyche, now in chairs for their bedside vigil, wearily rose.

"You were right, Lady. The infection is pseudonosis," said the physician, scrolling through data on his touch screen. "It's not necessarily a fatal one: with medication, seven out of ten patients fully recover."

Although the physician presumably intended this to reässure him, Periander gritted his teeth, not at all relieved by what he heard. A seventy percent recovery rate still meant that close to a third succumbed to the disease! "Are you going to administer the medicine now?"

"No, we can't administer any," said the physician nonchalantly, not bothering to look up from his pad. (Had he done so, he would have noticed the aghast look erupting on Periander's face.) "We're lacking one of the essential ingredients necessary to compound the—"

Before the doctor could finish his explanation, Periander had grabbed his pad and, with a great hurl, smashed it against the wall. Electrodes and transistors rained down upon the dry floor. "What do you mean you can't get him medicine?" demanded a panting Periander, gripping the collar of the physician's lab coat.

"It's alright," said Leonidas, interceding to separate him from the physician.

Discombobulated, the physician breathlessly mumbled, "As I was say-ing, we lack a necessary ingredient for the cure: a rare plant found only in eastern Libya. But we've sent a team to get some; as soon as they return, our pharmacist will compound the drug."

A whimper came from Jason, whom they had buried in ice packs to lessen the fiery fever consuming his body. Periander turned his head, wincing when he saw his son. "And just how long will that take?"

"A few hours."

"And what if he doesn't last till then?" hollered Periander, his body itching from the heat of furor. "Are you sure no one in the city has whatever root you need?"

"Exactly what plant is it?" asked Psyche.

"A species of wormwood."

Without a word Psyche dashed out of the room like a hyena in pursuit of fleeing prey. When she returned, she was holding a bottle, freshly fetched from her chest of drugs, which contained extract of Libyan wormwood. "I have some!"

"Stupendous!" exclaimed the physician, praising Psyche while casting tense glances at Periander.

As the physician departed with the lifesaving ingredient, Periander embraced his wife. "Thanks be to the Deity you brought wormwood."

"I'm glad my hobby could be put to a good use."

Periander slowly let go of her lithe body and gazed into her shim-mering, cerulean eyes. *If I'd left you unmarried in Egypt, if you hadn't come with us....* He gulped and stopped himself from dwelling on that counterfactual.

***

T HE MINUTES PASSED EXCRUCIATINGLY slowly for the fretful father and anxious stepmother. (The patient himself, however, was delirious and therefore oblivious to time.) Nevertheless, it took less than an hour for Jason's medicine to be compounded. The drug, administered intravenously, proved fast acting: in three hours Jason's temperature fell three degrees, which, while still high, no longer hovered at a dangerous level.

Now, as the night drew on, only Periander and Psyche remained with Jason apart from the occasional inspections performed by the medical staff. His condition beginning to be alleviated by the drug, Jason breathed more gently and his face, while still red and scaly, became a noticeably lighter hue.

Relieved that the most perilous phase had passed and that his son's health appeared to be making progress, Periander turned to Psyche. It was she who had found Jason, she who had the ingredient necessary for his salvation. She had, moreover, demonstrated herself to be more than a mere discoverer or herbal supplier. Psyche had been attending to Jason since she found him—tenderly dabbing his forehead with cold compresses, rubbing anti-inflammation ointment on his face, dispensing eye drops to ease the puffiness. Aside from himself, Psyche had stayed with him longer than anyone else; the sagging of eyes, the drowsy movement of hands, and the muscular twinges from sitting motionless for so long all bore witness to her conscientiousness.

"You should go and get some rest," said Periander, kissing her cheek.

"No, I'll stay a bit longer."

"You look worn out."

"I'm not," said Psyche, belying her words with a yawn.

A smile spread out across Periander's face. "I can't thank you enough, Psyche, for everything." She rested her head against his shoulder, and he stroked her soft, flowing red hair. "You've been so wonderful with Jason, acted so skillfully."

"I have seven younger brothers whom I tended to when they were sick. So, I have experience."

"Well, I'll always appreciate your loving care, and I know Jason will, too. When I saw him this morning, gasping for air, his face so red, I, I... I was so frightened." Periander sighed. "My poor boy has endured too much for his age! Besides watching his mother killed in front of him, he's had his own life endangered ever since Critias' attempt to slaughter us by night, driven from his home, forced to travel incognito to evade the bounty hunters, captured by perfidious Thrallis... None succeeded in depriving me of him. (The Deity be thanked.) Yet to think a bite from some nameless mosquito, billowing along the parched Libyan air, came so close to robbing me of him where all the others failed—that has unnerved me."

"You're a good father, Periander. Nobody would blame you for feeling scared," said Psyche, caressing the side of his neck reässuringly. "He's your only child. Even though he's not my son, Jason has grown very dear to my heart. I too was seized with fear and not only because of that natural dread which we feel towards illness. Death is mankind's oldest foe, the lone victor who cannot be defeated, only delayed. We all are sickened by death, for it reminds us we are mortal."

"I do not disagree with you about aversion to death; I certainly felt it when watching each of my parents die, their lives weakened by pitiless old age and then finished off by an epidemic that struck Atlantis. Yet I did not blame myself for their deaths whereas... I feel responsible for what almost befell Jason."

"What?" Psyche pulled away from him, her arms repulsed by his words. With her sea-blue eyes inundated with shock and her head shaking back and forth, she said, "How can you say that?"

"Because that's how I feel."

"But you didn't ask for any of this. You're not responsible for an insect's actions!"

"Aren't I?" said Periander gloomily, standing up. He turned away from Psyche and laid his forehead against the cold wall. "If it weren't for me, he would never have been within a thousand miles of that blasted bug." As he spoke of his son, thoughts of Cornelia likewise entered his mind, of her hand desperately grasping for his as she fell.

The sound of screeching chair legs echoed behind him, which Periander ignored.

"I have always strived to serve the interests of Atlantis and her people. My father always said, 'A king is the first servant of the realm,' a maxim I whole-heartedly endorse. Because of that sense of duty, I felt compelled to oppose Eudoxia and all the reckless, reprehensible things she sought to do. I was not one of the kings diverted from the right path by bribes or intimidation; I maintained my opposition till my last day in Atlantis. Yet what did that get me? What was the reward for my integrity? My home, my throne, my queen—all were taken from me." The wall chilled his forehead, which wrinkled with deep lines. "After my flight, the only thing left to me was Jason; and if it weren't for you and the Deity's grace, I would now have lost him too."

Psyche's warm breath washed over the back of his neck and her hushed voice entered his ears. "Periander, you've endured so much hardship, so much loss. I cannot mend what has happened. But I want you to understand that you are not alone: I will always be at your side! I love you so much."

Whirling around, Periander grabbed Psyche, pulling her close to him in a deep embrace. "I appreciate that," he said, patting her blushing cheek, "but your love only adds to my cares. For now, it is not just Jason I must look after, but you too. I know my duty to my country, and it is that duty which impels me blindly down an unclear road towards a final confrontation with Critias."

"But you are not blind," protested Psyche. She kissed his cheek. "I've heard your plans for how to invade Atlantis and overthrow the régime, and they are good."

"True, I have hope, great hope, that I shall prevail in the end... and restore good order to Atlantis. Yet experience has taught me that hope is by nature an expensive commodity, one that can delude men into gambling their all on a single throw of the dice—they don't even realize what happened until after their ruin is complete."

"Periander—"

He stood back and held his hands on Psyche's shoulders as he looked into her eyes. "I recognize this, which is why I fear that, in pursuit of my country's welfare, Jason and you—the two who, above all others, have a claim on my protection—will become casualties in my conflict." Periander broke his gaze off her and stared into the empty air behind her. "My fear is that, in these two distinct but overlapping duties—to family and to country—one will prove all-consuming and destroy the other. Already the latter has claimed Cornelia's life, and today came close to also claiming Jason's."

Psyche placed her soft hand on his right cheek and Periander's face tickled as her delicate palm ran through his platinum beard.

"I know you are besieged on all sides by manifold duties; such is the life of a king. But I am fine, and Jason shall recover. Do not let your worry for us sway you from what you must do. We will be alright. We both trust you. *I* trust you."

"Psyche—"

"You are devoted to your country and must save Atlantis. We will be at your side. As will Agathocles and the rest of your men: they all trust you and look to you and your leadership as their country's last best hope of restoration."

You truly know how to console a man's soul. Moved by her words, a resurgence of confidence washed over Periander. He formed a fist over his heart. "You are right, Psyche. Eloquently put. I cannot jump off the path I have been set on; I can only race down to its conclusion."

He kissed her lips and then, hand in hand, they resumed their seats alongside Jason; and, secluded within the melancholy chamber on this bleak night, shared their common angst.

***

H AVING SPOKEN IN PRIVATE, neither Periander nor Psyche knew that their conversation had been overheard. Outside the open doorway leading to the hall, sticking against the wall like a gravity-defying bug, stood Leonidas.

He had come to check on Jason's welfare and to cheer up his friend. Overhearing the dialogue between Periander and Psyche, Leonidas was about to knock on the door to announce his presence. But when his friend's anguished voice reached his ears, and the inner fears that it conveyed, not only did he not announce himself but, try though he might to stop, Leonidas kept listening.

He stood transfixed throughout their conversation, hiding outside the door, his skin perspiring and eyes darting every way lest any passerby should catch him eavesdropping. Yet with three tears (one shed for each person in the room) falling from his eyes and his heart weighed down with sympathy for his friend, Leonidas progressively became the more and more visibly tormented.

When the voices within died out, Leonidas could not bring himself to enter. He instead slunk quietly down the hall, depressed by what he had overheard.

CHAPTER EIGHTEEN

A WEEK HAD PASSED since the pseudonosis seized Jason. Receiving the proper medicine in twice-daily dosages, Periander's son steadily improved: his fever subsided, his breathing returned to normalcy, and his face no longer glowed red (even if the skin continued to flake in patches). While the physicians attending to him still ordered rest, an increasingly impatient Jason had been straying farther and farther from his bed, his strength regained much to his father's delight.

This was the sole encouraging development.

During the same period, horrifying news trickled into Athens about Critias' repression of the American insurrection: the unmitigated slaughter, utter devastation, vindictive indignities, and the cruelest tortures which he had inflicted on all of Teotihuacan's inhabitants irrespective of age, sex, or condition. Despite its brutality, the carnage had its desired effect: the rebellion had its wind knocked out of it as when a man's ribcage collides with a titanium-spiked steel ball, chained to a handle, which an exceedingly brawny giant hurled at him at a speed of over one hundred miles per hour.

Such extreme measures, however, scandalized the people of Athens. Leonidas was outraged by the atrocity, which only confirmed every warning Periander had made about the tyrannical High King; but what outraged him most of all was his father's indifference and stubborn refusal even to reconsider his friend's proposal. Now, armed with even fresher intelligence, Leonidas went to confront his father yet again.

Bursting into the royal library past the emerald-green garbed guards stationed on either side of the entrance, Leonidas espied his father sitting in his comfortable velvet-upholstered chair in front of the grand fireplace. There was an immense, crackling fire burning behind the fireplace's stained-glass screen while on either side of it two life-sized eagles, carved of black marble with their wings outstretched, towered menacingly above Athenagoras.

"Father!" shouted Leonidas, carefully navigating his way across the room so as to avoid tripping over the various books strewn pell-mell on the golden carpet.

Diverting his eyes from his tome, a pasty-faced Athenagoras looked up. From behind his small-framed rectangular reading glasses, his beady eyes narrowed, and his aquiline nose sniffed when he saw Leonidas. Returning his gaze to his book, he coolly asked, "What is it this time?"

"Father, reports have just come that Atlantis has sent troops into southern Italy! They've already seized control of Brundisium, Croton, Regium—all of the peninsula's boot—and are now staging an amphibious invasion of Sicily!"

"I know all that," replied Athenagoras whilst flipping through several pages.

He knows and yet so calm? "Then what are you going to do about it?"

"Nothing."

"What?!" Leonidas rubbed his ears to verify they were working.

"You heard me correctly."

Leonidas lost his composure. "How can you *sssssit* there perusing the moldy pages of some old novel, *sssssipping* your *preee-ccious cham-o-mile teeeea*, when the forces of war are pressing ever nearer to our shores?" As he spoke, he thrashed his arms and accentuated his words with fierce gesticulation.

A disdainful smirk erupted on Athenagoras' visage. He set his book down on the stand adjacent to his chair, next to the much-abused cup of tea that was still cowering at Leonidas, and slowly clapped his hands.

"Bravo, my son, bravo! Since your friend's arrival, you have honed your theatrical prowess with each succeeding performance. Endowed with histrionics such as these, the likes of which must be innate, it's clear you were born to be an actor, not a prince!"

"Are you mad, Father?" Shaking in disbelief, Leonidas' skull rose from his jaw. "Have you pawned your wits to some beltless huckster? As we speak, a butcher's army is massing within five hundred leagues of this city! And yet you do not act except to speak of actors' skills."

"Leonidas," said Athenagoras, dismissively waving his hand, "I have seen the same reports as you, and there is nothing that need concern us."

"War does not concern us?"

"Not when it does not involve us."

"How does the conquest of our neighbors not prefigure future wars against us?"

"You misrepresent the facts." Athenagoras shook his head and his ashen hair. "The governments of certain Italian states, engulfed by internal factions whose hatreds have spilled over into civil wars, have invited Atlantis to help restore order in their territories. King Critias is not conquering them; *au contraire*, he is banishing lawlessness from their lands."

What inverted insanity is this?! Thunderstruck by his father's blinkered interpretation of Critias' intrigues, Leonidas swiftly rejoined, "You mean he is crushing rebellion like he did in America, right? The whole world knows of the outrages he inflicted on Teotihuacan! Of the atrocities and tortures collectively inflicted upon the entire people—*after* they had already peacefully surrendered to his lieutenants on the promise of safety!"

"Harsh measures, I am sure. But they were inflicted on his own subjects, not ours."

"Are the Italians his subjects?"

Athenagoras' white eyebrows rose but his voice stayed level. "No, but their governments have invited him."

"They also have pledged fidelity, military alliance, and financial contributions to Atlantis," challenged Leonidas. "All are hallmarks of subjugation and vassalage."

Athenagoras sneered, "Are they not the same things that you keep proposing I give your friend?"

His nostrils flaring, his teeth gnashing from left to right, and his untrimmed nails digging into his clenched fists, Leonidas seethed at so blasphemous a comparison. "In no way can assistance to a wrongfully exiled monarch be equated with a belligerent tyrant exerting his empire's superior force to extort weaker states!"

"I do not see it that way."

"You mean you *choose* not to see it that way!"

Snarling, Athenagoras leapt to his feet, his sleeve falling down to reveal his bony arm as it swung leftwards and sent his cup flying. It flew seventeen feet, disintegrating as it impacted a bookshelf and drenched old tomes with tea. "No more of your insolence!" he growled, slapping Leonidas' left cheek. "I will not suffer this persecution any longer: I am your father and your king! If only your accursed Periander had never set foot in my kingdom! I have not had a moment's rest from your pestering on his behalf."

"Of course I seek his good. I owe him so much: he saved my life."

"You saved his wife! Your debt has been repaid. Why then do you so shamefully insist on being his lobbyist?"

"Because he is my closest friend on Earth, dearer to me than a brother."

"Your friendship with this foreigner will doom your real brothers born on native soil!"

"My love for Athens and Periander interlocks perfectly with one another," rejoined Leonidas, clutching the air with his fist. "That is why I want to help him overthrow the Atlantean régime that has been hell-bent on world conquest from the moment Eudoxia—"

"EUDOXIA IS DEAD!" spat his father. "So, stop your bickering about her when it's her son we are to deal with."

Leonidas wiped off the droplets of saliva that had hit his face and asked, "And will he deal with us as he dealt with his mother? He murdered her."

"I do not justify Critias' deed. It was most unnatural and evil. But his sins, against both his mother and his people, are between him and the Deity; it is not our place to intervene in another realm's internal affairs."

"But what sort of a man is he, who can callously kill the woman who gave him life? Who can devise demonic tortures and massacres of entire cities? He has proved himself a monster, a menace to all the world."

"Even so, he has done absolutely nothing to us!" protested Athenagoras.

"Not yet! Not yet! Will you wait to act until our streets run red with blood?"

"YES!" Athenagoras' forehead became crumpled with wrinkles, and taking his glasses off he slammed them on the table so hard that the lenses cracked. Standing two inches away from his son, staring into his eyes, he hissed, "Atlantis is the most powerful nation in the world, its military first class. I will not expose my kingdom to the bloodied claws of that behemoth by *choosing* to declare war against it when it has not committed any hostile act against us."

"But Father—"

"Have you forgotten the stories of my youth I've told you? What disasters befell this state when it last made war with Atlantis?" His voice falling to a hush, Athenagoras ignored Leonidas' protestation and began his tale. "I was three years old when my uncle Creon came to the throne. Like you, he was infused with the arrogance of youth. He wanted to avenge some diplomatic slights that the Atlantean government had inflicted on Athens during his father's reign. Thinking to exploit some domestic disorder that was then rocking Atlantis during Delphis' reign, he foolishly declared war."

"That wasn't the same as what I'm—"

"Listen to me!" roared Athenagoras, striking Leonidas when he was not expecting it, which caused him to lose his balance and fall backwards. Athenagoras' breathing became erratic, his chest heaving, and the whites of his eyes bulged prominently. "Creon's misbegotten war failed utterly! Whatever disorder prevailed among the Atlanteans ceased as soon as he declared war. Creon's planned invasion fleet was sunk at the Battle of Ibiza. Then the war became a stalemate, harshly fought, year after year, in lands bordering the Mediterranean. These were my earliest memories: watching bands of young men, vigorous and in their primes, shipped off to fight, half never to return. The other half still haunt my sleep—youths without arms, legs, eyes. They were everywhere! In every street and room... bearing the marks and scars of war—so many casualties clinging onto life but only half-alive! The screams of bloodied soldiers shipped home for medical treatment. The wails of wives and mothers when their men succumbed to their wounds. War. Death. Destruction. So went my childhood.

"And what did it profit Creon? What did he gain from plunging our land into the jaws of war? He fell in battle in my seventh year, his son Eteocles in my eighth. His youngest sons were too young to rule, their regents too stupid. It was on my ninth birthday that the enemy overran this city, after relentlessly bombing it for several days. Soldiers flooded through the streets, occupying buildings, killing, raping, looting. When the palace fell, I saw my cousins, Creon's sons, sweet Mopsius and gentle Faenus, put up against a wall and shot; their lifeless heads oozed blood all over, their eyeballs—still attached!—hanging limply down beside their mouths.

"My father was made king and forced to sign a humiliating treaty that made me a hostage! King Delphis took me back in chains to Atlantis City where he kept me as his slave, whipping me, disgracing me. I had to eat the crumbs that fell from his table—my allotment! Nineteen years I suffered there, till he died, and good King Cuculus finally let me return. I will never start a war with Atlantis! NEVER! Not after that!"

Throughout his father's speech, Leonidas had remained upon the floor, staring unblinkingly up at him as he raved on and on about Creon's War. He rose himself up and, on bended knees, beseeched his father. "I understand, Father, I really do. You experienced unspeakable horrors from your earliest life that you don't want ever repeated. I agree! We must not allow them to happen again. And it is precisely because I want to spare our kingdom from such horrors that I support Periander's plan—stop Atlantis and its voracious tyrant before they grow too powerful to be stopped."

"*No, no, no!* I built up our navy to defend us, not to start wars!" howled Athenagoras. "If they attack, we'll of course have no choice but to fight. But not till then! Not till we are openly attacked will I countenance talk of making war against Atlantis."

"But Father—"

Leonidas recoiled as his father snatched the book he had been reading and wildly clobbered the side of his face with it.

"Enough of you! *Get out! Get out!* AWAY FROM MY SIGHT!"

Clasping the side of his face, his hand becoming bloodied from where the book's hard metal covering had drawn blood, Leonidas rose to his feet; recognizing the futility of further talk, he made his way to the exit, soiling the carpet with droplets of blood wherever he went.

"Fine, Father!" Leonidas yelled as he left. "Cling to your stubbornness, you old fool! May it not lead to this kingdom's destruction!"

Chapter Nineteen

"OH, THAT MAN!" Leonidas pounded his fist against the wall. Having left his father's library, he stormed through the palace hallways, infuriated at both Athenagoras' rejection of Periander's alliance and the overbearing way his father had cast him out. Leonidas' face still stung from where he had struck him, although he had staunched the bleeding with an indigo handkerchief.

Now, standing in the throne room, his rage had still not abated. Alone though he was (for except when the king was present, this was the most deserted room in the whole palace), Leonidas nevertheless gave voice to his wrathful thoughts.

The throne of solid gold lay before him, on a daïs six steps above the floor. The backside was large and disk-like, molded so as to appear as though it shed golden rays; under the lights of the room, the solar throne flashed like the sun. On both sides of the throne were two silver statues of soldiers, depicted clothed in ancient armor and breastplates, and each holding a javelin in their hands closest to the throne. Their expressions were ever-solemn, gazing down at whoever stood before them; their lips were tight, eyebrows depressed over bulging eyes, and bulky noses protruded from their faces.

Looking up at these twin guardians of the throne, who had watched over generations of Athenian kings, Leonidas tightly clasped his handkerchief as the blood began to dry, encrusting his knuckles. "Oh, what a stubborn man you watch over, Guardians! Athens needs her king to be a lion, roaring at all foes and overlooking no marauders, who chases them all out of his pride's land—not a tortoise hiding in his shell, hoping no predator makes an attempt upon his defenses."

"How true, my prince."

Who's that?

Leonidas startled at the unexpected voice. Yet before he finished spinning his head around, he had recognized the voice. Yes, he recognized that sleazy pitch as it oozed down his ear canals—the distinctive, jarring, guttural voice that had been shadowing him for days now. "You again."

"Lord Leonidas." Twenty feet behind Leonidas, standing between the two propped bronze doors, was Gnatho. His eyes flashed from side to side mischievously and his oblong mouth formed a duplicitous half-smile that revealed his buckteeth. "Allow me to express my whole-hearted concurrence to your judgment."

"And what do you want, sycophant?" barked Leonidas, ready to vent his anger on this flatterer. "I am not in the mood to deal with vain conversations."

Gnatho cupped his well-manicured hands and pressed them gently onto his oily chin, whose fat undulated at his touch. "No vain conversation do I bring, my prince, but rather suggestions to save our state and that dear friend of yours, too."

"If you mean persuade the king, I doubt any idea of yours could move him. I just spoke with him: he's inflexible."

"Which is most deplorable since your arguments were by far the strongest."

"How would you know?" snapped Leonidas, putting his arms akimbo. "Were you eavesdropping on our talk?"

Gnatho's eyes withdrew to their sides. "I may have happened to be passing by."

"And you just 'happened' to stick around and listen." *It's no wonder this parasite knows so much: he's spying on us all.*

"To monitor where crucial matters are decided necessitates a shrewd mind."

"Fine, have your say," said Leonidas pithily as he motioned him to approach, irked by Gnatho's artfulness and yet forced to admire him for his persistence (if for nothing else).

Gnatho walked over to Leonidas and bowed. "My prince, you are quite right: Athens is in greater danger than I have ever seen. Our enemy is encroaching on our sphere of influence, massing armies so near to home as to be able to invade us effortlessly. There lingers on the horizon the greatest of threats that we must either overcome or be by it overcome."

"Yes, but try persuading my father of that; it is a hopeless task."

"Our way of life—our very life itself—depends on what we next do."

"So true," agreed Leonidas, shaking his head in his hand at his father's stubbornness. *This man is skilled at arguing my points himself... He does know how to speak well; I'll give him that.*

"Great forethought is needed for our state. I wonder what you would do, my prince, if, hypothetically, you were now king."

"Well, I would join Periander's alliance, invade Atlantis, overthrow—why are asking this, this hypothetical? My father still lives! You promised no vain talk, so restrict your speech to how things are."

"Oh," murmured Gnatho, "this 'hypothetical' is not like others: it is poised above the threshold which separates that which is from that which readily may be."

Leonidas' head cocked to the side. *What does he mean by these ominous words?* With each hand's outstretched fingers touching their counterparts, he ordered, "Speak plainly and not in riddles."

"I am proposing that Athenagoras' life be shortened so that you may succeed as king."

Leonidas' right leg involuntarily stepped back, his hands sprung back from one another, and without a sound or breath of air his mouth made the motions of a gasp. "Are you MAD?! You're seriously suggesting I kill my father?"

Such a reäction would have caused others to retract their propositions, or at any rate, upon seeing the disgust on Leonidas' scrunched-up face, would have softened their tone. Gnatho, however, kept his composure icy cold, his voice unblurred, and his eyes unblinking as he advanced forwards by as much as Leonidas had recoiled. "Yes."

Leonidas simply stared at him. *Even from this guttersnipe, I wasn't expecting a scheme so outrageous.* "This is treason you're talking! I could have you hung for it."

"Treason against whom?" queried Gnatho with a blank face.

"Don't play dumb! Against the king, of course! Treason is plots against his life."

Gnatho raised his eyebrows. "But is it not also treason to betray one's country?"

"Certainly, it is."

"And is it not betrayal for a man to wage war on his country, even if his war-making is limited to undermining its defenses?"

"Yes."

"Has undermining not been deemed under Athenian law to encompass omissions of such a nature, on the part of one in authority, that by his failure to take action when it was within his power so to do, he is held culpable for any mischief that might follow?"

"Well, of course. Numerous men over the years have been executed for such—" Leonidas closed his jaw so fast that he nearly bit his tongue when he realized what Gnatho was insinuating.

Gnatho's eyes gleamed as he leaned over to Leonidas, whispering, "By your own admission, King Athenagoras, in refusing to confront the Atlantean flood threatening to swallow up every land, is endangering not only our own country but the entire world."

"Y-yes, b-but, but—"

"Is that not what you believe?"

"To my core," answered Leonidas, standing wobbly. *Just because Father is endangering Athens with his obstinance, that doesn't justify...* Yet the more he listened, the more he felt himself being sucked into the whirlpool of Gnatho's gutturally mesmerizing voice.

Maintaining his onslaught, Gnatho clasped Leonidas by his shoulder and said, "Then are you not obliged to do whatever is required to safeguard our country?"

"Yes... but surely that cannot include what you propose! To kill a king is an unholy deed; to kill one's own father—unthinkable."

"How much more unthinkable is it to kill one's fatherland! Most unholy of all for its own king to kill it!"

"He is my father."

"The whole palace knows your terse relationship with him. He's never behaved graciously towards you, nor shown you fatherly love, but rather treated you like some contemptible slave."

Leonidas' mind overflowed with memories of his father—how he was always unfeeling, never expressing any love, forbidding Leonidas to do what he must do or criticizing him for it, such as the time Leonidas was berated for helping Periander rescue his bride... Then there was Athenagoras' recent scene in the library, his shocking behavior, and Leonidas' injured face.

Leonidas truthfully had no love for his father. But did that justify murdering him?

"Regardless of my personal feelings, duty still binds me to my father. Can I, denouncing Critias' matricide, perpetrate patricide?"

"What of your duty to Athens," pressed Gnatho. "Critias slew Eudoxia in furor because he hated her and her influence. Whereas you, my prince, would not be acting out of ignoble private passions but resolutely for the public good, the greatest good of all."

"You dare lecture me about the public good? From infancy my tutors educated me in statecraft, including the relations between king and people. A king is inestimably tied to his realm like no other man. He is the

Deity's vicegerent on Earth, the wellspring of legitimate authority. How can one attack him without attacking the foundation of the state, and thus the people too?"

"But what is a king without a people? Nothing! Therefore, the salvation of the people must come before the king's."

"But, but…"

"If you kill Athenagoras, you'll salvage the monarchy as well as the people; stand by, and watch him destroy your family's heritage along with the people you've sworn to serve. Isn't it foolish to choose the latter and not the former?"

Oh, what am I to do? wondered Leonidas, biting his lip. *Countless lives, entire states… the whole world is at stake. I am crushed by its weight!* Less and less could he summon intellectual argumentation from within him, being instead overwhelmed by an army of emotions: fear of Atlantean soldiers devastating Athens as in his father's recollection, resentment for his father's stubbornness, anxiety for his friend Periander…

When Leonidas did not answer, Gnatho, rubbing his manicured hands together, began to clinch his argument. "We cannot wait for nature to take her course. Our king is paralyzed by childhood traumas, preventing him from making a rational defense of this realm when it is most in need of it. You, my prince, must become my king while there is still a kingdom for you."

"I… I… Seize my inheritance…." Leonidas' drooped as he turned his eyes upwards towards the silver guardians.

"Before it is seized from you!"

Swinging his head around, Leonidas demanded, "What?"

Gnatho leaned in and whispered into his ear. "My prince, after you left your father, I overheard him cursing you with mighty curses and suggesting out loud that he should disinherit you in favor of your brother Cleomenes. Can you believe that? You must act at once before it is too late."

Pulling away from Gnatho, Leonidas shouted, "I have to think!" as he turned around and ran out of the room without looking back.

Rushing past pairs of conversing courtiers and servants dusting the palace chandeliers, Leonidas sped through palatial halls. He went down granite-floored hallways, through sitting rooms alive with potted plants, past offices wherein letter-dictating ministers answered petitions of those seeking royal pardon for their convicted relatives. All the while, his mind was whirling over what Gnatho had proposed.

It's too evil to be done, he told himself. *Yet Gnatho is right about one thing... Father's intransigence could lead Athens to utter ruin. I have a duty to Father, but also to my people. What do I do? So many lives hang in the balance! A king's life or his people's...*

Eventually Leonidas' feet conveyed him unwittingly to that part of the palace in which Periander and his entourage were lodging. Walking up the wide stairwell whose green carpet, slightly damp after being washed, glistened beneath the lights, Leonidas reached the top and turned down the hall. It was not until he came to Periander's door that he, still sifting through the overflowing haystack of his thoughts, realized where he had come.

Psyche was speaking as he entered: "Maybe Father could be persuaded to drop his precondition. *I'll* plead with him."

"Your offer is a welcome one," replied Periander, "and you may try it; but I seriously doubt Ozymandias will change his mind."

Periander was sitting upright on a red divan, hunched over with his hands clutching his bare knees that protruded from his navy tunic. Psyche sat on his left, with her right arm enfolding Periander while with the other arm she gently stroked his face. Demosthenes stood a few feet away from them along with Socrates; using an auburn wooden cane topped by a golden two-headed eagle for support, Socrates was whispering something to Demosthenes, who nodded somberly while twirling his sideburn. Not far away Agathocles, standing with his back turned from the rest, leaned against the wall; clearly agitated, his body heaving violently, he suddenly kicked the wall. As a result, several of the jade-painted tiles adorning the walls smashed into numerous pointed shards of glass that enveloped his thick black boot.

"What is going on?" asked Leonidas, rapidly looking at one and then another. There was in the room's atmosphere an unmistakable odor of gloom.

When Periander did not immediately respond, Socrates answered, "A report bearing adverse tidings has come our way."

"I'll tell him." Periander, freeing himself from Psyche's embrace, rose and took a couple steps towards Leonidas. "We just received word from Philip. He informs us that Indra is likely to reject our offer of alliance again, this time definitively."

Not Indra too! thought Leonidas. "Are you absolutely sure he will reject it?"

"Philip couched the news with the caveat that Indra's not officially declined. Yet, he said that, informally, the royal court is filled with every indication that a rejection looms."

Leonidas put his hand on Periander's left shoulder. "I am so sorry. Is there anything I can do?"

"You can't change Indra's decision," sighed Periander. "Though I don't suppose you made any progress in persuading your father, have you?" He looked wistfully at him.

His throat filled with the bitter bile of revulsion as noxious as fluoro-sulfuric acid when his memory regurgitated the acrimonious encounter he had recently had with his father. Leonidas felt ready, after hearing this, to disparage Athenagoras verbally. Nonetheless, lest he overburden his friend with the intensity of his father's refusal, he swallowed the resentment and instead replied with a quick and banal, "I haven't, unfortunately."

"Well, I am at a loss as to what to do next." Periander went to sit back down on the divan. He sunk his forehead into his palm. "Without a second great power on my side, there's no alliance of states; and without the combined military might that only the great powers can raise, there's no way to stage a successful invasion of Atlantis. And thus, all my plans to snatch my fatherland out of Critias' clutch perish."

"If you cannot make war from without, perhaps you should reconsider making war from within," offered Psyche. "You still have loyal subjects in your subkingdom and friends throughout the island; you could instigate a rebellion among the populace and then furtively enter the country to lead it."

Demosthenes mused, "A rebellion would have to be precisely timed lest Critias crush it in its infancy like he did in America."

"But you could provide it with greater cover," added Psyche, "by simultaneously throwing the imperial government into confusion. Have some of your friends in the capital, who live and work in Critias' palace, covertly slay him."

"You mean in cold blood?" said Agathocles tensely.

"Yes. I can recall learning of a couple instances during my grandfather's reign where a prominent governor of this or that province, conspiring to plunge Egypt into civil war, was dealt with by special operatives in that manner. By killing them in private, the public was saved from general calamity."

Periander looked up at his wife. "I've already explained my reservations about such a scheme. Without foreign troops to fight with us, our forces would consist almost entirely of untrained civilians whereas Critias has a professional military at his disposal. Furthermore, while my own subjects will doubtlessly rally to my banner, there's no indication we can count on much support from the other nine-tenths of Atlantis; and regardless of how valiant my tenth is, I just cannot see how we could possibly prevail against such devastating odds. Finally, there's no question Critias must die but... assassination has always gone against Atlantean tradition. Killing by stealth is the sort of dishonorable thing Eudoxia would do. It reeks of nefarious motives rather than the public vindication and administration of justice that I seek. (Assuming our allies are even able to make it past his bodyguards, there's not even any guarantee that his death would paralyze the government; one of his cronies might just take his place, like his loathsome aide Thrax.) On the other hand, Critias, like his mother before him, violates so many ancestral customs; one custom shouldn't be upheld at the expense of all the rest. And we clearly do not have many other options... this desperate move may in fact be the only course we have left."

When the conversation began to take this turn to assassination, Leonidas found it hard to concentrate on the matter at hand. For although Critias' name was spoken, he could only visualize his father. His heart beat faster, perspiration showed on his forehead, and his hands, resting on his sides, produced sticky sweat that made wet spots on his tunic.

Inching back towards the door, Leonidas made an excuse and exited the room, heading down the hallway. But he did not make it farther than forty feet away when, turning the corner onto the green-carpeted staircase, none other than Gnatho appeared.

"Ahh!" exclaimed Leonidas. He clutched his heart which was now pounding at a rate of over one hundred beats per minute. *Wherever I go, he's there!*

"My prince, I must know your intention at once if there is to be sufficient time to undertake the preparations."

Reeling from all that had happened that day—his fight with his father, Gnatho's counterpunch scheme, Indra's thwarting of Periander's quest, the dismal state in which he had left his friend—Leonidas' lips went numb and his tongue become as heavy in his mouth as a barnacle-clad anchor.

CHAPTER TWENTY

PERIANDER INHALED DEEPLY AS soon as he felt the cool, light breeze caressing his nostrils. He was atop the palace's highest tower; from here a panoramic view showcased all of Athens. The city still slept, for it was only three o'clock and the sun would not be stirred from his bed for a few more hours. Periander, however, could not rest.

The day's terrible news that Indra would reject his alliance—thereby frustrating his plan for the liberation of Atlantis—still haunted him long into the night. Nor was this an isolated attack on his mood. When Jason came down with pseudonosis, Periander's confidence was shaken; although his boy was now nearing a full recovery, his mind still bore the scars of parental fear. And now, with his domestic crisis about to be compounded by a diplomatic defeat, he felt all the more beaten by his troubles. His shoulders sagged from all the burdens they carried.

He had attempted to escape his waking anxieties but could not maintain sleep tonight. Repeatedly he staggered in and out of consciousness, groggily tossing and turning in his bed. After a few hours of this futility, he at last decided to spare Psyche from his insomnia by abandoning his attempt.

Wanting some fresh air, he went up to the tower. The cobble-stoned deck was circular with a diameter of about thirty feet; at its center was a brick-covered hut concealing the entrance. Periander leaned against the stone banister, formerly rough but whose hardness the weather had flattened into their current velvety state.

The sky was cloudless, and the constellations shone brightly. Below the acropolis the citizens' houses were dark, while the perfectly planned grid of streets was illuminated by the streetlights' greenish glow reflecting off the metallic gray buildings.

"What will you do?" said Periander aloud to himself. "Things are not going as I'd hoped they would. Critias seems increasingly secure in his hold on power, while my opportunity to stop him is slipping through my hands." He closed his eyes and rested his head upon the cold, smooth stone. "O Deity, strengthen me in my difficulty! If it be Your will that I succeed, arise and help me!"

"The Deity already helps you."

Periander was caught unawares, having thought he was alone. He bolted upright and spun around.

The sonorous voice came from a man standing about five feet behind Periander. He appeared around Periander's age and stood the same six feet high; his light hair was ruffled by the breeze and his beardless well-complexioned chin protruded powerfully. Though dressed in the apparel of an Athenian general, the aura he exuded contradicted his clothing.

"Who are you?" said Periander, his eyes contracting beneath his narrow eyebrows.

"Less important the Who than the What."

"Alright. What are you?"

"A Watcher."

"Hmm. Whom do you watch, Watcher?"

He smiled playfully while his eyes focused unswervingly on Periander's. "*You.*"

Me? His momentary confusion turned to anger, and Periander shot his finger at him. "Who appointed you to watch me? Was it Athenagoras? Has he decided I need to be watched like some common criminal?"

"No mortal's appointee am I: it was the Deity Who set me over you."

"What the—aaahhh!"

No sooner had Periander began to speak but the Watcher, who was in front of him, instantaneously vanished; and, in the twinkling of an eye, he reäppeared behind him as though he had been there the whole time. He placed his warm hand on Periander's right shoulder.

Falling to the ground, his body instinctively recoiling from this strange being, a dry-mouthed Periander exclaimed, "Who are you?"

"Be not afraid, Periander. The Deity commanded me to watch over you and that I will do."

"You've seen the Deity?" gasped Periander, his whole body still shivering. *What kind of creature is this?*

"Daily in His presence do we Watchers dance—a million years to your hour, to your century a millisecond."

"Why have you come to me?"

He laughed, his head bobbing gently. "Periander, you are well-loved by the Deity. He knows your dutifulness, and the troubles you've incurred for it. I have been watching you throughout all your travails, and I too am warmed thereby."

"O Watcher," murmured Periander, tentatively rising onto his knees and stretching out his open palms to him, "tell me what I am to do. So far, everything—"

The Watcher silenced him with a flick of his wrist. "Son of Themistocles, I know all your anxieties and worries. Recent setbacks have kindled doubt in you concerning your plans to invade Atlantis and make war against Critias. Be of good cheer! Know that your plans fulfill the Deity's will."

"They do?" said Periander eagerly. He licked his lips, and his body surged with vigor at the Watcher's words. "So, the Deity will bless my endeavor? All these setbacks will be reversed? I'll be able to kill that monster! Avenge Cornelia! Save my country! All that will happen?" His eyes widened, focusing unblinkingly on the Watcher.

The Watcher blinked slowly. "A war against the tyrant, this the Deity has decreed; and so it shall be. Yet as to how this great conflict will be resolved, and of the fates of its participants, that I do not know."

"But surely the Deity knows all."

"Omniscient my Master is; but I His servant know only what He tells me. He has revealed that Atlantis and her tyrant are to be chastised for their sins; but alas, I am ignorant of the chastisement's magnitude." He gazed deeply at Periander, who had lowered his head when he said this. "Be not crestfallen that you are unaware of the Deity's ultimate will. It is greater than us all and none of us could comprehend it all were it revealed in its plenitude: we must defer to His judgment on what we ought to know and content ourselves therewith. So, rejoice, Periander! Take comfort in that which He has deigned to tell you and know that you are not alone in your fight—a fight not merely against flesh and blood but against the forces of evil and a darkness that seeks to overwhelm your world. By the grace of the Deity, you will wage your desired war against the High King in his Atlantean realm. Though this struggle will be hard, and the outcome known only to my Master, you are not on your own. The Heavens themselves watch over you. Never forget that you've been called to play this part and always comport yourself with this in mind."

Periander opened his mouth to ask one more question; but before he could speak, the Watcher had vanished in a cloud of mist.

Rubbing his eyes as vigorously as one freshly dragged from bed, Periander glanced all around the empty tower deck. Only he and the stars of heaven were present.

Then he put his hand over his mouth and thought of what had just occurred.

Was I dreaming? Or did that really happen?

He looked up at the twinkling stars. Such vastness of space, and he so small by comparison. The stars had watched countless generations of men struggle upon the Earth before his own era and would watch countless more long after he was laid in his grave. His life was but a speck of dust that the cosmic winds would soon sweep away. Nevertheless, gazing at the endless expanse above him, Periander felt a surge of serenity course through his whole being.

CHAPTER TWENTY-ONE

A S PEACEFUL AS THE night was for Periander, it had been just as peaceful earlier that night—thirteen minutes after midnight, to be precise. At that time, most people in Athens had absconded the world of labor and retired to dreamland, and those in the palace (apart from Periander) were no exception. With the exception of the security forces and the nightshift members of the communications hub, whose never-ending labor processed all the kingdom's vital information, the rest of the palace was quiet.

This hallway was murky. When the clocks struck twelve, the lights had automatically dimmed. Total darkness did not descend; one could still discern the octagonal plaster moldings on the ceiling, the contours of the oil paintings hanging on the walls, the tiny tables jutting out from the walls along with the bowls of rose water placed atop them. Yet while the lights emitted white light during the daytime, now they shone pale, sickly green beams which choked everything in their unnatural, dark hue, thereby giving the entire corridor a dismal atmosphere.

Huddled behind the corner, his entire body rocking like a boat full of holes in the midst of a great tsunami, Leonidas breathlessly waited for Gnatho to create his diversion.

Crakkkhhh.

Hearing the sound of breaking glass, Leonidas cautiously peered around the corner. Of the two guards stationed in front of the door leading into his father's suite, one of them began walking down the hallway to investigate the noise while his comrade, now standing with his back to Leonidas, watched him go.

When the first guard had gone the forty or so feet to the end of the hall and vanished around that corner, Leonidas made his move. His leather moccasins, a specialty which Gnatho had given him, noiselessly sprinted across the floor. As swift as a cheetah, Leonidas locked his arms around the unsuspecting guard's throat, feeling the man's bulky Adam's apple in the center of his left palm. Meanwhile, using his right hand, Leonidas stifled the guard's mouth and nose with a cloth sopping wet with chloroform. The guard attempted to free himself, thrashing as much as he could; Leonidas' right shin howled agonizingly when the guard gave it a backkick. The combination of surprise and the chemical agent, however, proved invincible. In only seven seconds, the guard passed out from the chloroform and Leonidas gently guided him as he slumped down onto the floor.

Gnatho appeared just as Leonidas was positioning the guard up against the wall. "The other one is taken care of." Glancing at Leonidas' hands, which were still shaking, he added, "You placed me in charge of this operation, my prince. Do exactly as I say, and nothing will go wrong."

Leonidas merely nodded halfheartedly as Gnatho took out a small, brick-sized object, covered with dials and buttons. It beeped softly.

"What is that?" asked Leonidas.

"It's a jammer. This will jam any security surveillance channels and allow us to enter undetected."

"Won't the disruption be detected?"

"No, for it disguises the waves with reruns of what was previously transmitted. By the time they figure it out, we'll be long gone."

As this was the king's suite, there naturally were many security devices, the first of all being the door itself. Nonetheless, when Gnatho held his device in front of the door's biometric access panel, there arose a faint electrical snapping sound from it. Then the metal door slid open, and he bade Leonidas enter.

They passed quickly through the spacious antechamber, bypassing the various marble statues of men, women, children, and animals who were stationed throughout the room in a grid-like pattern. Leonidas shivered when his eyes met those of a sculpted old man whose face, profoundly wrinkled with eyes bulging out of their sockets, permanently bore a disapproving frown. Had that particular statue been there the last time Leonidas visited his father's room? All the others had been. Yet this one looked new, somehow, and newly-carved too.

Creeping down a short corridor from the antechamber, they came upon Athenagoras' bedchamber. There was no door to this room, only a silvery, shimmering drapery hanging above its entrance. Leonidas took hold of the drapery and brushed it aside. The material felt thick in his hands but was surprisingly lightweight; durable enough to withstand the blast of a laser-pistol, yet extremely glossy and smooth to the touch like undying bubbles. Leonidas' hands reveled in its texture, for they had not handled any material as soft as this in the two years since he laid his mother's funereal shroud over her casket.

The bedchamber was about forty feet wide by sixty feet deep. In the right corner at the end of the room was the entry to the royal closet. Scattered here and there were a few small pieces of furniture: a yellow divan against one wall, a desk adjacent to a waist-high bookshelf on another, and a rectangular granite pedestal on which the royal crown, orb, and scepter were resting. It was the bed, however, that dominated the room.

Gargantuan, with ornately-carved oaken bedposts, the bed stood in the middle of the room. Underneath white sheets, with ruby-red pillows propping up his neck, Athenagoras was asleep on his back, snoring loudly.

"Here," whispered Gnatho. From his sleeve he had pulled out a long, sharp dagger.

"Why a dagger?"

"The frequency from lasers would set off security sensors."

Alright. As agreed, Leonidas would have to do the deed. *Steady,* he told himself, reaching for the blade's handle.

Clank!

Owing to his palm's sweatiness, the handle slipped right through his hand and thudded upon the marble floor. Instinctively, Leonidas froze along with Gnatho beside him.

Guh-unck uuhhh, snored the king.

"At least your father is a heavy sleeper!" hissed an agitated Gnatho.

Leonidas apologized for his clumsiness and carefully picked up the blade. Tiptoeing leftwards, with Gnatho going rightwards, Leonidas came around the backside of the bed. He was breathing even heavier than before; his heart beat faster than ever it had before.

"Come, my prince," said Gnatho when Leonidas merely held the blade in the air without doing anything. "We've come this far. We cannot go back now."

Leonidas could not hear him. All he could do was stare at his father, so tranquil and peaceful in his sleep. The white tip of Athenagoras' beard was blowing towards him whenever he inhaled and scuttled away whenever he exhaled.

"We must act quickly before we are caught!"

"I-I don't, I don't think I can do this." *This is wrong. I should never have agreed.*

Gnatho pressed up against him, his hot rancid breath irritating Leonidas' eyes while his guttural voice clawed at his ears. "You have no choice. You have come too far!"

"How can I possibly commit a crime so impious and unnatural?" Leonidas took a step back, his tendons itching to run, but Gnatho seized his left arm to stop him.

"It's only one life. Remember what's at stake: the survival of Athens! It is better that one man die for the people than the whole nation perish."

Stepping forwards again, Leonidas held the dagger high but still hesitated to strike.

"It is imperative that you continue!" Gnatho's eyes bulged crazily; his oily, fatty jowls clashed with furor. "You must strike!"

Oh, what am I doing?

"DO IT! DO IT NOW!"

Leonidas grabbed his father's chin and slashed his throat. The blade tore through the air as he swiftly moved it to the left side of Athenagoras' throat. It cut deep into the skin. As the blade hacked all the way across the throat, blood gushed out everywhere from his arteries. The white sheets were stained red; the red pillows became even redder in hue. Athenagoras awoke the moment his throat was cut, gargling blood as it surged up into his mouth and thence shot out in every direction; but his son's blow struck true, and he died without even the time to look up and see the pained face of his assassin.

Of the blood that spewed out, some hit Leonidas in his face. Dripping down from just below his eyes, his father's blood made him look as if he were crying tears of blood. In realization of what he had done, Leonidas did produce a couple real tears—two from each eye—which mingled with the blood, a frightening concoction of the double bodily fluids.

Backing four feet away from the sanguine scene, Leonidas let his hands go numb. The blade fell to the ground, so copiously coated in blood that it seemed to act like a cloud of blood as it fell, drenching the floor with its foul rain. Once it hit the floor, a lake formed around the murder weapon; as a saturated sponge pressed down by an anvil oozes all its liquid out, so too did blood flow from the blade. Owing to a slant in the floor, the paternal blood lurched towards the son, the bloody tide washing over Leonidas' boots.

"An excellent job, my prince," said Gnatho as he nimbly picked up the dagger with a handkerchief. "No, pardon me, *Your Majesty.*" He walked over to the entry. "Come, we must go!" When Leonidas did not answer, he called, "Feel no regret: it was your father who pushed you into this."

I can't believe I've done it, thought Leonidas, gazing at his hands. They were soaked from under the tips of his nails to his palms and his wrists. The sleeves of his tunic were likewise bloodied. Slowly his feet began to drag him away; but as he left the room, even as he was turning the corner, Leonidas' head lagged back to see his father once more: dead in a sea of blood, his head half-hacked from off his neck, all his limbs shooting out from reflex albeit still disguised beneath the sheets.

Leonidas passed quickly through his father's apartments, and even quicker pass the antechamber's disapproving old man. Exiting into the hallway, his whole body froze at the sight that greeted him.

"What are you doing?!" he cried, gasping.

Gnatho, holding the same weapon used to slay the king, stood over the guard Leonidas had left propped up against the wall. He who mere moments ago had embarked upon a chemically-induced excursion through dreamland now slumbered in perpetuity, a bedfellow to his king. The guard lay dead, his cut throat still vomiting blood that the carpeting eagerly consumed.

"We can't risk any leak of our involvement," answered Gnatho matter-of-factly, slipping the blade back into its sheath. "Can't be too careful about these things."

Leonidas grabbed him by his upper arms and slammed him against the wall. "You never said anything about killing the guard!"

"Surely you don't think one can kill a king without eliminating some pawns? If the regicide is to appear the work of the enemy, it must also exhibit the ruthlessness that an enemy would inflict."

"But the guard was just doing his job!" protested Leonidas, pulling him slightly forwards and slamming him against the wall again. "He shared no blame with Father and didn't deserve to die!"

The eyes of Gnatho narrowed into mere slits and a sardonic smile crept across his face. "I do not think a man, his hands still dripping with his father's blood, is in any position to be giving lectures on the *sanctity of life*."

Seething and unable even to spat out a curse, Leonidas abandoned his hold on the scoundrel and staggered away. He went down the hallway in the opposite direction from where he had hid only minutes before; he walked briskly, his head down, and turned the corner.

Another one!

Less than ten feet from the corner, stretched out across the floor, was the facedown corpse of the second guard. A gash across his scalp where the blond hair had been scraped off from the blow revealed that some heavy object, presumably Gnatho's jammer, had been the murder weapon.

The acidic taste of vomit rose in Leonidas' mouth. Swallowing everything, he looked away from the cadaver and briskly continued on his way.

The hallway stretched far, and there were no doors on either side of it. At last, he reached the door at the end of the hall. He opened it and, checking to see if there was anyone around before going out, exited the king's wing of the palace.

Leonidas raced through the rest of the palace, vigilant so as not to be seen; his vigilance arose not so much out of fear of being discovered as out of shame of seeing any other living person after this death-begetting night.

It was forty-seven minutes past midnight when Leonidas finally arrived at his room, having completed, in under an hour, an event that would affect his country most profoundly. He slipped inside, slamming the door behind him and, as it were, cementing it tightly shut like one of the mausoleums in the royal cemetery. Panting heavily, he rushed into his bathroom and began washing the blood off his hands, off his wrists, off his clothes. He scrubbed, and he scrubbed, and he scrubbed; frantic to remove from his body every last trace of the regal blood, he removed myriad skin cells, both living and dead. Ceaselessly did he rub his skin until it was bright red and irritated.

Having disposed of all his soiled clothing, Leonidas distractedly took whatever new garments were at hand. He then staggered over to his bed and collapsed upon it, overwhelmed by the night's actions.

172

Chapter Twenty-Two

Periander, still lying on the tower deck, rose to his feet. As he reflected on what he had experienced, he paced from one side of the deck to the other. After a few minutes of contemplation, the woolen robe he was wearing proved itself insufficient to repel the predawn chill and so he turned to go inside.

Yet before he went in, a burst of light suddenly appeared on the northward horizon.

What is that? He moved to one of the binoculars built into the tower's banisters and peered through the lenses, adjusting the scope for the correct distance. *Oh, my. Is that really…*

Off the Saronic Gulf a few miles south of the city, there was a flotilla of landing crafts from which an army was disembarking onto the beach. Hundreds of vessels were either floating in the gulf or had already come ashore and lowered their ramps. Rank after rank of soldiers proceeded down those ramps along with countless tanks and other armored vehicles. One of the tanks that was still aboard its landing craft, evidently due to some mechanical failure, had ignited and engulfed the entire landing craft in a mighty inferno. From the light that those flames provided, Periander discerned the battle-flag of Atlantis proudly hoisted among the troops on the beach.

He raced inside and down the tower's stairwell. "Invasion! Invasion! The city's under attack!" shouted Periander, racing through one dim hallway after another until he had made his way to the communications hub and command center.

"What are you yelling about?" asked a grumpy middle-aged colonel, toddling over to him with a scowl.

When Periander explained what he had seen, the blustering colonel exclaimed, "That's impossible! No army could invade this kingdom without our sensors detecting its approach." He briefly questioned one of the officials monitoring the various computer screens and received instant confirmation that no hostile force had been detected.

"Then your sensors have failed—probably sabotaged!"

"Even if that could happen," said the colonel, folding his arms, "we have patrols around the city; if there were an army disembarking onto our beaches, they'd report it."

"I don't care what you say! An Atlantean army is massing outside Athens. Go look for yourself!"

Turning to a subordinate, the colonel shouted, "Contact the coastal patrol!"

Frantically buttons were pushed and dials turned as several officers attempted to contact the patrol. Static was the sole reply.

"That's odd." The colonel's voice lowered. He questioned when the patrol had last reported and was told it had been two hours.

"Colonel, you must ready the city's defenses!" urged Periander.

The colonel slammed his fist on a desk only inches away from a technician's hands. "Try the video feed!" he fumed, referring to the reconnaissance cameras that all their sentinels had attached to their uniforms. "Override and take control of the patrolmen's video cameras! I want to see what they're seeing."

Quickly the screens lit up with visual footage of what certain still-functioning cameras were recording. Through cracked camera lenses there appeared grainy videos of dead patrolmen, a burning patrol vehicle, and the unmistakable image of Atlantean soldiers gathered on the Attic coast.

The colonel gaped at the horrific imagery. "Great balls of fire! There really is an invasion! Quick—wake the general! Scramble the aerial defense ships! Mobilize the infantry! Prepare for an attack!"

"Colonel," said Periander, grabbing hold of his arm, "this is obviously a well-planned invasion. Because your sensors failed to detect anything, you must assume internal sabotage. It's logical they'd also try to disrupt the city's most crucial defense: its force fields. Without them, Athens would be easy prey to any invader."

"You're right. Make sure the city's force fields are operational!" he hollered to one of his subordinates.

As the officers and technicians leapt from their chairs and frantically rushed to execute their given orders, rushing throughout the room and bumping into one another amid the confusion, Periander left. He had notified the Athenian military, and now he had to see to his own.

His vertebrae vibrated with trepidation. *Even thousands of miles from home, I am being surrounded by Critias' forces.* Defiantly he fisted his hands as the Watcher's words repeated in his mind. *This changes everything. This is the beginning of when I defeat the tyrant. In your hubris, Critias, you thought you could stage a surprise attack on Athens, whose king was least likely to interfere in your affairs. A shrewd decision, indeed! All you've done is vindicate everything I said about you, made yourself the unquestioned aggressor, and set in motion the creation of a grand alliance to destroy you. The time for diplomacy and negotiations is passed: the world is now at war.*

On his way to his apartments, he bumped into Leonidas. His friend was still in his nightclothes and looked utterly exhausted. His eyes sagged, his limbs wobbled unsteadily down the hall, and his face bore a blank expression while his spittle-covered jaw dangled open. Beside him were four high-ranking military and security officers, madly waving papers and electronic devices before his face, and barking over each other an incomprehensible mixture of facts, conjecture, rumor, and hearsay that a groggy Leonidas was visibly straining to understand.

His eyes perked up when he spotted Periander, and dismissing them he rushed over to his friend. "Periander, what is going on? I'm being assailed on all sides by conflicting reports; all I know is that they say you saw armed men somewhere."

"I was on the highest tower and observed an Atlantean army storming the beach south of the city. I notified your high command to ready the city's defenses."

"What? Atlantis? Here? They've actually launched an invasion of Athens?" Leonidas reeled backwards, his forehead and neck perspiring profusely.

"They have. The so-called Italian Crisis was probably just a pretext for Critias to maneuver an invasion force nearby and then use Brundisium and the rest of southern Italy as a launching pad to strike Athens. But thanks to the Deity's providence and these eyes of mine, these forces will not catch Athens totally unawares. There is still time to mount a counterstrike and thrust them out of your land!"

Leonidas started pacing back and forth, nervously rubbing his hands, and acting clearly agitated. "This is precisely what I feared might happen—Critias' rapaciousness leading him to make war upon our people, invading our dominion. That's why I agreed with you that we should carry the war to him before this could happen. Why I worked so hard to persuade Father to accept—Father..." He broke off, slumping backwards against the wall and gripping it with his hands for support; his breathing became slightly erratic, and he appeared even more worn-out than he had before, his body shaking.

The poor man, thought Periander. *He looks so exhausted from this news! Of course, he must fear greatly for his countrymen. This is the gravest danger Athens has faced in his lifetime.* He remembered how hard his friend had labored these past few days to further his cause and to sway Athenagoras. Leonidas could not have gotten much sleep before being awakened to this nightmarish reality, which naturally would explain his shock and fatigue. *I must say something to encourage him at this critical juncture.*

"Fortify your spirit and strengthen your nerves, Leonidas. We shall prevail!" Periander laid his hand on Leonidas' shoulder and steadied him as he ambled away from the wall, seemingly more confident from Periander's heartening words. "Forgive me if this seems crass or insensitive under the circumstances—even in the most bottomless of holes we must seek the feeblest vine to pull ourselves back up—but the fact that Critias has made the first move is advantageous for us. His open act of aggression exposes him for all the world to see; his belligerent intentions are stripped of any pretenses the pacifists might venture. Even your father cannot skirt the obvious any longer. Though his obstinacy held out till now, all the arguments you presented him are proved by others' actions and your goal is achieved. We now stand together as brothers-in-arms: Egypt, Athens, and potentially other states too. United in a grand coalition of kingdoms, we will defeat Critias!"

With that, Periander excused himself and continued onwards to notify his men. Leonidas made no reply to his words; nor did Periander, having turned around to proceed on his way, witness Leonidas collapse onto his knees and feebly grasp the marble floor.

Returning to the section of the palace where he and the others were lodged, they were already assembled in his room's vestibule and greeted him as he entered.

"Periander, what is happening?" asked Psyche, still in her flowing pinkish nightgown, as she rushed over to him.

"The whole palace is in an uproar!" said Jason as he likewise approached him, his auburn hair even spikier than usual.

Periander put an arm around each of them and pulled them close. "An Atlantean army is drawing near to the city."

Psyche gasped while Jason, Socrates, Agathocles and Demosthenes all looked equally startled at the news. Their eyes all focused intently on Periander as he quickly summarized the situation.

"This is outrageous!" exclaimed Agathocles, clutching pockets of air with his fists. The veins in his forehead and skinny neck bulged. "Does Critias just think he can invade anywhere he wants and win? Is this just so he can capture us?"

"Is the city about to be overrun?" said Socrates.

Demosthenes, seated motionless in a chair, his legs crossed, coolly asked, "How large is the enemy army?"

"Enemy army..." muttered Jason, lowering his head and shuffling his foot while he slowly paced the floor.

Periander glanced at his son sympathetically. *It's so regrettable our countrymen and comrades are now forced by a tyrant into being our enemies.* He shook his head and sighed. "Very large. I couldn't discern the full size of the force, but—"

BOOOOOOMMMM! BOOOOOMMM! BOOOOOMM!

The floor struck Periander on his left cheek and bruised that side's clavicle when the blast of deafening force roared overhead. Instinctively, he clasped his ears as the bellowing continued at full strength for about eight seconds. The whole room shook: pictures fell off the walls and the potted plants' containers shattered. Afterwards, although it persisted, the noise was reduced to a bearable level.

Periander jumped to his feet and looked around. Slumping but still in it, Socrates struggled to rise from his chair. Psyche was underneath the red divan, frantically holding Jason close to her. Agathocles, covered with dirt from a potted plant knocked over in the commotion, lay on the floor in the corner; Demosthenes, a few feet away from him, had already risen to his feet.

With Demosthenes at his side, Periander dashed into the main room of his suite where there was a window. Pulling the vermilion silk curtains off so fast that they tore in three places, he scanned the vista.

Of the part of the city visible from that window, two districts in the distance had a bombardment of missiles exploding above them. Reds, oranges, and yellows burst forth in the sky, glowing like deadly fireworks.

Underneath the detonations, however, glimmered the faint amethyst glow of Athenian force fields. No matter how many missiles were lobbed at the city or bombs dropped from airships zipping through the sky, this manmade firmament absorbed all their blows. Not a single one penetrated the city's force field during this minute-long attack.

"The force field held," shouted Periander as soon as the missiles had ceased. He ran back into the other room. "I can see a few small sparks down by the coast; the Athenians' aerial ships must be counterstriking now."

"What do you wish us to do?" said Agathocles, dusting himself off.

Periander turned to him and Demosthenes. "Contact Philip and tell him to relate everything that's happened to Indra. Do the same for Ozymandias. News of Critias' aggression must be publicized immediately so that we can respond in force."

"I'll do that," said Psyche, signaling for attention with her arm. "Father will also want to know I'm alright."

"Okay. Socrates, come with me."

While the others left to perform their given tasks, Periander and Socrates went in the opposite direction, heading for the command center.

"It would seem we have gotten our war after all," said Socrates with a wry chuckle, holding the railing as he gingerly walked down the green-carpeted steps.

"This was not the way I envisioned it starting—I wanted to bring the war to Critias before he brought it to us. But perhaps this is to our advantage. Now Critias bears full responsibility for starting the war whereas I am blameless before all and justified in finishing it."

"That is true..." Reaching the bottom of the stairwell, Socrates mused, "Preëmptive war can prove quite successful in eliminating imminent dangers, if one can only rally the will to do so. Yet there is nothing that enrages the hearts of men to so great a degree as the desire of avenging an unprovoked wrong. Had Athenagoras consented to your proposal, the Athenians might have subsequently demonstrated themselves to be lukewarm allies and eager to surrender at the first setback; but now the whole populace will be consumed with a lust for vengeance that will not be quick to cool off."

"Indra may reconsider, too. He must after seeing war break out among the other great powers." His gait surged with newfound optimism. *Things are going our way—just as the Watcher said they would.*

"Athens is now an example that other states will be loath to emulate."

When they finally reached the communications hub, the room was still chaotic but less so than earlier. The entire staff had assembled, manning all the computer consoles, receiving reports from Athenian forces and relaying instructions to them, keeping in contact with city officials and security personnel on how best to safeguard Athens. A pale Leonidas leaned on a desk in the center of the room, watching the multiple monitors while he was surrounded by several uniformed advisors.

Periander approached him, first looking at his friend and then at the video images of the battle raging outside the city. "How are your forces faring?"

"The enemy have begun a strategic retreat in the direction of Megara," said a gray-haired, stout general with a prosthetic right leg who was standing beside Leonidas. "We are readying battalions to pursue them southwards and are diverting infantry from around the Peloponnese to corral them into Mantinea."

"They're already retreating?"

"After depleting their store of missiles in the attack," replied Leonidas, "the enemy was unable to counteract our retaliation."

Periander's eyebrows rose. "You mean they kept nothing in reserve for your counterstrike?" *Did they really count on seizing the city through their surprise attack?*

"I don't think they foresaw a counterstrike." Leonidas signaled to an officer, about Periander's age and build but with black hair and extremely long fingers. "Captain, repeat what you told us."

"As ordered, we began a manual inspection of all city defenses. We discovered that the force field generators had been severed from their power supply, although in such a way that our systems on this end still showed them to be operational. Thankfully, we were able to get them back online right before the bombardment began, or else—I don't even want to think about it."

"Sabotage!" said the general bluntly, curling his lips. "The enemy infiltrated and disabled our defenses, made it so we couldn't receive advanced warning from our sensors or patrols. When they surgically targeted the palace and our military bases with their missiles, they expected them to be destroyed by their surprise attack. Had they succeeded, nothing could have prevented them from taking the city."

"A risky but ingenious gambit," admitted Socrates. Bowing his head to Periander, he added, "We owe our lives to you, Sire."

"Yes, I'm told you were the one who alerted my staff," said the general, offering a salute to Periander. "And your hunch about sabotage was equally on the mark."

"It was providential that I was where I was," said Periander, downplaying his action as others began to thank him. Changing the subject, he asked Leonidas, "By the way, where is King Athenagoras? I must speak with him."

Leonidas' eyes turned sideways and he merely mumbled, "Uhhh..."

"He didn't answer the intercom. We just dispatched someone to his room," said one officer.

Another one added, "That was several minutes ago. He should have been—"

"Dead! The king's dead!"

Everyone turned around when a young officer burst into the room.

Sniffling, with tears in his eyes, he cried out mournfully, "King Athenagoras is dead! Cut down by an assassin's hand! The enemy has decapitated Athens!"

The room fell silent. While shocked glances were exchanged back and forth, nobody uttered even a whisper to his neighbor; all were overcome by the messenger's news.

What more evils will this day unfold? wondered Periander, shaking his head. Looking at Leonidas who was shivering beside him, he put his arm around his back. "Stand strong, Leonidas, in your adversity. Having lost Cornelia to Critias, I know what you must be feeling. Your loss is immeasurable, but your people need you."

"Lord Periander is correct," said the general. "We must lament our fallen king in the bright evening of victory; but in this dark morning of invasion, we must rally behind our new sovereign as we expel the enemy from our land. You are now our king, Sire." He knelt down on his good knee and shouted, "Long live King Leonidas!"

All the Athenians in the room likewise fell to their knees. "Long live the king! Long live the king!"

Leonidas looked flustered amid the acclamation, his face blushing and twitching as he bit his lip.

"Periander."

Periander turned around to see who was whispering.

"Periander," murmured Psyche, drawing him away from the throng. "What's happened?"

"King Athenagoras has been assassinated."

"The Deity preserve us!" she gasped, clasping her hand over her mouth. "How?"

"The enemy appears to have infiltrated the city, tried to disable its defenses. They must have killed Athenagoras to destabilize the government in case their first plan failed." He paused, frowning at what had happened, before asking, "Did you contact Ozymandias?"

Psyche's shocked expression metamorphosed into a proud smile. "Yes! Father says Egypt will fight with Athens and you, and he is mobilizing the Egyptian army at once. And Philip reports that King Indra has also agreed to join the alliance."

"That is excellent news!" Periander hugged Psyche tightly and kissed her sweet lips. *Oh, how great are the vicissitudes of life! Yesterday our outlook was so bleak; today a grand alliance against Critias is born!* The pebbly shores, the verdant meadows, the fertile orchards of Atlantis and cheerful shouts of his subjects—all would soon be welcoming him home. "Still..." His multicolored eyes glanced around at the sullen Athenians and orphaned Leonidas. "It is dreadful that this is how it had to happen."

***

"I CAN'T BELIEVE I listened to you!" yelled Leonidas, slamming the door shut behind him.

It was past noon; and with the Atlantean army now pushed back thirty miles from Athens down into the Peloponnese, any immediate threat to the city had been defused. Finally able to escape the deluge of advisers, counselors, courtiers, and officials who had been smothering him since he was acclaimed king, Leonidas had tracked down Gnatho to his room.

Backing away from him and holding his hands up in a conciliatory gesture so as to mollify Leonidas' rage, Gnatho meekly said, "Now, now, Sire. I—"

"I killed my father because of you!" Churning inwardly with wrath, Leonidas wanted to bellow Gnatho to deafness. He nevertheless hushed his voice lest anyone overhear the scandalous words.

Gnatho moved farther back and stood behind a wooden armchair. "Majesty, I sought only to help you!"

"By having me murder my father?" Leonidas threw the chair aside with one hand as though it were nothing and grabbed Gnatho by his scrawny shoulders. Panting, his eyes wide, he silently shouted, "You... you!"

"King Leonidas," groaned Gnatho, wiggling in an attempt to free himself from the bone-crunching clutch. His oily face became sweaty and twitchy, and he nervously eyed Leonidas. "You agreed your father would never consent to starting a war with Atlantis; his death was the only way that—"

"I'm sure an attack on our capital would have swayed him!"

"I am not blessed with a prophetic tongue, nor could I have foreseen the actions of Atlantis."

Leonidas relaxed his grip. He clenched his eyes shut. Then, speaking mostly to himself, he mumbled, "Had I only waited a few hours..."

"I am sorry, Sire."

"You? Sorry?" He squeezed the parasite tighter. "I should kill you for this!"

Regaining his composure, Gnatho coolly asked, "And will another murder assuage your guilty conscience?"

"Maggot!" hissed Leonidas, releasing his grip and letting Gnatho fall upon the cherry hardwood floor. He turned around to go, passing a table on which was a glass lamp and various other breakables. As he went, he ran his arm down the length of it and swept all the table's items onto the floor; the sound of breaking glass reverberated off the high stucco ceilings.

Using the fallen chair for support, Gnatho rose to his feet. "Sire, wait." Leonidas paused but did not turn around. "My King, please do not leave angry with me. I shall still serve you faithfully now that you are king."

Leonidas' eyes whipped around to glare. "King because I listened to you!"

"And as king"—Gnatho's eyes flashed, and his sweaty palms rubbed one another—"you will have full control of the war effort. Athens and Periander could find no better man than—"

"Gaarrhhh!" exclaimed Leonidas. He flung the door open. *Vile syco-phancy!*

CHAPTER TWENTY-THREE

UPON THE ATLANTEAN INVASION of the Athenian realm and the failed attempt to take the capital through a surprise attack, a colossal war broke out among the nations of the world.

Leonidas, newly ascended to the throne of the Athenians, promptly entered into an alliance with Periander, pledging all the resources of his kingdom to the war effort. Envoys specially dispatched by Ozymandias of Egypt and by Indra of Mohenjo-Daro, as well as representatives sent from Cyrene and a hodgepodge of minor states, likewise committed their states to Periander's cause by signing the *Treaty for the Reconstitution of the Atlantic World*. Therein the members of the coalition articulated the goals of the war: the unconditional surrender of Atlantis, the dethronement of Critias, and the conferral on Periander, as next in line to the succession, of the High Kingship. (A framework, moreover, was established for future negotiations regarding the disposal of the Atlantean colonies acquired under Eudoxia and Critias.)

The initial theater of war centered on Athens. After Periander foiled their scheme of disabling the city's defenses and capturing it by a surprise attack, the Atlantean army proved unable to cope with this contingency. Having counted entirely on the success of its plan, the Atlantean high command had sent an expeditionary force that was too small to sustain combat by itself deep within hostile territory. As a result, the Athenians drove the invaders southwards, trapping them in the Peloponnese and then annihilating them at the Battle of Mantinea.

Meanwhile the rest of the coalition were mobilizing their own forces for war. Pharaoh Ozymandias marshaled all the armies of Egypt, both the regular as well as the reserve and auxiliary soldiers. Totaling upwards of some three million men, the Egyptian infantry assembled in the Nile Delta after a four-week mobilization.

Far less time elapsed before Mohenjo-Daro's famous fleets of airships took to the skies. Indra allocated two-thirds of his air force to the Atlantic-European front while the remaining third he committed to combating Atlantean forces scattered around the globe, primarily their colonies in the Americas. The objective was to bog down Atlantean forces stationed elsewhere and prevent them from returning to defend Atlantis itself; and with a sizeable number of armies still deployed in America after the recent rebellion, their absence meant a much smaller number of troops were at home to fend off invasion.

In the earliest days of the war, Indian airships patrolled the Mediterranean to provide cover for the marshalling of Allied forces. Aerial battles of enormous size, greater than had ever been fought, consumed the skies above the sea, particularly off the coasts of Britain and Italy on account of the Atlantean presence there. Critias' pilots engaged Indra's in skirmishes night and day; with force fields pierced by lasers and hulls blown open by missiles, innumerable airships fell to the water and drowned beneath the waves. Despite each side suffering losses at roughly equal rates, Indra's airfleet far outnumbered Critias' and this disparity gradually led to the Atlanteans being pushed back beyond the skies of Europe.

By that point, twenty-six days after the assault on Athens, the Athenian invasion contingent was equipped aboard their underwater armada. Over one thousand submarines, each leviathan over two thousand feet long and two hundred feet wide, with the capacity to transport a thousand troops each, were launched from Aegean docks. Speedily they sailed to Egypt where, by the twenty-ninth day of the war, the Egyptian armies assigned for the initial invasion had finished embarking them.

This grand armada, under the protection of Allied aerial forces, then set sail for Atlantis.

Owing to the recurring attempts made by the Atlanteans to foil the impending invasion, the Allied armada frequently had to halt as aerial battles were waged overhead; Atlantean submarines also sought out and engaged them in subaquatic battles. Yet the Athenian submarines surpassed those of Atlantis both in quality and quantity, destroying the enemy's boats without losing more than thirty-nine of their own.

On the morning of the ninth day from their departure from Egypt and the thirty-eighth from commencement of hostilities, the Allied armada reached the southeastern coast of Atlantis. Here it had been agreed the invasion should commence because the southeastern sector was Periander's patrimony, inhabited by his subkingdom's subjects whom he expected to welcome his arrival. Nonetheless, only half of their forces would land here: the other half would simultaneously stage a second invasion on the opposite side of the continent. The goal of the two divisions was to begin occupying land between them and progressively work their way inland; eventually both invasion forces would converge outside the capital after having split the continent in half. In the meantime, the multiple points of invasion would prevent the Atlanteans from being able to concentrate what forces they had on the continent.

***

"**W**E'RE ALMOST THERE—PREPARE TO land!" shouted Periander. He gritted his teeth as an ocean swell swept over his face; the sharp taste of salt hit his mouth, irritating a canker sore on his lower right lip, while the pungent brine stormed his nostrils. He coughed out the belligerent water.

The forty men in his amphibious landing craft roared their responses to their commander. Their voices, however, were drowned out by the din of the battle.

At dawn Periander had given the order to begin the invasion. The submarines under his command had then ascended to the surface about a half mile off the southeastern shores of Atlantis; doors in their rears opened and out of them came landing crafts loaded with soldiers.

As they made their way across the choppy waters towards land, Critias' aerial warships and fighter-aircraft blared through the overcast sky. The larger ones, laden with bombs, sought to destroy the submarines before they could unload their men, leaving it to the smaller aircraft to use their lasers to blast the transporters already afloat out of the water. But they were foiled by Indra's sky fleet, which provided a safeguard for the invaders by intercepting the Atlanteans. In every direction red laser beams flashed like lightning; the sound of aircraft exploding in midair, their heated metal plopping into the water and setting it aboil, was deafening. Although there was no wind this morning, the swarms of aircraft buzzing through the sky stirred up great gusts for the men below.

Periander braced himself and held onto the side of his craft. Only thirty yards away an aerial fighter—spiraling too fast to see whose it was—crashed in flames on a troop transporter. Shrieks erupted that straight away fell silent. The surrounding water was dyed red. The reverberating waves caused by the crash washed over his vehicle.

Moments later, as they came within fifty feet of the shore, Periander thought, *It's time.* "Drop the ramp and go! Go!"

The engine stopped, the ramp lowered, and Periander began to lead his soldiers ashore. Like him, they all wore full-body armor, painted dark green with camouflage patterns. When all had disembarked, Periander slipped on his helmet that he had been holding. Immediately much of his peripheral vision was blocked, the polarized visor reducing his line of sight only to what was straight ahead of him; to compensate for this visual limitation, heads-up displays built into the helmet on either side of his eyes provided him with motion sensor alerts, weapons targeting assistance, and various other pieces of data useful for the battlefield.

The water came up to his waist as he waded forwards. A wave hit him, and an avalanche of drops dripped down his visor. Maintaining his balance, he wiped the frothy water off his helmet. A severed arm, bloody and with large hunks of skin flopping off it like the ears of a bloodhound, bobbed in front of his chest. Periander, grimacing, hurled the limb as far away from him as he could.

When he reached the shore, he looked around. The beach stretched about a hundred yards inland, a rolling flat plain without any obvious place where one could hunker down. Bands of Allied soldiers thronged the beach to secure their advance. Their comrades' lifeless and limbless bodies were sunk into the sand while their body parts, scattered here and there, intermixed with Atlantean corpses—a testimony of the price paid to take the beach.

Agathocles, whom Periander had appointed grand general and his second-in-command, ran up to him. "Sire, we've pushed the enemy—approximately twenty thousand infantrymen—back and secured the beachhead. They've retreated through that gap but we're unable to pursue because their redoubt's canonry is killing any of our men who get near it." He pointed to the end of the beach.

There the land sloped upwards, and the sand gave way to rocky ridges that rose fifty feet high. A wide gap occurred at one point and a gradual inclined path led through it from the beach to higher ground. Perched atop the ridge were three mammoth canons on the right of the path.

The cannons were at the cliff's edge, one in the center and the others stationed at ninety-degree angles from the first. Manned by a dozen gunners, their sides painted bright white with thin purple stripes wrapping around them at certain points, they loudly bombarded the beach with green laser beams—their power great enough to hurl, thirty feet into the air, four corpsified soldiers at a time.

"Contact our aerial forces and have them bomb it."

"We tried that," said Agathocles, "but they say they can't spare any aircraft—the aerial fighting is too heavy for a bombing raid."

Periander bent his neck to one side. "Not even one?"

"No."

Great. Biting his lip, Periander surveyed the enemy's redoubt. *That'll be hard to take...* Across the large gap between the cliffs, however, there were no Atlantean soldiers. He pointed that out to Agathocles. "Can we get up on that side and take the cannons out from there?"

"That's almost five hundred yards away. Our hand weapons can't fire that far."

"No, but this can!" Reaching to his back and removing it from the leather cross-body strap he was wearing, Periander brandished the Astrapë whose orichalcum sides gleamed even in the absence of a clear sky. "I've practiced with it: it'll be able to hit the target."

"Too dangerous, Sire," said Agathocles, waving his hands in objection. "Let me send others to—"

A particularly loud blast blared in the distance. Several Allied soldiers, their bodies disintegrating, soared skywards.

Unflinchingly Periander declared, "I am fighting to retake my country from a tyrant, and by fighting, I mean fighting! I will not hide behind the frontline and watch my subordinates die when I have it in my power to save them!"

Agathocles bowed his head.

Then Periander led his platoon through a cadaver-ridden section of the beach where fighting had ceased. Coming to the cliff opposite the cannons, his soldiers deployed grappling hooks and within minutes they were atop the ridge.

Crawling through the dust and wilting beachgrass to the edge, Periander took out his electronic binoculars and clicked them into the sockets for them on his helmet. They automatically zoomed in on the enemy redoubt; a few sentinels, the cannons themselves, and behind consoles the gunners aiming the firing mechanism instantly flashed before Periander.

He rested his left elbow on the ground to support the Astrapë, gripping it with his left hand. With his right index finger, he pressed and held the trigger.

Several blue laser beams were emitted from the Astrapë's bow. A prism made out of a rare elemental crystal, located at the center of the bowstring, fused the disparate beams into a single laser-arrow in front of the bow. The concentrated laser was first the size of a marble, and a second later that of a walnut, then a coconut, and after that a squash. Periander released the trigger, and, with a great whooshing sound, the laser-arrow darted through the air, clearing the gap between him and the redoubt in a second.

When it hit the left-facing cannon, a minor scraping sound erupted as the laser-arrow penetrated the metal casing of the cannon's laser generator. There instantly followed a flash of light as the cannon's inner workings were disrupted by the arrow; and with a loud bang the cannon exploded from the inside out. A whirlwind of heat and shrapnel radiated outwards as the cannon became entirely engulfed in flames, burning its gunners to death.

The other cannons' gunners were thrown into confusion by the explosion yet scarcely survived long enough to comprehend what had happened. For as soon as the first cannon was destroyed, Periander let loose another arrow, and then another, achieving the like effect. The billowing clouds of smoke, reeking of metal, plastic, and charred flesh, testified to the destructive power of the Astrapë and to Periander's skill in wielding it.

Excellent, thought Periander, glancing at the Astrapë and then at the enemy redoubt. *Many kings have wielded you in battles, but your potency in war has yet to be surpassed.* Removing his binoculars, he pressed the intercom button on the side of his helmet. "Agathocles, the cannons are destroyed. Begin pursuit of the enemy."

***

W ITH THE PASS CLEARED, the Allied soldiers pursued and over-came the fleeing foe. Greatly outnumbered after additional waves of invaders landed, the Atlanteans fought to the end; but at last, they were slaughtered to the man by Allied soldiers eager to avenge their fallen comrades. The aerial battle raging overhead likewise turned in the Allies' favor: Indra's sky-ships not only prevented Critias' from supporting the Atlantean army but progressively forced them away from the battle below. By noontime, with the last line of Atlantean soldiers being cut down by gunfire as the Allies established their foothold on the beach, the enemy's aircraft had all retreated.

Periander stood on the beach, his helmet in his hand. The tide, which had been choppy amid the amphibious assault, now gently lapped at his bloodied, sand-covered boots. The tops of submarines no longer surfaced from the sea like a herd of hippopotami; instead, having completed their initial task of transporting the Allied army, they had submerged with the intention of enforcing an underwater blockade of the continent.

O Atlantis, how I've longed for you! Periander inhaled the salty sea air, whose sharp tang elicited a lone teardrop from his blue eye. *The tyrant failed to kill me when he tried. He may have separated us for a season but at last... I am home. Soon, I will rid your shores of Critias and his tyranny. Then, the Deity-willing, we'll finally be able to secure a lasting peace...*

Reaching down, he scooped up a handful of sand intermixed with shell fragments and crumpled bits of seaweed. The grains trickled down from his gloved hand, leaving only the dead seaweed and broken shells clinging to him.

"Commander." A voice and feet kicking up plumes of sand as they ran interrupted Periander's contemplation. Tall, muscular, and possessed of an elongated face on a head that was completely shaved, an Egyptian brigadier was speaking. "We've exchanged information with the north-western landing forces, and I can report that they have successfully oc-cupied their foothold and are proceeding inland according to plan."

Periander brushed the debris off his hand, grinning as he said, "And so will we!"

Chapter Twenty-Four

The bodies of seven men convulsed terribly. Reflexively their hands dug at their throats, desperately trying to free their windpipes from the burning, choking ropes. Their feet, swinging a foot off the floor, thrashed wildly as they danced the hangman's waltz. Within a minute the last of these dancers expired. Lined up side-by-side, the seven blue-faced men swayed gently from the makeshift scaffold, looking peaceful apart from eyes which popped from their sockets and tongues which protruded from engorged faces.

Only several feet away, in the center of one of the imperial palace's audience halls, stood a panting Critias. His face was twisted in rage, the veins on his ivory neck and even his cheeks visible, and his tattooed fists choked the air. Glowering at these officers, these incompetents who had commanded the assault on Athens, he gave the cadaver on the far end of the scaffold a kick so violent that it struck the one next to it, which in turn struck the next one, and so on—the bodies behaving like the balls of a Newton's cradle.

"I was promised *victory*! TOTAL victory!" ranted Critias. He paced around the room, stomping on the central floor mosaic of a giant map of the Earth. "Too good an opportunity to pass up! Knock Athens out in a single blow! Kill Periander and conquer the whole Balkans to boot! And what have I got to show for this, this... oh-so clever stratagem devised by my generals, supported by my courtiers? WELL?!"

His eyes flashed frantically around the room as he glared at them all. The sheepish officers and courtiers, faces low, all hovered quietly around the edges of the room. None dared look up to meet his gaze.

"My kingdom is invaded on two fronts and my generals can't repulse the scum!" Critias lurched over to a golden throne and slunk down in it, his arms hanging limply down from the armrests. "What are you doing about it?"

There was silence. Everyone's eyes darted to his neighbor. Finally, one general, prodded on by his colleagues, nervously inched forwards. As he approached Critias, his facial sweat formed a moustache above his shivering lip. "Ma-ma-majesty, w-we are pulling back and regathering our forces behind the, uh, en-enemy's advances from their beachheads."

"WHY?" growled Critias. "Why not halt their advances to begin with? Why cede even one acre of my domain?"

"W-we-we dispersed our forces throughout the continent because we didn't know where the invasion would occur. The enemy's forces already number hundreds of thousands at both landing points and additional personnel are still arriving."

"Why are they still able to land their soldiers on my shores? Why haven't you stopped them?"

"Unfortunately, my Lord, the combined forces of the Athenian navy and Indian airfleets and their adept coördination has proven too much for our forces to handle. Against either power alone, Atlantis is unmatched; but together, those two kingdoms are limiting our ability to project power along our coasts. Consequently, our ground forces have borne the brunt of confronting the invaders. And since our legions were not united at the invasion points, the ones that happened to be in those vicinities were in no position to halt the enemy, although they did put up a good fight. Based on the two invasion spots chosen by the enemy and their subsequent advances, they appear intent on converging on the capital."

Another general, holding a handheld hologram projector, approached and a three-dimensional map of Atlantis appeared. "If they succeed and surround the capital while maintaining their occupations, they will have divided the continent in two, thereby cutting off our forces in either half from one another unless we can break through the enemy's lines. This result would be terrible: it would give the enemy a central launching pad to push back our divided forces even further. We cannot allow that to happen! It is imperative we defend this city and the surrounding regions."

"If we concentrate our armies here," said the first general, "they'll be large enough to withstand the Allied armies' advances."

Critias nodded. "Very well. Have our armies regroup; defend the capital at all costs." Eyeing the hanged men, he added, "Make sure you don't fail me."

"There is also the matter of conscription," said Thrax, from the right side of Critias' throne. He spoke without derision notwithstanding that his protruding jaw, bearing its yellow cavity-filled teeth, played the part of a snarl. "We need more men."

Critias rolled his black eyes. "Aren't my armies already the largest in the world?"

"Yes. But many of them are stationed in our colonies. Others that would normally be at home were diverted to the Americas during the revolt."

"Then recall them."

"It is a delicate situation, my Lord. Even if we were able to remove them from the colonies, we'd face the prospect of a new rebellion erupting. Or else Mohenjo-Daro might scoop them up without a fight."

After I showed Teotihuacan what befalls rebels, they wouldn't dare revolt, thought Critias, flexing his fingers. *Then again, Indra would love to steal my colonies. Must I really choose between my overseas empire and my metropolitan domain? That's unacceptable.* "Surely a garrison force left behind could safeguard the colonies? I know how vast my armies in

America were; many of them could be recalled without detriment to my overseas empire."

"We've made initial attempts to do just that," continued Thrax, "but for the same reasons we cannot prevent the enemy from landing more troops, we are struggling to bring our overseas force home. While our armies far outnumber theirs, our naval and aerial forces do not. The Athenians have imposed a naval blockade, which is further aided by Mohenjo-Daro's aerial fleets, and their joint effort is isolating us from our colonies. So far, it's proven difficult to break the blockade."

Critias growled. He clenched the throne's armrests with his fists; the sinews of his arms visibly bulged, the muscles stirring as though a pack of mice were running below his skin. "Are my existing forces here unable to defend this continent?" he hissed.

"Not at all, my Lord," said Thrax supportively while the rest of the room hastily voiced their concurrence.

You all vouch for success, thought Critias, surveying the room with a grimace. *But where are my Athenian provinces and spoils?*

Thrax resumed. "The home armies should be equal to the enemy's in size and undoubtedly will be able to drag them to a standstill. But in order to destroy them and win the war, our top military strategists say we need to augment our ranks domestically."

"Aren't my subjects rallying to my kingdom's defense?"

"They are, though voluntary enlistment is lagging what is necessary. For that reason, it is suggested that conscription should be imposed."

Critias rose and strode over to one of the colossal windows on the north-facing wall. His hands clasped behind his back, he leaned forwards to peer out. In the northern courtyard were crowds of his subjects, clustered together like vines copious with grapes. Whether on handmade posters still wet with paint, or in the lyrics sung by musicians gathered here and there, or in the sheer magnitude of the people congregating to express their support, patriotic slogans were seen and heard everywhere.

The chant "Long live King Critias! Death to the traitor Periander!" was deafening.

Critias chuckled when a larger-than-life effigy of Periander, intricately detailed all the way down to the multicolored eyes, was lit ablaze by the crowd.

The inhabitants of the capital were entirely loyal to their High King.

"I will not impose conscription," said Critias, still peering out the window with his back to his officers and courtiers. "The unpopularity of the act would demoralize my subjects and dampen their support for me; it would also give the appearance that I'm desperate. No," he said, turning around, "offer bonuses for enlistment. Be as aggressive in your recruiting as possible. Empty the prisons, even, and utilize that pool of manpower. But unless the capital itself is about to fall, there shall be no conscription. For I am High King in this land and beloved by my numerous subjects far more than the traitor could ever dream of being; I don't need to stoop to the desperate tactics of weak kings and depopulated kingdoms."

With that sweeping diktat, the matter of conscription was settled. Several more subjects were dealt with, and then Critias dismissed everyone except Thrax from the room. All left quickly through the bifold doors, opposite the throne, which then shut. The single gold-plated door on the southern wall of the room, however, opened and through it entered Dr. Anaxagoras.

"Your Majesty," he said, bowing excessively.

Critias acknowledged his arrival with a lingering blink of his eyes. "There's only one thing I wish to know from you, scientist. How long until Project Heliocalypse is ready?"

In Anaxagoras' right hand was a laptop computer. Reading from the screen, he said, "According to our astronomic observations, an asteroid possessing a mass sufficient for utilization in Heliocalypse will approach the Earth's orbit in three months, eleven days, five hours, forty-two minutes. We have dubbed it Phaëton."

"And you will be ready to weaponize it then?" asked Thrax, walking up behind the scientist over whom he towered menacingly.

"Absolutely!" Grinning, Anaxagoras pushed the small lenses of his eyeglasses closer to his pale face with his index finger. "We took the precaution of secretly launching the satellite before the... intrusion of unwanted guests upon our shores."

Critias snorted at the euphemism.

"As soon as the asteroid arrives," continued Anaxagoras, ignoring Critias' rebuff, "it will be immediately captured by the satellite and able to be used for offensive purposes."

Critias leaned forwards on his throne. "And do you expect Project Heliocalypse to prove as advantageous to me as you have promoted it in the past?"

"Master, the power of the asteroids, once harnessed, will give you a decisive advantage! Phaëton, moreover, is but the first of a group of asteroids—all useable!—that are nearing Earth. Five days later, three days after that, nine, two, four. You will have so many asteroids under your command, you'll be able to obliterate the capital city in every Allied land!"

"All of them?" Critias licked his pale lips which unrolled into a smirk.

Anaxagoras nodded. "And then some! In anticipation of this moment, we are readying additional satellites. These super weapons, high up in the exosphere, will be out of reach of even Indra's sky-ships: no hostile hand will be able to touch them. The Allies will find themselves defenseless against our coming cosmic onslaught. They'll have no choice but to surrender or die."

Rubbing his chafed, scaly-skinned hands together, Critias remarked, "So I have a secret weapon that will overawe the world." He glanced towards the window, his eyes narrowing and his ivory nose crinkling with pleasure. "Let Periander struggle for a while. If he and his still live in three months, then they'll learn what a calamity longevity can be...."

CHAPTER TWENTY-FIVE

D EVASTATION. COMPLETE AND UTTER devastation. That alone is how one could describe the scene Periander witnessed on this third morning after the invasion, when he beheld the remnants of his palace.

With Critias' forces hastily retreating before his army, in only three days' time Periander had advanced sixty miles inland and, in a generally bloodless manner, had occupied over half his subkingdom and begun reïmposing his authority over all that he reclaimed. Included within this territory was the city of Eumeleia, the subkingdom's administrative seat, on whose outskirts his palace had once stood.

Upon his arrival this morning, Periander sullenly surveyed the ruins of his former home, the abode of his father, his father's father, and countless forefathers before them. Generations of the House of Eumelus had dwelled within its mosaic-lined halls, heard lyres and fifes inside its conservatory noted for its stained-glass dome, slept peacefully in ermine-fringed beds, dined outdoors under its marble-columned porticoes, strolled through manicured gardens adorned with orange trees and water fountains...

The memories of his boyhood, his adolescence, his adulthood—gone.

All the trees and gardens had been overturned, reduced to an endless expanse of mud disturbed only by the occasional brick remnant. The building itself lay ruined. Blackened by soot and charred by the arsonists' hateful flames, most of the ground level external walls still stood defiantly; the interior walls, mere dusty jagged fragments scattered all the way through, had collapsed along with the roof.

Periander staggered through the destruction. The residue of ash assaulted the white tunic he was wearing. The acrid stench of smoke yet lingering in the air caused his eyes to water. Popping up amid the ruins were various vestiges: rusted doorknobs; cracked piano keys where the conservatory once stood; and bones, their flesh now nibbled away by rats, which once were ensconced in tender meats hanging in the kitchen's meat locker.

In what must have been a storage room, his eyes lit upon something that they had not seen in years, something that moved him more than anything else he beheld that day. Although only its curved back survived half-broken, sticking out from a pile of rubble, the white paint thereon chipped and spattered with green mold, he recognized the item instantly. This had been the crib that held Jason as an infant. Both Periander and Cornelia had so often stood beside it, admiring their newly-born child, all those years ago.

Many such memories had permeated Periander's mind when he visited his former home, and also afterwards. But right now, about to enter Eumeleia as part of his triumphant return, he rested a fist uncomfortably on his chest and forced those sad memories aside.

Periander stood atop the long black hovercar as his procession went down the city's main street. His soldiers lined the boulevard, wearing their camouflaged battle armor, and behind them were the townsfolk crowding around to glimpse their king.

Many clapped when Periander drove past and saluted him when he waved to them. Yet although hundreds congregated in the street, the city's size betrayed the fact that thousands did not. The tenor of the crowds present, moreover, was on the whole subdued. Enthusiastic supporters, cheering and gesturing applause, were outnumbered by those who only clapped halfheartedly or not at all—their minds compelling them to attend to show their loyalty but whose hearts would not let their eyes gaze up from the ground.

"The people seem less enthused at our homecoming than what we were expecting," Periander remarked dryly through gritted teeth, still smiling as he waved to the crowd.

From beside him Agathocles, an enormous smile gliding on his oval face and blue eyes beaming with unadulterated confidence, said, "I'm sure it's only shock from the war and fear for the future that keeps your subjects from erupting in pure joy. They undoubtedly welcome your return and look forwards to the day when you restore peace to our country."

For emphasis, Agathocles jumped down from the moving car, crossed the line of soldiers, and waded into the crowd of civilians. Grabbing a hand from two men and raising them in the air with a shout, eliciting laughter from a group of women by dancing a little jig, and wrestling a reluctant well-dressed gentleman over by the scruff, he steadily whipped the crowd up. In response to Agathocles' eagerness, the people around him began to chant loudly along with his booming voice.

Periander shook his head at the spectacle but could not suppress a chuckle. *With you at my side, Agathocles, I'll never be in want of fervor and support.* His comrade certainly appeared jovial, a great grin engulfing him. *Then again, why shouldn't he rejoice?*

While Periander had been surveying the remains of his palace, Agathocles had enjoyed a reünion with his family. Since his flight from Atlantis, his wife and three children had been forced into hiding lest Critias' forces punish them because of Agathocles' loyalty to Periander; but upon hearing that the Allied army would be arriving in Eumeleia, they returned to the city to await the beloved head of their household.

At last, the car approached the city center where the building, which housed the magistrates' offices, loomed over the street; its marble columns glowed beneath the sun. The street outside the building divided in two around a grassy strip of land opposite it. Periander exited from the hovercar, flanked by several advisers (apart from Agathocles, who was still somewhere in the crowd), and entered the building—a temporary headquarters from where he could direct the war effort.

Walking down a crowded desk-lined hallway, military uniforms ubiquitous, Periander handed several papers to one officer following him. "Get these orders to General Necho. Tell General Psammetichus that he must take Aspalax at once and secure a passageway for the Fifth Legion. Also, direct Cleombrotus to..." His voice broke off when he glanced down the hallway. "I'll get back to you in a few minutes."

Scurrying down the forty feet of hall that separated them from him, Periander asked, "When did you arrive?"

"In the last ten minutes," replied Psyche, her cerulean eyes glittering through batting eyelashes as she embraced Periander. "We left the submarine three hours ago and just arrived in Eumeleia."

He pulled her close, fondled her soft red hair, and kissed her supple lips which tasted of rosebuds. Next to her stood Jason, who wore military-style boots, khaki trousers, and a dark green tunic with a blue sash across his chest; standing tall at five foot ten, a resolute look upon his face, he resembled an immaculate officer apart from his spiky auburn hair. Periander leaned over and patted his son on the shoulder. "Why didn't you tell me before coming ashore?"

"We wanted to surprise you," said Jason with a smile.

Before Periander could respond, Psyche quickly added, "The route from shore is safely in Allied hands, so we were told it would be safe to travel here."

"Well, I might've waited a bit longer before sending for you. But now that you're both here, I am thrilled to see you. I saw something today, a very distasteful sight... but seeing you has cheered up my soul."

Psyche hugged him from his side, her blushing cheeks embracing the hairs of his beard. "We couldn't stay away when we can help you most by being at your side."

"Yeah, and you can't fight this war all by yourself," said Jason, excitedly grasping two pockets of air with his hands. "I am ready to fight, to avenge Mother and our House!"

"Fight?"

Jason nodded rapidly. "Yes, with you!"

"No, no," said Periander, patting Jason's shoulders while trying to banish those memories from his own mind. "There's no need for you to join the battlefield when there are plenty of—"

"No!" Jason brushed off his father's hand, eliciting a muffled gasp from Psyche. His green eyes determinedly met his father's. "For too long I could only watch one disaster, one setback befall us one after another: Mother's death, exile, Cyrene, the uncertain negotiations and outright rejections. Over and over, it did not seem as though things would ever come our way. But then they did. Now, with allies at our side, we are embroiled in the final stage of our journey: we're waging a great war to destroy Critias and avenge all who've been hurt by him. With victory actually possible, I'm not going to remain on the sidelines and just watch as the most crucial struggle in my lifetime plays out before me." His breathing quickened. "No, I want to play an active part now, to take some control, no matter how small, in this matter that's upended and overshadowed my life. Father, I want to fight alongside you!"

Several moments passed. At last, Periander, biting his lip, said, "Alright. I suppose I can find some position for you in the Allied army."

"Thank you, Father!" Jason hugged him before dashing off, a great smile enveloping his chin.

While eyeing his departing son, he was asked by Psyche, cocking her neck to one side as her eyebrows rose, "Do you really intend to let him go to war? He's your only son; and after everything you've told me, I'm surprised you would so readily agree to his request."

"I know, I know." To Periander's mind sprinted images of Jason in Thrallis's dungeon: the dark, dingy, straw-laden room; the bloodied cuts and bruises on his son's body; and, above all, the sweat-inducing dread that had seized him when his son was caught, the ignorance of whether he lived or not, or if he would be lost to him forever as was his mother. "I assure you I won't be sending him out into the thick of battle. But you saw his resolution."

"Must you really mollify such a sudden zeal?"

He stroked his beard. "I can't say I was not expecting it. He turned seventeen last month. War rouses the strongest passions in young men's breasts; like a magnet, it draws them from home and parents. When I was his age, I too was eager to prove my mettle; and if there had been a war then, I would have gone off to fight it no matter what. Yet unlike my younger self, Jason lost both home and mother to the enemy. He's endured much pain, witnessed far too much for his age. There is a trauma that can only be healed by inflicting retaliatory wounds. I can't squelch this yearning of his. No, but I can channel it. I'll keep Jason by my side, somewhere behind the line of fire where I can keep an eye on him."

That evening, as the shadows caused by the sun's dying rays joined the Allied soldiers in patrolling the streets of Eumeleia, Periander visited the city's temple, being accompanied by several guards for protection. Like most temples it had marble columns running along its outside to support the roof. Periander carried a cornucopia of fruits while another held the chalice and wine: thank-offerings for the Deity.

Outside the temple's edifice, with Periander already halfway up the steps, the voice of Socrates called out, "Sire, please wait a moment," as the old man ambled up the steps beside him. "Before you enter the temple, I must warn you that it is still in the blasphemous state we found it in."

"Whatever do you mean?" asked Periander, his intonation rising in perplexity. *What sort of profanation has Critias committed?*

Socrates had arrived yesterday with an Allied division when it bloodlessly took Eumeleia. Since then, he had exercised a provisional command over the city.

"As you surely recall, Sire, we were notified sometime back that Critias had enacted the innovation of styling the Deity 'the Bringer-of-Light.' Well, it would seem he also implemented... additional reforms."

"What sort of reforms?"

"You must see for yourself," answered Socrates, casting his gaze upon the ground.

Entering the temple, Periander gasped. The stone altar in the center of the building lay entirely encrusted with dried blood. Thickly coating every inch of it, the blood spilled over onto the floor and covered the white marble for several feet around it; a rotting smell of death hung in the air. Bloody scuffmarks from cattle, swine, and other beasts marred the floor here and there, while resting against the inner columns were the flesh-mangling iron prongs used to prod the sacrificial victims along. Higher up on the columns, hanging from pins newly drilled into the marble, were black-and-white masks depicting skull faces crowned with fire-red feathers for hair.

"What desecration has Critias wrought?" said Periander, his mouth agape.

Socrates coughed to clear his throat. "It would seem Critias ruled fruit and flowers insufficient sacrifices for his god, demanding the blood of animals instead. The animals are hoisted onto the altar whereupon their throats are slit and arteries cut; once all the blood is drained from them, their carcasses are incinerated in the name of the Light-Bringer. The priests conducting the ceremonies, moreover, don these masks to resemble the spirits of the dead while they do the killing."

What a sickening, wanton lust for blood! Periander stepped forwards to investigate the altar but gagged at the thick casing of blood. "Socrates, this is appalling. Critias' lust for bloodshed is limitless! All the blood of the innocents he's shed did not satisfy him: he needed to expand his bloodlust to the realm of beasts! And to defile temples with it to boot. What will he do next? Drink it?"

"That's only a rumor," mumbled Socrates quickly as he stroked his silver beard. "But we do have eyewitness testimony about one further thing Critias' priests do during the sacrifices. Something so abominable that I feel queasy even mentioning it." He leaned over to whisper into Periander's ear.

With his cheeks and eyes scrunching, Periander involuntarily retched. "That's sick! Critias ordered such *disgusting* deeds performed—and as centerpieces of *religious* rituals—and the people failed to rise in revolt and slay his sacrilegious hide?! I'm appalled." *What kind of devilish pervert could even dream up such things, let alone make it a public spectacle?*

"Regrettably," replied Socrates, "the people have come to accept the practice. The priests he appointed certainly do... gleefully, even. This, combined with the bloodshed, reveals Critias' inner psyche to be precisely what we always held it to be. Death and wantonness are his only companions. You must therefore overthrow him, my King, before he drowns the world in blood and pollutes all people with his perversions."

"I will cut him down like the ogre he is!"

CHAPTER TWENTY-SIX

PERIANDER SLEPT SERENELY IN his bed, his body held in the warm embrace of Psyche's arms. The room was in the Eumeleian hotel that had been requisitioned for him and leading members of his army. Bright colors—neon oranges, greens, yellows—characterized the room from the hot pink carpeting to the blue ceiling; abstract paintings, framed on the walls, were all obscured by various maps and military papers which Periander had hung up everywhere.

For the past week Periander had busily directed from this headquarters the final reconquest of his subkingdom. Allied armies had so far peacefully taken control of this sector of the continent, capturing towns and cities without resistance from the populace. The absence of formal protests or open resistance from his subjects delighted Periander, who alone among the Allied commanders refrained from imposing martial law on the territory he occupied.

Which is not to say, however, that Critias had no supporters in this part of Atlantis.

"My King! My King!"

Shouting and banging on the door roused Periander from his dreams. "Wh-what?"

The door flung open and Agathocles, panting, rushed over to the bed.

"What's happening?" cried Psyche, sitting up and pressing herself against Periander.

"Sire," screamed Agathocles, his blue eyes squinting and face twisted with distress, "you must come at once! I'll explain on the way."

With his heart pounding and a cold sweat breaking out on his forehead, Periander grabbed a nearby bathrobe, threw it over his pajamas, and went with Agathocles out of the room while Psyche followed behind them.

In the hall were bodyguards waiting to accompany them.

"Tell me what's going on," said Periander.

While leading him down the hallway to the stairs, a wide-eyed Agathocles said, "Horrible! A conspiracy to kill you and hand over Eumeleia to Critias was just foiled!"

"Who? Where? How? Why?" Adrenaline surged through Periander's veins, killing whatever drowsiness in him yearned to return to bed.

"Senior civil officials, loyal to Critias, we've captured. I'm taking you to them. You'll find out everything. But you need to know, Sire... Socrates is dead."

Not Socrates! Periander clenched his jaw and his fists.

After descending three floors, they reached the room wherein the captives were detained. All the furniture had been removed except for seven chairs in which the men, their hands and feet shackled, sat. Demosthenes and several Allied officers were also inside; their faces looked wearied and their eyes dim, partially because it was three o'clock in the morning but mostly because of the seriousness of the situation.

You! Periander startled upon entering the room. He pointed at the prisoners. "I know you. I know each one of you. Three of you I know quite well. What's the meaning of this?"

An Athenian officer spoke. "Sir, these men used their high rank to access city hall. They were planting explosives in the basement, which they intended to detonate once you and all your senior command were inside. General Hippothontis," he said, referring to Socrates, "stumbled across their scheme and radioed for help. We arrived before they could escape but not soon enough to save the general."

"Which of these *maggots* murdered Socrates?"

"None," answered the Athenian officer. "The assassin engaged our men in a firefight and perished."

Good. Periander walked up to the prisoners and glowered, his arms crossed and his knuckles white. "Parmeno, you were a page in my palace. Though only twenty-one, I made you chief of public works because I detected great leadership abilities in you. Davos, I appointed you mayor of Eumeleia when others said your earlier drunken antics should've forever disqualified you from holding any office. And Geta... you served both me and my father as grand treasurer. You were welcomed in our home, attended my son's birth. When you embezzled royal funds to pay for your dying mother's medical expenses, did I not pardon you, even give you all the money you needed?"

He turned his back on them. "That you three, out of all my officials, should betray me... plot to kill us all... slay my father's faithful confidant whose advice I've always sought—it utterly disgusts me." His head craned back to glare at them. "*You* disgust me, you worthless traitors."

Parmeno, Davos, and Geta gazed silently down at the floor; but their co-conspirator and the chief judge of Eumeleia, Phormio, defiantly spoken up. In his mid-thirties with slim limbs but fatty jowls, he had a large nose which was bruised and covered with dried blood. Phormio spat, "And we're disgusted by your treachery to King Critias!"

Periander's nostrils flared as he spun around. "I never," he said, sniffing in indignation, "betrayed Critias or his mother: I voiced my opposition to specific policies, but I never contested the High Kingship itself. If there were any betrayal, it was their betrayal of our ancient laws and customs—*including the prohibition of one king unjustly attacking another.*"

Phormio reäcted to Periander's response by spitting at him and snarling, "We don't care about your stale archaic customs! Atlanteans want a vibrant king who'll expand our empire, enrich our people, and destroy everything and *everyone* that hinders our glorious destiny! Your decaying system of subkings is an outdated relic of an idiotic age. A multitude of rulers is *never* a good thing: it only provokes domestic conflict, as my grandfather described Delphis' reign to me. As there is one sun in the sky, so too must Atlantis have one ruler, one king. And that king is Critias! He and the Light-Bringer shall give the people more than they could ever want!"

"Shut up!" yelled one of the guards as he slapped Phormio's jaw.

Periander shook his head and thought, *How is Critias this appealing to Atlanteans who ought to know better?*

Leaving the room, he was followed by Psyche, Agathocles, Demosthenes, and some officers into the hall. He put his forehead in his palm. "Even in my ancestral lands, Critias' foul allure draws men to himself. I cannot believe so many of my subjects, even officials whom I myself appointed, could prefer that wretch to me—me!—their king of eleven years. Oh, Socrates, Socrates... how I need your counsel now!"

Psyche gave him a sidelong hug.

"I know the death of your adviser is upsetting," said Necho, an Egyptian general. His thick eyebrows weighed heavily on his wrinkling forehead. "But this conspiracy, which could easily have succeeded, exposes the extremeness of danger we face. Any significant resistance behind our lines threatens the entire Allied force. That possibility must be neutralized *immediately*."

"What do you propose?" asked Periander, blinking. *Though I doubt I'll like the answer...*

"First, we must extract from these prisoners everything they know. Then, once we are assured that there aren't other co-conspirators afoot, we ought to publicly execute them most horrendously in order to make an example of them and deter future plotters. Furthermore, while it is laudable that you sought to maintain civilian administration after reclaiming your throne, the treason of these men exposed the naïveté of it. There's only one course: impose martial law. Have the Allied army govern and police the country. Establish curfews and watch the populace. Try all transgressors before military tribunals; judges like Phormio prove there's treachery in the judiciary."

A bitter taste washed over Periander's mouth as Necho listed his counterinsurgency program. "What do the rest of you think?"

"I agree with Necho," said Demosthenes, twirling his right hazel sideburn. "The extreme danger of the times warrants extreme measures. All other Allied-occupied territory is already under martial law. Though unpleasant, the alternative is far worse: we cannot allow Critias and his partisans to prevail."

"Well, I disagree!" shouted Agathocles. "These are just a handful of conspirators. It doesn't mean the whole people need to be put in a straitjacket."

"They're civil officials."

"So what?" Agathocles shoved his finger at Demosthenes. "Are you angry at all civil officials because you just learned your wife ran off with one during our exile?"

Demosthenes frowned and glared at Agathocles as he spoke. "If we leave our territory under the command of persons possibly loyal to Critias, we risk being undermined at every turn. We must leave the government in hands we trust: the army."

"Sire, this isn't the rest of Atlantis," said Agathocles as he turned to Periander. He pounded his fist into his other palm. "This is our home! These are *your* subjects! It's never been the Atlantean way to have the military be in charge of everything. That's what Eudoxia wanted, what Critias is doing."

Oh, how I hate this! To save my people from Critias' tyranny, I might have to browbeat them into submission... Periander sighed; his ears burned. Glancing at Necho, he said, "I know that Egypt utilizes harsh methods to maintain a well-ordered state, but I did not wish to import them for use against my people."

"But they are effective," said Psyche. She nodded to Necho. "Even Father has had villains conspire against him. You probably don't know it, since it wasn't publicized, but a year ago several high-ranking courtiers plotted to stage a palace coup. Necho, however, uncovered the conspirators and eliminated them before they could strike."

Periander moved away from the rest.

Psyche followed him. "Please, Periander, listen to Necho. He's a good man and thoroughly acquainted with rooting out subversive elements."

"This isn't how I envisioned returning to Atlantis," he whispered to her. "Driven into exile by that tyrannical woman and her murderous spawn, I wanted to return and destroy them both. Critias beat me to Eudoxia, leaving him alone to suffer my wrath. Yet I don't wish to triumph over him by emulating his tyranny and cruelty. I opposed Eudoxia every time she sought to usurp more authority over Atlantis, to demolish one more custom to concentrate absolute power in her hands." He took a few steps back towards the rest before glancing at Psyche. "Am I now to employ foreign armies to subjugate the people to *my* will?"

With a steady, reässuring calm in her voice, Psyche gently shook her head. "Periander, do not equate measures—however harrowing—with cruelty. Critias is cruel because he inflicts pain for pleasure. (You told me of his demented look when he pursued you and slew Cornelia; the world knows with what gleeful abandon he massacres cities.) He is a tyrant because he presumes to rule others purely out of selfish ambition while being himself enslaved to his own passions and maniacal lusts. Whereas you..."

She approached to rest her soft cheek on his; she laid her hands around his wide shoulders. "Love for your country, for your family, for all who are under your protection—that is what motivates you. You are the epitome of the good king, a shepherd who tenderly cares for his flock. You didn't return with an army of mercenaries to enslave your people: you returned with Allies to liberate them from the clutches of a tyrant. Whatever harsh measures you enact now are merely temporary until you have overthrown him. Critias' cruel measures, on the contrary, are all designed to subjugate our countrymen to his every whim. *Permanently*."

Periander clasped his eyes shut. "I know, I know," he muttered, stroking Psyche's fragrant hair. Blinking, he looked to Demosthenes. "So, you agree with this plan?"

Demosthenes slowly nodded. "Your wife is correct. There is nothing inherently wrong with the steps Necho is proposing; all are reasonable under these extreme circumstances. As to the charge that they too closely resemble Critias' ways, we must remember the great distinction that exists between means and ends. And unless Critias is defeated, Atlanteans will suffer far worse things than martial law or irksome curfews."

"And are you still opposed, Agathocles?"

"Yes, Sire, and vigorously so. Yet if that's your will, then, as a faithful subject, I'll bite my tongue and obey."

Periander went several paces away, his head gazing down at the floor. He looked back, first to Psyche, then to Agathocles and Demosthenes, and then to that empty spot where ought to have stood another sagacious counselor. Gnawing his lip, he made his decision. "Very well. Necho, you may do whatever you judge necessary to suppress disloyalty and sabotage."

Necho saluted Periander and returned to the room where the prisoners were held. Demosthenes followed him inside, while Agathocles went his own way down the hall.

Returning to his room, Periander leaned his face against the window's icy glass. Darkness held sway over the city. Only the flickering of cold, fluorescent streetlights interrupted the gloom; in the aura around the lights, it was possible to make out the torrential rain that pounded down, overflowing the streets. Strips of cloth, empty metal cans, and other debris floated along.

"I hope," murmured Periander, "when the bright morning sun emerges to banish the soldiers of darkness, the sordid deeds of night will also evaporate beneath his rays."

Psyche, standing close enough to hear his words, embraced him from behind. Her small hand glided into his right hand, her fingers interlocking with his. "I can feel the pulsing passion of the sun," she said while eyeing his hand, "and I know that not even the commander of the whole dark force will be able to resist him."

He smiled. "Your words encourage me, Psyche. All of them." Periander scowled and closed his eyes as memories of the bland looks on his subjects' faces when he entered Eumeleia, the pain he felt after his flight from Atlantis, his years as king and all the good he did, replayed in his mind. "Before the invasion, I had expected my return would elicit as great a joy in my subjects as my longing to return to them. I thought for sure my subjects would rally to me; I now see they have no zeal for me. Where is the loyalty? I always thought theirs equaled my love for them. Yet if this conspiracy is any indication, it would seem I misread my people. Even Parmeno, Davos, and Geta betrayed me—their ingratitude far more hurtful than their traitorous actions."

"Remember you're a faithful man, even if some of your subjects are not. Perhaps the majority were not wildly enthusiastic at your return; but that doesn't mean they won't come around to support you in the end."

"But it means my subjects don't detest Critias' tyranny enough to welcome the chance of overthrowing him," he protested, withdrawing his hand and slamming it against the window. "And if my own subjects don't, then the rest of Atlantis must love him all the more. Critias *must* go. Yet the people find him sufficiently tolerable that they won't rebel against him. Many even *like* him. This distresses me: to find out just how tyrannical a ruler my fellow Atlanteans will abide and what evils they'll let him get away with."

Psyche put her hand on his face, gently rotating his head so as to look him in the eyes. "Periander, I'm sorry that the people can't yet see whom they should abandon and whom they *truly* should rally behind. But in Egypt there is a proverb: 'As a chameleon the terrain, so too emulate subjects their king.' Between Critias and his mother, Atlantis has suffered two decades of malevolence, delinquency, and venality emanating from its heart, metastasizing throughout the body-politic. That's enough to weaken and corrupt a whole nation's spirit."

"Psyche—"

"If the people have grown blind to this wickedness, it is because their tyrants have deprived their eyes of essential nutrients in order to enfeeble their eyesight." She cupped her hand over his beating heart. "*You* have the power to restore their sight."

CHAPTER TWENTY-SEVEN

"It appears King Timocles is commanding them," said Periander, removing the binoculars from his helmet.

Periander stood atop one of the grassy hills that overlooked the plain below. Down there were forty thousand Atlantean soldiers led by Timocles, scion of the House of Mestor. They had encamped there two days before, determined to halt the Allied advance. The presence of Timocles, who at fifty-five-years-old was a veteran of multiple campaigns and proven to be one of the best generals in Atlantis, attested to how important it was to hold this location.

The Plain of Cleon marked a change in the region's geography. Behind Periander's position the land alternated between hilly ridges and deep ravines; forests intermixed with riverbeds in this out-of-the-way section of Atlantis. This was prime territory for defenders to fortify themselves and stave off advances, so it was fortunate that the Allied army had occupied as much of this land as it had without encountering heavy resistance.

Beyond the plain, however, lay a flat expanse of grassy land that stretched for thirty miles to the capital, open and without any gully or rock formations that could be easily fortified. If the Allied army could defeat Timocles' forces, they would be able to make a sprint to the capital and besiege it. Periander commanded thirty-five thousand soldiers; although slightly outnumbered, he held the advantage of having the high ground whose ridges his men had fortified with numerous cannonry.

"We should join battle immediately," said Demosthenes, "while the sun is behind us and in front of them." An Egyptian general concurred with his assessment.

Periander nodded. "Give the order."

"I'll get to fight too, right, Father?" Dressed in full military body armor, the light reflecting off his helmet's visor, Jason eagerly questioned his father.

Periander exhaled deeply, flexing his fingers, before turning to face his son. "Jason, after careful consideration, I've decided you would best serve the army by heading up the rearguard."

"What?" exclaimed Jason, moving a step back and putting his arms akimbo. "I don't want to be stuck in the rear! I want to see action on the frontline."

"The rearguard performs a vital function." Periander placed both his hands on Jason's shoulders, their helmets coming within an inch of each other. "You will be responsible for protecting our canons and their gunners. If the enemy should maneuver a contingent behind our line and assault our artillery, we would lose a decisive advantage. You see, your mission is a critical one, and I am counting on you to follow your orders like a good soldier."

With a muffled assent, Jason went off to his designated station. Periander meanwhile walked down the hill to his vehicle of war. While his legions were marshaled into order, he picked up the Astrapë and climbed into his hover-chariot.

The gleaming bronze-colored vehicle hovered nine inches above the ground. The chariot box had enough room only for Periander and its driver. The anti-gravity propulsion engine, which kept the chariot sustained above the ground, was contained in its own separate structure levitating seven feet in front of the chariot box and connected to it by thick metal coils. Able to accelerate rapidly up to seventy miles per hour, the hover-chariot could maneuver well on the battlefield.

Periander took off his helmet and looked skywards. A cerulean expanse towered overhead, dotted by occasional puffy clouds stacked upon each other in patterns reminiscent of mountains; a two o'clock breeze nudged these along, while the sun shed his warm rays on the Earth like blood from a pig. Quiet permeated the air. With the Atlantean air forces bogged down in an engagement miles away, this battle would be won purely on *terra firma*.

"The army is ready!" cried an officer.

Donning his helmet, Periander commanded, "Begin artillery barrage! Infantry, forwards, march!"

The air reverberated as the cannons fired in unison at the Atlanteans, eliminating at a blow the handful of artillery the Atlanteans had with them. Then Periander's army, divided into hundred-man companies, began marching down the hills as his charioteer steered his vehicle alongside them.

Below on Cleon's Plain, Timocles' army sustained the fire. Similarly divided into companies that were positioned a hundred wide by four companies deep, the Atlantean troops held their ground while the bombardment continued. The canons' lasers destroyed men here and there, sending bloodied bodies flying upwards. But as soon as the Allied soldiers had descended the sides of the hills, the Atlanteans marched to meet them with laser-rifles firing.

The opposing armies collided like two equipotent stags. Shouts and shots erupted everywhere. Red laser beams soared through the air, piercing armored soldiers who withered on the grassy plain that thirstily soaked up the bloody monsoon.

Two down, thought Periander, killing two men with two shots from the Astrapë. "Head for those tanks threatening our men."

Guneus, his charioteer, veered the vehicle. Zooming across the battlefield, the chariot weaving around foe and friend alike, they reached the spot where two large tanks had cornered a group of Allied soldiers. The tanks were twenty feet apart from each other, and Periander's chariot halted behind them.

He quickly shot a laser-arrow which bored through the first tank's rear. Knowing that the rear was where the engine for Atlantean tanks was, his shot penetrated the tank's weakest spot and crippled it. The other tank's barrel started turning to fire on him, but it was too late. Periander shot it in the same location and disabled it.

Periander smiled. *Tanks are no match for the Astrapë! What wondrous things the ancient armsmakers could make.*

"Sir, another tank's coming behind us!" cried Guneus, his voice cracking.

Periander spun around. The long barrel from another menacing gray tank was just twenty yards away. The tank trampled over corpses as it sped towards them, churning up the mangled flesh. As Guneus turned the chariot, the barrel followed them. Periander's eyes locked onto it. *Here's some lubricant!*

He strung the Astrapë's bowstring and hurled forth a laser-arrow. In an instant it zipped down the hostile barrel. The tank exploded: its turret blew off and smoky flames shot out of it with a bang.

Raising a fist to the wreck, Periander directed his eyes elsewhere. He zipped across the battlefield and fought where he was most needed.

Periander's chariot soon came to the end of the Atlantean line. Here was Timocles, surrounded by a dozen Allied soldiers. Though they had cut him off from his men, none could get closer to him than thirty feet.

Timocles wore armor that was dark gray with yellow stripes along the limbs; his visor, instead of just slits for eyes, filled up the helmet's entire front piece. In his hands he held a long trident that had been forged in the same era as the Astrapë and had been in his family's possession ever since. It was the color of aquamarine and red laser beams were discharged from its tips. Depending on which of the handle's buttons Timocles pressed, the lasers could be steady bursts or intermittent blasts; the three beams, moreover, could either fire in unison in one giant blast or diverge in three separate directions so as to cover a greater range. Whenever the Allied soldiers approached, he cut them down; if they fired on him, his triple beam blasts provided him cover to dodge.

"Stop here!" ordered Periander. The chariot stopped and he hopped out.

"Sir, we've surrounded the enemy's general but can't neutralize him!" shouted one soldier who rushed beside Periander.

"Go. I will handle him. Just keep the Atlanteans away." Periander took several large steps forwards as he tightened his grip on the Astrapë. "Timocles!"

Timocles rested his trident's top on the earth and looked up. "Is that you, Periander?"

"Yes," answered Periander, removing his helmet, "it is I."

"Periander: the traitor who's led hordes of foreigners into our land." Timocles pushed a button on the side of his helmet and his visor slid up. His grizzled gray hair covered his wrinkled forehead, his round face displayed several scars, and his narrow brown eyes stared with clarity at Periander. "It's been a while."

"Indeed. Last we met, you were standing alongside me in opposition to the dark disorders of the present régime—fighting to preserve our ancestral customs and institutions from Eudoxia's power grabs, to stop her insane lust for world domination. Now you oppose me by defending her murderous son, a tyrant who equals Eudoxia in ambition while exceeding her only in cruelty and madness."

Timocles' matted unibrow rose. "I am defending Atlantis. You are the one killing your country by siding with her enemies."

"Enemies, that is true. Enemies of *Critias*, not Atlantis!"

Timocles let out a deep laugh. "Enough with words that cannot reconcile. If we are to fight, my boy, then let us begin."

Periander nodded, donning his helmet again. He raised his bow and shot off two arrows.

Timocles jumped aside, evading the lasers. "I see the Astrapë is as excellent as I heard it to be. But it will have to be better than that to match my trident."

Periander ducked as three red lasers flew less than two inches above his head. He started running, firing several arrows as he went. Impenetrable clouds of dust pursued him wherever he went because Timocles trained his trident after him, setting it to discharge continuous lasers that plowed up the earth behind him. *Such dreadful firepower!* thought Periander, the adrenaline surging through him. *I've got to score a hit, and quick.*

He ducked behind his chariot, which was the only covering around. He managed to unleash a burst of arrows in Timocles' direction. Suddenly the hard jolt of the chariot hit his back when Timocles' lasers pounded the vehicle's opposite side.

Sweat cascaded down Periander's forehead; his heart pounded. He held the Astrapë's firing button down, allowing the laser-arrow to grow before firing it. He spun up and around, rested his left elbow on the chariot's side, and shot his big arrow at Timocles.

A gasping sound came through the air. Yet the dust was so thick that Timocles could not be seen. *Did I get him?* Periander remained hunkered down, charging another arrow. "Timocles!"

His call was answered by another blast from the trident. The side of the chariot that had been sustaining fire flew off, the warped metal landing with a thud only three feet from Periander. His eyes frantically darted from side to side. There was nothing else around he could use as cover, nor anyone to help him. The rest of the chariot was about to give way.

He was trapped.

"Surrender, Periander," Timocles hollered, trudging out of the dust cloud and over towards the chariot. He let up on his lasers so that he could be heard. "You've fought valiantly, like your father before you. But as so many witnesses in the underworld would avow if only the dead could testify, my trident's power is too great. You'll never breach my offense."

That's it!

The chariot shook when the trident resumed firing red laser beams. Ducking his head, Periander ran several feet behind the chariot. He had been amplifying the same laser arrow all this time: now it was the size of a watermelon. Being about as large as the Astrapë could muster, the whole bow quivered from the arrow's intensity. Periander crouched down and, aiming at the chariot in front of him, let loose the Astrapë's arrow.

Larger and more powerful than any he had previously shot, the arrow impacted the chariot with such force that it exploded into a maelstrom of fiery shrapnel which hurtled through the air towards Timocles. While his adversary was attempting to dodge the incoming shards of metal, Periander jumped up and shot four arrows in swift succession at him.

Once the shrapnel had been distributed across the field and the explosion's echo had died down, the sound of groaning could be heard. When the dust began to settle, Timocles' motionless body became visible, only seventeen feet away.

Periander ran over to him. His armor showed three places—his chest and right thigh—where either Periander's arrows or the shrapnel had pierced him. But his left shoulder was completely destroyed; the arm formerly attached thereto lay inches away. Blood gushed from Timocles' body as Periander removed his helmet. He gently put his hand under the neck to feel for a pulse.

"Timocles?"

"Gahhhhh." Timocles moaned and coughed up blood. His pupils focused on Periander. "I am slain."

"I regret that this was where our paths had to cross."

"I don't blame you." Timocles coughed again, the blood trickling down his face. "You did what you had to do. For I see, like Themistocles, you will go unwavering in your support of what is right. The blame falls on me, for yielding to Eudoxia and abetting Critias' tyranny."

"What made you yield to them?" asked Periander. "Although our relationship didn't extend beyond professional collaboration and jointly dissenting to Eudoxia's policies, you always seemed to me to be an upright man and a faithful king. I remember that speech you gave three years ago in the Council, when you eloquently defended Atlantean traditions to Eudoxia's face. That speech stirred my soul and those of the whole opposition—as much as your unexpected defection shocked and disheartened us."

Timocles shook his head and shut his eyes. "My betrayal is unforgivable, although I think you'll find it understandable. I was a widower whose only family consisted of three sons: Strabo, Daphnis, and Lycus. To me they were my world, a fact that... that witch Eudoxia divined. She called me aside one day to witness three chickens destined for supper. Would you believe she named the birds after my sons? After telling me that detail, she personally snapped each of their necks, her gaze locked on to mine as she ruthlessly killed them."

"She threatened your family?" A shiver went up Periander's spine as the memory of Cornelia's death revolved in his mind.

"Yes. She made sure I understood. And overcome by fear for my sons, I complied: whatever she wanted, I did it, readily if not enthusiastically. I selfishly put the interests of my own family ahead of my country's welfare. And you know what? Want to know what the kicker was?" Tears began flowing from his eyes. "After selling my soul, I still lost my boys: Strabo died repressing the American rebels, Daphnis in the assault on Athens, and Lycus in the Allied invasion."

Periander bit his lip. Jason flashed through his mind as he thought, *How horrific to outlive all your children!*

"I shamefully submitted to Eudoxia to save my boys from her," sniveled Timocles, "but her boy and his wars deprived me of all three. I forsook my duty to my country, my principles—everything!—only to lose everything in the end. O Periander..." His voice became hardly a whisper, forcing Periander to lean in close. "Periander, succeed where I failed. Overthrow Critias. Restore Atlantis to her former self."

"I have vowed to do so, Timocles. Critias will pay for all that he has done. I…"

A final breath was exhaled by Timocles, a man broken both in body and spirit.

Periander withdrew his arms and gently closed Timocles' eyes. "Farewell. Despite your misguided actions, I commend your spirit to the Deity."

In the course of his fight with Timocles, the wider battle had not intruded on them but did continue without them. Rising from the bloodied earth, Periander took several steps away before the cry of, "They're retreating!" hit his ear.

His forces had broken through the center of the enemy's line, dividing them in two. Now Atlantean soldiers had dropped their weapons and were running madly away in two opposite directions, aggressively pursued by Periander's soldiers.

Moments later Demosthenes arrived aboard a chariot. Descending, he announced, "Sire, we have achieved victory. The enemy's forces are dispersed. The path to Atlantis City now lies open before us."

"Excellent," murmured Periander, still thinking of Timocles.

Demosthenes noticed the body lying nearby. "I see you repaid Timocles for his defection." He spoke evenly but with a narrow-eyed gaze fixed on the corpse.

"No, Demosthenes, I didn't. Timocles himself realized his error; he brought more pain upon himself than any I could have inflicted on him."

"Sire?"

Periander climbed into the chariot. He drew in a deep breath. "Come, Demosthenes," he said with a small smile, "I have business to attend to in the capital."

Chapter Twenty-Eight

━━━━━━━━━━

P ERIANDER EXITED HIS QUARTERS, a private building located in the center of the camp, and stepped out into the overcast afternoon.

After routing the Atlanteans on the Plain of Cleon a fortnight earlier, he had led his army here on a breakneck thirty-mile march through the undefended countryside. Shortly before reaching Atlantis City, however, one of Critias' armies emerged from the capital to greet them. It did not fight to defeat Periander's forces but merely to halt their advance long enough to allow another Atlantean army, chaotically converging on the city after a crushing defeat elsewhere, to retreat behind the city walls before being overtaken by their pursuers.

Indra's sky fleet had coördinated with their ground assault, flooding the skies above Atlantis City with airships to shoot down all of Critias' ships and protect the Allied troops below. The ground battle ended quickly. As soon as their comrades were inside, the Atlantean army facing Periander likewise retreated into the city. Neither side inflicted much damage during this engagement; but the Allies won insomuch as they surrounded Atlantis City, thereby cutting the capital off from the rest of the continent.

Periander's camp, the headquarters of the besiegers, was named Andreia. It was larger than the four other encampments around the city, whose campsites were teeming after days of additional soldiers pouring in. Pitched two miles southeast of Atlantis City, Camp Andreia lay atop a large flat hill that sloped so gently upwards as to make it nearly impossible to detect its incline. Well-organized, with drab olive-colored tents and some prefabricated metal structures meticulously arranged in concentric rows, the camp housed fifty thousand troops whose endless trampling of feet had kneaded the hilly grass into a single expanse of bare earth.

As Periander walked towards the camp entrance, he passed by many soldiers. Some were eating vegetables and soups straight out of their cans, some were being marched in formation by their squad leaders, and others were sitting beside their tents either scrubbing the muck and blood off their body armor or performing maintenance on their weapons; all paused to salute their supreme commander. Overhead roared the sound of Indra's aircraft, their protectors in the sky.

With a smile forming on his face, Periander waved his hand and shouted, "Leonidas!"

Leonidas, a hundred paces from the entrance, called out a greeting. He was donned in Athenian body armor, painted aquamarine with yellow shoulder plates and a black utility belt, but he carried his helmet in his hands. Several Athenian advisers surrounded him.

"At last, you have joined us at the frontlines, my comrade," said Periander, welcoming him with a quick embrace. "Now no obstruction will withstand the Allied army!"

Leonidas said with a laugh, "I'd have thought Atlantis would have fallen to you by now!" as he glanced around the camp. "Had I known you could barely eke out a foothill, I would have come all the sooner."

"Yes, then we would have two foothills!" Periander shared a laugh with his friend. *It's good to see him so cheerful.*

Despite the merriment, Periander was familiar with the sort of hectic problems that had prevented Leonidas from arriving earlier. Since ascending the throne, all manner of demands would have been made on him: to mobilize his military and appoint commanders of new forces, to oversee the damage caused by the Atlantean attack, to familiarize himself with the most intimate details of government policy and state secrets, to safeguard himself from any malcontents' subversion... Every transition from one reign to another entailed difficulty; possibly the greatest was the onerous awareness that the fates of countless subjects, among whom you were yourself so recently numbered, now suddenly depended on you for their safety and wellbeing.

Periander remembered when he succeeded his father. He had lamented his death; but service to his people compelled him to put aside private grief and to take up the reins of sovereignty. *How hard this must be on you*, thought Periander as he eyed Leonidas. *To be brought to power due to a heinous villain's crime, at so difficult a juncture, and given no time to mourn your murdered father before being thrust into the maelstrom of war....*

"So that is the great Atlantis, source of this war." Through buck-teeth came this observation from Gnatho. He rubbed his hands together, looking past the camp perimeter to the city in the distance. "Such boundless wealth its walls are said to hold."

Leonidas flashed a cross look at Gnatho before turning affably to Periander. "So, tell me, how is our war effort progressing?"

"Come." Periander motioned with his hands. "I'll show you."

He led Leonidas and his entourage to the camp's command center, housed in one of the prefabricated buildings. Inside were many desks, computers, monitors, communications systems, and the personnel to staff them. Periander walked to the center of the room where a large holoprojector, fifteen feet by fifteen feet, displayed Atlantis City and the surrounding regions.

"Here are our positions. Approximately two hundred thousand soldiers, plus our tanks and aircraft, have completely sealed off the city. No one can get out without encountering our resistance."

"Tomorrow you'll be able to add thirty-five thousand more men to that," said Leonidas, referencing the fresh recruits he had brought with him from Athens. "That should help in taking the city."

Periander nodded. "Yet it will still be difficult. Atlantis City's force fields are the strongest in the world; not even Indra's largest bombers could breach them. So long as they're operational, we can't take the city by storm."

"Do we know how long it can hold out? I mean, with food and stuff?"

"The city's blessed with vast internal springs that will indefinitely supply its water needs, and historically we always maintained a year's worth of food reserves." Periander gritted his teeth, his lip curling in disgust. "But who knows what Critias has been up to? Expand the reserves, sell them off—he's unpredictable. And my sources inside the city haven't reported anything on that, nor will they now that the siege has commenced."

"So, we don't know how long the siege may take..." said Leonidas, crossing his arms as his wide shoulder blades slumped. "Any developments in the rest of the island?"

Periander fingered a touchscreen, and the hologram zoomed out, displaying a three-dimensional map of the whole continent. "Battles were fought here, here, and here the last couple of days, our forces prevailing in two out of the three. King Pindar of the House of Ampheres was slain at Acheron Canyon." He pressed the touch screen and the parts of the continent controlled by the Allies became highlighted in red. "We've gained additional ground this week, though at a diminishing rate. The scattered forces of Critias have thus far entrenched their positions in these two disconnected sectors of the continent; it will be a war of attrition in those areas with our current allotment of soldiers."

"I have a question." Gnatho, slithering towards Periander from the rear of the room, spoke. "If this siege, which is monopolizing our forces, is not expected to succeed for quite a while, why not redirect those same forces to capturing the rest of the island? Once all else is under our control, we could then resume the siege of the capital (assuming they do not then surrender in light of our island-wide conquest)."

Periander cocked his head and blinked. Sizing up this little man, who alone of Leonidas's entourage wore civilian garb, he asked, "Are you a military adviser?"

Gnatho, his eyes focusing on Periander as his oblong mouth opened to reply, was interrupted by Leonidas, who growled, "No! He has absolutely no grasp whatsoever of military affairs; he shouldn't even be here."

Taken aback by his friend's fierce response to a member of his own staff, Periander attempted to defuse the flare up. "I appreciate your... interesting suggestion; but to abandon the siege would allow the many armies trapped within the capital to pour out and vie to retake the land we have already occupied." He patted Gnatho on the back. "You should leave military strategizing to us."

***

L EONIDAS SPENT THE REMAINDER of the afternoon with Periander, plotting the next course of the war with him and their respective advisers. As the sun began to set, Leonidas and his entourage were escorted to a building on the outskirts of the camp, newly erected to lodge them.

"Thank you," he said to the soldier, a fellow Athenian who saluted his king as he left. Bidding his advisers to go inside without him, Leonidas caught Gnatho by his tunic's rumpled sleeve. "Not you!"

Leonidas jostled him around the corner of the building and slammed him against the cold metal wall. Looking around to see if anyone was about, he nevertheless lowered his voice to a whisper. "What did you think you were doing back there?"

With a frosty and unflinching gaze, making not so much as a whimper at this undignified treatment, Gnatho calmly answered, "I do not know to what you are referring."

"Like the Deity you don't know!" Leonidas slapped him hard on his left cheek. "Who told you that you could speak at a war council, much less spout off military proposals which your senile old brain can't comprehend?"

"I am one of your advisers, Master: I must give you my advice."

I would heed Critias' advice before I would yours! "You are no adviser. You are a *sycophant* and a *parasite*, leeching your way here on my back! The only reason you're here is because you inveigled me to come, and I foolishly said yes on the condition that you do *nothing* and say *nothing* without my express command." *Although I suppose it would've been too dangerous to leave you unsupervised at home...*

"Forgive me, Sire, if I displeased you." Gnatho spoke without either the tenor of his guttural voice or the appearance of his oily body betraying sarcasm; his eyes, their pupils enlarging, seeped with sincerity. Yet in his mouth the words sounded ironic while his eyes were notoriously peerless in their acting prowess.

Leonidas grunted at this faux apology, which turned out to be not at all unwarranted given what Gnatho seamlessly appended to it:

"I am but an old man, wishing to see the famous Atlantis before my years are spent. I am not too many years removed from your father's age when you..."

There it is again! thought Leonidas as the final, patricidal words were left to dangle unspoken before him. "Get out of here!" he yelled, shoving Gnatho onto the ground and befouling his tunic with mud. *How I hate your worthless guts...!*

CHAPTER TWENTY-NINE

P ASSING UNDER THE MARBLE archway, Lysander stepped outside onto a balcony overlooking the palace's grand courtyard. The palace grounds and avenues of the city leading up to it were decked with colorful streamers; musicians stationed here and there were playing songs whose tacky verses lionized Critias; and firecrackers, emitting billowing clouds of pink and purple smoke into the night air, were being continuously set off by the boisterous mob.

Lysander glowered at the thousands of his fellow Atlanteans below, who thronged the courtyard as do aquarium fish at feeding time, screeching their praises for Critias like hyenas about to be given blood-dripping meat. *Look how easily the people are led astray by the tyrant's ploys, with what pleasure they beg for his yoke!*

A moment later he was joined by Timaeus. "Good, there you are."

Timaeus did not return his son's greeting. Clasping his gray cloak close to his body with his fat fingers, Timaeus approached the balcony's edge. He had a grave look on his face; the wrinkles under his eyes appeared especially pronounced tonight, the skin sagging an inch downwards. He nervously glanced back and forth, and his tongue repeatedly moistened his paler than usual lips.

"What's the matter, Father? You look like you've seen something terrible."

"I'm not sure yet if it's anything—it may turn out to be nothing." Glancing over the side to peer at a balcony on a lower floor, Timaeus muttered, "He's starting," before Lysander could question him further.

About thirty feet lower and fifty feet to their right, Critias began speaking from the central grand balcony—a myriad of loudspeakers conveying and amplifying his voice to them and to the crowd below.

"My beloved subjects! Though that infamous traitor not to be named, who abandoned our land in his flight from justice, has returned to assail my precious crown with his vassal hands and to destroy our government and dismember our empire; though he has brought with him swarms of mercenaries—*foreigners* recruited from the most barbarous nations—whose mouths water at the thought of ravishing our land, our wealth, and our women; though he has occupied part of our continent, terrorizing my subjects there, and has even (momentarily) cut our capital off from the rest of our blessed isle, I promise you this: we will triumph! The Light-Bringer watches over us! He will illuminate us with his wisdom and destroy the forces of darkness seeking our destruction! We will kill the invaders and eat their cowardly livers!"

The crowd roared ecstatically. They waved flags depicting images of Critias' face. At key points in the High King's remarks, they threw hats, bottles, and chairs into the air.

"From the crowd's reäction, you'd think *he* was winning the war," Lysander remarked snidely. He nudged Timaeus with his elbow.

Timaeus nodded absent-mindedly, his wrinkled face staring down at Critias.

Now ranting about the Allied forces' alleged atrocities, now charming the people by announcing increased food rations, Critias' honeyed words and madly gyrating arms stirred the people into riotous applause.

Lysander meanwhile listened irritably, the scar below his lip stinging afresh as he heard one diatribe after another hurled against Periander. *I pray King Periander will scale these walls soon and rip your precious crown from off you—head and all!*

He struck the bronze railing with a clenched fist, his anger at Critias equaled only by that which he felt towards the citizens of Atlantis City. For the thousands of enthusiastic shouts testified to Critias' enduring popularity in the capital; and so long as the people adored him, alas, there could be no internal revolt to depose him and surrender the city to Periander. Were it possible to stage one, Lysander would be the first to rush into the streets, rip down one of the ubiquitous posters of glossy Critias, raise his fist in the air and shout, "Down with the tyrant!"

After an agonizingly-long forty-seven minutes, Lysander shut his eyes and hung his head over the railing as Critias spat out his last syllable and returned into the palace. Opening his eyes again, he exhaled profusely. "I thought he'd never finish. Right?"

Timaeus was gone.

What? Where'd he go? This is so unlike him. Lysander stepped inside and glanced both ways down the hallway. Apart from the red-and-purple tapestries hanging on the wall, he was completely alone.

Mystified, he wondered, *What could he know that gnaws at him so?*

Chapter Thirty

"Retreat! Retreat!"

Periander yelled the command to his charioteer Guneus, who swiftly executed a U-turn. Just as the chariot turned around, a blast from a laser cannon hit the earth where the chariot had been mere seconds before.

Buffeted from the blast, his back becoming caked with dust, Periander gripped tighter onto the chariot before glancing over his shoulder. Dozens of his soldiers lay dead or dying on the field, being trampled by the fresh squads of Atlantean soldiers who were streaming out of the Southern Gate.

How did this happen? wondered Periander, his helmet covering his gaping mouth.

As recently as twenty minutes earlier, his side had held the advantage, outnumbering the enemy. Their line, although collapsing into a semicircle, had nevertheless withstood the initial Atlantean thrust. Yet as reïnforcements emerged from the city, the burgeoning Atlantean ranks managed to break through Periander's line and divide his force in half. After that, the battle quickly turned in the Atlanteans' favor.

Not another defeat! With his heart weighed down by anchor-heavy resignation, Periander transmitted the order to retreat to his subordinate officers. Guneus steered the chariot southwesterly, driving a thousand yards to a knoll from where Periander could observe his troops withdrawing. The killing field was ceded to the enemy.

Periander returned to Camp Andreia. Dismounting from the chariot, he removed his helmet. The smell of blood and fear, of burned flesh and pungent medicines, filled the air as the wounded trickled into the camp. The men arrived either on their own feet or on the backs of their comrades. Physicians and their assistants darted from soldier to soldier, flinging armor away to measure pulses and analyze the extent of wounds; their foreheads gleaming with sweat, they frantically were deciding whose injuries needed instant treatment and who should be left to die.

The poor fellows, thought Periander. *You won't have died in vain. I swear, Critias will suffer for all the harm he's wrought...*

Reaching the camp's headquarters, the stench of death had left Periander's nostrils, but the images of the dying still clung to his mind.

As he entered the building, he was greeted by Psyche.

"Oh, Periander, I'm so glad you're safe!" Undeterred by the grime and coagulating blood of his enemies that coated his armor, she threw her arms around him. "Jason told me your legion was overwhelmed—hundreds killed."

His son, whom he had assigned as an aide-de-camp to the command center's officers, was seated across the room. Though attempting to appear nonchalant by remaining at his designated station, Jason's repeated, furtive glances at his father betrayed his concern.

"I'm quite alright," said Periander, speaking loud enough to be heard throughout the room. He kissed Psyche and freed himself from her embrace just as Leonidas entered.

"You're already back," murmured Leonidas haggardly. His suit was drenched with dried mud. "I hope you had better success."

Oh, not you too... Periander bit his lip. "There were too many of them; they just kept pouring out. We had to fall back and reform the perimeter a mile from the city."

"At least you maintained a perimeter," sighed Leonidas, shaking his head while gazing up at the ceiling. "Our lines were utterly overrun. The Atlanteans regained control over the hills a mile north from the city and are *en route* to Camp Phronesis; General Chromis has already ordered his units to pull up camp and move it six miles back."

"But weren't you responding to an attack from the Western Gate?"

"Yes, and to suppress it I diverted a number of our forces from the north side to the west. But as soon as they arrived, the Atlanteans started streaming out of the Northern Gate. I rushed over there to mount a counterstrike just as soon as the first battle ended, but by then it was too late. They had the momentum and forced us back."

Grinding his teeth, Periander turned towards a colonel. "Contact General Sesostris and have him move his men to the northland! Get him air support too; we can't let Critias' forces regain territory beyond the Traconite Hills or he'll be in a position to reëstablish his supply lines and nullify our siege."

As the officer scampered to carry out the orders, Periander slammed his white-knuckled fist down on a table. "So, we lost two battles today, almost three," he growled. "These losses are becoming intolerably frequent."

Leonidas, sitting down and gulping a glass of water which a subordinate handed him, asked, "Are you sure? I've been here eight days and our loss-to-win ratio in the skirmishes seems about the same."

"Well, the skirmishes didn't start until around the time you arrived," replied Periander. "Before then, there were only a few instances of Critias' troops mounting an attack from within the city. We crushed both of them. Looking back, I suppose they were just testing us, and now we have to endure the real thing." He wrinkled his nose and grunted. "If only we could've laid siege before Critias' armies retreated inside! We wouldn't be facing these skirmishes..."

A gasp came from across the room. "Sir! Sir!" shouted one of the communications officers as he rose from his desk. Shakily, he removed the headsets and earpieces from his pallid face; his eyes were agog and his mouth agape. "We're receiving reports! Atlanteans outside the Western Gate! Our men are being slaughtered!"

"That can't be! I pacified that battlefield—drove them back in," protested Leonidas, jumping to his feet. "Don't tell me they've unleashed a second wave."

"They have and this time..." The officer's voice trailed for several moments before, gulping, he said, "King Critias is with them. Fighting."

Periander was not alone in exclaiming, "Critias? In person?" *That lout is actually going to risk his own life in a fair fight?*

"Himself. And he's—the reports are unbelievable!"

I have to see this, thought Periander. "Get us video from one of our drones!"

Within seconds, the giant monitor on the wall began displaying the live video stream from an Allied drone. The whole expanse before the western wall of Atlantis City appeared on the screen, with small pixels scarcely larger than a hair representing soldiers, tanks, trees, and bushes. After a click here and a button pushed there, the screen zoomed in. Toggling the screenshot back and forth to locate Critias, it was not difficult to find him: his presence dominated the battlefield as much as it now did the screen.

Clad in body armor, completely jet-black with the exception of a white skull painted across the thorax as well as vertical silvery lines upon the helmet, his thick-soled boots boosting his already tall height by an additional three inches, Critias towered above all the other combatants like a giant over windmills. In his left hand he bore a large round shield, the color of a gleaming full moon; with his right he wielded a frictional axe.

This weapon operated on the principle of friction whereby momentum and physical contact produce heat. The mechanism inside its blade was designed to super-compress molecules within it and thereby amplify the heat generated by the molecular collisions. In doing so, this allowed the battleaxe to be cool to the touch when static but, as soon as its wielder swung it through the air, its blade would near-instantaneously reach a temperature of six thousand degrees Fahrenheit—a temperature hot enough to dissolve almost anything it touched except tungsten (the same metal that the blade was made of).

Critias charged two Allied soldiers. They fired their guns at him, but he held up his shield to deflect the salvo. Reaching them, Critias thrust his shield at the soldier on his left, knocking the gun out of his hands. Simultaneously he used his axe to hack the other soldier's thorax. The blade fleetingly glowed light blue as it tore through the air. It liquefied the soldier's armor and seared the man's innards: the extreme temperature instantly cauterized all his blood vessels before even a single drop could mar the blade.

Withdrawing the unbloodied and now un-hot blade from the corpse, Critias turned to the other soldier whom he was still crushing with his shield. His victim defenseless, Critias shoved him to the ground and neatly severed his head from his shoulders.

Critias rose and looked around. Three soldiers were advancing towards him, two about a hundred feet away on his left and one only forty feet to his right. Dodging the latter soldier's gunfire, he sped over to him; great clumps of sod and dirt soared upwards with every step he took. Critias overtook the soldier who had no time to reäct, and, from behind, he cut him down too.

Of the other two soldiers, one arrived sooner than his comrade. A slash through his pelvis and another through his ribcage finished him off. Critias, his unscratched armor gleaming beneath the rays of the sun, stood erect as he turned to face the remaining soldier.

Though only twenty feet away from his target, that soldier suddenly stopped his charge. He hesitated a second, dropped his gun, and redirected his advance in the opposite direction. He went seven feet.

Then Critias, throwing his right arm back like a rearing horse, hurled his axe. It hurtled through the air and hit the soldier straight on his spine.

With one giant spasm all his limbs convulsed, thrown backwards even as the torso thrust forwards, before the soldier collapsed, lifeless, to the earth.

What am I seeing? Periander could not blink as, one by one, Critias scored kill after kill. *How is he doing this?*

"You never said Critias could fight like this."

Leonidas had approached beside him. His head was in his right palm as it slowly swayed back and forth.

"I'd never witnessed him fight a fair fight," mumbled Periander, "and no such report ever reached my ears. Yet, evidently, Critias can kill people who are not unarmed." He gritted his teeth as Critias dismembered another Allied soldier. *I must confess he's a far better warrior than he should be... It would seem his stay in the Americas was not limited to visiting brothels.*

Psyche's arm gripped his own; her pale face was cold against his. "What kind of a man can fight like that? Kill so many—so fast!"

"One who's been well trained."

"And what sort of weapon is that, that axe of his?"

"Must be something new from his arms developers. His mother was obsessed about creating new weapons—establishing all sorts of programs to that effect. I never knew the details because she kept it all extremely secret." He let out a dry laugh. "Well, everything except the exorbitant expenses. Her black budget was a fiscal black hole."

"He is terrifying."

Periander put his hand over hers and spoke some reässuring words. But inwardly he had to agree, however grudgingly. Critias had already killed at least twenty men; he would probably have killed even more had not the remaining Allied soldiers fled the field. Periander could only seethe and flex his fingers as the monitor zoomed in closer to Critias, who now stood with his right leg resting triumphantly upon one of his kills. His helmet was in his hand as his ivory-colored face loomed ever larger on the screen, growing until every filthy pore could be seen in high definition.

The High King was laughing!

His ebony hair flapped to the bobbing of his head, and his cheeks soared high as his mouth swallowed his face which was belching laughter. But despite his outward gleeful countenance, Critias' black eyes, gyrating from side to side, did not have the sheen of one overcome by joy.

They resembled those of a rabid dog.

Chapter Thirty-One

The sun was scurrying westwards through the sky, eager to reach his bed and sink beneath its horizontal covers, when Leonidas made his way through the camp. He clicked his jaw, and his hand guided his neck as it moved from side to side. He was ready for rest after another day of fighting. Thankfully there had been no repeat of yesterday. The Allies halted the Atlantean advance and retook lost terrain on the northern outskirts of the city.

Walking past an outdoor training ground, Leonidas called out a greeting to Jason. The lad was attentively watching some soldiers do target practice. Stationed at the opposite end of the yard were life-sized mannequins. Wherever the soldiers hit the mannequins with their training guns, the plastic bodies glowed bright red in that spot to mark the hit and the whole body turned green whenever a lethal hit was made.

"How are things?" asked Leonidas as Jason approached.

Jason was reticent at first; but as he followed Leonidas, he soon divulged his mind. He was saying, "I want to help the war effort."

"But you are. Is serving in the headquarters' staff not important?"

"Clerical work is not the same," protested Jason. He raised his chin and his fist; his spiky auburn hair smoldered in the dying sunlight. "I wish to fight, like you and Father. I want to serve by killing my family's enemies, by proving my courage on the battlefield."

"Have you spoken with your father about your aspiration?"

"Yeah, but he won't let me join the fighting."

"Hold on," said Leonidas as they were entering his building, "didn't Periander already take you along with him in some battles?"

Jason snorted. "He deliberately kept me on the sidelines, away from the fighting."

He must be protecting him, thought Leonidas. *After what happened to Cornelia, I can't say I blame him for wanting to safeguard his son.* He put his arm around Jason and made him look him in the eye. "You must listen to your father. I've known him since before you were begotten and I have no doubt he's only doing what he thinks is right."

Jason mumbled a frustrated assent before venturing, "Yet perhaps if you were to speak with him..."

"NO!" screeched Leonidas, his outburst causing Jason to take a step back as a shocked look spread across his face. With his throat tightening, Leonidas swiftly drew his sweaty palms to his sides. "I mean, I'm not going to interfere in a father-and-son dispute."

When Jason did not respond, Leonidas forced a laugh in an attempt to calm the situation. "I've learned from experience that third parties only exacerbate conflicts."

As they wordlessly turned the corner down the hallway to Leonidas' room, he tried to regain his inner composure. *Stupid, stupid, stupid! There was no reason for that outburst. He was talking of his father and their quarrels, not mine and ours. And yet they still flood my mind. If I can't better control my—wait, what?*

At the end of the wall was the door to his room, the same door that he had locked before he left but which now was slightly ajar. Light from inside was visible.

"This has been an interesting conversation, Jason, but I am tired now and need my rest. I'll see you later." Leonidas waited until the boy had gone around the corner before approaching his door.

Taking his pistol out of its holster, he pressed himself against the wall. Leonidas inched closer and closer to the door. He inhaled deeply. Then he kicked the door open and rushed inside, brandishing his gun. "You!"

Standing by the desk adjacent to Leonidas' bed, a corpulent old man spun around. As he clasped his heaving chest, several papers fell from his hand to the floor. "Sire!" he gasped. "I was not expecting you till later."

Gnatho was the intruder.

"Well, of course you weren't!" Marching over to him, Leonidas seized the papers to peruse. They were classified reports about the progress of the war as well as confidential messages between him and his lieutenants in Athens! He struck Gnatho's greasy head and shoved him onto the bed, greatly rumpling the sheets. "You thief!"

"No, Sire," whimpered Gnatho whilst feebly raising his bony hands in front of his face. "I only wish to be apprised of what is happening—the better to advise you!—but amid your many cares you have inadvertently neglected to inform me of certain things."

Leonidas punched Gnatho's back and a tiny flash drive rolled out of his tunic's pocket onto the bed. "What is that?"

"Nothing." Gnatho shoved it back into his pocket.

"Nothing?!" Despite Gnatho's pleas, Leonidas forced his hand down his pocket and recovered not only the flash drive but also a miniature camera to boot. He loaded the flashcard and pressed the replay button. Immediately, images of various documents of his were flashing before his irate eyes. *Aha, so this is what you've been up to!* "Get up."

Gnatho stared unblinkingly as his breathing subsided. His oily face was white as salt.

"I said, GET UP!" Leonidas grabbed him by the collar of his tunic and forced him to his feet. "Let's see how far your treachery goes." He marched Gnatho out the door into the hall. Gnatho's room was only two doors down from his, and Leonidas dragged the parasite's flailing body there.

Slamming the door shut behind them, Leonidas proceeded to ransack the room. He swiftly went through the desk drawers, casting all the papers and contents onto the ground in turn. He looked under the bed, slashed open the amethyst-colored pillows, and then turned to the wooden dresser; red tunics and blue cloaks flew through the air as Leonidas flung each garment out. But he did not find anything. Panting, he seized the oak dresser in both his hands and slammed it to the ground. The wood cracked and splinters became strewn across the floor. Glued beneath the bottom of the dresser, however, was a metal box.

There it is.

Inside there was a communicator, about the size of a brick, encased in sleek white plastic and dotted with lime-green buttons. Snatching it Leonidas rushed over to Gnatho, whom he had left sitting in front of the door. "A secret communicator, I see," he said, looming over him. He thrust it under Gnatho's nose, ramming it against his oblong mouth. "Should I bother to ask who's been the recipient of your illicit communications? Or is the answer all too obvious?"

Leonidas shuddered as a grin appeared upon Gnatho's slimy face.

"I guess I can dispense with my pretenses now, Leonidas." His wrinkly brow rose, and he cackled, "You've caught me!"

"So, you've been feeding Allied intelligence to the Atlanteans. Why?!"

"As you say, I am a sycophant and a parasite—I aid my master for my own gain."

"But you're an Athenian, my subject! You should be toadying to me, you traitor!"

"Do you not remember what I once said to you?" Gnatho shut his eyes. "For a sycophant to retain his position, year after year, requires him to exercise great dexterity and... forethought. Yes, yes. He must not only be able to recognize the risks and opportunities pervading the present day but also reckon in what direction they will take in the future. And when the time shall come that his horse has grown old and weary, he must be prepared to forsake his former beast and to pursue his destiny upon the youngest and most vibrant stallion that his eye spots."

You sleazy, conniving, perfidious...

"Had things turned out differently, you might have been that horse. But..." Gnatho's eyes flew open like a hyena's mouth and his giant bloodshot pupils assaulted Leonidas. "THE FUTURE BELONGS TO ATLANTIS! Critias shall win this war, and become World-King, and I will eat every day from the banquet of his spoils!"

"Gaaahh!" yelled Leonidas, grasping Gnatho by his scruff. His knuckles whitened as he lifted the old man up and slammed him against the door. "Sorry to disappoint you, but that banquet will spoil when Periander slays your tyrant-master. Not that you'd be there." He drew out his pistol and put the cold metal against Gnatho's left temple. "You have manipulated me, embroiled me in your schemes, and betrayed every natural allegiance which you ought to hold."

Gnatho slowed his breathing, his expression undaunted save for one single drop of sweat materializing upon his oily forehead.

"Have you anything to say before you die, traitor?" asked Leonidas.

"Yes." Gnatho looked straight at him with unblinking eyes. His hot rancid breath enfolded Leonidas. "As I just explained, I foresaw this day. Which is why I took measures to dissuade you from killing me."

Pressing the gun closer into Gnatho's head, Leonidas growled, "What would make me spare a murderous thug and traitor to the Alliance such as you?"

"Would it not disrupt the Allied war effort if it became known that the King of Athens murdered his father to attain his crown?"

"You're the only one else who knows. I'll do to you as you did to those guards."

"For now, I'm the only one who knows." Gnatho smirked and a glint came into his eyes. "Before we left Athens, I entrusted one of my associates with a sealed package to be opened in the event that *anything* befell me. In it is the murder weapon (covered with your fingerprints) that you used to kill Athenagoras."

Leonidas flinched, losing his hold on Gnatho. "You told me you disposed of it!"

"I told you many things."

No, no! This rat has been plotting against me all this time... The tangy taste of blood hit Leonidas' mouth as his teeth tore his lip. *That's exactly the sort of thing I feared he had up his sleeve...*

"There is also," added Gnatho, "an audio recording of us discussing how to kill Athenagoras."

"A recording?" Leonidas put his gun back in its holster. "Even then you were planning this? To blackmail me? And let me guess, if something more promising had come up you would have used it to denounce me to my father?"

Gnatho chuckled and a wry smile crawled across his face. "You're a quick learner, Leonidas. That's what I always liked about you."

"But if it's released, your duplicity will also be revealed."

"If I am dead, then what is that to me?"

Leonidas unhanded Gnatho and took several shaky steps away. *Again, you ensnared me, you little snake!* He put his hand to his forehead; sweat from each mixed together, being whisked by the rapidity of his pulses. *I should've killed him long ago, but fear of his tricks and his subtle hinting paralyzed me. Now he openly confirms my suspicions. Ohhhh... what am I to do?*

"There is nothing you can do," gloated Gnatho as though he could read his mind. Touching his fingertips together, he rested them on his nose above his grinning mouth. "Kill me, you kill your legitimacy. You'll simply be known as another—what was that king's name?"

"Patraloäs." Leonidas pronounced the name dolefully, as though his lips were coated with poison. Ever since his father's death, his mind's tongue had been squirming over the name of that Athenian king from centuries ago, the one whose palace portrait was painted over with black.

"Ah, Patraloäs, that young prince and heir to the crown, famed for his downy golden locks, rosy cheeks, and mirthful countenance," remarked Gnatho, nodding along to each historical factoid. "Who would have thought him capable of poisoning his father to expedite his inheritance? I believe it was two years he reigned before the truth came out. Then his subjects turned on him, paraded him in golden chains through the streets of Athens, and in due course flogged him to death. Hmmm…" His eyebrows rose. "What do you think our modern Athenians would do?"

Leonidas flew back to grab him again. "If I kill you in secret," he hissed, placing his gun on Gnatho's head again, "how will your friend find out you're dead?"

Gnatho yawned. "I call him weekly. Failing that, he is to publicize all."

"How I hate you!" Leonidas stepped back, inwardly cursing Gnatho and also himself for having fallen into his trap. He gritted his teeth and glared at the parasite. "You've spun your web well. I have no choice. If I let you depart in peace, you'll reveal nothing?"

Gnatho held up his left hand, grimier than his right, and said, "On my honor."

You dishonorable wretch! He raised his fist but sighed instead of struck. "Go."

Gnatho quickly opened the door. He was halfway out when Leonidas commanded him to stop.

"I must know something. The attack on Athens, the force shields sabotaged—exactly at what point did you decide to switch your allegiance to Critias? Was it after the war started? Or have you been in his employ this whole time?"

Gnatho shrugged his scrawny shoulders. "What difference, at this point, does it make?"

As soon as the sycophant had slipped out, Leonidas closed the door. Glancing at the ransacked room, the secret communicator on the floor, he buried his head in his palm.

What have I done? What further evil will come from this? Cursed be the day I first inclined my ear to him. I should have plunged a blade through his putrid heart!

CHAPTER THIRTY-TWO

*N**O, NO... WHY? WHY is this happening?*

Lysander pulled his cloak's hood tighter around his pallid face as he cringed on the upper balcony of the palace temple. He was alone on the dark balcony. Yet on the ground level a hundred feet below him, visible if one would only peer over the golden railing, were the flickering lights of torches. If one were still blind to them, smoke from burning frankincense kept wafting upwards to assault any nearby nostril.

Amid the fiery glow walked the priests. Dressed in their all-black robes and gray turbans (as prescribed by Critias' liturgical reforms), the twelve men ambled up the column-lined aisle to the altar, swinging their noxious thuribles as they went. After them came a similarly appareled Critias surrounded by his bodyguards. He assumed his place at the head of the altar, oozy-eared Thrax standing on his right, while his priests divided into lines of six on opposite sides of the altar. Then he signaled with his hands for a group of soldiers to approach.

They marched up the aisle, encircling an old man whom they violently jostled. The prisoner, bound with manacles and fetters, had bruises all over his face and cuts that still bled. The rest of his body was likewise injured; shoves from the guards pushed him farther than his feeble legs could carry him. When they reached the altar, the guards grabbed the old man and slammed him atop it. They removed his shackles but only to replace them with larger ones which they fastened to four iron poles drilled into the floor at each corner of the altar.

Lysander began weeping heavily, the snot dribbling from his nose and running down his chin. The man strapped to the altar, bound, and gagged like a lamb about to be slaughtered, was none other than his father Timaeus.

"We are gathered here tonight, in the sight of the Light-Bringer," proclaimed Critias, gesturing wildly to the small crowd of officials, "to dedicate to our great god the body and soul of this abominable traitor. His treasonable deeds have been exposed: communicating with the Unnamable Traitor in a grand conspiracy against my crown. Now he shall suffer a penalty appropriate for his crime."

When he snapped his fingers, several guards ripped Timaeus' rags off.

While they were doing this, Critias threw his head upwards. His tongue lashing wildly between his cavernous jaws, he roared, "O Light-Bringer, you who enlighten me and my realm, who will give me victory over the vermin waging war against your son, accept this offering—the first of many!"

The priests began chanting: "*Nos illuminati, cultores Luciferi, ut ferat lucem aetheriam nobis Princeps Potestatis Aeris, omnes proditores infidelesque sacrificabimus!*"

Receiving a large pot from Thrax's hands, Critias set it on the altar and opened it.

Lysander gagged, his mouth curling in disgust, as Critias took out leeches and placed them on Timaeus.

Critias let loose a haughty laugh. "This leech sought to drain my royalty away. Now let him have his lifeblood sucked dry by his own kind! Then, once they've infused themselves with his foul life's essence, we will boil them in a stew, a sweet savor for the Light-Bringer! Mua-ha-ha-ha-ha-ha-ha!"

Vilest tyrant! cursed Lysander. He rubbed his eyes with his vein-bulging fists. *Impious miscreant! If I could smuggle a gun into the palace or get a blade past your guards—ohhhh! How I would make you suffer!* Unable to watch Timaeus' torture any longer, Lysander crawled several feet away from the railing. He lay down on the cold stone floor, sobbing, and curled up in the fetal position. *O, Father... If only there were something I could do...*

Ten minutes passed with him in that position, his eyes burning from the rising plumes of incense and his ears from the torturous chanting.

Then the chanting stopped.

Lysander raised his head and sniffed. The scent of incense was less than before. *Could it be done?* Steadying himself, he stood up and crept over to the railing. He tentatively leaned forwards and, forcing his eyes to open, looked down.

Critias and all the rest had left. The room was empty. Empty, that is, except for Timaeus, who was still chained to the altar. His writhing body confirmed that life yet pulsed in him.

Whirling around so fast that his hood blew backwards, Lysander bolted down the balcony's zigzagging stairs. When he reached the bottom, the ground level was still empty. The room was now dimmer, since only several oil lamps affixed to the ancient marble walls remained after the torchbearers left.

"Father, Father!" whispered Lysander, racing over to the altar.

Timaeus raised his bruised head, quite white except for patches of dried blood, and trained his dim eyes on his son. "Lysander, is that you?" He coughed and a tremor surged up his body as Lysander removed his cloak and began using it to swat the leeches away.

"Yes, Father. I'm here." He tugged on the nearest chain; but it was bolted tight, and he did not have the key.

"Forget it, Son. I'm done for."

"No, I have to save you," Lysander insisted through gritted teeth, the tears running down his cheeks.

"You can't save me. (Even if you could free me, there's not enough life left in me.)" Timaeus coughed more, thick spittle flying from his mouth onto skin still bleeding from where the leeches had sucked. "But you can, and must, save our king, Periander."

Lysander sniveled, "How, Father? What can I do now?"

"Out on that balcony where we watched Critias' speech to the masses last week—you remember the one?—there's a tile to the right of the door, the third one down. Press on each of its corners simultaneously and it will pop up. Underneath it I hid a flash drive before they captured me."

"What's on it?"

Timaeus shut his eyes, his facial skin wrinkled, and laid his head back with a grimace. "I discovered something dreadful: a weapon that will give Critias immense power once it's operational, enough to overawe the world. That is how they discovered my espionage. In order to obtain the information, I had to take some risky moves. It was dangerous, but I had to do it; from what I'd heard about it, no risk was unjustified." His eyes flew open and locked on to Lysander's. "King Periander must get this information! The flash drive contains everything he needs to know about it. That is what I need you to do, my son. Get it and get out of the city. Don't come back. I never told my tormentors about your espionage; but even if you were the most fanatical of all Critias' subjects, I wouldn't count on your safety now that your father's been condemned. Go!"

"O Father..." He stomped on a leech on the floor; his hand feebly tugged once more upon the poles' chains.

"Lysander, that's enough," murmured Timaeus. "You've been a good son, a faithful servant to our king... I'm so proud of you. I know you'll do what I'm asking you."

"Yes, Father. I'll... I'll do it. I won't let you down. I love you."

"And I love you." Timaeus coughed out his final lungful of air while his neck crashed down onto the altar's stone slab. Even in death his eyes, glazed over, rigorously gazed at Lysander as though emitting an intense plea.

Lingering a few moments, not even conscious that a couple of leeches had crawled onto his leg from the cloak in his hand which dragged on the floor. He brushed the biting pests off and turned around to go.

He's with the Deity now, away from Critias' cruelty, he told himself. His irate nails dug into his palms as two fists were born. *I will deliver the information to our king, Father. With your help, he will defeat Critias. He'll avenge every indignity and agony the tyrant made you suffer. And I will be there—a witness to your justice!*

CHAPTER THIRTY-THREE

As Guneus steered the chariot up the body-strewn hill, the sound of cannons and tanks blaring in the rear, Periander observed the battle still raging below.

For the two hours since the Atlanteans emerged at ten o'clock, Allied soldiers had been clashing on the fields outside Atlantis City's eastern wall. Critias' forces numbered at least seventy-five thousand men; Periander matched them by diverting men from the other camps, making this the single largest battle yet of the siege. The thousands of soldiers lying dead in their own blood or in that of their enemies, their bodies pierced by gunfire, whole limbs obliterated by cannons, bodies crushed beneath the tracks of tanks and being ground up within their armor like noodle soup inside a can, testified to the battle's ferocity.

The chariot reached their mobile battlefield command station atop the hill. A giant olive tent, surrounded at each corner by a portable force shield generator, housed four lines of tables inside. On them were computers, monitors, and communications equipment; thirty officers and technicians, howling commands to one another or broadcasting them to troops on the battlefield, rushed frantically inside the tent.

Dismounting, Periander hollered to Demosthenes who was coming to greet him. "Our right flank needs support. Divert the Thirty-Seventh Battalion to them."

"At once," said Demosthenes.

Periander approached a table on which a hologram of the battlefield was being projected. He removed his helmet, accepted a glass of lukewarm water from a corporal, and guzzled half of the liquid while the other half flowed down his platinum beard.

"Periander," called Leonidas, helmet in hand, coming up behind him, "how are we holding up?"

Eyeing the hologram, Periander said pensively, "We haven't lost yet, but they've got the momentum and are pushing us back. If we don't break their ranks soon, they'll break ours, and then we'll have no choice but to retreat." *That means relocating Camp Andreia…*

Having said that, he left the chaotic tent and went thirty paces away to just within the edge of the force field. There he could observe the orderly lines of soldiers, both Allied and Atlantean, stretching across the fields below.

Why aren't we winning these skirmishes? wondered Periander, his hand supporting his chin. *The invasion landings went better than could have been hoped for; next to those, a siege should be easy. Instead, these recurring skirmishes are draining our forces, our supplies, our morale. These foreign troops, as brave as they are, do not love this country as I do; they are not fighting to save it, but to stop Critias. The Athenians want vengeance. Indra wants to augment his realm's security (and, as I increasingly suspect, to seize all our American colonies for his own). And my own countrymen are either too decadent or apathetic to rally behind us. Only the prospect of victory unites the Allies; and if that falters, the whole Alliance is in jeopardy.*

Periander shivered as a chill jockeyed from his tailbone to his neck. *What if Critias can hold out long enough, and the Allies lose their stomach for endless bloodletting? Might some of them seek a separate settlement with him? I know Leonidas will stand by me, but what about the others…? Egypt suffers the brunt of casualties. Would Ozymandias quit? We must win. We must stop losing ground outside the gates of the city. O Deity, what are we doing wrong?*

"By blood must bloodguilt be assuaged."

That voice!

Behind him, appearing this time in the guise of an Egyptian infantry-man with a suntanned scalp, was the Watcher. He smiled. "Salutations, Son of Themistocles."

"Watcher, what do you mean 'bloodguilt'?"

"It is the answer to your question."

"I don't understand."

"Periander," said the Watcher, putting one hand on Periander's shoulder and with the other directing his gaze to the battlefield below, "the Allies undergo defeat and losses because among you there is one who has polluted the Earth with innocent blood. Even now, the stench thereof rises heavenwards, which the Deity abhors; wherefore He has withdrawn His blessings from the Allied forces till the innocent blood is atoned for by the blood of him that shed it."

Periander's eyes swelled, and his mouth withered, the moisture of his body fleeing through his skin. "Can one man's offense bring disaster down upon whole armies?"

"If the offense be grave enough." The Watcher, his heavy-set eyes focusing on him, spoke forcefully; his chin and lips stiffened with solemnity. "And foulest of all this murder is."

As Periander observed the battle, and witnessed his soldiers fall, indignation arose in his heart. His hands became fists, and his eyes turned red. "Whatever man has done this foul deed, transgressing both divine and human laws, let that villain die! I will permit no coldhearted butcher, no callous slayer of the innocent, to stand by me in my fight against another of his ilk!"

"Your piety is admirable."

Periander shut his eyes and flexed his fingers. His hand's tendons were burning with rage. Picturing the criminal, he declared, "Tell me the man, and with these own hands of mine I will extinguish that wretch's life!"

He opened his eyes and the Watcher was gone.

"Lord Periander, Lord Periander!"

Before he could absorb what he had seen and heard, Periander startled more at the shouting sergeant who was rushing towards him than he had at the appearance of the Watcher himself.

"Lord Periander, we're receiving a holoprojector message from King Critias himself. He wishes to speak with you."

Slapping his face a couple times to recalibrate himself for earthly cogitation, he wondered, *Critias? Now? Why?* This was the first direct contact that Critias had sought with any of the Allies since the beginning of the war. "Whatever could he want?" Leaving the question to dangle and the grass on which he stood, Periander reëntered the tent.

Everyone stood around the table where the emerald-green hologram of Critias was being projected, their faces drooping and eyebrows sagging. Noiseless were all that were in the room, gazing at the hologram. Not even two moths exchanged a whispery theory on why Critias had called.

"Ah, here's the little man that's stirred up the whole world against me." Critias glowered haughtily at Periander, his cheekbones high, and his voice seeping with scorn. With the exception of his helmet, he was wearing his full armor; it was as black as his hair that scruffily overflowed onto his forehead. Around his lobes danced his skull-shaped earrings.

"You stir the world well enough yourself," spat Periander, his nostrils flaring. "Just tell me what you want, Critias."

"Well, I for one have been busily slaying your soldiers all morning." Critias stepped aside briefly to reveal the blood-soaked field behind him. "And now I've grown bored. Your men are *just too easy* to kill!"

Periander growled and grinded his teeth.

"Sssoooooooo," continued Critias sneeringly while gesturing with his bone-tattooed hand, "I thought I'd help you save your soldiers' lives by asking for your surrender—now. Why wait for the inevitable? Just capitulate already. You've lost."

"We will never surrender to you!" Periander declared, slamming his fist down on the table only inches away from the holoprojector. Leonidas and the other commanders seconded his defiance. "Until the last huff of air escapes my lungs, I will fight you. And I will defeat you. Then I will exact retribution on your head for every single crime you have committed against Atlantis and the world, starting from when you murdered my wife!" His eyes whirled with heated rage and cool sweat oozed out of his body's pores.

A frown spread down his chin as Critias shook his head. "Tsk, tsk, tsk. I feared you would reject my humanitarian proposal—I really did. Oh, well. I see your heart is set on revenge. So let the war continue! I'll prevail eventually; I've seen it written in the stars."

"You can only dream!" retorted Periander.

Chuckling, Critias said, "I find your rage and its intensity stimulating, your passion appetizing." He rubbed his hands together. His long tongue moistened his thin pale lips. "Want to fight, Periander, just the two of us? End the endless clash of pawns. Let us go king-to-king, finish this game in the style of our ancestors, winner takes all. Huh?"

Before Periander could respond to so unexpected a proposition, Leonidas, who was standing to his right, answered for him. "Don't bait my friend with your guileful plots," he shouted, wagging his finger at the hologram. "Periander does not have to fight alone. He has me at his side along with the Athenians, the Egyptians, and many more! We all are looking forwards to sacking your palace."

Unamused, Critias dryly replied, "The High King did not address you, *Prince* Leonidas. Leave the talking to us kings."

"You are addressing the King of Athens," rejoined Periander, rising in defense of his friend. "A king more than your equal."

"Oh, so foolish of me," said Critias as he banged his head in jest. "How could I forget Leonidas's grueling quest for kingship when I was just regaled by his squire recounting it?"

What in the Deity's name is he talking about? thought Periander, his forehead wrinkling in perplexity and his eyes narrowing as they focused on Critias. His range of vision had contracted so as to overlook Leonidas who, arms a-twitching with his blushing head lowered, was shuffling awkwardly beside him.

Alternating his gaze between Periander and Leonidas, Critias chuckled. "Don't tell me your dearest friend in the world hasn't confided his secret in you." He turned his ivory head to his side and smirked. "You were right."

"Secret? What's he talking about?" asked Periander, putting his arm around Leonidas.

Leonidas did not answer but freed himself from Periander's grip.

Critias grinned and said, "I am speaking of how your friend Leonidas, willfully and with malice aforethought, murdered his aged father in his sleep!"

Gasps erupted throughout the room. Everyone's eye lenses clouded over with Leonidas' face.

"*Murdered* him that he might take his crown for himself." Critias shook his head. "And you Allies claim to represent the forces of morality! Defenders of human rights! Ha!"

"No, you lie!" yelled Periander, looking at Critias and then Leonidas. There could be no way that that was true—no way that Leonidas, a man whom he had known for years, a man whom he knew to be conscientious and upright, a man who came to his aid when almost no one else was willing, could ever commit so unholy and evil a deed.

This was obviously slander. A vile, cowardly attempt to subvert the Alliance.

Yet why did Leonidas remain silent instead of defending his honor?

"Oh, it is quite true." Critias nodded to his side and an elderly man appeared before him on the hologram.

I recognize him! That's—

"Hello, Leonidas," said Gnatho nonchalantly. He grinned. "I have told Critias every sordid detail about your patricide: how you plotted with me, how the guards were killed, and then how you slit Athenagoras' throat before you left me to clean up the evidence of your crime."

Saying nothing, Leonidas gazed at the floor.

Periander grabbed Leonidas by his shoulders and moved his face within an inch of his. "Say something! Tell me these are lies!"

Blinking slowly, with his cheeks reddened like autumnal leaves, Leonidas whispered, "It's true." As Periander recoiled, his shocked hands covering his dropping jaw, Leonidas turned towards everyone else in the room. "What he says is true. I killed my father."

You are the man the Watcher spoke of! No, no, no!

"He admits it!" gloated Critias, who had pressed himself so closely to his holoprojector's camera that his giant laughing head monopolized the hologram.

"Grrrrrr!" Periander grabbed their holoprojector by its edges, raised it above his head, and threw it outside the tent. It landed twenty feet away, computer chips and metal gizmos flying this way and that, while smoke rose from its ruined hulk.

Leonidas glanced at the others, all of whom had backed away from him.

"Why did you do it?" said Periander, scarcely able to comprehend the revelation. *You're the last man I'd have suspected.*

"I did it for you, Periander," said Leonidas. "For you and for my homeland threatened by Atlantis's tyrant. When I saw you, when I saw what Critias had done to you—to you, sweet Cornelia, and Jason—as your friend I yearned to help you in your fight, to destroy Critias. And not just you! Hearing of his lust for domination and of the terrors he was inflicting on any that dared challenge his tyranny, I feared for the safety of my own nation. I wanted Athens to join your coalition to stop Critias before he could attack my country and do to it what he did to Teotihuacan. Time after time I explained all this to my father, only to have him categorically reject everything I proposed. He was a fool, an old fool too blinded by the horrors of his youth to take the preventative measures appropriate for the present. My heart overflowed with despair at what to do."

"Leonidas..." said Periander, inching towards him.

Leonidas put his hand up to halt him. "I committed the double atrocity of slaying not only my king but my father. Although it was that sycophantic snake Gnatho who urged me to do it, who offered every conceivable sophistry for regicide, who callously manipulated my feelings and my fears—despite all that, I was the one who feebly yielded to his chicanery and consented to his plot. I was the one who murdered my father, betraying him, my country, and the Deity too through my noxious crime.

"I allowed myself to be deluded into thinking, if only I could become king at once, all would be well: I could help you and save my country. But I was wrong. No matter how wrongheaded I thought my father was, I was duty-bound to obey. My disagreement towards his policy justified no murder. And it was especially wrong to use my country's safety as a pretext's bludgeon to try to overcome his will. I erred in putting my father and Athens in a false dichotomy. Truly, as I now realize, no one can attack a king without also attacking the king's country. Yet I did it. And you know what?"

Leonidas chuckled as tears began streaming from his eyes to inundate his russet beard. "It was all for nothing! The same night I killed him, Atlantis attacked. We were going to go to war regardless of what I did! I didn't have to kill him. Can you believe it? Oh, how tragic life can be..."

"What will you do now?" ventured someone, an Athenian by the looks of him.

"What can I do?" Leonidas' tearful eyes blinked despondently, and his hands and shoulder blades rose like those of bleak pallbearers. "I've forfeited my royal legitimacy by treason, my claim on life by murder, my humanity by iniquity. There's only one course left for me. But before exiting life, I will try to redeem myself by performing one final, heroic deed."

"NOOOOOOO!"

***

As Leonidas tore out of the room, rivers streaming down his guilt-ridden cheeks, Periander leapt towards him. His right hand stretched out before him, the fingers extended like the claws of a lion, and his feet departed the ground. Periander grasped wildly for him; coming within an inch of Leonidas' shoulder, his hand fluttered past a thousand-eyed fly that was as bewildered by this situation as was everyone in the tent.

Hard though he tried, Periander failed to take hold of Leonidas. And as his body fell earthwards, landing facedown on the dirt floor, Leonidas sped out of the tent.

Outside, parked nearby on the edge of the force field, was Leonidas' chariot. His charioteer sat with his back against it, drinking from a thermos; but when he spotted Leonidas, he rose to climb aboard.

"Stop, Aratus!" cried Leonidas, running up beside him. He climbed into the charioteer's compartment, grabbed its metal railing with one hand while he flipped the ignition switch with the other. He told the visibly perplexed Aratus, "I must go solo on this mission," before speeding off in the chariot.

From behind came Periander's fading voice: "No, Leonidas, you'll be killed!"

I know.

Steering the chariot down the hillside, a helmetless Leonidas headed straight for the thickest part of the battlefield. With his heart thumping in tune with the cannon fire that he was passing on his right, Leonidas removed his gun from its holster.

"I don't deserve to live!" he cried, shooting several Atlanteans as he barreled through the throng. "Father, forgive me for what I've done!" Leonidas was jolted as the chariot zoomed over two new victims of his gun.

Swerving to avoid an enemy tank, Leonidas said, "O Deity, I am not worthy to address You. But please, please let me atone for my sins by my death." He approached an Athenian, pinned beneath an Atlantean's foot, at five yards per second; and by a quick blast of his laser saved his countryman's life.

Then the stench of burned hair flooded his nostrils when an enemy's laser hit him in the rear. The hair around his neck was charred, but that was all.

Clenching his jaw, Leonidas prayed, *Just let me take out one man with me in death,* as he eyed the Eastern Gate, looming a thousand yards ahead of him. He sped towards it because it had been visible in the background of Critias' hologram.

And Leonidas intended to kill him.

Now, only five hundred yards away, it was possible to make out the dimmest figure of Critias who still remained outside the wall, conversing idly with Gnatho.

Steadying his gun in front of him, his unblinking eyes dry from the whooshing air as they appraised their target, Leonidas waited till he was in firing range. As he drew near, he must have been spotted, for Critias and Gnatho suddenly began to move away.

Not so fast! With his finger hovering over the trigger, Leonidas moved his gun and—

BOOOOMM!

From behind him, from some unknown soldier ignorant of the identity of whom he targeted, a laser beam smashed through Leonidas' skull.

But before his chariot sped out of control and crashed upside-down, taking out three Atlanteans with it; before his lifeless body, flung out in the crash, landed in the bloodied soil; before soldiers' boots trampled over him, pressing his corpse down into the earth and covering it in muck as though to improvise a burial, Leonidas, dying, managed to pull the trigger.

The laser shot forth from the gun with as much intensity as did Leonidas' soul from his body. Hurtling through the air, it neared its target. Critias' eyes grew wide when he saw it. Then, as the High King fell backwards in his seat, the laser, only three feet from him, struck Gnatho in the adjacent seat. It hit him in his heart. He was wearing no armor.

Thus perished King Leonidas of Athens and the sycophant Gnatho.

Chapter Thirty-Four

"**I** STILL CANNOT BELIEVE he's gone."

Five hours had passed since Periander's dearest friend slipped out of his grasp and charged headlong towards his death in battle. Lugubrious though he was, Periander had maintained his composure and stayed on the battlefield to command the Allied forces until, two long hours later, he oversaw their victory. With the battle won, he quickly retreated to Camp Andreia, sealing himself up in his room. Here he now lay, collapsed on his bed, in the lithe arms of his wife.

"I know," said Psyche gently as she caressed his platinum locks of hair. The sunset's glow, the only light in their dusky room, filtered through the windowsill and brightened up her face; the burgundy, ruby, and crimson rays were dancing around her blushing cheeks, forming a gorgeous ensemble of reds. "It's shocking to hear Leonidas' name mentioned in the same sentence as parricide. For such a good man to have been misled down that path, to do what he did, to be torn by the crushing weight of guilt while knowing his crime was all for naught, until at last the truth emerged and, in remorse, he cast away his life—that is the whole soul of tragedy."

"He did rush into the thick of battle because it would likely result in his death, but don't say he threw his life away: he died with his gunhand pointed at the enemy, not at himself. He fought heroically before being killed. And at least he took out a few of the enemy with him, including that wretched parasite that seduced him," Periander remarked acrimoniously, looking up at the ceiling. *You died honorably in battle, Leonidas, just as you lived honorably your whole life (except for that one thing).* He sighed.

"Do you feel alright?"

"No, I don't," he muttered, his eyebrows falling angrily as he sat up on the bed. "I can't help but feel I played a lead part in this tragedy."

"Please don't say that, Periander."

"But it's true!" He tapped his chest. "It all revolved around me. If it weren't for me, King Athenagoras would still be alive. But because he wouldn't help me, my greatest friend in all the world—that devoted fool!—allowed himself to believe that he could only help me by killing his father. He told me so himself..."

Psyche encircled his abdomen with her arms. "You can't blame yourself for Leonidas. So, he did it for you. You never asked him to! You're not responsible for his actions. He bore his own guilt."

"I know all that, and I wrestle not to blame myself. But it's the same way as how I feel about..." He left off without uttering Cornelia's name. "I regularly condemn and acquit myself; I don't know why, but I feel like I must, and... it's excruciating."

"Oh, Periander." Her warm lips kissed his cheek.

About to reciprocate, he was interrupted by pounding on the door. "What is it?"

"Lord Periander," came the muffled voice of one of his officers, "we have a situation involving one of the enemy combatants we captured."

Not being in the mood to deal with so mundane a matter, he grunted irritably, "We've taken many captives. Can you not handle one more?"

"But this is no ordinary prisoner. He deliberately sought us out during the battle to surrender. He claims that you know him, says his name's Lysander Besa."

Lysander! Periander bolted from his bed just as a starving lion pounces upon a boar. He flung the door open. "Why wasn't I notified at once?"

The officer, his hair blowing backwards and his cap shuddering from the door's gust, stuttered, "W-w-we've only just now sorted out the prisoners. It's been hectic all day."

"Bring him at once!"

The officer scurried away, returning within minutes with Lysander. Apart from the Atlantean infantryman's uniform he wore, the shackles on his wrists, and several scrapes around his bruised left eye given to him by an overzealous soldier during his surrender, Lysander otherwise appeared the same as he did before Periander's exile from Atlantis.

"It's so good to see an old friend again!" said Periander with a smile, ordering the shackles removed. "And so unexpected."

"Majesty," said Lysander as he kneeled and bowed his head, "my father and I have been your eyes and ears in Critias' den, faithfully serving your interests and relaying what news we gathered when we could. You must be wondering why I've abandoned my post."

"It must be of great consequence."

"It is." Lysander looked up, sheepishly. His eyes swirled, his teeth-chewed lips trembled, and his perspiring chin wavered. "Timaeus Besa is dead, horrifically executed by Critias when his spying was discovered."

Oh, not Timaeus, too... Periander lowered his head and his eyelids. "He was a true friend to my father and a most dependable subject to the end."

"I assure you, Sire, his death was not in vain. He risked his life to obtain information vital to the outcome of the war. With no way to send it to you due to the siege, I had to bring it myself. Hence my present appearance: blending in among the departing infantry was the only way to leave the city."

Periander told Lysander to postpone his report, ordering the officer who had brought him to summon Agathocles and Demosthenes at once. After a pause, he added Cleomenes, Leonidas' younger brother and successor as king.

While waiting for the others, Periander and Psyche sought to lessen Lysander's discomforts. They had a glass of white wine, fruit, cheese, and bread fetched for him; Psyche dabbed his scrapes with a cloth dipped in hydrogen peroxide and put an icepack to his swollen eye; and Periander took out some articles of clothing from the royal wardrobe for him to change into.

As soon as everyone gathered, they were all seated on stools that had been brought in apart from Periander and Psyche, who sat at the end of their bed.

Standing among his listeners, Lysander began to speak. Per Periander's instruction, he recounted the minutiae of the whole affair—starting with Timaeus' arrest and ending with his own escape from Atlantis. With his arms flying energetically and his voice modulating its pitch according to the scene, a teary-eyed Lysander narrated the horrors of the palace temple with more passion than the finest stage actor. Psyche wept and Periander juiced an apple in his hand as Lysander vividly described Timaeus' tortured death. For his finale, with his audience focused on him, he revealed the existence of Project Heliocalypse by inserting the flash drive into a holoprojector and displaying the satellite's schematics.

Silence engulfed the room as the listeners exchanged glances with one another.

"So, we have a month," said Periander at last, "before Critias will be able to harness the power of the asteroids against us. One month to defeat him before he acquires this... super weapon capable of obliterating cities." He rested his cupped hands on his chin. *First Leonidas, now this... What a cursed day this has been!*

"We do not yet know if Heliocalypse will prove as decisive as Critias' scientists believe," cautioned Demosthenes, twirling his hazel sideburn. "No one has ever attempted to weaponize space. Frankly, this whole scheme sounds fantastical. Even if Critias' people have built a device with the intention of trapping and redirecting asteroids over the Earth, designing and execution are two quite different things. We do not know if this device is operable or can become so; even if it could become so, the time required might stretch beyond the period of the war. That being the case, Critias' 'wonder weapon' would turn out to be little more than an idle hope of his."

"My father didn't die over an 'idle hope,'" said Lysander angrily. "He died because he knew Heliocalypse was a colossal and very real, very imminent threat. We have barely a month until Phaëton is in position to be weaponized. The Deity help us all if Critias succeeds in doing so."

Agathocles swung his right fist up into the air. "Then we really shouldn't underestimate the risk it poses." He flashed a perturbed look at Demosthenes, who pointedly looked the other way.

"No, we shouldn't," said Periander, rubbing his chin. "While Heliocalypse's status is still unverified, I wouldn't be surprised if they've been working on it for a long time. (I know for a fact Eudoxia, going back years, was spending money wildly on her black projects and this scheme smacks of her.) And Timaeus was always a meticulous man; if he thought the project was nearing completion, then I'm inclined to believe the danger is real. We should definitely develop contingency plans in the event such a terrifying weapon is operational: the consequences of not acting are too dire. And after what Critias did to the American rebels with his atrocious slaughter of Teotihuacan, it wouldn't surprise me in the least if he sought to wipe entire cities off the Earth."

"If Critias does gain the power to redirect an asteroid and cause it to crash on a location of his choice," began Cleomenes, "where wouldn't he be able to strike? Athens, Memphis, Mohenjo-Daro? I don't know about the other cities, but Athens' force field would very likely buckle upon impact of such a concentrated mass as Phaëton careening down at so high a velocity."

Agathocles added with a nod, "Cities' shields are designed to absorb blows from missiles and lasers, not to deflect mammoth asteroids."

"If it didn't penetrate initially, the colossal strain on the shields would eventually overwhelm them," remarked Periander, gazing down at the floor. "I believe even Atlantis City's shields would collapse under Phaë-ton's weight."

"If the worst case comes true, Critias will have a powerful weapon," said Psyche dolefully. "It's just a question of whether it will materialize or not before we can defeat him."

Periander leaned his head back while his hand went over his platinum hair from front to back. Sighing, he muttered bluntly, "Perhaps I should accept Critias' challenge and settle the war king-to-king—assuming he *meant it*." The bile rose in his throat as specters of Critias surfaced from his memory, two images of him predominating: his crazed, blood-lustful mug from that night when he pursued them to the death of Cornelia, and his more recent fit of cackling upon watching Leonidas writhe with guilt.

Critias must suffer for all the suffering he's caused....

Although he was only thinking aloud, Periander's brusque suggestion triggered fiery reäctions from the rest.

Cleomenes spoke first. "I do not think it best serves," he said formally, clearing his throat, "the interests of the Alliance to agree to such a stip-ulation proposed by the High King."

Periander frowned and eyed him warily. While he had always been able to trust Leonidas implicitly, he was not yet familiar enough with his brother or his brother's goals to make a judgment of him, much less to depend on him.

Then Psyche clutched Periander's arm so hard with both her hands that the nails all but dug into his skin. This caused the folds of his skin to darken where they were grasped. "Periander, you can't fight Critias!" she cried, her voice almost cracking. "He fights like a demon! He'd kill you."

"Nonsense!" declared Agathocles as he rose from his stool. Placing his left foot atop the stool and his left elbow on the thigh, he pointed towards Periander with his right hand and said, "Periander is the greatest warrior in our army! We see him daily cut the enemy down in battle after battle; few have notched more kills in personal combat than him! You can beat that snake, Sire. I have no doubt!"

Demosthenes remained seated serenely while casting an icy glance at Agathocles. "Our king is undoubtedly a fierce combatant, but as his queen correctly points out, so is Critias. No duel between them could have its outcome predicted. It would therefore be highly foolish to gamble the entire war—risk all the gains we've made—on a single fight when we still possess immense military forces."

"Precisely why Athens could not support it," interjected Cleomenes, saying the words quite hastily as if that could tack Demosthenes' analysis onto his earlier statement.

"Nor could Father," said Psyche.

"Alright, alright," said Periander, raising his hand just as Agathocles was about to make a retort. "Really, I was only thinking aloud. But if not that, then what are we to do?" He looked at Lysander. "Lysander has confirmed that we shouldn't anticipate either mutiny or starvation occurring before the asteroid arrives. If the siege is to be broken within a month, before the window for Heliocalypse opens, how are we to do it?"

Several unconvincing or infeasible plans were proposed before Lysander said, "What about tunneling underneath the force fields to enter the city from below?"

"We tried that early on," said Periander. "Each time their sonar and other sensors detected our diggers, and they destroyed the tunnels."

"I know all that," replied an undeterred Lysander. "I heard reports of it. Which is why I looked into the matter and learned that the scanners have a blind spot over at the Mitallophagous Hills due to the orichalcum deposits in them. If we can tunnel under them past the northeast section of the wall, a specialist team could infiltrate the city under cover of dark and disable the force fields from the inside."

"Allowing us to take the city by storm!" Periander leapt up with a grin. "Yes, that could work." *This is the kind of windfall that can turn the fortunes of war.*

"But how can we get close enough to dig?" protested Cleomenes, his baritone voice conveying his perplexity. "I don't care about electronic scanners: if we bring out the borers, the Atlanteans will spot them with their own eyes!"

His mind racing with excitement, Periander replied, "I've already thought of that. First, we'll push our line all the way to the Mitallophagous Hills. Then Camp Dicaeus will relocate as near to it as is safe, becoming itself the cover for the digging crews. Indra's air force, of course, will have to increase its presence to safeguard the camp's relocation. I'll contact him on a secure channel and inform him of these developments; Psyche, I trust you can likewise inform Ozymandias."

Quickly everyone agreed to Lysander and Periander's plan except Cleomenes. His silence lingered several moments before he slowly turned towards Periander and said, "You have my support as well."

"Great!"

"Periander," continued Cleomenes, "I know you had a special relationship with Leonidas, and he with you. We know he would have done anything for you. I am not my brother. Nonetheless, I want you to know that I am committed to maintaining my country's freedom and avenging the attack upon it. Even if the worst should happen, Athens will never capitulate to that madman."

Periander thanked him for his pledge. Then, a scintilla of hopefulness surging through his veins, he announced, "We have our plan. Guard it with the utmost secrecy. If anyone has an alternative idea, we can try that too. In fact, we will try everything, no matter how implausible, from now until Asteroid Day! And, by the grace of the Deity, we will defeat Critias and avenge all our fallen comrades!"

CHAPTER THIRTY-FIVE

TWENTY-SEVEN DAYS PASSED SINCE the Allied leadership was astonished by Lysander's information. While restricting the knowledge of Heliocalypse to their highest echelons lest their forces become dispirited or the Atlanteans realize their plan was divulged, Periander oversaw the amplified assaults on the capital. Endless aerial barrages struck the city's shields to no avail, swelling ranks of ground troops pushed the Atlanteans back up to the walls that they themselves could not breach, and many other failed attempts to storm the city were frantically made. Despite the surface failures, round-the-clock work had begun beneath the Mitallophagous Hills on a tunnel; and the miners were now on the verge of penetrating the city.

The sky above Camp Dicaeus was the darkest it had been in days. The new moon was unreflective, and the dimly blinking stars were obscured by ominous clouds. Thunder resounded in the distance. *This is good*, thought Periander as he glanced skywards. For the nocturnal veil would aid the special forces he was about to send into Atlantis City.

Flanked by Agathocles and Demosthenes, Periander entered the building in the western corner of the camp that covered the site of the tunnel excavation. From the outside it looked no different than any other camp structure: an austere-looking prefabrication whose shabby metal siding blended in among the rest.

The inside of the building, however, was hollow without any internal walls. Its floor consisted of dirt. In the center was a hole whose diameter stretched twenty feet. Deep tracks caused by excavating machinery led up to it from the door, and electrical wires descended down the hole to give light to the miners' work. Emanating from it came the sound of grunting workers which echoed throughout the building.

An officer in charge of the tunneling, clothed in a dirt-covered mining suit, approached Periander. "Sir, we've removed the excavator and have set the explosives at the tunnel's end." He held up a detonator. "Give the word, and those five inches between us and the city are gone."

"Excellent," said Periander. Rubbing his hands, he turned to survey the team of troops lining up in front of the hole.

There were twenty men, half of them shaven-headed Egyptians, nine Athenians, and one Cyrenian whom Periander recognized from his stay in Cyrene. All wore black uniforms and had camouflaging black stripes painted beneath their eyes; the Egyptians even donned black caps lest under city lights their reflective scalps betray them to the enemy. In their hands and satchels on their backs they had guns, grenades, ropes, and tools to sabotage the city's force fields.

"Men," began Periander, "tonight you embark on what may be the most crucial mission of the war. If you succeed, and disable the city's shields, then Allied airships now on standby will converge here, bomb the urban defenses, and allow us to capture the city in one fell stroke. The capital will fall, Critias will be dethroned, and the war will be all but over! Be valiant and know our prayers are with you."

Having spoken, Periander saluted them and they him. With the detonation ordered, the soldiers marched down the tunnel towards their destiny. Periander stood by, leaning over and breathlessly watching till the last soldier had disappeared from sight. Then he went over to the makeshift mission headquarters where Agathocles and Demosthenes were.

For several minutes they and seven commanders and technicians monitored the computers and transmitters whose monotonous beeping filled the air. After the special forces started entering the city, Periander turned to one of the officers.

"How long until we hear from them?"

"Well," murmured the Athenian, rubbing under his chin as his tongue peaked out the side of his lip beneath his bushy gray moustache, "they'll maintain radio silence till they complete their mission. It's about thirty minutes to the nearest force field station, so... maybe a couple hours."

Periander nodded. *Finally,* he thought, gripping his tunic excitedly, *we will break this siege! Then, Critias, nothing will stand between me and you....*

Approaching him, Agathocles leaned over his chair and whispered, "Sire, I've sent dispatches to the other camps to begin preparations to storm the city."

"Good. By the time they're geared up—"

"Mayday, mayday!" ranged the team leader's voice over the speakers.

Periander jumped to his feet, and everyone gathered around.

The moustached officer grabbed the transmitter. "Mother-Cat to Kindle, Mother-Cat to Kindle, what is the problem?"

"We've walked into a horde of enemy soldiers," responded the team leader, his voice crackling over the receiver as well as being interspersed with the sound of gunfire.

"How many? Can you continue the mission?"

"No, no. There's got to be four, five thousand of them. They had to know we were coming. *It was a trap!*"

Periander clenched his fists. "Order them to retreat."

The officer hollered, "Abort the mission, Kindle. Repeat, abort the mission."

There was no response.

"Do you copy?"

Everyone glanced at one another while the radio crackled with dead air.

At last, Periander exclaimed, "We've lost them!" as he kicked a metal cabinet propped up against the wall, causing it to wobble with a thud. He looked over to the hole. "Get the miners to cave in the tunnel pronto. We don't want the enemy to be able to use it to infiltrate *our* camp." He shut his eyes tight and massaged his temples with his fingers.

"I'm sorry, Sire," said Agathocles glumly. He put his hand on Periander's shoulder. "I can't fathom how they could've known we were coming!"

Demosthenes ambled over, twirling his sideburn. "They must have either installed newer, more accurate sensors since Lysander investigated them, or they detected our tunneling another way. In either case, this was an untimely setback."

It certainly was... We're only two days away from when that asteroid is supposed to pass the Earth's exosphere. If it works the way it's supposed to, we're in for horrific troubles. We need to destroy Critias before he gets this weapon. But this was our best chance, and it's failed...

***

S IXTY-FIVE MINUTES LATER, AFTER seeing through the end of the fiasco, Periander returned to Camp Andreia. The sky was still oppressively dark and gloomy. Or was it even darker now that it was past midnight? There was not a flicker above, no, not a single scintilla of starlight.

His eyes and limbs sagging under the weight of drowsiness but his mind whirling on account of his disappointment and frustration, Periander entered the building in which his quarters were. He did not walk far into the building, scarcely making it past the entrance area before he was set upon by his son in the hallway.

Jason was leaning up against the beige wall with his arms crossed, one foot resting on the wall's metal plating. "Father," he called upon seeing Periander. He approached him.

"Why are you still awake?" asked Periander as he greeted his son with an affectionate slap on the cheek. "You should be sleeping."

"There was a camp-wide alert earlier," huffed Jason, his eyes wide and focusing on Periander. "It sounded like a massive operation was about to get underway. Then it was cancelled—no reason given."

"It's not your worry."

"Father, I want to know what's going on."

Periander sighed. "If you must know something, I'll tell you this much. We thought we had found a way to break into the city, to break their resistance and take it by storm. Tonight was to feature such an operation. But our gambit was discovered—neutralized. So, there is still no end in sight for this long-drawn-out siege."

"Is that why we've stepped up our attacks so much lately?"

"Yes, yes," murmured Periander, frowning and rapidly tapping his right foot upon the floor. "It would be preferable for us to take the city sooner rather than later."

Standing before him in the narrow hallway, Jason blocked his father's path. Taking hold of Periander's tunic's sleeve, he asked imploringly, "If it's so important to take the city, then you need all the fighting men you can get. Father, please let me prove my mettle on the battlefield! Take me with you into battle!"

"No, Jason. We've already discussed this. I want you behind the lines for now."

"But I could be of such great use —"

"A battle won't be decided by your presence: you're just one boy."

"I'm not a boy—not anymore." Jason leaned forwards, higher on his toes; his eyebrows scrunched up, and the stubble above his lip jumped up in protest. "I am a man!"

"A young man, a very young man."

"Others my age are soldiers in our armies."

Periander did not contradict that point. Instead, exhaling deeply, he put his arm around Jason's shoulders. Then, with calmness of voice, Periander said, "I am tired now and need to sleep. The next few days are going to be an especially trying period. Coping with that will be challenging enough. Please, just follow the orders I've given you like a good soldier. We can discuss this another time."

For several moments Jason squinted and chewed on his lip. Finally, casting his eyes upon the ground, he mumbled, "Very well, Father."

CHAPTER THIRTY-SIX

"**I** CAN'T BELIEVE HE won't let me fight!" said Jason to the others.

Still chagrined over his father's persistence the prior night, he had sought sympathy from his friends, the young aides and junior officers serving at the Allied Headquarters. Having arrived there this morning, he found four of them not too encumbered by their duties. So, Jason gathered those fellow aides into a vacant conference room at the rear of the building where he now vented his grievances.

"Yeah, your father's just hogging all the glory for himself," remarked a twenty-year-old named Sethos. He was Egyptian, with a shaved head apart from a single sidelock of black hair, and he stood an inch higher than Jason.

The Athenian Akasion, who was about the same age as Jason, seconded that sentiment. "That's what all these old men running the war do: monopolize the battles and victories for themselves while holding us back to run their errands for them." He shook his fist and curled his lips. "I enlisted to get revenge for the attack on my country, not to fetch file-folders and cups of wine for old generals."

"It's so unfair," said another. "We're in here doing nothing when we could be out there winning the war! If they need busboys so bad, why not let the cripples do the job? Or, better yet, the cowards? We actually *want* to fight."

Sethos grabbed Jason by his left arm from behind and raised his hand into the air. "And Jason here has actually fought at close range. He's an experienced fighter!"

"That's right; it makes no sense," agreed Jason, nodding his head eagerly as he recounted once more the incident in the Phoenix Tavern in Cyrene, and how valiantly he fought until that Thrallis took him by surprise. "Yet my father won't acknowledge my abilities! He says I don't have good enough experience for the battlefield. Well, how will I ever gain more battle experience if he won't let me on the battlefield? *To fight*!" He emphasized the last words in reference to the battle of Cleon's Plain, about which he next proceeded to gripe.

They continued talking among themselves, voicing their resentment over their respective assignments, and exchanging tales of battle they had heard from soldiers in the camp. After a few minutes, the door opened, and a colonel entered.

"Hey, you there! Stop slacking off, boys, and report to the command center! There's a battle raging outside in case you didn't notice; the Atlanteans are pushing hard against our ranks."

Jason and the others followed the colonel to the command center. Upon several of the large screens were live feeds of the battlefield off Atlantis City's southern wall courtesy of Allied drones. The battle was essentially fragmented into two pieces: one that was right in front of the wall and one about a mile away where the Atlanteans had pushed back the Allies.

The officers in the room were either in their chairs, leaning over desks or keyboards, or else they were standing to view the main screens and bark orders to subordinates who attentively carried them out. Amid this absorption that everyone had for his own task, no one had noticed that Jason was not at his station. He was still by the entrance, having been pulled aside by Akasion.

"What is it?" asked Jason, brushing off his sleeve where it was pulled.

Akasion grinned and his little eyes glinted. "I think I found the perfect opportunity for you." He signaled another aide, who had not been with them in the conference room, to come over. "Arsenio," he said, pointing at one screen displaying a skirmish of about a hundred soldiers, "is that what I think it is?"

"Yes. Seventy or so Atlanteans have surrounded thirty of our troops around the bottom of that hill. They're cornered on three sides. The only way out is over that hill; but additional Atlanteans are arriving to scale the hill from the rear and prevent any escape route."

"If they do, they'll completely box our men in and be able to slaughter them all," remarked Jason wearily as he eyed the Allied soldiers' situation.

Arsenio nodded. "The Atlanteans don't yet have enough men on the hill to hem in our troops below, but more are on the way. Unless they're stopped quickly, our men won't have a chance to escape alive."

"Why is no one on our side coming to help them?" asked Jason.

"They're too distracted at other parts of the battlefield."

"That's where you come in." Akasion put his arm around Jason's shoulders. "Look, those Atlanteans are all heading up and over to the side of the hill facing our troops. They're not even looking back; they've left their rear completely exposed. Now's your chance! Just gear up, take one of the chariots, surprise them from the rear, and kill them."

Jason's jaw dropped and his spiky hair soared higher in shock. "But I can't just go into battle all by myself." *Father would kill me if I went behind his back...*

"Sure you can." Akasion's hot breath tickled Jason's cheek. "Chariots are fast. Those guys are all lined up... sitting ducks. Just zoom by, shooting as you go, and bam! Instant war hero."

"But he's not authorized to undertake such a mission," said Arsenio, cocking his head as he looked at Akasion. "He'd be guilty of insubordination."

Jason's eyes darted between the two of them while his hands began to sweat.

"So what?" asked Akasion, disdainfully raising his nose high and rolling his eyes. "Jason, your dad's Supreme Allied Commander. What could he do to you for seizing the moment instead of letting these old bozos waste time strategizing stuff until it's too late? Shoot you? Pshaw! He wouldn't punish you; if he did, it wouldn't be too bad. And if you score a big win, he'll have to honor you. 'Cause you'd be a hero."

"Ummm..." murmured Jason, chewing on his chapped lower lip. He had never defied his father in such a way. His comrade's suggestion sent an itchy, sweaty heat surging all over his skin. *And yet if I succeeded...*

Akasion clenched Jason's shoulder tight. "Come on, you've been arguing about how unfair it is, your father saying you can't fight. Show him he's wrong. Show the whole world what you can do! Do it for all us lackeys stuck on the sidelines."

Jason hesitated a moment. Then he clenched his fists. *He's right. I can fight—I'm a warrior just like my father!* "Alright, I'll do it!"

Cheered on by Akasion and (to a lesser extent) Arsenio, Jason slipped out of the room. He hastened across camp to his quarters. There he put on his thick-soled boots, his body armor, his gloves, and his helmet. Checking his pistol to make sure its power supply was optimum, Jason proceeded to the hanger where the camp's chariots were kept.

Due to most of the soldiers being on the battlefield, he encountered few persons along the way. Jason nevertheless kept turning his head from side to side as he went, watching out for any camp guards who might approach him: being all alone, and without an official explanation for what he had resolved to do or why he had abandoned his post, a stop by a guard might end his mission before it could begin.

To make up for that deficiency, he sought to present a self-confident walk. But try though he might, holding his chin high, swinging his arms wide, and taking long strides with pointed toes, Jason's awkwardly artificial gait betrayed his jumpiness.

He was, however, neither stopped nor questioned; and upon reaching his destination, no one there took notice of him. Jason first stopped inside an armory, helping himself to another pistol and a rifle and draping a string of grenades over his shoulder. Then he located a free chariot. As he stepped into it, a soldier from across the hanger called out and started running towards him.

Oh, no!

Jason froze. Not even his eyelids moved. His mouth became dry.

Before he could speak, the man identified himself as a charioteer and apologized for not knowing another chariot was supposed to be heading out.

Whew, thought Jason. A drop of sweat rolled down from his forehead inside his helmet whilst the charioteer started up the engine.

When they arrived at the camp gate, a squint-eyed sentry met them. His intense glare made Jason gulp.

"We received no word of another chariot going out." The sentry paced beside the chariot. He rested his arms on its side and stared at Jason. "Where are your orders?"

"I-I," stammered Jason, inching slightly backwards from the sentry. He clenched his fist and his resolve. "I was ordered to join battle by Periander himself."

"Reeaaalllyy? Show me your orders!"

"They were, uh, verbal."

The sentry raised his slender eyebrows. "What makes you so special as to warrant personal instructions from the Supreme Commander?"

A scowling Jason yanked his helmet off. "I'm his son!"

"Whoa!" yelped the sentry, jumping back.

"Are you going to let me pass or do you want to explain to my father why you detained me?" said Jason, unblinkingly shoving his huge eyes at the sentry.

The man glanced at his fellow sentry, who merely shrugged his shoulders. "Then open the gate!" Turning to Jason, he said, "Forgive us, Sir. We didn't realize. We were only doing our job."

"Very well." *Yes, they bought it!* Jason inwardly let loose a cheer as the gate opened and his charioteer drove them out of camp. *I'm heading out to battle!*

Once they were outside the camp, Jason directed his charioteer where to go. The sounds of gunfire, of dying men's screams, and grenades exploding on the earth grew louder and louder as they approached.

On the outskirts of the battlefield was the hill. The situation there appeared the same as it had on the video. The Allied troops had hunkered down on the dusty earth at the foot of the hill. Surrounding them on three sides, the Atlanteans trained their lasers on them while in turn sustaining gunfire. About a dozen Atlanteans were stationed on the hilltop in a row, using the high ground and their united firepower to prevent the trapped Allied soldiers from ascending.

Jason's chariot approached the hill from behind and sped up towards the enemy. Before they could turn around and see him, let alone reäct to this unexpected combatant, Jason had grabbed one of his grenades. Gritting his teeth, he pulled its pin and lobbed it at them. The grenade soared like a rock dropped from a vulture's claw.

BOOOOMM!

Dust and earth, mixed with blood and flesh, flew into the air as the grenade exploded. Bits of body armor, the pungent plastic warped and still melting into little droplets from the blast, scattered everywhere.

"Yahoo!" cried Jason, throwing his arms up. *I've done it!*

The fact that the high-speed chariot quickly brought him to the next in the line of Atlantean soldiers forced him to postpone his celebration. With two pulls of his pistol's trigger, Jason shot him dead-on in the chest as he spun around. The enemy clasped his chest and keeled over, rolling ignominiously down the hill. Then Jason shot the next soldier, and another one after that, killing them both.

But after killing a fourth one, the remaining hilltop Atlanteans became conscious of his presence. Soldiers farther down the line began to move closer together while the couple closest to Jason spun around and pointed their gleaming rifles at him.

Jason shouted, "Evasive maneuvers!" to his charioteer as a hail of lasers raced towards them. The chariot zigzagged this way and that, dodging the gunfire. Jason held on tight. His rifle he steadied on the chariot's rail under his left shoulder, clasping the rail while using his right hand to fire at the Atlanteans. His upper and lower teeth clanked with each shot he fired. But he hit his mark, leaving a trail of victims behind him as the chariot roared down the hill.

By the time Jason reached the hill's midpoint, the Atlanteans farther down had formed a wall of six soldiers, all lined up a hundred feet away. They greeted him with synchronized gunfire.

"Ughhh!" Jason was rocked sideways as the chariot made a sharp ninety-degree turn, zooming down the hillside away from the fighting before the lasers hit. Having lost his hold of it, the rifle flew out from under Jason's shoulder. He grasped wildly for it. But it evaded his hand, tumbling into an upturned patch of weeds. So, he grabbed one more grenade and cast it as far as he could before he was out of reach.

Reaching the bottom of the hill, the charioteer said, "Sir, look!"

Jason, recovering his balance from the jarring ride, craned his neck upwards. He expected to see the enemy regathered, rifles a-firing, so he drew his pistol from its holster. But, instead of firing, he smiled.

Allied soldiers were slogging up the half of the hill that he had cleared of enemies. Already seven were atop it, exchanging fire with the remaining hilltop Atlanteans; and that number kept swelling as more soldiers made their way up the hill, having escaped from the trap below.

Jason dismounted from his chariot and ran up the pebbly hillside. He arrived in time to help his comrades take out the last hilltop Atlanteans who only minutes ago had been on the verge of slaughtering the trapped Allied troops. Now, their lifeless bloodied bodies tumbled off the hill's verge, landing in dusty heaps. Their Atlantean comrades below, moreover, now were the ones in danger of slaughter. The Allied troops, having taken control of the high ground, now targeted the Atlantean troops below who had started to scatter in multiple directions.

I've actually done it, thought Jason, his pistol-holding hand falling to his side as he surveyed the hilltop. His right eye moistened and he sniffled. *I've fought in my first true battle, and I've defeated the enemy, saved my comrades...*

"Jason, what are you doing?!"

He flinched when a livid voice boomed over his helmet's communicator. "Father!" he exclaimed, pointlessly glancing from side to side as though he would be there.

How had he learned of what he was up to so fast?

"Jason, you've deliberately disobeyed me!" The pitch in Periander's voice rose. "Did I not forbid you—on multiple occasions—to go into battle?"

"Yes, but—"

"Then why do I see you on my video feed, fighting, instead of being back in camp at the command center?"

Jason guided his swaying head with his hand for a moment, thinking. Then, inhaling deeply, he answered. "I've tried to obey you, Father, I've really tried. Till today I remained a spectator, watching as you went out to battle day after day. While the greatest war in history waged outside our camp, and my innards burned to join you, I stayed in my place, consigned to the sidelines, out of deference to you. But today I couldn't remain there anymore. When I saw a group of our soldiers about to be slaughtered, I knew I could destroy the enemy first. I'm sorry, but I had to seize the opportunity! I could no longer stand by and just watch: I had to take the field and face down the enemy. I did. And you know what, Father? I triumphed!"

Jason's last words were seconded by shouts from the Allied soldiers gathering around him. Already some of them had left the hill to pursue the fleeing Atlanteans; those that remained audibly made themselves known.

Crackling static echoed over his communicator.

Please, Deity, make him understand. Jason gnawed at his lower lip, awaiting his father's reply.

"Jason," said Periander at last, his voice softer, "you're young and want to distinguish yourself on the battlefield, to avenge our family for the wrongs Critias has done us. I understand your feelings. Believe me, I do. But I want you also to believe that I have only had your best interests at heart. It has not been easy being a father since... our exile. While on the run I had to look out for all our lives, then recruit allies to our cause; now I must oversee the whole war in addition to the siege. Starting with your mother, our family's been oppressed by the weight of the world...."

The speed with which Periander's words shot forth continued to slow. "After losing her, I couldn't bear the thought of losing you, too. That is the true reason why I've kept you close by, away from the fighting: to protect you."

"But I'm not a child anymore. I don't need protection." Jason then clenched his eyes tight, drew in a deep breath, and said after exhaling, "But I understand why you did what you did. I miss Mother so much. You just wanted to avoid having to experience something like that again."

"I'm glad you understand." Periander sighed. "You should not have disobeyed me, although perhaps I should have been less strict about your involvement in the war. By a purely disinterested measurement, I now see that you are able to hold your own on the battlefield."

"I can."

"You truly are my son, and generations of our forefathers would be proud of what you can accomplish. I love you, Jason. Now, as long as you are there, stick close with those troops for the rest of the fight. After the battle, we'll have a real discussion about your future military service."

Jason could hardly speak, the words welling inside his chest. This is what he had wanted! He had shown that he could fight as well as any soldier and, finally, after countless appeals, got his father to acknowledge it. He sniffled. "Thank you, Father—"

BOOOOOOOMMM!!

CHAPTER THIRTY-SEVEN

"NOOOOOOOOOOOO!"

Dropping his helmet and communications transmitter, Periander rushed out of the mobile command center and hopped onto his chariot. He pressed the ignition switch and streaked across the battlefield like uncontrollable lightning through the sky. With his hands, chest, and forehead flooding with sweat, his heart pumping twice as fast, and his eyes blinking as frequently as a marble statue's, Periander kept praying, *Please, Deity, let him be alive! Let him be alive!*

Two minutes passed as slowly as two centuries.

At long last he arrived at the hill. There still hovered above the hilltop the remnant of a black cloud of acrid lung-killing smoke, now only light gray and scarcely bitter-smelling as the breeze scattered it eastwards. Several Allied troops were gathered around the body of an Atlantean lying facedown in the bloody, muddy dirt. Repeatedly they fired their guns at the corpse; again and again they shot him, riddling his body armor with dozens of holes.

Twenty feet away, his body being hoisted up by a couple of other soldiers, was Jason.

"No!" cried Periander, shoving past them. Falling down beside him, he took hold of Jason and laid his son's bare head against his chest. "What happened?"

"That villain," snarled one soldier, pointing towards the dead Atlantean whose body was still being defiled, "apparently wasn't dead. When he regained consciousness, he chucked a grenade at our rescuer. It detonated right in front of him, blowing his helmet clear off." He wiped a tear from his eye. "If it weren't for your son, Sir, we'd all be dead right now."

Periander ran his trembling fingertips an inch above Jason's face. The skin, seared from the heat of the explosion, was brown, yellow, and white in many places; portions of it were peeling off in large patchy flakes interspersed with droplets of blood oozing up from beneath the epidermis. Shrapnel had torn a larger chunk of flesh on his right cheek; though it remained attached to his face by a few fibers of skin, the chunk was bobbing up and down, thereby exposing the raw dermis underneath it. Jason's left eye, having closed forever, had a bit of jagged metal wedged therein and was surrounded by the sad concoction of yellowish pus, tears, and brownish blood.

"Oh, Jason, Jason," murmured Periander, his voice breaking. "What have they done to you, my son?"

Jason looked at him with his one good eye. "Father..." he gasped, coughing copious quantities of blood, stomach acid, and other stinking fluids that ran down onto his body armor and seeped into the cracks.

"My son..."

"I'm sorry I disappointed you."

"No, never," Periander insisted as he held Jason tighter. "You are like me: you had to take charge and do what you thought was right. You saved all these men. You defeated the enemy. You're a true hero, Jason. I-I... I couldn't be prouder of you." Clenching his eyes to staunch the flow, he could not prevent the fugitive tears from falling down to intermingle with the tears of his son.

"That makes me so happy." Trying to smile, the blackened edges of Jason's lips rose while bloodied drool poured down onto his chin. "Oh, Father, why must my first taste of victory be swallowed up by death?"

"Don't say that," murmured Periander, addressing himself as much as his son. "You'll fight many more battles after this. I just know it."

Jason gently shook his head.

"No, help is on its way." Periander kissed his charred forehead. It was cold.

"I can see Mother," whispered Jason as his eye glazed over.

"No, just hang on," begged Periander, his voice cracking as he pressed his face up against Jason's. "Don't die. Please don't leave me. I can't lose you too."

His plea was futile.

Jason had already left his father's embrace and gone to join his mother.

"No, nooo... NOOOOOOO!" howled Periander, thrusting his tearful head up towards the dark and unforgiving sky. *O Cornelia, I'm so sorry... I've failed you. I've failed both of you...*

For several minutes Periander's arms remained tightly wrapped around his son, seemingly locked in place as though it were they that had experienced rigor mortis.

Periander let go only after a couple medical personnel arrived, climbing the war-torn hill with a stretcher in their hands. It did not take them long to read the situation. Expressing their condolences, they put Jason on the stretcher and carried his body down the hill to their medical transport which already had several wounded soldiers loaded in it.

Periander stepped aboard his chariot and followed behind the medical transport as it, escorted by the troops whom Jason had saved, returned to Camp Andreia. His face was strangely vacant during the journey back. He neither wept nor sniffled, nor did his body convulse in grief. He stared emotionlessly straight ahead.

Although it was not visible from the outside, Periander's mood was undergoing a thorough alteration. From the moment that his arms had yielded up his son, his lugubrious heart began to change as his mind was overwhelmed by one image.

Critias!

That monster in the form of man, haughty and smarmily contemptuous, haunted his mind. Three figures of him—two that were and one that would soon be—kept clawing at Periander's eyes. The daunting mass of Critias looming over Cornelia, like a rabid wolf over a doe, was the first. The second was the nauseous laughter that Critias belched forth after tormenting Leonidas to the point of making him rush headlong towards his death. And the last one, which had not yet happened and therefore could only be imagined, was what sort of demonic laughter, what kind of uncontrollable slobbering glee, would seize Critias as soon as he learned that his soldier had slain his archenemy's only son.

As when gold and silver, the ancient money of the land, are overwhelmed by an influx of brass coins minted with nominally equal value, and the baser metal drives the precious straight into hoarders' jars so that the brass alone remains in circulation to pass from hand to hand, so too was Periander's anguish supplanted by unbridled fury. His body itched all over from the heat of his rage. His dry eyes, having first grown red from tears, now resembled the color of his wrath. His upper teeth gnashed the lower stratum with such force that would have made a weaker man's teeth shatter.

When they entered the camp, their vehicles stopped at the head of the main path. Periander stayed in his chariot until the medical personnel, conveying his tarp-covered son to the morgue, were out of sight. The whole time he was gripping the chariot's rail. When his hands finally let go, the fingers were stiff and slow to flex.

About twenty feet away, standing motionless on the main path, was Psyche. Periander got down and trudged over to her.

"Periander," she said as he came within earshot. Her quivering mouth was open, her head slowly shaking while her red hair was rustled by the breeze. "I heard. I don't know what to say." She threw her tender arms around him.

"What can be said?" asked Periander dryly, gazing unblinkingly at the harsh clouds. "My son is dead, my only child. He shouldn't be. But he is."

"Oh, Periander..." She nuzzled her supple cheek against his own, which was still streaked with the dried blood from Jason's face. "I can't begin to imagine what you must be feeling. Just, whatever you do, don't blame yourself; you're not responsible."

Grabbing her by her upper arms so suddenly that she squealed, he lifted and set her a few inches away from him and held her there. "Blame myself? I don't blame myself." The blue veins on his forehead bulged as he yelled, "I BLAME CRITIAS!"

"Periander—"

"He's responsible for this war! He's responsible for all the blood that's been shed! He's responsible for taking those I love from me. He murdered Cornelia and Timaeus; his partisans killed Socrates; he drove Leonidas to his own destruction; and now his killers have taken Jason too. That bastard son of a whore stole my whole family from me! AND I WILL KILL HIM FOR THAT!"

Periander let go and brushed her arms away as she reached dazedly for him. Ignoring the fading sound of her voice, he stomped through the camp to the command center.

Everyone inside fell silent when he burst into the room. Of the senior commanders, only Demosthenes was present; the rest were still out on the battlefield.

"My King," said Demosthenes, stepping towards him with palms up-turned and jaw dropped down. "We are all dumbstruck by this calamity, seized by the greatest grief."

"Treasure up your grief for later. Now's not the time to succumb to heartache, nor to indulge in tears and lamentation. Now is the time to overcome our weaker feelings and to rouse ourselves to do our duty to the dead. My son is slain. I will avenge him!"

"Sire—"

"Demosthenes, contact Critias. Tell him I do accept his challenge: I shall fight him one-on-one, tomorrow morning, unless he should prove to be a coward."

Demosthenes' eyes were wide as he approached, his pupils great. "Majesty, no. Please wait. Do not make a rash and momentous decision in the aftermath of so traumatic an event. Please reconsider!"

"I considered it enough. Critias is only hours away from having a wonder-weapon at his disposal. We've tried everything we could to take the city before that point. Are we any closer now than we were a month ago? No! Disaster hangs over us."

"But we can't know for sure if Critias' weapon will work. Only wait and—"

"And if it turns out it works, it'll be too late!" snapped Periander, his saliva assailing Demosthenes. "I must do *something*! Fighting him is my only option. Call him."

"What of your Allies? Surely, they have a say?"

"Cleomenes has returned to Athens. Ozymandias is in Egypt, Indra in Mohenjo-Daro. As Supreme Allied Commander, I am entitled to make binding decisions in their absence." When Demosthenes did not respond, Periander narrowed his eyes and poked him with his finger. "Are you going to arrange this duel, or shall I? If necessary, I'll march up to Critias' palace, knock on his front door, and deliver my message myself."

Demosthenes bowed his head. Exhaling loudly, he murmured, "I shall do it, Sire."

Chapter Thirty-Eight

In the hours after Jason's death, Critias was notified that Periander would accept his proposition and that he expected him to honor it.

Although he had proposed it extemporaneously, making it more in jest than in anticipating its actual acceptance, Critias made no retraction when confronted by the belated answer. He agreed to it. Salivating at the prospect of killing the father in his grief, Critias hankered all the more to taste on his thin pale lips the spilled blood of his enemy and to feel between his fingers the gooeyness of his entrails. Indeed, upon learning of the demise of Periander's son, his face had contorted in ecstasy far greater than anything Periander had imagined.

Periander, meanwhile, was in his room. He had withdrawn here after checking that his message was sent to the imperial palace. Removing his body armor and sending it off to be refurbished for his duel, he gave orders not to be disturbed. Then he slumped down across his bed and shut his eyes, his languishing limbs falling asleep while his mind whirled like a tropical tsunami.

The antlike crawl of sunbeams through the window marked the passing of hours. As dusk came on, Periander, not yet moved to wash his blood-soiled beard, began practicing for tomorrow's fight.

There was a full-length mirror on one of the room's walls. Having pushed all the furniture against the other walls, he trained in the cleared open space. He kicked, he punched, he shadowboxed. Grasping the inactive Astrapë, Periander worked to improve his draw.

Thud, thud.

"Sir," came a voice from the door, "your wife still persists on seeing you. She's—hold on, no! Come back!"

"Periander," exclaimed Psyche, pushing the door open and shoving past the officer.

Glancing at his wife, Periander turned to the exasperated officer. "Leave us."

As the departing officer shut the door behind him, Psyche approached Periander. Her cerulean eyes were wide, staring blankly at him; her little hands fiddled with one another. "Have I been informed correctly?" She cocked her neck. "Have you actually agreed to meet Critias in single combat?"

Periander stood there for several moments. His multicolored eyes gazed at Psyche's, blinking rhythmically as though attempting to dispatch optical messages to one unable to understand them. Then he replied with a laconic, "Yes."

"How—why—for what reason—" Psyche's flailing voice gyrated in pitch before normalizing. "How could you agree to that?"

"Critias must die. The war must be ended. This is what I have to do."

"You mustn't fight him!"

"Critias already accepted. We fight tomorrow, 9 a.m."

She grabbed a hold of his sleeve. "But what about all the things that were said before? How can you jeopardize the entire war, imperil our ultimate victory, on one lone duel?"

"Our victory is already in jeopardy," said Periander matter-of-factly, brushing her hand off his arm. "After tomorrow Critias will have a super weapon to deploy against us. Unless I stop the war before then, we face devastation."

"How can you even trust Critias' word that he'll surrender if you beat him?"

"When I duel Critias, only one of us will walk away from that fight: it's victory or death."

Her face twitching and jerking, Psyche exclaimed, "But this isn't the right course! There must be something else we can do."

"We've tried everything else! It all failed." He closed his eyes. "We don't have any more time."

"How can you do this without your Allies? They lent you their armies."

Does she think I've forgotten? Periander formed a white-knuckled fist beside his thigh, the veins positively bulging. "They made me Supreme Commander of our forces to make decisions such as this. I've informed them of mine."

"But remember what Cleomenes said last month," protested Psyche. "Athens won't support it!"

"Not that I need it," hissed Periander, "but I've received the blessings of both Indra and Ozymandias. Without them on his side, there's nothing Cleomenes can do."

Upon hearing her father's name, Psyche winced. She moved even closer, wrapping her arm round his like a boa constrictor around a wren. "Please, Periander," she begged, "please reconsider. I don't want you to fight Critias."

"Why not?" His narrow eyebrows rose in concert with his broad shoulders. "Don't feign surprise. You knew I would eventually confront him. My soul will never rest so long as that man breathes the same air my loved ones once inhaled."

"The magnitude of it did not hit me till just now." Psyche's hot moist breath struck his cheek as her red nails dug into his arm. "It was dreamy and remote before; but now, to hear you'll fight him tomorrow—my whole body quivers with fear."

Periander moved his free hand to dislocate her grasp. "I have been going into battle almost daily, fighting amid the thickest hordes of soldiers, assailing blasting tanks, evading the payloads of enemy airships...

and you never implored me to forsake the field of war before. Why then does a duel between two champions, agreed to by both sides—free of the distractions caused by other warriors roving on a common battle-field—terrify you so?"

"Because Critias is no ordinary fighter!" shrieked Psyche, uncoiling from him as he recoiled. Her face was pale. "Periander, you are a great warrior, gallant and peerless among all Allied men. (I am so proud you are my husband.) But Critias fights unlike any of his minions. He's unnatural! More a monster than a man! You yourself saw the video with me that day, when he first ventured onto the battlefield... how fiercely he fought. Well, since then I've monitored all his fights—observed from our command center how many men he's slaughtered with as little effort as a boy steps on some ants. I've even scoured through our infirmaries for any who might have fought him, to see if they might have advice on how to face him. And do you know many survivors I found? *Zero*. Absolutely nobody. Of all our men who've gone against him, whether attacking or being attacked, none have survived—not a single one!"

"Then I'll be the first!" Periander shot back, raising his voice and his arm. He madly waved his right forefinger as he paced about the room. "This duel is the culmination of everything. From my expulsion from Atlantis until now, I have been striving to reclaim my country from that beast and bring down upon his wicked brow recompense for all the blood he's guilty of. Tomorrow, I fight Critias. I finally have the occasion I've long sought. Face-to-face with him, will he escape from me? *No*. I'LL KILL HIM! I don't care how formidable a foe he is. With my goal so close to me, there is a greater chance water will flow uphill than I will back out of this fight."

"I know how much pain Critias has inflicted on you..."

"That devil robbed me of my wife and son."

"Yes, and you want revenge for those he's taken from you. I don't fault you for it, Periander; it's completely understandable. But..." Psyche's lip wavered, and her eyelike dams burst as she whimpered, "But what about me, Psyche? Must you leave me a widow just to satisfy your vengeful wish?"

How dare she say that! Periander raised an accusatory finger and glowered at his wife. "This is not mere sentiment, woman, but a duty which I must manfully perform. I will avenge my family."

She gently nodded. "Of course you have your obligations towards them," she said sympathetically. "Jason was an extraordinary boy. Pressed on all sides by sorrows and difficulty, he remained constant and never gave up; I loved him so. And Cornelia... I realize she meant so much to you, being your first love. Her loss caused you such grief of heart that will never go away. But..."

Doubling over as the tears flowed down her cheeks, Psyche clasped her abdomen. With her tear-moistened lips warping into an erratic frown, she asked, "But what about your duty to me? Am I not equally your wife? Is little Psyche not your family?"

"Of course you are. Don't be ridiculous," said Periander through curling lips, his fingers flexing. "Since our wedding, I've fulfilled every husbandly duty towards you."

"Yet now you risk all that, chasing your revenge. If you die tomorrow, you won't just forfeit the war or fail to avenge the dead: you'll leave me all alone. I love you, Periander, from the first time you entered Egypt!" She straightened up and gazed evenly at him, her breathing quickening. "I never told you this, but I was the one who wanted us to marry. I asked my father, who would not hear of it; he refused to let me go. But I persisted till I'd won him over because I wanted to be with you so much. I willingly left my homeland, despite how dangerous your situation was, because I wanted to be with you. I still do!"

"So, I was right in suspecting you had Ozymandias make me marry you as a precondition to our alliance," remarked Periander, rubbing his chin. "That went against all Egyptian custom. Nor was I blind to how much he loved you; I'd have never guessed he would willingly send his only daughter away. What? You look as though you're surprised I knew?"

A baffled Psyche blinked. "I'm surprised because you never said anything."

"What's there to say? When he told us to wed, I saw how you looked, noted how you acted, heard the words you spoke. It was quite clear you were smitten with me. And when I thought back to how I'd behaved around you—always letting you stick around, bidding you to sit too close to me for modesty, speaking so freely to you and without the due reticence—I realized I'd unwittingly led you on. It was only natural you fell in love with me."

He paused a moment, scratching his forehead, before continuing. "Yes, I knew our marriage was not arranged in the same way as other royal marriages; amorous affection was the driving force behind it. But I was fine with it. You were an excellent bride to be had. Any king would have been fortunate to wed a princess such as you, even one who did not bring a martial alliance for a dowry."

"You're right. I did fall in love with you," said Psyche, sniffling and rubbing her eyes. "And in case you hadn't noticed, I still love you. That's why I don't want you to *die*! Please, Periander, husband... do not fight Critias. Anyone but him! Stay with me. Find another way. Anything. Just don't forsake me... I want always to lie down beside you in your bed, not in your coffin. Please, let me continue to serve you as your wife, not as your pallbearer."

The seconds went by like millennia as he strained to find an answer. Finally, Periander gently placed his battle-worn hand onto her tear-washed cheek. "Psyche, dear Psyche, you keep speaking of my death as though it already transpired." He kissed her salty lips. "Look! I live! And living I will live, as do we all, until that set time appointed by the Deity for me to die—and not one nanosecond before or after! And yes, I am convinced that I am doing the Deity's will in this. Regardless of tomorrow's outcome, I will meekly commit my life into His hands."

"Y-you won't reconsider?"

"No."

"Fine, then." Backing slowly away from him, her eyes having exhausted their downpour and turned bright red, she thrust her hands down at the air and shrieked, "I hope your precious fight is worth it!" She spun around and darted out of the room.

"Psyche, wait," called Periander. He took a step forwards, his hand reaching out to the air that was still buffeted from her rapid departure.

Sighing, his hand became a fist that he rested over his heart as his eyes closed tight.

He returned to his shadowboxing.

Chapter Thirty-Nine

W HILE Periander grieved in his solitude, his servants and companions spent the day arranging for a royal funeral. At a quarter past nine, with the moonlit sky having swept the clouds away so that every flickering star might see and lament, Jason's funereal rites commenced.

The camp huddled in the main square for the ceremony. The pyre was built upon a marmoreal base whose white sides, freshly polished but still indelibly blackened here and there by its prior victims, stood in the center of the square. Standing near it was a golden urn perched atop a knee-high stand. Shaped like an amphora, with two coiling pairs of handles—a diminutive pair resting on the larger one below it—on each side of the neck, this urn had been salvaged from the remnants of Periander's palace. Ancient goldsmiths had emblazoned it with Eumelus' crest: a lion's head whose finely-detailed mane billowed with majesty. Herein would Jason's ashen bones lie, mingling with the dust of his erstwhile flesh.

The voices of the crowd hushed when Periander arrived. A gray-bearded priest, whose white vestments clashed starkly with his own garb, accompanied him. Although his body had slipped into the black robes of mourning, Periander's face still wore the clotted blood of Jason. Refusing servants' helpful hands, he forswore all washing until he had placed his son upon the pyre.

Making their way through the crowd, Periander glanced at all the somber faces. He caught sight of Psyche, dressed all in black from her shoes to her mourning veil. But when he looked at her, his foot halting for just a moment, her eyes evaded his and she bowed her head earthwards. His fingertips gripped his palm; his feet marched firmly on.

In front of the pyre, on a stretcher that had been rolled there from the morgue, lazed Prince Jason beneath a dark-felt shroud. Periander delicately removed the smooth, weightless shroud.

Oh, that face! Once so reminiscent of Cornelia, yet now appearing so pitiful and torn.... Blockading his tear ducts with his forceful will, Periander took his son into his arms. How heavy he was! When was the last time he had carried Jason? He had been only a boy then, not yet weighed down with so many years and muscles....

Periander laid the corpse upon the pyre and took his place. As was Atlantean custom, three torch-bearers stood on either side: Periander, Agathocles, and Demosthenes on the body's right and on the left Sethos, Arsenio, and bawling Akasion, Jason's friends. The torches burned so fiercely that Jason was bathed with a golden-orange glow. He looked almost peaceful in repose.

The priest stood at the head of the pyre, resting his liver-spotted palm upon Jason's scalp. To the accompaniment of a dirge and sporadic laments from the throng, he began reciting the traditional hymns and prayers in Old Atlantic while his other hand waved a thurible emitting strong incense.

His sonorous, mellifluous voice soothed Periander, who stood resolute throughout the rite. Then, as soon as the priest had said, "*Tibi, O Deus, corpum animamque ejus commendo,*" Periander took his torch and, in concert with the others, ignited the oil-soaked pyre.

The crackling flames leapt upwards, being fanned by the cool evening breeze. The other torchbearers withdrew along with the priest, and soon the crowd too had dispersed.

But Periander stayed behind. Entranced by the conflagration of what had been his son, his legs swayed back and forth.

"Oh, my son..." he murmured. "Jason, I... I was wrong to sideline you like a child. You truly had become a man. You proved that when you saved all those soldiers' lives. They shall be forever grateful; for their salvation came at a price few men can repay..." The heat from the flaming pyre warmed his blood-soiled cheeks; to cool it, his eyes let out some tears. "I'm so proud of you...."

He laid down beside the pyre's base and shut his eyes. In the deserted center of the camp, Periander was all alone.

"Periander," came a great voice.

He jumped up from the ground as did his heart in his chest. "Watcher!"

The Watcher stood beside the pyre. His face was grave-looking, yet calm. With muscles rippling beneath the skin, he formed a slight smile; his whole body stood in a relaxed posture. His eyes, however, were heavy-set and cloudy to behold. "I see you are distressed in soul."

"My son is dead," replied Periander, gripping his fists.

"Do not mourn too terribly for the dead." The Watcher, nodding with his head towards the pyre, waved his hand over Periander's face. Instantly, the coated blood re-liquefied and was absorbed into his hand. "Your son is with the Deity in Paradise."

I never doubted he was... "My heart rejoices to hear Jason is where eternal bliss prevails. (This ghastly world was not worthy of him.) But... why, Watcher, have you come? Surely not to speak of my son?" He bit his lip as a drop of sweat ran down his temple. *You've only appeared to me right before horrific events unfolded...*

"I have come because you are about to duel the High King Critias. Rare are events such as these, which steer whole nations' fates, and they must be watchfully attended to."

"Does that augur well for my cause?"

"With all things the Deity is concerned. It does not mean all things are to go well."

"Are you saying the Deity disapproves?" His face flushed with heat. "I love the Deity and will obey His will. But I must fight that monster Critias. I must!"

The Watcher blinked leisurely. "The Deity does not disapprove. Your duel is fulfilling His will."

"But what is His will? Will I win and destroy Critias, avenge his victims, and save my country? Or am I destined to...."

After Periander's voice had trailed away, the Watcher looked skywards. "Wars, famines, tyrants, earthquakes, pestilence—these are some of the Deity's instruments wherewith He punishes wicked nations. The Atlanteans have, by their actions, greatly offended Him; He intends to chastise them. The majesty of Atlantis is to be brought low, that great city and her continent, the crown of human achievement... brought down by her own opulence and greed, iniquity and perversity. How low I know not: the Deity has not revealed it to me, and I know only what He tells me."

"It vexes me to hear of my nation's fate," said Periander, grimacing. "Yet I cannot express surprise. Seeing firsthand how willingly my countrymen were allured, first by Eudoxia and even more by Critias, to do what should not be done—even my own subjects, whom I loved and nursed like a mother hen, had to be cajoled by force to return to my fold!—I knew great judgment must have accrued against Atlantis. We are guilty. I'll make no excuses, offer no rationalizations. We have been condemned justly because we receive the due reward for our deeds. Even so, I pray that so great a country is not brought too low. For Atlantis was once truly great, back when it was good. Perhaps Atlantis could be made good again."

The Watcher's rosy cheeks bulged out to form a smile. "Concerning your country's fate, do not be anxious. What is to come has already been decided."

Nodding slowly, Periander pressed his original question. "What is decided about my duel? Who will live or die—me or Critias?"

Only one of them could outlive tomorrow's fight. Yet would it be better to know if knowing meant knowing he would die, or to remain ignorant so that he could retain hope of his prevailing? Periander did not know which was best.

The Watcher's smile evaporated as his body turned away from Periander. His head sagged towards the ground. "As I said, I know only what the Deity reveals to me. When you fight Critias, a mighty king will fall; that much I know. Which of you it will be—the Deity has not deigned to tell me."

Periander swallowed awkwardly, half frustrated by this response and half thankful. *Perhaps ignorance proves best in this one case*, he told himself. *It precludes cockiness from foreknowing certain victory, or despondency in the case of...*

Before Periander could respond, the Watcher turned to face him. "Though ignorant of your fate in battle," he said, his body fading with the breeze, "I do know, as your Watcher, how much strength and courage is in you." By now only a faint outline of his face remained. A voice pregnant with conviction came from him before he was entirely dissolved: "I have great confidence in you, Periander, Son of Themistocles. Fight that villain and avenge your family...."

CHAPTER FORTY

TENTATIVELY ROSE THE ALL-SEEING sun to dawn the day. Camp Andreia hummed with talk as soldiers waking in their dormitories, eating in packed mess halls, or going about their rounds, all speculated one with another over the forthcoming duel.

Periander, meanwhile, arose before first light, resolute in soul and body. He visited the camp chapel and, grasping the altar's sides, prayed fervently to the Deity. Then he ate a vigorous breakfast: bacon, sausages, scrambled eggs, toast, hash browns, fried tomatoes. Afterwards he spoke with Agathocles, Demosthenes, and his other closest friends and advisers; among them was Philip, who had left his post commanding armies in the northwest sector of the continent to wish his master well. All offered Periander advice on fighting Critias. He did not solicit it from them; he much preferred reminiscing about life before his exile. Yet with courteous nods he accepted all the proffered counsel from his fretful friends.

Gradually the sun progressed across the sky, searching for the best spot from which to view the duelists. Periander retired to his room. There his servants had brought his armor from its refurbishing; resplendent and glossy, every scratch and nick had been worked out so that it appeared as beautiful as the day it was fashioned. Periander put on his boots first, fastened the greaves about his legs, and donned the heavy breastplate. While reaching for the arm plates, there was a knock at the door.

With Periander's assent, the door was opened and through it entered Psyche. Lysander followed behind her, holding in his arms a greenhorn shield.

"Psyche!" exclaimed Periander, rising suddenly from the bed. *I wasn't expecting to see her after last night's row.* He stepped forwards to meet her, opening his mouth to speak. "I want you to know that—"

She placed a long petite finger on his lips to shush him. There was a washbasin and white towel on the nightstand. Psyche dipped the towel and applied it to his face. Working intently on this task, her eyes focused on his beard and not his eyes, she gently cleansed his mane, massaging the warm water into every pore.

Remaining straight-faced, he nevertheless was moved by her gesture. *Oh, Psyche,* he thought, shutting his eyes, *it was such a blessing to have received you into my life...*

When she finished, her arms embraced Periander. Though his thorax was blocked by the breastplate, his arms were still free to enjoy the warmth from the body of his wife. She held this embrace for many seconds, resting her head on his shoulder and making not a sound as she neither looked at him nor avoided his gaze. Finally, murmuring, "The Deity preserve you," she turned and bolted from the room.

After she was gone, he shifted his attention to Lysander, who had all this time been standing in the corner, awkwardly balancing the shield in front of him. "What is this?"

"Please accept this gift, my King," said Lysander, his head bowing whilst his arms presented the shield.

Shifting the circular shield between his hands, the gray metal imprinted with seven concentric rings, Periander remarked, "Thank you, Lysander, but I already have a shield. This one seems much heavier."

"Yes, but that is because only this one can withstand Critias' battleaxe." Lysander summarized how he had spied out the details of Critias' favorite weapon of choice and learned how it operated. "Hence only tungsten, the same metal the frictional axe is made of, can endure its heat."

"Then that explains why his axe has been so lethal... Given that, I'm shocked the whole Atlantean army isn't equipped with these."

"Tungsten is extremely rare in Atlantis. They were only able to construct Critias' axe and shield before the naval blockade commenced. I, on the other hand, was able to send to Egypt for some in order to fashion this shield for you. Sire, it's made of pure tungsten!"

"So, it won't yield to his blade?"

Lysander nodded. "Not at all."

Slipping his arm through the strap and weighing the shield, Periander smiled. "You've done an excellent job, Lysander. You anticipated what would help me the most in a fight with Critias."

"I appreciate the praise, Sire," answered Lysander as he bowed his head, "but it's Queen Psyche whom you should really thank. It was she who approached me, inquiring about Critias' weaponry, and subsequently told me I should make a tungsten shield for you...."

***

"THERE HE IS."

After about a thousand soldiers and courtiers emerged from the Southern Gate, including technicians who quickly erected a large video screen so that the rest might watch the duel via drone video feeds, Critias finally appeared. He was in his distinctive black armor, his helmet held by Thrax beside him. A great sneer spread across Critias' face when he spotted Periander. Licking his pale lips with his long tongue, he pointed derisively at him. Then he shared a boisterous laugh with Thrax and whispered something into his companion's oozing ear.

Not wishing to show his own feelings, Periander merely put down his binoculars. He and his men, equal in number to Critias' men, were standing in a row a thousand paces away from the wall. As had been arranged beforehand, a breathless Atlantean envoy ran over to the Allies. He took out of a brown canister a large parchment on which were written the terms of the treaty. Atlantis agreed to surrender to Periander if he slew Critias; but if Critias won the day, then the Allies agreed to withdraw their forces from the continent and to allow a ten-year armistice to pass.

Expeditiously perusing the circuitously discombobulating idiom of ambassadorial conventions, Periander signed his name to the document and returned it to the messenger. A similar scene then transpired on Critias' side of the field.

Next each side prepared a sacrifice on behalf of their champion. Dressed in white robes, a gentle breeze lifting up his flowing gray beard, the priest who had officiated at Jason's funeral offered up a sacrifice for Periander. He set some fruit upon a makeshift altar of stones, poured a libation of blood-red wine, and ignited it. The billowing smoke ascended heavenwards. His counterpart on the other side of the field, meanwhile, clothed in a black tunic which bore the emblem of Critias' crown, brought out a kid of the goats. Placing the unsuspecting creature upon their altar, the priest slit its throat with a knife he had been concealing up his sleeve. He positioned the goat so that its blood would drain completely onto the earth before dousing it with oil to incinerate the victim.

While these rites were being performed, Periander waited with his companions.

"Remember, Sire," counselled Demosthenes, "Critias prefers to fight at close range; stay at a distance and take him with the Astrapë."

"Yes," murmured Periander, rubbing his chin. He turned to his charioteer, Guneus. "Remember that advice." Gazing at his new shield, he thought, *Yet if he comes at me, he'll find I'm prepared to meet his axe.*

Agathocles, his blue eyes wide and blond eyebrows high with enthusiasm, punched the air and shouted, "Go kill him! I know you will!"

Periander nodded. *It's time.*

He marched halfway across the field while Critias approached; the two halted as they came together.

"It's been a while since we were so close," said Critias. He shoved a couple fingers from his bone-tattooed hand into Periander's chest. Both his cheeks were smeared with blood from the goat, the scarlet red dancing in the rays of the sun. Affectedly crinkling his nose, he sneered, "Ah, I'd almost forgotten those ugly eyes of yours! Your pathetic mother couldn't even birth a normal child."

Periander, narrowing his eyes to slits and swallowing the bile in his throat, said serenely, "My mother was no goddess; that I freely confess. Despite her human imperfections, she at least never drove me so insane that rage compelled me to murder her. But, then again, *my* self-control has always been impervious to mental castration."

Critias spat on Periander's right boot. "I've wanted this since you escaped my clutch. You should have been mine then. I'll enjoy yanking your guts out from your worthless hide and using them to decorate my boots."

"At least I have guts; I don't have to stoop to slaughtering defenseless women and children."

Critias bared his reeking, cavity-eaten teeth and snarled. "If my advisers had their way, this duel of ours wouldn't even happen. But I am High King: my will prevails. And my face will be the last thing your hideous eyes ever see."

Both their chariots had by then arrived and Critias went over to his. Grabbing his battleaxe out of it, he pointed its glinting edge towards Periander. "Come on, old man. Mortality beckons you home. Prepare to greet your dear wife and child."

Periander gritted his teeth and climbed aboard his chariot. He donned his helmet, strapped his shield to his left arm, and from the cache of weapons strewn across the chariot's floor he picked up the Astrapë. Gripping it tightly, he thought, *To battle once more, trusty friend. May the Deity direct your arrows!*

Then he gave Guneus the command: "Go!"

CHAPTER FORTY-ONE

P ERIANDER SHOT TEN LASER-ARROWS in quick succession. They soared towards Critias, but his chariot dodged them. Speeding alongside the southern wall, Critias picked up a handgun and fired at him.

"Grrrr," rumbled Periander, being jostled as Guneus steered their chariot out of the line of fire. Puffs of smoke rose from the chariot's metal side when a couple laser beams struck it. "Get us to one side of them!"

Air whipped against Periander's visor as the chariot went into overdrive. He steadied his bow on the guardrail and held down the trigger. Swelling by the second, the blue arrow sparked with energy. Then, when the two chariots were lined up opposite one another about fifty feet apart, Periander let loose his arrow that was the size of a large zucchini.

BOOOOMM! A swirl of solid smoke enveloped Critias' chariot.

Did I get him? Periander's eyes forgot how to blink, and his neck's thumping arteries choked off the flow of air inwards. *No!*

Emerging from the smoke, Critias was triumphantly holding up his shield. Although it had absorbed a tremendous jolt of energy, it bore no visible sign of damage; its glossy black paint glinted in the sunlight. Critias had no sooner appeared than he disappeared again as his chariot made the turn around the southwestern corner of the city wall.

Periander gritted his teeth. His chariot zoomed around the corner. As it did, a grenade hit him. The lobbed weapon collided with his chest while the chariot was in the middle of turning the corner. It consequently hit him at a diagonal, harmlessly rolling across his breastplate and continuing past the chariot. Immediately the grenade detonated with a thunderous boom, and a mound of unearthed dirt pelted Periander from behind.

"Uggh!" Periander swatted away the dirt that had managed to overshoot him and cloud his helmet.

Critias' chariot sped to within hearing distance. He called out, "What's the matter, Periander? If you want to beat me, stop playing in the sandbox!"

"You're the one who wasted his grenade. Want some of mine? Here!"

Grabbing a couple from the string of grenades around his shoulder, Periander threw them in Critias' direction. Critias, however, gracefully batted them away with his shield as though they were tennis balls and he an expert player. The grenades flew into the wall. There they detonated, causing some dusty chunks of concrete to fall to earth.

Periander braced his shield while sustaining more gunfire from Critias. He shot more arrows at him, and the two continued exchanging fire as they completed their first circling of the city. Then they circled it again.

As they approached the capital's northeastern corner for the third time, Periander ordered Guneus, "Don't let them get ahead of us!"

His chariot pulled to the front. Squinting, he aimed the Astrapë. Critias was raising his shield again, ready to deflect the laser. But Periander was not aiming for Critias. Targeting the spot on Critias' chariot where one of its engines was located, he fired. A blinding whiteness flashed. Beginning to give off a trailing billow of smoke, the chariot began to lose speed.

Ha! That will slow him down! Periander grinned while his chariot rounded the corner. *Come on, Critias.* He kept his finger glued to the bow's trigger, prepared to fire as soon as Critias appeared around the corner.

But Critias did not appear.

Periander barked at his charioteer to halt. They stopped.

A full minute passed and still Critias did not appear.

"Guneus," said Periander, his eyebrows crumpling and forehead wrinkling within his helmet, "shouldn't their chariot still work with one engine?"

"Of course! It won't go nearly as fast, but one is all that's necessary to go."

"Hmmmm. Take us closer."

They advanced to within twenty feet of the corner. Periander looked up. A faint cloud of smoke, about two hundred feet around the corner, was still rising upwards without moving from the spot of its origin.

"This could be a trap," cautioned Periander, biting his lip. Nevertheless, he told Guneus to make the turn around the corner.

The northeastern corner of the wall was, of course, the spot where the Allies had attempted to tunnel under the city. About a half mile away one could still discern where Camp Dicaeus had been temporarily relocated; the earth and dislocated rocks still bore the marks of where buildings and tents had been erected, not to mention the filled-in mound where the excavation team had worked.

Owing to the sloping rocky Mitallophagous Hills, the chariot had to slightly deter away from the wall in order to reach the other side of it. As they snaked around the slope, the puffs of tear-inducing smoke grew farther away before coming closer again.

Periander braced himself as they arrived on the other side. *What?*

Critias was not there nor was his chariot. The only thing there was the damaged engine. Having been severed from the chariot (presumably by Critias' battleaxe), it lay shattered on the ground as flames consumed it.

"Ahhhh!" screamed Guneus, pointing up to their right.

Periander spun his head upwards. Racing down the slanting hill towards them was Critias in his chariot. In one hand he held his battleaxe and in the other a laser-pistol that he began firing at them.

"Get us out of here!" shouted Periander, even as Guneus had already started steering them away.

It was too late.

Their chariot managed to move a few feet away but did not escape Critias. His chariot, speeding down the hill, swerved right up beside theirs on the right. Then he lunged at it with his super-heated battleaxe. Periander, scarcely saving himself, leapt back against his chariot's left rail before he hit the earth.

From the rear to the front of the chariot, the blazing blade sliced through the middle of its whole side as though it were made of straw. Whatever metal touched the blade was instantaneously liquefied upon contact. The metallic liquid, its boiling point lower than the battleaxe's inferno, next transitioned into black lung-killing steam that rose thickly from the wound. Yet as soon as the blade had finished passing through, the dissolved metal solidified anew. This resulted in a great creaking sound as the metal coagulated in a most misshapen way.

Periander gasped and his hands grasped the railing as his chariot reeled violently before overturning. All the weapons and items in the chariot pummeled him as up became down. Using his shield to prop up one of the chariot's sides, Periander crawled out from under it. His helmet had been pierced by a jagged bit of metal; it did not reach his skull but still came within a quarter inch of his skin. He carefully wiggled his head out.

Smoke engulfed the chariot since both its engines were in flames. Coughing due to the foul-tasting metallic vapor that had entered his mouth, and with his eyes burning from the smoke, Periander's voice was scratchy as he called out, "Guneus!"

His charioteer's blood-gushing head rolled out in front of him from the chariot. The glazed eyes stared blankly at him through their shattered visor. Clearly Critias had been slashing more than just dead metal.

The villain! A growl rumbled through his jaws. He glanced around.

Critias was about twenty feet away. He had abandoned his chariot and was running towards Periander, his feet kicking up a hurricane of dust.

Gritting his teeth, Periander planted his feet into the red earth and raised his shield.

Critias' axe smashed into it with the force of a thunderbolt. The shield vibrated from the blow. Straining, Periander's feet slipped a few inches back; but the muscles of his thighs forcing them to dig in, he halted the attack's momentum. Critias struck his shield again and again. Yet the tungsten shield withstood each blow.

"What's this?" mused Critias, a twinge of disbelief in his voice.

"Surprised?" Periander grinned. "This shield was made to counteract your axe."

"You used tungsten? *Gaaahh*! Well, let's see you counteract this."

"Ahhh!" exclaimed Periander. A laser hit his left shoulder from the rear. He swung his head back and clenched his jaw.

There was Critias' charioteer, gun in hand, converging on him. He fired again.

Purposely shifting his shield and feet to the side, Periander maneuvered Critias in between him and the other's line of fire. "Call off your charioteer! His participation in combat is against the terms of our agreement."

"Then consider the agreement altered," came the snort through Critias' helmet.

"You perfidious devil!" Periander grunted as he blocked another blow of the axe. Without more than a cursory glance at the distance between them, he grabbed his penultimate grenade and chucked it over Critias' head.

BOOOOOMM!

"Oh, well," said Critias nonchalantly, shrugging his shoulders. "He wasn't that good a charioteer anyway. I've many more where that came from."

Periander shoved his shield into Critias' chest and broke off from him. Lifting up the Astrapë from his side, he fired a round of laser-arrows. "Do you respect any of your subjects' lives?" he called out.

Critias nullified the arrows with his shield while hollering back, "Bah! I respect what they can do for me. When they can do no more, what more need have I of them?"

"What a coldhearted, so-called 'king' you make!"

"Keep your priggish hypocrisy! At least I don't send my children off to die for me."

Periander's brow boiled with rage; his skin itched with hatred. "And exactly what children would those be?"

"Ha," laughed Critias, rushing forwards to strike again. "With all the baby-making I do, I must have at least a few bastards by now. And I think I'll beget my next one off your new wife. What's her wittle name, *Pssssy-cheeee*?" He slammed his axe against Periander's axe-blocking shield. "She'll do nicely!"

Disengaging between blows, Periander turned around and dashed off. He was panting. Although his shield had kept him unharmed, Critias kept striking with such intensity—like a ten-ton hammer on an anvil—that Periander's limbs began to feel heavier, his muscles less limber. *I must finish this quickly, before he exhausts me.*

But where to make his stand? He darted his multicolored eyes from side to side. There were no trees, boulders, or other natural objects around to offer shelter. Weeks of battles and skirmishes, fires and earth-treading tanks, had reduced the landscape to a dusty wasteland.

So Periander knelt down, fixed his shield into the ground, rested the Astrapë atop it, and let loose another barrage of arrows.

"That won't work!" Critias once again deflected Periander's arrows with his shield as he charged towards him, axe a-swinging.

Periander was still in a kneeling position. Groaning, he braced his shield above him. Though the muscles in his arms labored their hardest, his tendons cursing Critias amid their exertion, they soon began to give way.

Before Critias could beat away his shield, however, Periander dropped the Astrapë onto the ground. He used his free right hand to support the shield while he extricated his left arm from the shield's strap. Then he leapt backwards. Without anyone to support it, the shield was whacked so hard by the next blow of the battleaxe that it was driven seven inches into the earth. A mound of dirt sprang up all around it as Periander scrambled away.

"Ha, ha, ha!" Critias lifted up the bow and triumphantly waved it in front of his chest.

Meanwhile Periander, twenty feet away, turned around to face him. His hands became fists, and he grated his teeth.

"Looks like even your own weapon has defected to me," gloated Critias. "Now your life is all that's left for me to—"

BOOOOOMM!

A fiery-red explosion, its almighty glow as that of a supernova, radiated outwards from the Astrapë. Parts of the bow flew in all directions. Critias' armor, screaming with fright, was shredded by the shrapnel. His helmet was blown clear off his head. He himself was hurled twenty-two feet by the blast. Face down on the ground, his limbs straggling like a frog's, the once fleet-footed king lay motionless.

Periander, hunched over and leaning on his bruised knee, smiled. *That was for everyone you've killed!*

While concealed behind his shield, he had taken his final grenade—which also happened to be the most powerful of all his thermal detonators—and pulled its pin. Then he had jammed the grenade up the overhanging rear arch of the Astrapë, a place where it would wedge and also be less visible. As he had predicted, Critias could not resist picking up such plump spoils of war and brandishing it like a toddler with a new toy. The bow was destroyed, but it was well worth it to—

"No, it can't be!" Periander gasped.

"Grrrr-ehh-uhhh!" groaned Critias, struggling to his feet. Blood trickled down from his left nostril onto his chest. All of his breastplate had been vaporized; charred and smoldering, the thick armor nevertheless had stopped the blast from reaching his skin. His limbs, however, were less fortunate. Most of Critias' arm plates were gone; scarcely any armor still clung to him from his belly to his shins. His gloves had melted away, with some of the black plastic now sticking to his bright red, burned hands.

I can't believe he survived that explosion! And at such close range!

"You can't kill me!" roared Critias, standing upright. He rubbed his bleeding nose with his blistery knuckles and spat bloodied spit upon the ground. His bloodshot eyes, their pupils tiny dots, glared at Periander. "My father won't let me die!"

As Critias crouched to pick up his axe, Periander started to run away from him. Fumbling for the pistol in his holster—his last weapon—he glanced back.

"Grrrrrrrr!" snarled Critias as he vehemently shook his axe back and forth. Its frictional mechanics had been damaged in the explosion and the blade failed to heat up.

O Deity, what do I do now? thought Periander, his heart racing faster than his legs could run. "What the—?"

A small shadow appeared before him. Now it was a large shadow!

"Uuuggguuhhhhh!" Periander screamed and his whole body clenched as pain seized his back. He involuntarily bit his lip; warm blood filled his mouth.

Critias had grabbed his shield and flung it at Periander. Although Critias' strength had declined from what it had been at the start of the battle, and notwithstanding that the shield's weight reduced the speed with which it flew, the shield still landed with enough power to force Periander to the ground.

Spitting the bitter chalky dirt out of his mouth, Periander tried to cast the shield off him despite his muscles' rebellion. He stood up and fell back down. As Critias approached him, he reached for his handgun that had landed a tantalizing four feet away.

He could not reach it.

"Caught at last!" exclaimed Critias, grabbing him.

Wheezing heavily, Periander resisted as best he could until Critias shoved his hands under his arm pits and hoisted him up.

Foam and blood sprayed Periander's face as Critias panted, "I told you how this would end, old man! You die. I live."

"I ain't old," snapped Periander, his fidgeting feet dangling a foot above the ground.

"You're over thirty-five. Your body's strength has already begun wasting away." Critias snorted. "Youth will always triumph over the decrepit past. Just as all your stupid traditions and antique nonsense had to fall one by one, so too did your limbs succumb to me. You fought well enough, but you could never beat me. Hey, cheer up. Look on the bright side. Perhaps someday your son can avenge your death—oh, wait, he's dead. *You're* the one who was trying to avenge *him*. Bwa-ha-ha-ha-ha-ha-ha! What a sad, pathetic avenger *you* turned out to be!"

"I hate you so much!"

"Hate me when you're dead. All the living will love me while cursing your name from generation to generation."

"There'll be millions after me to hate you!"

"Then I'll crucify millions!" Critias laughed. "Even if ninety men out of a hundred should hate me, all I have to do is kill those ninety haters and then all the remnant of mankind will love me—one hundred percent!—because dead men's opinions don't count."

Periander's hands trembled, and his arms were hanging limply at his side. He so desperately wanted to hit Critias, but he was too exhausted. *I'm so sorry Cornelia... Jason... Psyche.* An orphan tear fell from his blue eye. *I've failed everyone.*

"What a worthless fellow you are," said Critias, droplets of spit bathing Periander's face. "It's incredible anybody would have allied himself to you, let alone given you his daughter. Mortals are such *fools*! For you've lost them everything! EVERYTHING!"

Periander gritted his teeth. "I was bound by conscience to oppose you!"

"Yet all your precious principles failed you! Power is the only thing that counts in this world. Power is what defeated you. Power will seize what was yours. *I AM POWER!*" Critias drew him closer to him; his hot breath, stinking of sardines, tickled Periander's face. "A loser like you never deserved to have a crown, a palace, a gorgeous wife. Yours is now mine—and better off for it! Starting tonight, little Psyche will provide me with great pleasure. And I'll enjoy her for *sooooo* much longer than I did your last woman."

"What drivel are you spewing?" demanded Periander, blinking in confusion as memories of Cornelia being shot by Critias and falling to her death, her body lying in a pool of blood, flashed through his mind. "You never had Cornelia."

"Ooh, that's right," said Critias, smacking his thin lips. "You don't know, do you? Well, let's just say that after you so ungentlemanly abandoned your wife, I was there to take her in my arms and play the husband's part with her."

"You lie! I saw her die!"

"Hey, Periander," snickered Critias, his eyebrows wickedly jumping up and down on his wide forehead, "have you never baked bread in a cold oven?"

Then, as a wide-eyed Periander slowly shook his head, Critias began laughing uncontrollably, loosening his grip. His sides heaved, his head bobbed back in hilarity, and the grating sound of his cackle radiated in every direction like blood from a shark's victim.

Yet there was no amusement in Periander's heart. Rather, his sides stiffened steellike, his throat bubbled with hateful bile, and his eyelids flung back with fury. Sweat gushed from his pores like lava from the Earth's molten core. And as when a dam bursts and floods the riverbed below, so too did the adrenaline surge through his veins to give him one final bout of strength.

His mouth curling into a snarl, Periander interrupted Critias' hysterics by grabbing for his greasy hair. His fingers wrenched a handful of hairs. He pulled the High King's head back. Then he lunged for his ivory neck.

While Critias gasped, Periander sunk his teeth into the flesh. Blood bathed his tongue and coated his molars. His jaws strained as he bit harder than ever he had bitten before, his mouth muscles overworking. Then, with his teeth still holding onto the jugular vein squirming between them, Periander garbled, "Damned tyrant!"

Losing his grip on Periander, Critias plummeted to the earth as Periander's teeth still latched onto him. His body sprawled across Critias, Periander drew his teeth out of him. Blood trickled out of the corners of his mouth; his whole beard was dyed red. Panting, Periander shakily forced himself to his feet. He staggered the short distance over to the gun that had flown out of his hand. Snatching it, he returned to stand over Critias.

The High King was flat on his back. His right hand was pressed against his neck, frantically staunching the flow. Blood continued seeping out, staining his knuckles and forming a pool beside his head. His eyes were wide and rotating rapidly. As his facial and neck muscles thrashed in agony, he mustered a rasping voice that murmured a word it never had before: "Mercy..."

"Mercy? You ask me for *mercy*?" Hovering above him, his left hand steadying his right as he aimed his weapon straight at Critias' face, not even Periander's twitching green eye was moved by the appeal. With his spitting mouth returning Critias' blood to him, he bellowed, "NO MERCY FOR THE MERCILESS!"

The first laser penetrated Critias right between his fearful black eyes.

"Cornelia strikes this blow!"

The second bolt dissolved Critias' pelvic area into a gory mash of burnt flesh.

"Jason damns you to the hell below!"

After shooting him this third and final time, Periander dropped the gun. His knees buckled, his heart faltered, and he slunk onto the ground. Lying there, tasting the red earth, his eyes turned skywards.

CHAPTER FORTY-TWO

*W*HO'S *THAT?* WONDERED PERIANDER, stretching his neck up.

Scarcely ten minutes had passed and already another chariot was approaching on the horizon, fast. It was heading straight for him.

Was this some agent of Critias who had been hiding in ambush? The pact had been violated before. Or was it a committed partisan intent on avenging his fallen master? Whoever it was would soon be known. Inhaling deeply, Periander picked up his gun.

"Periander!"

It was Psyche! Her charioteer slowed the chariot down as they approached. While still twenty feet away, Psyche jumped down from the moving vehicle and, with her hands holding up the bottom of her azure dress, she raced over to Periander.

"Oh, Periander!" she exclaimed, her soft hands gliding under his bloodied head to prop it up.

"I'm alright, I'm alright," replied Periander, wincing as she helped him sit upright. He placed his hand upon her rosy cheek, which immediately submerged beneath a tearful torrent.

"We need to get you to the infirmary! You must be in so much pain," said Psyche, her head whipping back and forth to examine him.

Periander shrugged his shoulders. "Pain? Nah. Just some scrapes and bruises... a few pulled muscles... maybe a broken rib or two." A large grin spread across his face, revealing teeth dyed red that, combined with a beard covered in clotted blood, made him look quite ominous. "Don't let all this blood fool you. Most of it is his. I'll be fine, believe me."

"Periander, I'm so, so... so thankful you're alive...."

"I am too." He chuckled; and while stroking her cheek, a little smile appeared around the corners of her quivering lip. *I am infinitely grateful to You, O Deity, for letting me prevail. I have avenged my family... my first family. Now the dead can rest. And... we the living can resume the labors of this life.*

She threw her arms around him; and he, suppressing a groan as they touched that part of his back struck by Critias' shield, clasped her tightly to his bosom.

"I should never have doubted you," sniffled Psyche, pressing her face against his even though the dried blood began to rub off onto her. "I was just so worried, said things I shouldn't—"

"No, you were right to be concerned." Periander's fingers, going through her supple, strawberry-scented red hair, turned her head to his. Her moist breath washed over his face as his multicolored eyes trained themselves on hers. "A year ago, I'd have never expected such a fight from Critias. His strength and dexterity were... inhuman. He survived one attack of mine that he shouldn't have. He almost survived the battle. I really thought I was going to die in the end. My strength had drained away; I couldn't resist when he hoisted me up. He could have killed me easily had he tried. Yet in his hubris he had to goad me with the only words capable of unleashing one final source of vigor still left in me. And by the Deity's grace, I killed that vile man."

Psyche's soft warm cheek, still pressed against his, was again wetted with tears as she murmured, "I'm just so glad you're safe! I saw everything on the video feed. My innards clenched throughout the battle. I nearly fainted when he picked you up; I couldn't even breathe. But you won! You won, Periander! As soon as you killed him, I commandeered the first chariot I saw."

"It surprised me to see you arrive first," said Periander, "when the Allied party that accompanied me is just over—"

Before he could finish his sentence, the selfsame party came into sight, having made the trek from the Southern Gate. All the troops, their armor gleaming under the sun, their chins held high, took giant triumphant strides. Filled with the chief dignitaries, several hover cars shot ahead of them and arrived first.

"Majesty!" shouted Agathocles, jumping down from the car. With a giant beam engulfing his oval face, his long blond beard blowing in the breeze around his skinny neck, he ran over to Periander. "I knew you'd win! Hail King Periander, Slayer of the Tyrant and Restorer of Atlantis!"

Demosthenes disembarked from the same car. Appearing more circumspect than Agathocles, a smile nevertheless formed above his beardless chin and his sideburns rose high with joy. "Your decision to overrule my counsel is most gloriously vindicated." He bowed his head. "We are all thankful you have prevailed in your duel, Sire."

"As am I." Periander grimaced as the two of them carefully lifted him up and set him in their hover car whilst Psyche, fidgeting and making frantic gestures with her hands, oversaw them. Sitting back in the blue-upholstered seat, Periander said, "How have Atlantean forces greeted the outcome of the duel?"

"Well, as soon as you killed Critias, one of his ministers attempted to renege on the treaty," began Demosthenes, twirling his sideburn.

"Yeah, that Thrax fellow," said Agathocles crossly, narrowing his large blue eyes. "He drew his pistol and started shouting, 'Attack, attack!' while pointing wildly at us. We thought we'd have to fight a battle right there and then! But would you believe, before any of us could respond, one of Critias' own generals shot him?"

"Dead?" Upon hearing an affirmative, Periander remarked, "I hope that means the surviving government intends to honor the treaty." *If Critias appointed them to their offices, then they must be the kind of men whom diplomats despise...*

Demosthenes signaled three men from another car who forthwith approached and knelt before them. "Sire, these three wish to speak to you about that."

They were dressed in gray Atlantean armor. Their shoulder plates displayed the gold fringed epaulets that revealed their status as high commanders. Yet with their helmets removed, their youth was quite apparent: the eldest could not be more than twenty-six.

Periander looked them over without recognizing any of them. "Who are you?"

"Lord Periander," said the middle one, bowing his blond, shortcut head, "I am Callimachus, heir of Evaemon. This is Moschus, successor to Diaprepes; and this is Nicander of Autochthon. Apart from yourself, we three kings are the remnant of the sons of Poseidon."

"You three?" Periander stared unblinkingly, his body immobile. "I've never seen any of you before. What happened to Bion, Cleanthes, Apollonius?"

"My Lord, the kings you knew all perished by order of Critias, as did their successors, and their successors, and their successors after them. He and his crony Thrax, under color of law or through outright murder... systematically eliminated all the dynasts of five of the ten regal families. We are the last offshoots of the other three, none of us being kings longer than two months."

They all fell facedown, burrowing their chins into the red earth.

"Lord Periander," cried Moschus, not daring to look up, "as the new High King of Atlantis by right of both inheritance and conquest, we beseech you to have mercy on us. We served your predecessor, not out of zeal for evil but from fear of him."

"Mercy," cried the other two in unison.

Periander gestured for Lysander to approach the car's other side. Leaning into him, he whispered, "Is what they say true?"

"My Lord," said Lysander, "a crown had just passed to Callimachus when I fled; the other two I've never seen. As a witness of many contrived successions and royal demises under Critias, however, I'd wager their story is true."

Periander turned to the three and shut his eyes. With a dull pain irking his sides, he breathed in deeply while slowly nodding. "My animosity has always been against Critias and his mother before him. They were the ones who were intent on upending Atlantis, corrupting religion, violating our ancient constitution, unleashing unending wars on the world... Apart from those who insinuated themselves into Critias' circle out of greed or ambition, or who spearheaded his wicked acts for their own malevolent gratification, I bear no grudge against anyone. He that merely executed his duties, or submitted to the tyrant out of self-preservation, shall receive no condemnation from me."

The three kings rose to a bow, their wide and watery eyes gazing up at Periander.

Propping himself upon the car's side, he waved his arm over all the throng of Atlantean soldiers who had arrived, and with a great voice said, "My countrymen, hear me! Although I came to you at the head of armies and have won the kingdom and High Kingship by the sword, I do not want you to be in fear. The prior régime tyrannized this country for its own aggrandizement; I have only the good of Atlantis at heart. Let no soldier who opposed me and mine on the battlefield dread the outcome of this day. I will not inaugurate my reign with a new round of terror—my eyes too much abhor the sight of children snatched from parents' arms, wives from husbands'... We shall have peace in our divided land and reconciliation, not further bloodshed and divisiveness!"

Shouts of relief arose from the assembled Atlanteans who proceeded to bow their heads while the three kings profusely thanked Periander and praised his clemency.

I hope the rest of Atlantis will acquiesce as readily, thought Periander as he sat back down, still waving to the throng. Psyche pressed herself up against him and he caressed her head on his shoulder. "I think it's time for you to see the capital of Atlantis, Psyche." He called an officer. "Are our forces ready to secure control of the city?"

"General Necho has just led his troops through the Southern Gate, and Camps Phronesis, Sophron and Elpidius are about to converge from the Traconite Hills and western plains."

Wow. Finally, after so many years, Atlantis is free of Critias and Eudoxia... How I've longed to see this day.

Psyche's breath tickled his ear. "You've done it, Periander! You have avenged the fallen and retaken your country." Her eyes sparkled and her eyelashes danced. "Now you can restore it as you've often told me you would."

His bloodied lips smiling with joy, Periander took her hand and was about to speak when an officer ran up beside the car.

"Sir, sir! We've recovered a strange device off the decedent's corpse."

He handed Periander the device. It was a cylindrical gadget, about the length of a hand. Emerging from the blood-splattered gray metal were several flashing neon buttons on its sides, a dodecagonal knob in the center above a screen depicting a two-dimensional map of the Earth, and at the top of the device, underneath a popped-open plastic case, was an unmarked red button that was visibly pushed down.

"Where was it?" asked Periander, warily weighing it in his hands.

"In his left hand. He had his thumb pushing the red button; we got it from him just before rigor mortis set in."

Strange. I didn't notice him going for this; then again, at the end of the fight I had a fair case of tunnel vision. Periander moved the device within six inches of his eyes. "I wonder—"

"I know what it is!" came a voice from the crowd.

Periander looked up. A small, pasty-skinned gray-haired man wearing a white lab coat had approached the perimeter around the hovercars. Several Allied soldiers, guns drawn, were halting his advance. Periander ordered them to let him pass.

"Who are you?"

"Dr. Anaxagoras," he said with a bow, "chief state scientist."

Periander's brow curled crossly. "I've heard of you. You were one of Eudoxia's favorites; she funneled vast quantities of money your way to develop new weapons. It was *you* who set about to harness the stars for war—to rain asteroids down upon us all! I know all about your warped scheme."

"You know?" Anaxagoras's eyes went blank behind his glasses and his palms began squirming against each other; his right cheek twitched relentlessly, although it had been doing that even before he learned that his most secret project was a secret no more. Kneeling before the High King's angry face, he confessed, "That is true, my Lord. I did develop the capacity to weaponize asteroids. That is how I know what that device in your hands is."

"And that would be...?"

"An orbital calibration and trajectory targeting mechanism for the Project Heliocalypse satellite. To put it in layman's terms, it's a remote control that allows the user to reposition an asteroid in the exosphere with the satellite's tractor beam and, by pushing the red button, to hurl it earthwards."

"His finger was on the button!" exclaimed the officer who had brought it.

"Lord Critias did insist on carrying it on his person at all times," explained Anaxagoras, rubbing the back of his neck. "When he asked if it were possible to make a handheld remote control for the satellite, we thought nothing wrong in making one for him. Evidently, we erred..."

Periander's body went limp, his limbs cold, his agitated mind ablaze. "Are you saying that a mammoth asteroid is now hurtling down somewhere because of this device?" He held up the remote in his sweating hand.

"Regrettably, that would appear to be an accurate assessment of the situation," answered Anaxgoras, shuffling his foot.

"Where will it land?" cried Psyche, ignoring Anaxagoras' mumbled explanation for why Critias was given the unilateral capability to launch an asteroid. Her voice breaking, she asked, "Egypt?"

"Or Athens? Or Mohenjo-Daro? Or Cyrene?" came a cacophony of voices from the various soldiers of the Allied army who were still gathered around them.

Taking the device from Periander's hand, Anaxagoras examined it for but a moment before announcing, "The coördinates entered in here are for Atlantis City." The world went mute as he, adjusting his glasses, added dispassionately, "Apparently programmed about two hours ago, before the battle."

So even while dying, Critias' thoughts were on our deaths... and he planned his final assault ahead of time, just in case. With the words dreading to scale his throat and go forth into the choking atmosphere of terror, Periander managed to say, "A flaming rock's about to hit us? How long do we have?"

Anaxagoras did not reply. He took a pocket computer out of his coat and, focusing his eyes dead-straight on its screen, started typing. His skinny fingers struck with the rapidity of pistons; he maintained an icy composure whilst every eyeball gawked at him. "The asteroid Phaëton was launched," he said at last, "but the satellite was not yet in the orbital position necessary for it to hit its intended target. According to my calculations, the prematurely-fired asteroid will fall southeasterly over America before crashing off its coast, approximately four hundred miles southwest of Bermuda."

Periander's sprinting heart slowed to a saunter and his bursting lungs exhaled. *I can't believe Critias almost killed me twice today!*

"Thank the Deity! Atlantis is saved!" exclaimed Psyche, the first of many among the crowd to express thankfulness.

Periander turned to her and, wiping the fretful sweat from off her brow, said, "You've been saddled with far too many cares today, as have we all. Now come, my queen, and off to the city we go. The hour of war is over, the day of woe past: next comes the merry supper for belabored souls, and the night of blissful sleep."

CHAPTER FORTY-THREE

I T WAS A QUARTER past four, the late summer sun moving lower in the sky, when Periander pressed his head against the window and gazed out at the city.

"There've been a few disturbances throughout the city, but the army's suppressed them," reported Agathocles. "Critias' death has mostly over-awed the populace."

They were in the room habitually reserved for Periander whenever he had spent the night in the palace prior to his banishment. The arching silver canopy above the bed, the black-and-white checkered floor, the gold-footed mahogany armoire, and the fading fresco of frolicking shepherds and shepherdesses on the wall opposite the window were all familiar sights. Since his last stay, only dust had lodged here. But the servants had deftly cleansed it upon Periander's rejection of the High King's suite for his accommodations. While he might now be High King and rightful claimant to the suite, he nevertheless did not wish to even set foot in that room, which for so long had been befouled by its former occupant.

"And the rest of the continent?"

"Most of the Atlantean-controlled sectors have surrendered, though there are still pockets of resistance manned by hardliners."

"Hmmm." Walking away from the window, Periander winced and clasped his chest. The pain medication had not fully mollified his bruised and bandaged sides. "Subduing the remnants of Critias' forces is a problem, but a good problem—the remnants, I mean. Just think how far we've come! From fugitives to conquerors. Soon enough we'll have the whole land in obedience."

Agathocles bowed his chaplet-wearing head. "I always knew you'd lead us to victory, my Lord."

"I'm eternally grateful for your faith," said Periander, patting Agathocles' back, "especially during those days when victory seemed as easy as finding a specific grain on a beach of sand. Yes, I was always prepared to fight for our cause; there was no other course I could have taken. Yet that doesn't mean I didn't recognize the odds we faced. But now, triumphant, Atlantis delivered, the tyrant dead along with his mother, my soul can finally begin to heal." He wiped a tear away from his blue eye. *Oh, that Jason were here to share victory with me!*

Periander braced himself as the room began to quake, and Agathocles steadied him on his feet. A glass goblet fell from the nightstand and shattered on the shaking floor. This tremor lasted twenty-four seconds, the fifth one since noon.

"When will these quakes end?" asked Agathocles, glaring at the floor's tiles as though they were responsible.

Periander shook his head. "The scientists say they're tectonic plates reverberating from the asteroid's collision under the ocean. They should end eventually."

Agathocles snorted. "The sooner the better."

"Thankfully, it's only tremors we must deal with—not great balls of fire from the sky. Now come, let's go to supper."

They exited the chamber and proceeded through the palace halls to the grand banquet hall. This enormous room stretched over a thousand feet long, pairs of mammoth chandeliers hanging down at twenty-foot intervals. Of the many tables spread throughout the room, the one nearest the front stood upon a marble daïs. Psyche, dressed in a vibrant green silken dress, was sitting there as were the other chief dignitaries. Leading away from them throughout the room were the tables around which

Allied officers had gathered. Each wore his finest dress uniform: the shaven-head Egyptians wore white, the Athenians blue, and several other colors were interspersed among them. Beyond these tables, occupying the latter two-thirds of the room, thronged the common soldiers of the army. Boisterous and loud, they rose repeatedly in toasts to their comrades, which sorely taxed the servants striving to keep their cups full.

Periander and Agathocles took their seats around the highest table, and their feast began. Sumptuous steaks, roasted duck, and whole lambs on the rack were served to them; and after half an hour, the jellies and sweet meats were brought out. Yet sweeter still was the aroma of Psyche's lemon-scented perfume that titillated Periander's nostrils. Throughout the feast the husband and wife held hands beneath the tabletop, sharing flirtatious glances and cocoa-covered truffles.

As the din of soldiers grew louder, Periander signaled a steward. "Tell the servants to cut off the men's flow of wine," he ordered, surveying the room. A table had just collapsed beneath the weight of soldiers attempting to form a human pyramid atop it, and elsewhere half-filled goblets were soaring through the air to awaken fellow revelers. "I think they're drunk enough."

"I'll try, Sire," gulped the grimacing steward.

Periander shook his head and sighed. "Such excess…"

"The men are just over-exuberant from the thrill of victory," said Psyche nonchalantly, gently rubbing around his shoulder that had been shot. "They mean no harm."

"You'd think if they had the restraint necessary to achieve victory, they wouldn't allow themselves to be conquered by the thrills of victory," protested a frowning Periander. He gazed into his goblet. The purplish wine was calm like a tranquil sea, lapping at the shore of the cup's edge; a crumb from a cherry tartlet bobbed on the surface. Suddenly the calm began to ebb. Massive waves erupted, violently tossing the crumb out of the cup.

Periander latched onto Psyche as the room started shaking. Their chairs fell backwards in unison. He hit his head on the floor but quickly got up. Pulling her under the table, he grunted but ignored the pain it caused his wounded ribcage to shield her head beneath his chest while rolling plates and glasses smashed onto the floor in front of them. A custard pie slipped and went splat; some cream shot out and assaulted Periander's eyes. Screams resounded from farther down the room when one chandelier collapsed onto a mob of men.

For forty seconds the hall shook.

"Are you alright?" exclaimed Periander, wiping the stinging cream out of his eyes. Blinking, his eyes were drawn not to Psyche but to a figure straight ahead. There, one elbow reclining against the wall and his chin cupped in his other palm, lay the Watcher, staring at him. His eyes were wide and his voice heavy.

"Periander, you must go."

"Go where?"

"Away from this land that will soon be no more."

What? Periander's mouth was open, but no words came out.

"Remember what I said when last we met," said the Watcher. "The Deity's verdict has come. Atlantis has been judged. Tonight, it falls."

"No, no, it can't be!" His throat drew tight. "It can't be that final! Isn't there any opportunity to make amends?"

The Watcher shut his eyes and sighed. "It is done. The Deity has decided." He gazed at Periander, his heavy-set eyes penetrating him. "The asteroid you call Phaëton has sunk into the Atlantic seabed, burrowing deep beneath the Earth's crust. It's disturbing the tectonic plates; the pressure is escalating. Of the horrors that shall soon occur, these shockwaves are but bland foretastes. At exactly 8:51 p.m., this entire continent shall be overthrown."

"But why?!" demanded Periander, pounding his fist down on the cream-covered floor. "Why did you lead me on like this? Encourage me to fight Critias? To sacrifice so much, try so hard to save my country... only to have it all snatched away from me in the end? Why?!"

"Periander, who are you talking to?" asked Psyche, placing one hand on his forehead and the other behind his neck. "Are you okay?"

Ignoring her, Periander shouted, "Answer me!"

"What was taken from you?" said the Watcher, crossing his arms while his eyebrows pressed down upon his eyes. "Vengeance for your family? Vindication against a tyrant? These you have accomplished, as was the Deity's will."

"But my country, my people... I wanted to save them, to reverse all the evils Eudoxia and Critias unleashed... make Atlantis good again."

The Watcher shook his head. "Your destiny was never to redeem Atlantis from her sins."

Biting his lip, Periander bowed his head. *O blessed Deity, this is so hateful to me! But I know it's futile to resist Your will...*

"This land is irredeemable. Nevertheless, a remnant thereof may yet be saved. Periander, gather your family and friends and whatever of your countrymen you can. Forsake this desolate rock while time permits. Go, go quickly!"

The Watcher vanished.

Periander emerged from the table, Psyche close behind him, and he glanced around. His tattered tablemates appeared alright; but the rest of the room was anarchic as half-drunk men staggered out from under collapsed tables. Frantically gesturing to Agathocles, Demosthenes, and the others at their table, he exclaimed, "We must leave Atlantis at once! The whole land mass is about to be destroyed!"

Everyone gazed perplexedly at him. Gossipy whispers ruffled ears. Psyche stood beside him, her head cocked and eyes wide as she took his trembling hand. Finally, Cleombrotus, the highest-ranking Athenian general present, asked, "What do you mean the island will be destroyed?"

"I've had a vision from the Deity," murmured Periander, explaining what he was told. When their only response was silence, he clenched his fist. "We have just three hours! These earthquakes are preludes to unparalleled destruction."

Twirling his sideburn, Demosthenes said, "While these quakes may inflict damage, it's impossible, my Lord, for any quake to cause this continent to sink."

"That's right," agreed Psammetichus, the highest ranking Egyptian general present. "You've endured much today, Periander, but I think now's the time for you to rest."

"No, it's time for us to leave!"

"Atlantis can't sink! Your own man says so. It's impossible."

Fools!

Before Periander could respond, a new voice from behind them said, "Not necessarily."

Periander and the others turned around. Approaching the daïs from their rear, sporting his white lab coat and fidgeting his eyeglasses, was the pasty-faced man himself.

"Anaxagoras!" exclaimed Periander. "You agree with me?"

"Can it be true?" ventured Cleombrotus, raising one eyebrow.

"Atlantis *is* sinking? That can't be!" cried Psammetichus.

"The Deity has decreed it," said Periander, nodding his head but grimacing at the finality of what he was saying.

Motioning his hands to silence the rising cacophony, Anaxagoras explained, "I did not say Atlantis *is* sinking." He took his handheld computer out of his pocket. "I said it was not *im*-possible for Atlantis to sink. On the contrary, it is perfectly possible for Atlantis, if the asteroid penetrated the Earth's crust at the correct gradient, with an appropriate amount of kinetic energy, and if the compounding of the two factors were to disrupt the tectonic plates from their current configuration—then, yes, it would be possible for the continental landmass to sink into the planet's crust. *Possible*." Smirking, Anaxagoras adjusted his glasses as he remarked, "Yet it would be highly fallacious to infer from my prior negation the proposition that Atlantis is, in actuality, sinking."

"Screw your enthymemes! Screw them behind the apple orchard! Speak plainly, man, and just tell us if the island's sinking or not!"

"Well, calculations predicated upon *a posteriori* indications are inherently exclusive of categorical certitude. But, based on the preliminary calculations I've run, I would wager there is only a zero point six six six percent chance that Phaeton's impact will lead to the destruction of Atlantis."

"That's less than one percent!" sneered Cleombrotus. He glared at Periander. "I'd wager there's a greater chance that lions, tigers, and bears decide to turn vegetarian!"

A nodding Psammetichus clapped his hands. "Yeah, or that I'll dance *The Nile's Overflow* on my head!"

"Hey, you know," said Cleombrotus, placing a hand on Psammetichus' shoulder, "I once saw a man who could dance on his head. His name was Hippoclides, and he—"

"Stop it, the both of you, just stop!" Periander began to pant. His face flushed with heat. "I am telling you Atlantis *will* sink! The Deity has told me so!"

Agathocles inched forwards. "Sire, I believe you. I'll follow you if you lead us away from these quakes."

Demosthenes huffed, as Psyche said, "I, too, trust you."

"I'm not debating this," declared Periander, glaring at the disbelievers. "Demosthenes, go with Agathocles. Commandeer every vehicle you can find, gather all the supplies available, recruit as many... evacuees as we can take with us."

"But such orders will surely cause mass panic."

"It must be done." *The people should panic at what is about to befall them...*

As they went off, Cleombrotus said, "This is ridiculous! I'm not ordering my men to leave; even if I wanted to, half of them are in no condition to do anything."

The chief Egyptian commander concurred; but the deputy of Indra, biting his nails, sided with Periander and ordered that his aerial forces prepare to depart.

"Stay if you wish, Cleombrotus. But as Supreme Allied Commander, I order you to dock your submarines so my people may use them."

Cleombrotus wrinkled his nose, sneering, "Fine. Use my boats. My sailors will take you wherever you think you're going to. I, however, did not come to Atlantis just to conquer and then throw it away. Go, I'll rule your people for you."

The insolence of his tone rankled Periander, whose hands instinctively formed fists. But, gritting his teeth, Periander nevertheless forced a smile and thanked him for the use of the submarines. Now was not the time to become entangled in argumentative quagmires.

As Cleombrotus and those who agreed with his opinion left to drown themselves in wine, and those siding with Periander rushed off to perform the preparations for evacuation, he was left with only Psyche at his side.

"Periander, I'm scared," she said, intertwining her arm around his.

He pulled her close and embraced her like an oak around ivy. "So am I," he murmured, stroking her head, "so am I. The world I knew is dying. But, by the Deity, we will escape this catastrophe and find a new home."

"Where will we go?" Her eyes, their pupils swollen, flickered while her lip quivered.

He cupped her cheeks with his hands and kissed her velvet lips. "Wherever Providence shall lead us...."

CHAPTER FORTY-FOUR

P ANDEMONIUM SOON EMANATED OUTWARDS from the palace, spreading to every corner of the continent as fast as rumor travels. Yet unlike wildfires that incinerate whole forests, this pandemonium was more akin to a controlled burn: smugly spurning Periander's warnings, the high growth looked down on those below that were ablaze with fear.

Although only a minute fraction of the Atlantean populace, drawn mostly from the bottom strata of society, heeded their sovereign's call to action, nevertheless these were the folk who were inflamed into acting. Ignoring the mocking taunts and jeers of kith and kin and the pomposity of those long profiting from the spoiling of Atlantis, these would-be survivors and perpetuators of the ancient civilization began their work.

The bulk of them quickly trekked to the coasts where they boarded the fast-arriving submarines, carrying on their backs what meager belongings they could—the relics of a dying empire. On directions from above, some gathered foodstuffs, seeds, and the supplies that would be necessary for replanting civilization elsewhere. Meanwhile, others sought to salvage what they could of their culture: moth-eaten scrolls and rusty antiquities were spirited away while digitized copies of books and imagery, encapsulating more than one thousand years of Atlantean literature, philosophy, historiography, fine arts, and sciences, were feverishly downloaded from libraries and archives. They labored under duress as catastrophe loomed. With the earthquakes increasing in strength and frequency, artifacts were dropped, papers torn, workers injured. Despite these hardships, the Atlanteans heeding Periander's proclamation perse-vered in their endeavors up to the moment they entered the submarines and airships that would whisk them away from the coming cataclysm.

Periander now waited on a launch pad outside the palace, thirty feet from a large airship whose whooshing engines signaled its impatience to depart for the safety of Egypt. He kept glancing at his watch as he nibbled his lip: 8:41 p.m. "Where is she?" *Of all the times to be late!*

"Lady Psyche," answered Agathocles, who stood beside him, "said she had one more item to fetch; she took a crewmember with her."

An item?! "Well, they better get here fast! We're running out of—"

Periander's face sprinted to the sour-tasting ground as the land rum-bled yet again. The launch pad's concrete, which had thus far held up in the prior quakes, now began to crack—the cracks widening and deep-ening as the strongest tremor hitherto continued. Several lamp poles lining the path connecting the launch pad to the palace toppled over and smashed upon the ground with deafening thuds. Thick clouds of dust wafted in the distance as part of the building's upper edifice collapsed.

Periander crawled to his feet once the quaking stopped. Feeling his scraped cheek, his hand reddened with a minor amount of blood. His watch displayed 8:44 p.m.

"Sire, we must leave!" exclaimed Agathocles, touching his shoulder.

Periander shrugged his hand away and glared at him; he formed fists beside his thighs. "No, not without Psyche!" *I'm not fleeing wifeless a second time!*

Down the airship's platform raced Demosthenes. Two hours earlier his face had glowed with that smug serenity derived from disbelieving warnings of impending doom. Now, however, his twitching face had blanched from the realization of what was coming; sweat streaked down his forehead and nose; his eyes were wide and bulged with dread. With his voice uncharacteristically emotional, he screamed, "Master, we must go!" as he grabbed Periander by his left arm.

"No, no!" yelled Periander while Agathocles seized him by his other arm. "Psyche!"

"I'm so sorry, Sire."

"We both are," panted Demosthenes, tightening his grip, "but we must escape while we still can!"

"NOOOO!" Striving to resist, but with his body still weakened from his duel, Periander began to be pulled back towards the airship. Swinging his head around, his eyes grew wide, and he yelled, "Look, look, it's Psyche!" *Thank the Deity!*

Her form had appeared at the end of the path, shadowed by a crewmember.

Breaking away from their grips, Periander darted towards his wife, neatly clearing fifty feet in fifteen seconds.

"I'm sorry we're late! We had to go around a wall that collapsed," shouted Psyche as he approached.

Before he could reply, another tremor began. Grabbing her sleeveless lower arm that felt clammy in his hand, he stopped her from falling earthwards. "Hurry, let's go!"

Huddling together, the three of them made their way back along the path. Agathocles and Demosthenes, who were in front of the aircraft's ramp, were frantically waving their arms at them. Yet the quaking earth, not subsiding but growing still fiercer, slowed them down as giant cracks opened up in front of them.

Psyche shrieked.

O Deity, help us! prayed Periander, his heart running at a gallop and his palms flooding.

One of the remaining lamp poles came crashing down. As the towering mound of metal fell, it cast its shadow over them. Periander's arms instinctively grabbed Psyche, and his legs thrust them sidelong. Just four feet from them, kicking up dirt from the newly exposed earth beneath the concrete path, the lamp post lay strewn across the path.

"Come on!" Periander urged, helping Psyche to her feet. He looked at the crewmember who managed to stand without assistance.

They climbed over the fallen post. When they got within ten feet of the airship, Agathocles and Demosthenes rushed over and helped drag them over to the ramp. His arms firmly locking into place around his wife, Periander rushed them up the ramp; and, jumping inside the ship, they landed onto the cold metal floor. The rest also safely boarded and immediately a blast of air whooshed past them as the airship began lifting off before the external doors had even finished shutting.

Panting, his sides aching, Periander glanced at his watch. It was 8:48 p.m. He rolled onto his sore back and, shutting his eyes, exhaled deeply. *We made it.* After a moment he blinked and turned to Psyche. "Are you alright?"

Her red hair was frayed, her green dress had multiple tears below her knees, and her pupils filled her eyes; but she nodded affirmatively.

"You scared me so much!" exclaimed Periander. He wrapped his arm around her neck and began kissing her aggressively.

"I thought we'd get back quicker," replied Psyche, articulating the words as she could in between kisses.

"What was so important you had to go back for?"

From a pocket on her dress, Psyche took out a bunched-up lace handkerchief and handed it to him.

Weighing it in his hand, he unfolded the handkerchief and stared at what was inside. It was his House's signet ring, bearing the lion-headed crest of Eumelus. How did that get there? Was not this symbol of his lineage and kingly authority always safely wrapped around his flesh? His eyes darted to his naked finger. *But I thought...* Suddenly he remembered. He had taken the ring off and dispatched it with a servant when the Allied physicians brought him to the palace infirmary to bandage and inspect him after the duel. In all the excitement of the day, he must have overlooked it in his room and left without it.

Psyche placed the ring on his finger.

Periander smiled as the familiar ring returned to his hand; but as soon as the dead metal encircled his finger again, he frowned. "You shouldn't have risked going back for this."

"But it's an heirloom of your family. I knew you'd want it saved."

"Not if it cost me you!" He casually removed the ring and slammed it on the floor with a clink, his palm completely covering it. "You're worth more than a thousand heirlooms!" His shivering hands stroking her blushing cheeks, and his nostrils greedily sucking up the sweet lemon fragrance exuded from her body, Periander ogled her shimmering eyes. "Even if all the relics and accumulated treasures of Atlantis were mine, yea, all the rubies and gold in the world, none of it would offset my losing you. Never! For you, sweet wife, are dearer to me than my own life. You, Psyche, are as precious to me as my soul."

"Oh, Periander..." She nuzzled her head against his cheek, making him wince happily as some salt-laden tears worked their way into his scraped skin.

"Everyone, come look!" came the pilot's voice over the airship's intercom.

Periander and Psyche sped up to the bridge. There were large windows all around this circular compartment and several of the crew were pressed against them, their mouths open and palms leaving moist imprints.

"The Deity save us," murmured Periander. Psyche took his hand, and he pulled her close to him.

Five hundred feet below them, the quaking land was crumbling like a soufflé in a tornado. Inflamed buildings and woodlands were leveled. Colossal chasms opened up here and there. In other places jagged land soared upwards, ripping apart everything: primeval mountains were gobbled up whole by seconds-old sinkholes and lakes became tall ridges whose sides wept with fishy water. Those persons who had mere hours ago scoffed at the prescient evacuees now wailed their regrets; drunken soldiers and their proud officers cursed their disbelief before death snatched their mid-sentence breaths away.

Such devastation... millions dying before me... and there's nothing I can do...

While the airship careened south-eastwardly over the continent, all aboard were gripped with terror, their eyes unable to turn from the devastation. Then someone cried out, "What's that?!"

Coming on the southern horizon, colored amber by the dying rays of the sun that illuminated it, was a gargantuan wall of seawater. It crested to a height of over three thousand feet, sweeping up and pulverizing whole buildings and corpses the moment it made contact with the land.

As this tsunami barreled towards them at a speed of seven hundred miles per hour, Periander shouted to the pilot, "Get us out of here!"

"I'm trying!" spat the pilot through gritted teeth. "We'll go higher than the waves."

Periander landed hard on the floor as the airship abruptly soared upwards at a steep angle. Clenching his teeth, he braced himself by grabbing the bottom of a bolted-down chair. Then he called to Psyche, who had fallen to the other end of the bridge.

Before she could answer, the airship, although maintaining its ascent, began violently to spin out of control. Periander's legs floated off the floor and hovered in the air as though gravity had ceased.

"Hang on!" bellowed the pilot. "The tsunami's whipped up harsh air currents, pushing them our way. Arrrrrrgghhh...!"

Periander raised his arm to guard his face. All the objects in the room that were not bolted down were whirling around in the zero-gravity environment. He batted away whatever hurtled towards him: pens, electronic pads, widgets, even a fetid sock-filled shoe. Some he averted, some buffeted him. Then a foaming fire extinguisher flew towards his head.

Periander saw nothing further after the extinguisher hit him. He was not a witness to what further devastation occurred below.

The tsunami submerged the entirety of the continent, drowning any residue that still gasped for life. Nor would the land reëmerge after the waves subsided: for at the same time that the tsunami was pressing down on the continent from above, the tectonic plate beneath Atlantis was shifting on the Earth's mantle. As a result of this shifting, the continent started to sink beneath the planet's crust just as when a luckless traveler drowns in quicksand.

These horrors continued through the night. By dawn the next morning, when the fearful sun had to venture forth to catalogue the damages, there remained merely a scattering of petite isles a thousand miles off the Iberian coast—the archipelagic rump of a once-mighty landmass.

Yet the destruction did not end with Atlantis: it reverberated far beyond it.

The tsunami, far from weakening after it had submerged the continent, grew more intense in its strength. Having originated in the West Indies, its mighty tidal waves radiated outwards in all directions. Atlantis's colonies and outposts in the Americas were easily swamped by its westward and southerly progress. To the north and east, however, the Atlantean homeland had played world buffer so long as it withstood the surge. But as soon as the continent plunged into the planet's crust, further disturbing the shifting tectonic plates, the earthquakes responsible for the tsunami intensified. And with Atlantis no longer present to mitigate the waves, the aquatic wall marched relentlessly onwards.

The tsunami overpowered the Pillars of Hercules and breeched the Strait of Gibraltar. Quadrillions of gallons of water inflated the Mediterranean Sea, causing it to submerge Cyprus, Sicily, Crete, Sardinia, Corsica—all its islands—and to overflow its banks.

The waters washed away all the Mediterranean civilizations. The plains of North Africa were swamped; the once-cluttered streets of Cyrene had all their litter swept away along with everything else. The Nile's delta channeled the deluge into the innermost recesses of Egypt, the river doling out death to its children whom it had formerly succored. Greece suffered asymmetrically: its islands drowned under the salty surge, as did Athens and other low-lying plains, whereas Olympus and other high mountains in the north surmounted the flood, saving the herders and countryfolk who dwelt upon them. Indra's kingdom fared little better because the same pressure on the Atlantic plate affected the neighboring tectonic plates. This led to earthquakes breaking out beneath the Pacific too, which formed its own tsunamis that devastated vast parts of Asia.

When at last the water level fell, the fall of these civilizations became clear. It had taken thousands of years for them to mature and reach their climax—a mere day to be obliterated!

Across the globe countless millions of humans lay dead, many of them reposing beside the very carrion-creatures that normally would have consumed them. Cities had become clusters of collapsed buildings now functioning as enormous sepulchers. Lifeless fish were strewn throughout deserts; bears and camels bobbed along oceanic currents. Hover cars, computers, and other tools of human ingenuity were smashed here and there, their metal quickly rusting. The whole planet reeked of salt.

Oh, what destruction and lethality can one asteroid wreak! In but a single dreadful day and night a famous continent was lost, tectonic plates moved, nations smashed, civilization exterminated. No matter how many chronicles one might peruse, or histories sought, no disaster anywhere had ever equaled this cataclysm in either its scope, magnitude, or consequence. Universal was the devastation. Hopeless was its aftermath. The world of Periander, being overflowed with water, perished.

CHAPTER FORTY-FIVE

Periander's world had gone dark. His limbs were immobile, and his head bobbed along in an unconscious daze until suddenly a sound, so great and so sweet, began tickling his ears.

"Ugghhhh," moaned Periander, starting to stir. He blinked but was met with only darkness. Rubbing his eyes, the faint twinkling of lights appeared. He reached his hand out to prop himself up off the ground; but although his hand acted as though it had touched a solid floor, once the light had grown stronger it became apparent that he was floating in empty space.

Where am I? thought Periander as he rose to his feet. When he glanced down, he gasped.

Beneath his feet was the Earth—not in the way it had been his whole life, beneath his soles, but rather separated from him by many miles. As the planet slowly turned on its axis, Periander observed its surface: the continental land masses, the seas and oceans, and one place in particular which captivated his attention. The site in the middle of the Atlantic, where once his homeland of Atlantis had stood for untold ages, was now a plot of water indistinguishable from the rest of the ocean; nothing visible remained of the lost continent apart from a few tall mountains whose peaks poked up about a thousand miles off the Iberian coast. Periander could only gape at the geological destruction.

Suddenly, rousing him from his stupor, came a familiar voice.

"Yes, Periander, the prophesied destruction has come to pass. Atlantis is no more."

Periander spun around and blinked. A gray-bearded man in a white robe, who appeared to be no more than in his sixties, was approaching him. He was wide in his shoulders and muscular in his limbs. His face, though marked by a scattering of wrinkles, exuded a serene expression and his blue eyes flashed with warmth.

Periander popped open his eyes and shuddered. "Father? Is that really you?"

Smiling, the old man rested his hand on Periander's shoulder. "Be not afraid, my son. I am indeed your father Themistocles."

"Father, what is happening? Where is this place? Why am I here?" Suddenly memories of the airship spinning out of control—of objects hurtling towards his head—flashed before his mind. *Did I... die?*

"You were always the inquisitive one, Periander—even as a young'un you were always climbing up onto my knee to quiz me on how I was ruling our subkingdom. That is a trait most fitting in a king. It pleases me to see you still exhibiting this kingly quality: for you have conducted yourself well as my successor."

Periander lowered his head. "I tried, Father, I really tried. You were always an exemplar of kinghood after whom I tried to model my actions. I wanted to prove myself worthy as your son. For a long time, I thought I was on the path of succeeding in that. But I failed. Despite my best efforts, I've let you down."

"No, my son. Far from it! You have gladdened my heart by what you have accomplished."

"What have I done?" He cast a glance at the devastated planet. "Our fatherland is no more, our people destroyed. Everything you left me has been undone."

Themistocles shook his head. "What happened was not of your doing. Atlantis and her people suffered the just condemnation of the Deity. There was nothing you could do to forestall it. But in what little avenue you were allotted, in the alternative paths subject to your free choices, you demonstrated your excellence as a king and as a man. Periander, you succeeded!"

Grabbing his son's hand, Themistocles pointed down at the ocean below. Suddenly little flickers lit up against the dark deep, which steadily grew until whole submarines and airships, buffeted by wind and waves, became visible.

"You see, my son, a remnant of our people survives and will soon replant the better part of our culture on foreign shores. Although it was never in your power to save Atlantis, you saved what was possible to be saved. And that, my son, is what I call success. Kingship never promised us utopian outcomes; too often, merely minimizing the damage is all that we kings can do."

"Your words are sensible, and I am truly grateful to have earned your praise, Father. No man's judgment is more valuable to me than yours! It pleases me to no end to learn that at least some of our people have survived (and what wouldn't I have given to save them all!). Yet, despite whatever feats of kinghood I may have done to the benefit of our people, I still cannot help but feel defeated as a man. I couldn't save my sweet wife Cornelia, or my darling boy, or..." *Psyche? What has happened to her?*

"Yes, you have borne heavy heartache. To lose one's family is a terrible pain, one which I am thankful never to have experienced... But you mustn't blame yourself for things that were outside your control."

"But had I done things differently..." Periander buried his head in his arm. "Perhaps my family might have still lived."

Themistocles gently moved his arm aside and looked into his son's eyes. "And had you never married Cornelia, you would have been spared the pain of losing your family. Earthly life is full of possibilities and the ramifications of all our choices are never fully knowable to us. Nevertheless, we must strive to make the best choices that we can: that is all we can do. And if you will not believe me when I tell you that you have nothing to regret, then perhaps you will better receive the message coming from another. Look, do you not see who is approaching you?"

Periander turned his head around and followed where his father was pointing. His mouth became dry, and his eyes forgot how to blink. Approaching from twenty feet away was the curved figure of a woman. She wore a billowing sapphire dress; its fabric glimmered with starlight that was yet less brilliant than her white flesh. Long strands of golden hair flowed around her neck and past her shoulders. A demure smile was etched across her oval face and her eyes sparkled brighter than the stars which seemed to arrange themselves behind her in a celestial frame. In sum, she was a beauty to behold.

His heart pounding, Periander could only whisper, "Cornelia."

"Yes, Husband," she answered, halting only a foot in front of him. "It is I."

Pouring forth a flood of tears, Periander embraced her and started kissing her ruby lips. "Oh, how I've missed you, Cornelia!"

"Periander, don't weep." She wiped his tears away with her soft finger. "Don't mar that handsome face of yours with tears. I want to see those differently colored eyes again without water blocking them; you know how much I adored them."

He cracked a small smile. "Yes, you always did. Just as I adored you. O Cornelia, Cornelia, I'm so sorry. When you reached out to me, I didn't grab you. You needed me and I couldn't save you; I couldn't even give you a proper funeral. Forgive me."

"There is nothing to forgive. Periander, you were the best of husbands to me. From the moment you first laid eyes on me, you always looked out for me. That is why I was able to be so calm in life: because I felt secure under your loving protection. You were my rock, Periander. I trusted you to give it your all, always, and you did. No one could have caught me in that fall, not even you. And though that fall separated us for a time, I did not die. Only my body died. I, however, continue to live and now enjoy the presence of the Deity. So, you see, dear husband, you mustn't feel bad about what happened. What was to be, was. Now you must turn your sight onto what is to come."

"Your words have purged my heart, left me feeling better than I've felt at any time since I last saw you. Thank you for everything. I love you so much, Cornelia. You and Jason were the most precious things in my life."

"And you were as excellent a father as a husband. I already knew it while I was with you both. And when our son arrived here, I saw in him the final fruits of your fatherly influence."

"The Watcher told me he was with the Deity in Paradise. I am glad to know that you were here to greet him."

"And I was so proud when I saw him. When I left him with you, he was still a boy. But when he returned to me, I saw that he had grown into a man—a good man, like his father."

Periander, his face beaming, pulled her even tighter into his bosom and stroked her hair. "I've missed you so much. You were such a major source of happiness for me."

"There is nothing sad between us apart from our temporary separation." Looking into his eyes longingly, Cornelia gently disentangled herself from his embrace and began to inch backwards. "No matter how long it may seem in earthly time, remember that it will last only a twinkling of the eye in comparison with eternity. Then, Periander, I will once again be yours and you will be mine, for always."

"What do you mean? Why do you speak as though we will be separated again? Why can't I stay with you now?"

Although her body started to fade and grow transparent, Cornelia's voice remained as stable and warm as before. "Because, dearest Periander, you must return to your other wife and complete your allotted years."

What?!

"Really, Periander!" interposed Themistocles, having approached him from behind. He touched his frozen shoulder and asked, "Did you think you were dead like us?"

His face flushed, he blurted, "Well, frankly, yes! It's not usual for the living to converse with the dead."

"It's not ordinarily the case that the living speak with one of the Deity's Watchers either," chided Themistocles, shaking his head in mock disapproval. Glancing at his son, he smiled and added, "The Deity honored you with not only a Watcher's visitation but with the opportunity to speak with someone capable of settling your spirit once and for all. Consider yourself doubly blessed."

"So, I'm really still alive?"

"Yes, Periander. You are alive!"

"But I, but I... The airship was entering a tailspin!"

"A bumpy ride, for sure, but your airship survived the journey."

"But what of me? I remember something flying right at my head."

"A bump on the head, a severe one but not mortal."

Periander held out his hands and stared at them. "So, I'm really alive..." He glanced at the Earth still revolving beneath them. "And I'll be going back down there...."

"Yes, but only for a while, until you are mine again," called Cornelia, now only an outline that was soon to fade entirely. "In the meantime, Periander, love your new family as much as you did ours. Psyche is a good woman, worthy of calling herself your wife. Cherish her just as you did me. But don't forget that I had my claim on you first!"

"I could never forget, Cornelia. I'll love you always!"

Just as the last faint appearance of her body vanished, Cornelia exclaimed, "And I love you, too!"

Staring at the starry spot where she had been moments ago, Periander took a deep breath and exhaled. *Thank you, Deity, for letting me see my Cornelia again.* He turned to his father and asked, "What now, Father? Will you too be vanishing, or will I? How much time do we have left?"

"Not too much, I'm afraid," answered Themistocles. He wiped a single tear from his eye and hugged Periander. "My son, I am truly proud to see the kind of man and king you have become. Though our time now is short, your wife spoke truly when she said we will be united again. When that day comes, it will be my honor to have you beside me in Paradise. Your mother will rejoice too."

"And is Mother also here with you, Cornelia, and Jason?"

"Of course she is, that noble woman! Where else would she be? And rest assured, there are many others whom you will recognize when you return, such as my confidants Socrates and Timaeus."

"And what of...Leonidas?" Periander clenched his fist at his friend's name.

His father nodded his head. "Even he. Despite his monstrous sin, he repented before his end and merited absolution."

"That is excellent to hear. Leonidas was a troubled soul; I am glad he is now at peace."

"We blessed ones are at peace here, the truest peace. Therefore, after you descend to the Earth, do not mourn those of us above who preceded you but concentrate on living the rest of your mortal life and setting a good example for those who will in turn follow you."

"Please tell me, Father: if this is truly life, and unending happiness is here, why should I linger on the Earth? Why shouldn't I hurry to you here?"

"My son, do not entertain such foolish thoughts. What was it that I always told you was incumbent upon all men, and upon kings especially?"

"Duty, Father."

"Yes, duty. Earthly life not only imposes many duties upon a man, but life itself constitutes a duty of his, even the principal one. Where we are now is the endpoint that awaits every soul which keeps itself within the path set for it by the laws of nature. But unless the Deity, to Whom the whole universe belongs, has released you from the custody of your body, the entrance to this place cannot be opened to you. For men were endowed with rational souls by the Deity for this reason:

that they should govern that part of His creation which is called the Earth. You are a microcosm of your world. By virtue of your flesh and bones, which are made of mere matter, you participate in that lowest form of existence common to all corporeal entities; by virtue of your bodily senses and lower appetite, you participate in that mode of life which inheres in all your fellow animals in the world below; and by virtue of your soul, specifically the highest part thereof which is called the mind, you perform operations of intellect and will—immaterially transcending the sensible particulars of your world by the contemplation of their abstract essences, and thereby glimpsing at the universal good that all things desire. By performing these spiritual operations, you participate in the act of existing to such a high degree that you may rightfully be called the image of the Deity. No creature below the heavens exists in such a noble and transcendent manner as does man nor has, as its duty, so great a task as bringing into its mind the forms of all things in the corporeal universe—thereby becoming, as it were, all things. In this way, you imitate your Creator, Whose divine Mind contains the paradigms of all things and without which nothing that was made could have come to be nor now persist. This is the task, nay, the privilege that has been allotted to the human race. So, my Periander, you and all good men must allow the soul to remain in the custody of the body, nor without His command, by Whom it was given to you, must you leave your earthly life, lest you should be guilty of having deserted the post assigned to men by the Deity.”

“Your words are wondrous, Father, and frame earthly life in a whole other light. At such profound wisdom I can do nothing else but marvel and comply.”

“Excellent. It is good that you see the necessity of duty. For you are no mere man, Periander: you are my son and, what is more, one on whom the Deity has assigned a far grander destiny than most men can dream. So do not think that you have already accomplished all the tasks set before you. Oh, not at all: your journey is just beginning! Beyond your ordinary allotment as a man, you yourself have the additional task of taking the remnant of our people and preparing them to rebuild civilization. It will be a grueling undertaking, and a thankless one at that. You should know well enough by now not to seek the reward of kingship in the ingratitude of men. Your true reward will come from Him Who alone rewards men according to their works, Who dries every unmerited tear and exacts pain for every unrequited misdeed. Your labor at restoring civilization will therefore depend upon the Deity's grace for its deserved compensation. But know this: nothing of all that is done on Earth is more pleasing to the Deity Who rules the whole universe than the assemblies and gatherings of men bound together in justice, which are called kingdoms. And you, Periander, shall reässemble and regather our people into a new and juster kingdom."

Periander bowed his head. "I will do it, Father. No matter how tiring it shall be, I shall persevere. For the outcome will be well worth the labor."

"Not that you will live to see the fruits of your efforts. Generations of arduous work were required to build the Atlantis of old; generations more will be needed to establish a new Atlantis. But just because a man will not personally stand to benefit from his labor does not excuse him from his appointed mission. Indeed, there is no better image encapsulating the majesty of a flourishing civilization than that of old men planting trees in whose shade they will never sit."

"I give you my solemn vow, Father, that I will make you proud and do all that the Deity requires of me. I will brace myself to my duties, and so bear myself that no soul will ever doubt that I was your son."

"That is the highest hope I could have for my posterity, Periander. In you I am placing my unwavering confidence. And while you are embroiled in this mission, always remember that I am with you in spirit. I love you, my boy."

"I love you too, Father."

"Farewell, my son."

Chapter Forty-Six

*O*HHHHHHHH... PERIANDER'S THOUGHTS WERE hazy as he slowly awakened. *Where am I?*

As his crusty eyes blinked open, artificial light slashed past his eyelashes. Squinting, he raised his head and glanced around the room.

He was lying in a bed whose white guardrails matched the many pillows propping him up. Beside it stood some medical equipment, including an intravenous tube hooked onto his right arm. A dull peeping sound emanated from a stack of machines on the other side of the bed that monitored his heartbeat and other vital statistics. The rest of the room was screened off by a floor-to-ceiling green cloth.

Is this the airship's infirmary?

He was perplexed by where he was, particularly since he felt so well in body. Pushing away the blanket, he pulled up his hospital gown and his mouth became agape. All the bandages and bruises that he had received on account of his duel were gone, as was all the feeling of soreness.

I'm already fully healed? Then why am I here? And where is everyone? What's going on? He called out, "Hel... hellooo!"

Muffled voices arose in the distance. Footsteps brought one voice closer, which was censured by its low-speaking companion; but the first voice, growing raucous, ignored the second. Heavy footsteps trod into the room.

"Sire!" cried Agathocles, thrashing the curtain aside so hard that it came off its track. His mouth curved into a giant smile as soon as he saw

Periander. "You're awake!" Behind him a physician threw exasperated arms up in the air.

"Agathocles, what's going on?"

"You hit your head during the flight from Atlantis. You've been in a coma for eight months."

Periander placed his hand on his head and ran it through his hair. "Eight months! I can't believe—did anyone else get hurt?"

His throat and pulse tightened as images of Psyche flooded his mind. Where was she? If he had been knocked into a coma, had she sustained any injuries?

"No, no, she's in excellent health after everything," replied Agathocles, clearly intuiting Periander's concern. "We all survived that flight, even—Demosthenes!"

"Majesty," panted Demosthenes, rushing inside and kneeling beside the bed. His sideburns jolted upright with delight. "I am most thankful for your recovery."

Periander laid his hand on Demosthenes' shoulder and said, "I feel quite refreshed," while the physician checked his vital signs. He chuckled. "The Egyptian soil has always bolstered me."

As soon as he had said that, Agathocles and Demosthenes turned their heads sideways and awkwardly exchanged glances. "Uh, Sire..." began Agathocles, fidgeting his hands.

"Periander!"

Everyone spun their necks around.

Dressed in a flowing black gown, her rosy cheeks providing a brilliant contrast, Psyche lingered in the infirmary doorway as a tearful smile unrolled across her face.

"Psyche!" cried Periander joyously. As his wife drew near, he lowered the bed's guardrail, slinked back, and patted a spot on the mattress where he bade her sit.

She threw her arms around him with the force of a boa constrictor. "I'm so happy you're awake!" Psyche nuzzled her soft face against his.

"It's been so long—the physicians talked so grimly—but I knew you had to recover; I just knew it!"

Entangling his fingers in her soft red hair, Periander imbibed a deep breath and kissed his wife until her quivering lips responded with firm kisses overflowing with amour. *You too, Psyche, are such a major source of happiness for me.*

"I love you, Periander." After tightly embracing for a minute, neither of them having any more need to verbalize their feelings, Psyche rose to her feet. "There's someone I want you to see." Without another word, she left the room and him confused.

"Is she fetching her father? I will need to discuss with him about Egyptian assistance as we seek to salvage our culture."

Demosthenes shook his head and Agathocles said, "Not Ozymandias—that's what I was trying to tell you."

Periander stayed silent while his men explained to him that they were not in Egypt.

They summarized the events of the preceding eight months, starting from the tsunami that had wrecked devastation across the Mediterranean region. Their airship had managed to land after the deluge in northwestern Iberia where three submarines from Atlantis also came ashore. Some other submarines were destroyed in the tsunami; most of them, however, survived, landing around various portions of Europe and possibly beyond it. Communication signals were difficult beyond a five-hundred-mile radius, limiting the extent of their knowledge as to how the rest of the world was faring. They knew Egypt and Athens had been ravaged by the tsunami, although it was probable that some of their inhabitants survived; but they had not yet been able to establish contact with anyone in those lands to verify their hunches.

Despite the disagreeableness of their report, Periander soon learned of more positive developments. Their own settlement, however isolated it might be, was steadily progressing. Trees were felled to house four thousand settlers. Newly minted farmers tilled and sowed virgin fields, and greenhorn herdsmen corralled flocks of wild sheep and cows. Deep chilly caves were transformed into makeshift ice lockers for meat and storage bays for the artifacts salvaged from Atlantis.

Placing his sweat-moistened palms on his forehead, Periander slid his hands down his face and rubbed behind his neck. His eyes somberly gazed at a coin-sized ring of rust on the metal floor. "So not only did the catastrophe snatch away our homeland from the face of the Earth," he remarked dryly, "but it's sent Atlantean—no, all human civilization—back by centuries, too." *Father told me I would have to rebuild our civilization but... he didn't prepare me for a world where all the major civilizations have fallen, where there may be no outside help at all. Did one flood really cause global devastation? It's breathtaking. Nonetheless, we will have to persevere, show the world what stuff we are made of and make our ancestors proud. If they could found Atlantis in those olden times, then today we can establish Atlantean offshoots. We have no choice but to do so.*

Exhaling a heavy-laden breath, he stood up and shakily put his feet down on the floor. "It seems our labors have only just begun: our forefathers' age has cycled back to us. Show me the settlement."

"Perhaps you should wait a little more," cautioned Demosthenes while nevertheless supporting him by his arm as they exited the infirmary.

"No," said Periander, gesturing for them to let him go, "I must go on my own two feet, see with my own eyes..." *Into what sort of world am I resurrected?*

Descending the airship's ramp, Periander held his hand above his multicolored eyes and looked around. The aircraft was parked atop a pebbly hill, about two hundred feet north of the settlement. Beyond it stretched miles of cultivated land that gradually transitioned to hilly terrain penetrating the innermost parts of Iberia. The mild smell of salt wafted on the breeze from the ocean that lay a mile behind the airship.

Well, the settlement is larger than I envisioned based on their report. (Truly, there is no substitute for first-hand knowledge.) Looks like a hundred buildings in total, all made of wood. I wonder how they'll hold up in winter... What are Iberian winters like? There are fields and livestock, so at least we won't starve. All the settlers appear busy but not too overwrought. That's good: they've accustomed themselves to the necessities of toil. Periander nodded slowly, puckering his lips. *Yes, yes, I can foresee where this is going. This has the makings of a fine city.*

He drew the woolen blanket wrapped around him closer as a chill see-sawed up his spine. "Is it always this cold around here? By my reckoning, it should be spring."

"The equinox came last week," said Demosthenes.

"The cold's another thing you need to know," said Agathocles. He pointed up at the murky gray sky. "The sky's been clouded over since the catastrophe."

"Why?"

Demosthenes explained. "The same disturbances in the Earth's crust that caused Atlantis to sink beneath the ocean also stirred up the subterranean magma. Volcanoes everywhere began erupting, pumping vast quantities of sulfuric acid into the atmosphere. Their ash, which you now see covering the sky, decreases the amount of sunlight able to reach the surface while the aerosols produced from the volcanic gases reflect solar radiation. Lower temperatures are the consequence."

"When will the ash dissipate?" Periander held his hand in front of his eyes and stared at a diffuse brown halo surrounding the sun.

Demosthenes sighed, his sideburns sagging. "We don't know. It looks almost as heavy now as it was when the volcanoes first erupted; it was an unbelievable amount of material discharged into the air. Months, perhaps years may pass before the sun returns to full strength. In the meantime, we must pray that enough of our crops can grow in the dimness."

Periander shut his eyes and formed a fist. Before he could dwell anymore on the harrowing subject, there arose a high-pitched sound behind him. He turned his head and looked.

Psyche had returned, and in her arms was the cause of the noise: a baby.

"Who's this?"

"Periander," murmured Psyche as she came closer, "this is our son."

"Our son?" repeated a dumbfounded Periander.

"Yes! He was born eight days ago." She gently handed the child into his arms.

"Our son..." Periander carefully cradled the baby.

Wrapped in scarlet swaddling clothes, he had a few tuffs of strawberry blond hair. Two greenish-blue eyes reflected a bubble he was blowing. When it popped, the child frowned and wrinkled his little nose as though about to cry; but Periander quickly tickled him under the chin and in lieu of screams elicited spit-infused giggles from him.

Periander kissed Psyche's soft cheek and asked, "What's his name?"

"He doesn't have one yet." Her bosom released a playful laugh as her arms curled around his right. "I was waiting for you."

Periander smiled and held his son's head against his joyous heart. He laid his forefinger on the infant's shoulder. "His name shall be Athanasius."

"I like that."

Lifting his son up above his head, Periander said, "My son, the world into which I was born is no more. I am the final son of Atlantis. But you shall be the first father of this embryonic world that lies before us, and a thousand sons shall call you 'Father.' Your path will be difficult. Nourished by hardship, and forced to clothe yourself with resourcefulness, you will thus grow to manhood. And, as ruler of the remnant of our people, you shall forge from them a new nation in this wilderness, establishing its foundations and setting its course for the age to come. In you shall all the olden virtues that built Atlantis be revived: plant and cultivate them that they may come to fruition among your posterity. May the Deity bless you and preserve you in your travails as even He preserved me in mine."

A REQUEST FROM THE AUTHOR

I greatly appreciate the time you took to give my book a read.

If you have 60 seconds, it would mean the world to me to hear your honest feedback on Goodreads or, if you purchased this online, on the retailer's website. It does wonders for the book and I love hearing your thoughts on it!

To leave your feedback on Goodreads, visit

https://www.goodreads.com/book/show/230830759

Or

1. Open your camera app

2. Point your mobile device at the QR code below

3. The review page will appear in your web browser.

Thank you!

Joseph Bringman was born and raised in Seattle, Washington. He loves studying the history and cultures of the ancient Mediterranean, reading works of classical literature, and learning ancient languages. Joseph earned his PhD in Classics at the University of Washington.

Language is Joseph's passion and he enjoys teaching Latin and Ancient Greek to his students, guiding them through the great literature of the past and expounding on the artistry of antiquity's greatest writers. Now he is putting his own boisterous imagination to work and has begun publishing his own contributions to literature.

More about Joseph, including his social media presence and newsletter, can be found on his website:

www.BringmanPublishing.com

Acknowledgements

To all who had a hand in helping me bring my book to market, especially my mother Laurie for her superb proofreading, thank you.

ALSO BY JOSEPH BRINGMAN

Ahab sits on the throne but lacks the heart and stomach of a king. Jezebel exhibits kingly qualities galore but has no throne.

Most Israelites follow Ahab in submitting to his wife's gods. But a tenacious remnant led by the prophet Elijah seeks to restore the supremacy of the Hebrew God. And that means toppling Jezebel along with her gods. Although dynastic diplomacy forced Jezebel to marry Ahab, she has made do all these years... tirelessly working to remake Israel in her image. No one will oust her without a fight! But then Ahab becomes infatuated with his latest concubine. She not only worships the Hebrew God but also witnessed her family being slaughtered by Jezebel's goons. Is she really a devoted companion and sweeter than any man deserves? Or is she a Hebrew Anne Boleyn scheming to get Ahab to swap out his religion and his wife? Suddenly Jezebel is seized with fears of having her life's work undone, her faith outlawed... even being driven out of her own home by the other woman—just like what happened to her mother.

So what is Jezebel going to do? Win! No matter what it takes!

Full of intrigue, betrayal, and suspense—get your copy of *Ahab and Jezebel: A Match Made in Hell* today!